MW01626211

KEN KIRKBY

KEN KIRKBY
A Painter's Quest for Canada

GOODY NIOSI

libros libertad

First published by:
Libros Libertad Publishing Ltd.
PO Box 45089
12851 16th Avenue, Surrey BC V4A 9L1
Ph. 604-838-8796
Fax 604-536-6819
www.libroslibertad.ca

THIRD PRINTING

Library and Archives Canada Cataloguing in Publication

Niosi, Goody, 1946-
Ken Kirkby : a painter's quest for Canada / Goody Niosi.

ISBN 978-0-9810735-7-6

1. Kirkby, Ken, 1940-. 2. Painters--Canada--Biography.
3. Inuksuit in art. 4. Inuit in art. 5. Canada, Northern--In art. I. Title.

ND249.K546N55 2009 759.11
C2009-904138-3

Front cover photo by Diane Lyle
Cover photo of Isumataq by Roberto Lissia

Some photos shown in this book are from Ken Kirkby's personal collection and photo credit information was not available

Design and layout by Susan Mellor
Printed in Canada by Printorium Bookworks

Acknowledgements

Writing a book is a solo process – no question – but only the physical, actual writing part. Believe me, this book would never have seen the light of day and never found its way into your hands if there hadn't been a magnificent team of people dedicated to getting it out there. And so I find myself with a list of people I want to acknowledge and thank – from the bottom of my heart.

First, of course, Ken Kirkby. This is, after all, his story, and there are times I am sure he worked much harder telling it than I did writing it. Ken believed I could write his story and for that vote of confidence, I am eternally grateful. This is a story that I believe needed to be told, not only for the sake of the great tale that it is, but for the pieces of history it contains – a history that everyone needs and deserves to know, particularly our younger citizens.

I want to thank my friend and long time mentor, Thora Howell, who has always had faith in me. Thora is a sort of magnificent guardian angel for writers and aspiring authors on Vancouver Island. She is the biggest fan of books and reading I have ever met and a true champion of the written word. Thora read the manuscript, encouraged me with wonderful advice that jogged my brain in new directions and even more importantly, cheered me on years ago when I wrote my first book. Every budding author needs a Thora in their life.

Thank you to my publisher, Manolis, who loved the manuscript and was eager to publish it. His enthusiasm is contagious and a huge confidence builder in every respect. A gigantic round of applause – in fact, never mind the applause, let's just make it a standing ovation – to Pat Tripp, my editor. I heard a story once about an author who was bemoaning the fact that there weren't any good writing teachers out there. The other person answered, "Oh but there are – they're called editors." Pat taught me so much and did the most magnificent work. Some of her suggestions were so subtle as to be almost undetectable – and they made a difference. Other suggestions were hand-slapped-against-the-forehead obvious and I'm eternally grateful that all those ideas were offered – and that I humbly and gratefully implemented them. I want to thank Susan Mellor, the book designer, who took a concept Manolis, Ken and I had wrestled with for weeks and with deceptive ease turned it into a gorgeous cover. And also, a huge thank-you to Susan for the wonderful work she did and all the mistakes she found (and corrected) before they got to press.

I could go on to thank many more people including my family and my dog but I'll save that for the Oscar speech. Stay tuned.

One last thank-you – to you, the reader, for buying this book and, I hope, being thoroughly entertained by it.

A word from the painter

I had not intended to become engaged in the telling of this story. After a lifetime of living it and recounting this or that part of it to what became a blur of audiences, telling it yet again was the furthest thing from my mind. It has for me become simply the story of a promise made and a promise kept.

At this stage in my live all I wanted to do was go and live at my favourite place, a small village near a stream on the east coast of Vancouver Island. Most of all, I wanted to live an ordinary sort of life which had so far eluded me, a life where I could sleep when tired, eat when hungry, fly-fish whenever it pleased me and paint all those paintings that had become stored up in me like water behind a dam constructed by the events told in this book.

It was out of frustration at how some were mangling this story that convinced me to give it to Ms. Niosi, an author and journalist, who became a friend during the marathon of Friday mornings it took to recount. For the reader it is probably just a book. For me it was an exorcism since much of what is spoken of here I had kept to myself.

The events and conversations are true – as I remember them. Some were told to me and some happened to me but most were of my own doing. With the passage of time they have melded into each other like a myriad of tributaries dissolving into a river. I cannot with any certainty tell you if every detail is accurate. What I can say is that the story is true.

~ *Ken Kirkby*

1

A Painter is Born

It was a late blustery morning: March 28, 1992. A lone man walked slowly along the sidewalk, the wind whipping last fall's dead leaves around his feet. The man was oblivious to the wind, the chill, and the crows scolding from the lampposts overhead. He was aware of only two things: the intricate texture of the curved wrought iron fence that he was running his fingers along as he walked and the visions swirling through his mind.

The Canadian Houses of Parliament loomed ahead. Soon he would open the doors, walk across the stone floor, and make the presentation he had dreamed of and worked toward for what seemed his entire life. To arrive at this place he had covered five hundred and seventy linear feet of canvas with thirty-nine thousand, three hundred and sixty ounces of oil paint, applied by millions of brush strokes during six thousand eight hundred and forty hours of painting time spread over almost twelve years. The end product was Isumataq, the largest portrait in the world – a portrait of the Northwest Passage against a sky fired by the Northern Lights with two Inuksuit standing guard. Today he would reveal the painting in Parliament – today he would address Canadians and tell them his dream – his reason for pouring his soul into this work.

But Ken Kirkby was thinking of far more than the painting and the sheer audacity and will that had brought him here. His mind drifted to the women he had loved and who had helped shape him and his vision. He thought about his father and most of all he thought about Francisco, the old fisherman who had told him tales of the Arctic when he was a young boy. His imagination had fed on those stories. Through all the events of his young life, the dream of the Arctic never died – it took him to Canada's far north and to adventures most people never imagined.

He thought about his heritage – the Viking blood that flowed through his veins but perhaps most of all he thought about the people of the Arctic – the grandmothers, the men, the women and children and the orphans. Isumataq was for them – for their dignity, their freedom and their own land.

As his footsteps carried him closer to the doors, he considered how everything in his life, even his birth, had led him to this place – to this most perfect place and time. Just before he pushed through the doors, he thought once again about Isumataq, an Inuktitut word that means, *an object in the presence of which wisdom might show itself.* Would wisdom come to those who stood in front of it? Had his own insight and knowledge grown? Perhaps he had been born wise and simply grown into the wisdom he had always possessed.

Today, many years after the unveiling of Isumataq, the casual observer might conclude that Ken Kirkby is a man of great confidence. Some have called him arrogant. Very probably, his father, Ken Sr. was given the same epithet. But Ken recalls that although his father, like himself, was very much in the public eye, at heart they are both private people. Like his father, Ken enters the large public stage with considerable flamboyance and much noise. But when the show is over, he covets his private space and guards it fiercely. To begin to understand Ken Kirkby – the artist, the crusader, and the man, it is necessary to see him through the lens of his history.

Ken's father, Ken Sr., was born in England near the turn of the century, the youngest of four children. He was his parents' last hope for an heir to their wide-ranging interests in the steel industry. He had other plans. After a stint in the Merchant Marine, he travelled to Australia where he wandered along the coast and into the outback. When he was down to his last shilling he went to work in a steamy, sweaty laundry in Sidney. Within ninety days he was a partner and made the business so successful that it was franchised across the country. When he sold his share, he purchased a farm in the Blue Mountains in Queensland where he lived the life of a recluse reading all the great literature of the world. In 1937, when he judged his reading and education complete, he gave the farm to his staff and returned to England.

On August 17, 1937 Ken, freshly back from his Australian adventures, walked into a hotel in London where he planned to quietly celebrate his birthday by treating himself to a nice meal. It was there that he met his future wife, Louise May Chesney, and they were married a year later.

Because he had developed a reputation for being a young man who had the ability to make a business successful, the Rover Motor Company hired him. He played a key role in changing their factory from an old-fashioned hand-made automobile company to one with a more modern American-style assembly line.

On September 3, 1939 Britain declared war on Germany. Shortly after the beginning of hostilities a black limousine pulled up outside the Rover factory. A man stepped out, and introduced himself to Ken as Lord Beaverbrook. His job, he told him, was to take one of the Spitfire factories and find a way of making it more efficient and effective. "We've studied you. We know your past and your capabilities. This is your new job."

When Ken protested, explaining that he was a pacifist, Lord Beaverbrook explained that he was under direct orders from "The Old Man" – Winston Churchill.

Ken took on the assignment on the stipulation that he would only earn one pound a year. He was so successful at getting Spitfire manufacturing on track that Churchill took a personal interest in him and the two became close acquaintances.

Ken Sr.'s son, Ken, was born on September 1, 1940 during one of the first air raids of World War II, in the hospital in Golders Green. While Louise May was giving birth, two unexploded bombs lay directly below her, buried deep in the sub-basement of the hospital.

Before his family left England in 1946, Ken collected one special childhood memory. He was about to celebrate his fifth birthday and his father asked him well in advance of the day what he would like. Ken said he wanted three presents: first he wanted to see the Spitfire that had been placed on the grounds of Buckingham Palace because it had survived one hundred and eight bullet holes in one wing; second, he wanted to go to Trafalgar Square to see the V2 rocket that had been erected beside Nelson's Column; third, he wanted to walk on the decks of the HMS Victory.

Ken Sr. delivered all three gifts. On the morning of Ken's birthday, the two went to Buckingham Place and there, behind the locked and guarded gates was the Spitfire. As they approached, the gates opened and they were escorted directly to the airplane. A stocky man wearing a long, dark navy blue coat and smoking a fat cigar was waiting for them.

"Master Kirkby, it's a pleasure to meet you," he said. "I hear you would like to see this Spitfire." Then he lifted the young boy up and placed him on the wing. An officer helped him into the pilot's seat.

Ken was in heaven. For a few brief moments, he was a pilot, pushing the buttons, twisting the knobs, imagining soaring through layers of white clouds, into an ocean of blue sky.

An air force officer lifted him back down to the ground and the man with the cigar said, "I gather this is your fifth birthday. I have a present for you."

He reached into his pocket and pulled out an American five dollar bill. "I should like you to have this," he said. "I won it from a man you will hear about. His name is President Roosevelt – so this is a very good, lucky five dollar bill."

Then he patted him on the head and before turning on his heel, said, "I have no doubt things will be interesting for you in your life, young fellow. Good-bye."

Ken Sr. had made a promise before marrying Louise May that after the war he would make a permanent home with his family in Spain. So, in

1946, he organized a caravan of five Rovers, donated by the automobile manufacturer, to take his wife, son, baby daughter and in-laws back to their home.

Ken's maternal grandfather, James, was known in Spain as Don Hymie Chesney. He was a gentle giant with a laugh that threatened to topple large buildings. He traced his family line back to a Dane named Rurik of the Russ. The family history, beginning in Iceland, dated back to 746 AD and was one of the first ever recorded.

Ken's father had some trepidation about going to Spain, which had remained neutral during the war but was tacitly on the side of Hitler. He would have preferred going to neighbouring Portugal, which had remained neutral but was in support of the British. Don Hymie had been one of the most well-respected and well-known men in Spain before the revolution. He was no friend of Franco's and had worked behind the scenes as an ambassador for Britain and the United States, trying to keep Franco in Morocco.

The caravan of Rovers drove across France through a devastation none of the passengers could have imagined. The roads were rubble, water mains destroyed, fields burned to barren ground and houses reduced to piles of stone, crumbled brick and charred timbers.

They passed through France and crossed the border into Spain, where they climbed high into the Pyrenees before winding their way down to the plain.

After settling his family in the ancestral home in Valencia, Ken Sr. travelled to Portugal. One look was enough to tell him he couldn't stay in Spain. The country was broken. It had not been brutalized by others but by its own people and that fact seemed to have affected the national psyche on a deep level.

Compounding his dislike of the country was his conflict with his wife's brother, James. The two men grated against each other and controlled their animosity with difficulty. In Portugal, Ken drove up and down the country roads and walked the streets of the cities. He saw the potential in the country. It needed roads, railways, docks, shipyards – every piece of infrastructure had to be rebuilt. England was experiencing similar hardships and because Englishmen needed jobs, the country put them to work in factories building all the things that countries like Portugal needed – and then melting them down and rebuilding them again just to keep the men busy. Ken Sr. presented a plan to the British authorities and to Antonio Oliveiria Salazar, the dictator of Portugal, to export surplus goods from the British factories to Portugal. After successfully brokering the deal, he dedicated himself to putting the new infrastructure into place, working from his offices in the Plaza de Allegria, in Lisbon. At the same time he had a house built for his family in Parede, a small seaside village about 25 kilometres north of Lisbon. A year after leaving Spain, Ken Sr. went back to fetch his family.

In trying to define himself, Ken once wrote about his adopted country.

I grew up in a land where everything lasted forever and things were the way they were and needed no better explanation – a place where things were made by hand and machines were considered contraptions of the devil, thieves of the art of man's hand – where superstition was used in place of logic and a passing question would bring a priest to dinner the following day, a messenger of an unkind God – where the wealthy were opulent, the powerful omnipotent and the poor a magnificent sea of wretchedness, a society meagre in the middle.

Life was judged not by the quality of its rewards but by the volume of tragedy it contained. The land was home to a short, squat people, half Romano, half Moor that grew, in the manner of cork trees and grapevines, from a stone-laden and parched soil –with a harsh angular language hewed from stone quarries and spoken in daggers. They were a people swimming in an ocean of past glories, frozen in tradition and apprehensive of its thaw. The men were vain, proud, stony creatures that worshipped their land and loved the sea more than their women.

They built houses, walls around fields and churches of stone – each one carved to fit its final resting place. The roads, twenty generations old, were made from black cobblestones that defied vehicles and made them ache.

The women were called Maria, after the Virgin Mary. They dressed in black by their twentieth year, hurrying down the avenue to age, drenched in fascination with death. They all but lived in their churches of stone and gold, where the Bible was forbidden and services were conducted in Latin and words unintelligible, out of interpretation's reach – places where Christ might well have quietly wept a thousand times.

It was a place where West met and married East and stayed on to raise an enduring race that survived its own prejudice, illiteracy, hunger and the amputation of its intellect.

If we owe a debt for what we are beyond mere circumstance, then mine is owed to this meagre land and her people: gypsies, children of the street, her ever present weeds, who invited me to live with them on the Avenue of Princes, who struck the match that caused the fire in my belly.

Ken's childhood in Portugal is a story of a young boy growing up wild in the streets – a boy adored by his father and encouraged by his mentor, an old Portuguese fisherman, to become a painter and to explore the Arctic wilds of Canada. Ken was dyslexic. At school he was alternately called a moron and a genius. He overcame ridicule and unwarranted praise and grew strong, with a sense of self that no one could shatter. His inner sense of assurance drew disparaging comments all his life, the most frequent being, "Who the fuck do you think you are?"

Ken's response to the proverbial slings and arrows was and is, "To the best of my capacity I am not arrogant." Popular conviction has it that you are either a hero or a bum. Ken sees himself as neither.

I'm a human being with passionate desires who is naïve enough to be able to just go on in the world regardless of people's opinions. No matter how gray the day was, or the past was, I could get up the next morning and start again. And so I have seemed to get to places where I think most people don't go and I think the sadness of our species is that the greatest things that have not happened, have not occurred because we have not tried.

Ken was enchanted by his new surroundings. He had never lived in a new house and had never smelled the pungent perfumes of fresh mortar and whitewash that a new house emits. In his memory these odours are intricately laced with the salt smell of the Atlantic Ocean.

On the first morning Ken woke in his new bed, he opened his eyes to a raging storm. Big balls of white fluff spun and danced past his window. Entranced, he pulled on a pair of pants and a sweater, slipped his feet hastily into shoes and tore out the front door. Bending against the ferocious wind, he staggered down the cobbled street to the top of the cliff two hundred feet above the foaming waves crashing on the rocks below. He clung to the rocky path that led down to the beach, where the roar of the waves pounding against the reefs drowned out all other sounds. The wind tore the white foam from the tops of the waves, carrying it inland, like thistledown.

Ignoring the cold and wind, he peered into the tide pools where tiny crabs scuttled and little fish swam in tight circles; he waded into the shallows until the water slapped against his chest. Then, over the roar of the storm, he heard a voice. He was not sure what the voice was saying but he turned and there behind him was a tall, old man.

"Come," he shouted. "Come."

Ken slogged through the water toward him and the old man picked him up. "You're not allowed to be here," he chided him. "You could kill yourself. How old are you?"

"I'm seven," Ken said.

"Oh well, if you're seven then I guess it's okay. And what is your name?"

"Ken."

"Huh! Well my name is Francisco. Mine is an easy name. Say your name again."

"Ken."

"Do you have a middle name?"

"Michael."

"Ah!" He nodded his head. "Miguel. I like your middle name." And for Francisco, Ken would always be Miguel.

Still holding him, the old man took Ken to his fishing shack halfway up the cliff, cantilevered out across the rocks. Inside, it was small and cozy. The back of the shack opened to a cave that was piled high with oars, nets, fishing poles and an eccentric collection of gear. Ken felt like he had found the mother lode of all things wondrous.

A wood fire burning briskly in an old cast iron stove warmed the shack. The old man helped Ken off with his wet clothes, which he hung in front of the fire where they steamed and filled the air with warm beads of moisture.

"Do you know how to cook?" the old man asked him.

"No."

"What woman in her right mind would want a man who can't cook?" Francisco said, tearing up a great head of lettuce.

"The trouble with this modern world is that we have made certain things and we do certain things with them. Do you know that we never put metal in a salad? You never use forks or knives or anything metallic with a salad. And you never cut anything – you break the things up by hand. You tear them apart. Never forget that – I hope you're paying attention to me. This is very, very important."

Ken was mesmerized. For the first time in his life he knew that he was being treated as an equal. He knew that this was a man who would not hold back, who would not tell him half-truths, who would never underestimate him or shield him from life.

Here he was, starting out with something that is common to all humanity – making food and eating. And of course, the two great things in Portugal are language and food. I think it is one of the marks of a great, great culture that they take those two things and put them at the front of the list. My lessons in the realities of the world began while I was sitting on that counter, damn near naked, watching my clothing dry in front of the stove. And it seemed to be the most natural thing on earth.

Ken's first lesson in food preparation, although technically precise, was also enormously romantic. In Francisco's world, there was no separation between science and the soul – it all blended into one. To Francisco the world made sense on a large, universal scale – and though Ken had no words to explain it at the time, that view of the world made sense to him.

While the salad absorbed a dressing of olive oil, in an old wooden bowl, Francisco opened a cupboard door and brought out some crusty rolls, a hunk of cheese and a bottle of Vino Verte. He poured two glasses. "Salud!"

Ken took his first sip of wine and thought it very fine indeed. Then they set about devouring the bread, and cheese and salad, eating their entire meal with their fingers. While they ate, they talked – Francisco in Portuguese and Ken with a mixture of English and Spanish and the few Portuguese words he had learned – and they understood each other perfectly.

What Ken didn't know was that Francisco and his father had become friends long before the family had moved to the village, and his father would have thoroughly approved of the impromptu meal and the dawning friendship between the old man and his son.

When Ken finally tore himself away from his perch by the hot stove and walked home in his still-damp clothing he was full of a deep, thrumming joy. His mother was anything but pleased. She had awoken that morning to find that her son had disappeared in the middle of a raging storm. His father, however, shared his excitement about the wonderful old man on the beach, about the life in the tidal pools and about the spumes of white foam eddying in the howling wind.

The incident deepened the rift between mother and son that had been growing since Ken had learned to walk and talk. It was not an intentional rift. Louise May strived to be a good mother but it was evident that the two would spend their lives in intense opposition to each other. More than one observer of their relationship suggested that the problem was, they were both warring Vikings – one polite and the other not. And so, Ken learned quickly to do the dance of the scorpion with his mother – keep at a respectable distance to avoid catastrophe.

The cultures in that region of the world were very much frozen in tradition. There were ways things were done and there were ways they were not done and they were not to be questioned. Anybody who did question was immediately suspect and was pushed to the perimeter. No matter how hard I tried to live so that I could be with others in a reasonable way, it never worked. Although I didn't know it at the time, this was the ideal training ground for this creature that we call an artist. But I don't see myself as an artist. I'm a painter; I'm a politician; I am occasionally, potentially, a philosopher but we don't really know that yet.

Ken had received no schooling in England. He had been born during the war and the family had moved constantly – thirteen times in seven years. Despite his lack of schooling, Ken's mother and father had tried to teach him to read and write – with no success. There was no doubt in their minds that their son was bright. His conversation was mature and clever and he could draw brilliantly. He had started drawing from the minute he could hold a crayon in his hands and he used every available surface.

Ken Sr. was curious that his son could draw anything he saw but could not form a letter. He gave him a sheet of paper and a pencil and cut a 'W" out of a newspaper column. "Make me a drawing of that," he said.

Ken tried, but the shape eluded him.

His father gave him a larger sheet of paper and asked him to try again. He failed again. His father produced an enormous sheet of paper that he tacked to the wall. "Draw it as big as that piece of paper," he said.

Ken made a shaky but creditable "W".

His father bought several large rolls of newsprint and tacked huge sheets up on the walls. "Now draw a "W" there," he said.

For the next two-and-a-half-years, he experimented with scale and with combinations of letters and objects, trying to discover how his son's particular disability worked. In 1948, he wrote a paper on a condition he called *dyslexia*, a word with Greek and Latin roots, meaning, "can't read."

He told Ken to let whatever he was looking at simply come into his eye, without interpretation or judgment, and in his mind's eye, to project it on a giant movie screen. Gradually, Ken began to untangle the meaningless jumble of printed letters and to read and write, all the while imagining his hand engraving letters on a giant screen.

And so, scale has always been a very, very important thing for me, emanating out of this practice.

While Ken was learning to read and write, he was also honing his skills as an artist. The neighbourhood where the family lived had been built specifically to house the world's deposed leaders. The King of Spain and his family, the King of Italy and his family, Batista and the Maharaja of an Indian Province all lived there. Portugal's foremost architect, Rui de Andrade, lived a couple of streets over. After seeing some of Ken's drawings, he took a deep, personal interest in him and arranged for him to pay regular visits to his house where he was given all the materials he needed to create his drawings.

Ken didn't wonder why this man should make such an offer. It seemed as natural as going to the beach to meet and talk with Francisco. And so Ken would sit and turn out drawings as though he was working on an assembly line while Rui's pet monkey sat and watched.

Several weeks after this arrangement had begun, Rui talked to Ken's father. "The wisest thing you could do is not send him to school. Let him develop what he has. He is a primitive. I have never met one before now. He obviously has an immense talent and he has an immense desire. I have never seen anything like this. The best thing you can do is just leave him alone to do what he does. You can tutor him. Teach him to read and write – and do arithmetic and the other basics – but let him develop, as he will. It would be a crime to interfere with him."

Two days after Rui had delivered his opinions about Ken's schooling, Ken and his father were having breakfast in the small room off the kitchen where gauze curtains filtered the early morning sun. His father took a sip of coffee and looked up from his newspaper. "I have an idea," he said. "As you know, we all have our jobs in life. I have mine and now you shall have yours. You love to draw so much so why not make drawing your job? If you like, I'll make an arrangement with you. You draw all week and help Francisco doing what he does. And sometimes go to Rui's house and draw there. At the end of the week, after breakfast on Saturday, show me the drawings – but not all of them. Take the best ones and stand up over there and explain to me what they are and why they are good and what it is that is good about them. Give me an understanding of what it is that you see in them and why they are the best."

"I want you to think very clearly, and then I want you to speak very clearly. And I want you to speak in a voice that could be heard at a distance without yelling. I want you to find that voice that allows people at a distance and up close to hear. One of our problems is that we don't know how to think and so we don't know how to articulate. This is one of the difficulties of our age. So this is what I expect of you."

Ken had no fear of making his presentation but he wanted to do it right. That first Saturday he stood up and explained each drawing and what it meant.

"The labourer is worthy of his hire," his father said when Ken had finished, and he reached into his pocket for some coins.

"This is what I would like to pay for those drawings," he said. "What would you like to have for them?"

"I don't know," Ken said.

"Well, you have to know and you have to think about it." He handed his son the coins. "Those drawings are mine now," he said and picked up the dozen or so drawings, squaring off the sheets and tapping them on the table until they were a neat, uniform stack. Then he tore them in half, put the halves on top of each other and tore them in half again. Then, picking up the newspaper, he disappeared behind its outspread pages.

Each Saturday the exercise was repeated. One day, Ken's curiosity could no longer be silenced.

"Why are you doing that?" he asked while his father ripped up another dozen of his best drawings. "Those are the very best drawings I made. Why don't you rip up some of the ones that aren't the very best?"

His father put his coffee down. "I'm doing it because you seem to be on the path of becoming what we call an artist. This is how artists are treated by society. This is what you have to be aware of – this is what you have to become acquainted with and you have to find ways of dealing with this. This is just one of your first lessons. I know very little about art, but it seems to me that the point of art is to present to the world a different point of view or a different way of seeing something and to point out shortcomings and better ways of seeing or doing. "

"Many, many years ago, before we were born, they used to take artists and burn them at the stake and burn their works. They were called heretics. As time passed they stopped burning the artists but they shunned them and continued to burn their works. Sometimes they jailed them. Nowadays, you're simply ostracized because if you don't fit the mould of the ordinary you will be put aside."

"Essentially, your job is to be a shit disturber. That is a prime requisite for being an artist. Having all the talent in the world is just fine. Having all the capacity is just fine. But what do you do with it and how do you handle yourself in the world? That is the big question."

"You're living in this wonderful world of yours and now you have to present that to a world that probably doesn't understand it – not that they should unless you can make them understand. There is great resistance to what is new. We live in a world that is caught between the two boundaries of compulsory enthusiasm and cultivated boredom. In order to stay stable we try to stay in a steady state in the very centre. You apparently are not one of those. You're roaring off with your own vision and your own agenda and you are very fortunate to have a means of expressing it. But this is how the world is and it's not going to be an easy road. Artists are known to have a rough road. That's why I tear up your drawings. As long as we keep doing this I shall keep tearing them up so that you will never forget."

2

Religion and Education

The beach where Francisco lived was rough and wild. About 300 metres from shore was a large reef comprised of great slabs of barnacled stone and rock, tossed there eons earlier by a great upheaval of the earth's crust. It was a magical world, where all you had to do if you were hungry was go out to the reef and catch a fish or dig for clams. They were all there for the taking, and Francisco taught Ken how to dig and how to fish.

Ken thought the beach was perfect – not so Francisco. He complained, "If only we had a nice beach. It would be so fine if we had some sand so that people would come and sit on the beach."

"Why do you want people to come here?" Ken asked.

"People like to come to a beach," Francisco said. "They bring their parasols and picnics – why shouldn't they come here?"

Ken wasn't sure that he wanted to share either his beach or Francisco with anyone else but the old fisherman approached Ken's father, who made a presentation to city council; telling them, they should build a wall from the beach to the sea at a particular angle to the reef. Then, when the storms came, driving waves laden with sand, the wall would trap the sand and deposit it on the beach.

Ken learned many new skills. He helped Francisco drill holes in the rock and set dynamite sticks and blow them up. When the rocks were the right size, they moved them to the beach and then, as the wall progressed, farther and farther out during low tide. The tide and the weather dictated when the work should be done and Ken learned another valuable lesson: don't mess with the ocean. And especially, don't mess with the weather – it rules everything.

The colours and flavours of Portugal were all around, especially in the local market, which played a big role in Ken's new world. It was the largest market in the area and served many nearby villages. Every imaginable vegetable, fruit and variety of fish, imported from Portugal's far-flung colonies, could be found in the noisy, crowded stalls. Chickens and ducks hung suspended in the air by yellow, gnarled feet; fish of every imaginable size and colour glared at shoppers with cold, dead eyes; coconuts jostled for room with bananas, oranges and lemons.

For Ken, the colour and the sheer numbers of people and objects were thrilling. It became one of his habits to take his sketch pad to the market and draw whatever his eye fell on – the possibilities were endless – carts, wagons, stalls, fruits, the black-clad fishmongers and the men who sold protesting chickens and ducks.

The activity in the market was like a dance that had been practised, performed and perfected for countless generations. There were patterns of movement, symmetry in the arrangement of vegetables and rituals in the transactions, all of them synchronized with delicate precision.

For Ken it was a marvellous and exotic world. For the local people, Ken was the exotic – a small eight-year-old boy always armed with a sketch pad and drawing without stop. They became used to seeing him wandering through the market with his drawings and when they admired his work with a smile and a nod, he would give the drawings away. One particular fishmonger, a large woman with a smile that threatened to split her face in half, took a particular fancy to Ken and his art. He always gave her a drawing and she always had a little gift for him in return. In time he became part of the dance.

Ken had been living in Portugal for almost a year when an invitation arrived at the Kirkby home requesting the presence of Ken and his sister, Louise, at a birthday party for one of the neighbouring children. A wrapped present was provided to the children to take to the party and they were sent off up the Avenue of Princes. Louise was as nervous as her brother and clung tightly to his side as he knocked on the door. The first question that was fired at him when his young host opened the door took him by surprise.

"Have you been baptized?" the boy asked. The other children crowded around, anxious to hear the answer.

"I don't know," Ken said. "Why?"

"If you're not baptized you go to hell."

"What? Right now?"

The other children joined in, peppering him with questions. What about religion? What about baptism? Ken felt a slow thread of heat crawl up his neck. He wanted to turn and run back home with his little sister in tow.

"We don't talk about religion in our house," Ken said. "And if I'm not baptized, why would I go to hell?" He took a breath, feeling his courage gather. "Yours must be a very angry God. Mine is a happy God and he loves me very much. We have wonderful times together and wonderful conversations."

Two days later a priest rang the doorbell. From his room upstairs, Ken could just make out the words. "Your Excellency," the priest said to Ken Sr. "I need to talk to you about your son."

"If it's my son you want to talk to, he's upstairs drawing. I'll go and get him." Ken Sr. called up the stairs.

"No, I don't wish to speak to him, I wish to speak to you on a rather serious matter," the priest said.

"If it's to do with my son, I want him present."

Ken Sr. ushered the priest into his study and Ken followed.

The priest delivered a stern lecture. Children are not theologians, he said, and they are not to comment on theological matters.

Ken's father interrupted. "What are you talking about?"

The priest explained that the children had gone to a birthday party and Ken had talked about God and religion and had given the other children his version of God and heaven – a blasphemous view. Ken was not to behave like this anymore.

Ken's father listened calmly until the priest was finished. "In this household we do not dictate how people are to be to each other or to anyone else," he said. "Each individual has to find his own way through this life and our mottoes are very, very simple. When you get up in the morning, you do as you please and you hurt no one. Before you go to bed at night, you have to do something very fine for someone else, that will be unspoken. Whatever you make today, by way of material goods, you give half of it away. Those are the things we run our lives by. Beyond that we don't dictate terms."

The priest's eyes narrowed. "You son is behaving in a very anti-Christian way."

"Well," Ken Sr. said. "It's a very interesting thing about Christians. I have met many Catholics and I have met many Protestants. My quest now is to see if I can find some Christians."

After the priest stalked out with a last warning, Ken asked his father why it was an issue. He told his son, "The main driving force of humanity is fear – fear of whatever is not known. So we have to invent answers. We have to invent a God. We have to invent this God's rules. When the first people stepped out of their caves and looked up at the sky and had no understanding of what they were seeing, they had to invent a story to try to make sense of it. The purpose of these stories was to try to make the unknown known – to make it less frightening. The idea that we might be here for no particular reason other than we are here is intolerable. The whole thing is driven by fear. There are those who understand this condition and they have been able to use it for their own interests. They may be the heads of corporations or of churches or of countries – they all play the game. The majority of people are so easily taken in by fear that they readily believe the stories they are told. This is the beginning of turmoil and it is the mother of war."

A few days later when Ken went to the market with his sketch pad, he smiled and waved at the big fishmonger woman. Her eyes opened wide and she backed away behind her stall, waving her hand at him. "Go, go," she said.

Ken stood still.

She waved both hands at him, "Go!"

Puzzled, Ken walked away and as he wound his way past the stalls he noticed the silence that fell when he approached. No one smiled at him; no one nodded or called out a cheerful "good morning." People avoided looking at him and stepped deliberately out of his way.

Ken left the market with an ache in his throat. The next day he went back and still no one would talk to him. He went to the market for a third day and was again chilled by the rejection he met. But that day as he turned to go, he heard one woman say, "You're the anti-Christ – go!"

At home he asked his father, "What is the anti-Christ?"

"That's the devil," he answered. "Why do you want to know?"

He explained the scene at the market and what the woman had said to him.

"That's very interesting," Ken Sr. said, his lips drawing tight across his teeth and turning the colour of ash.

Ken Sr. picked up the telephone. "Don't leave the house," he said. "I want you to stay here."

A short while later the same priest who had visited the house before came to the door. "Something very interesting and potentially important has just taken place," Ken Sr. said. "The other day you called my son's behaviour anti-Christian. For the last three or four days he has gone to the market where he likes to make drawings. People have shunned him and he was called …" he turned to Ken. "Say the words."

"The anti-Christ," Ken said.

Ken Sr. leaned back in his chair. "There seems to be a link between your words, 'anti-Christian' and their words, 'the anti-Christ.' Was that their interpretation or was there someone, perhaps you, who actually said those words? This is how they now feel and whether you realize it or not, you have made me the second most important man in history – I'm the father of the devil is what you're telling me. I expect it's you who started this. If you ever refer to my son or any member of my family again, I will truly make you wish you had never been born. Get out of my house and don't ever come near it again."

The priest listened in stony silence and left, wrapping his black cassock tightly around him.

It was at that moment that I first recognized that I was different. We had conversations about being different and it was from those that my dad's morning greeting emanated. Every day when I'd come to breakfast, he would give me a big long hug, and kisses and say, 'And how is my special, different friend?' And that's how it was to the end of our days.

Out of their long discussions on being different, some of his father's words stayed with him all his life. "Fortunate are those who come to get a sense of themselves early in life. Many don't have a sense of themselves and their opinions and visions are really prefabricated. They simply function by rote. They have never begun to exercise their minds and that is, partly at least, how to get away from this terrible condition of fear."

Ken went back to the market again after that conversation, but in a half-hearted way. It was never the same. The people no longer told him to go away and they no longer called him the anti-Christ. But they looked through him. To those people he no longer existed and their attitude underlined his feeling of being different.

But secretly, Ken liked the idea of being special and it added to his growing sense of confidence. He had a clear sense of who he was though he could not express it in words. Rui called him a prodigy and a genius and talked about him to his many well-connected friends. Consequently, adults didn't often treat him as a child.

But he was different in other ways as well. In the summer he tore through the streets in shorts and bare feet like a street urchin. He didn't go to school and spent most of his time with Francisco and his peasant friends – all this while the children of the well-to-do families on the Avenue of Princes attended school, wore proper uniforms and mingled with people of their own class.

Ken's father, too, was considered an eccentric. He loved gardening and began to dig an enormous vegetable patch on his property, to prove a theory about future food production. He also fished, which was not a sport in Portugal but a job. He brought the Boy Scout movement to Portugal and encouraged the children of the poor to enrol.

I've never seen anyone who was as loved as he was. No matter what was going on he seemed to go through the world with an incredible fearlessness. He had a gentle quality that was so attractive. Everyone was attracted to him. He was a magnet. Being the son of such a person allowed one much latitude.

It also gave the young boy great responsibilities at an early age. His father taught him that he was utterly accountable for his own behaviour and that he should consider every action with great care. However, that didn't necessarily mean he should be careful. In the end, he only had himself to answer to. "We all end up in the same place," his father said. "We all end up alone in bed and we have to face ourselves and how we have lived."

He didn't advocate revolution but he did say that a person should live by his own code, which required that a person should have one – and that required thought and making the effort to come to know oneself.

Ken was exposed to many opportunities to learn about himself, often through finding himself in company with some of the great thinkers of the day. His father carried on voluminous amounts of correspondence with some of the most brilliant minds in Europe. They exchanged ideas and theories and many of them came to stay for a day, a week, or longer, to talk and to theorize.

Ken and his sister were supposed to be in bed at sunset, a rule Ken balked at. Only two circumstances permitted them to stay up later – if they were not at home and couldn't be found, or if a distinguished guest was visiting and intriguing conversations were taking place. Then the children were permitted to stay up late, and encouraged to take part.

Much as Ken loved these discussions, they still couldn't equal his best times with Francisco, especially once the dolphins arrived. One day he was on the beach with the old man when he poked him gently in the shoulder and pointed, "Look out there."

The tide was rising on a calm day without a hint of a breeze. At first, all Ken saw was a great school of mullets coming in through the openings in the reef to feed on the sea lettuce. Then he saw the great, gray shapes that were herding the mullets into the shallows.

"Here," Francisco said, tossing a ball to Ken, "Throw that far out into the water."

Ken heaved the ball out as far as he could. It had barely touched the crest of a wave when a dolphin surfaced under it, picked it up and pushed it with his snout back to shore. Ken waded out, picked up the ball and threw it again. The dolphin knocked it back, squealing. To Ken's ear it sounded like laughter.

Ken threw the ball again. The dolphin squealed, pushed it back, put its head up in the air and shivered. Ken was sure it was laughing and he was instantly smitten. He was falling in love for the first time in his life and it didn't strike him at all odd that his first love should be an animal.

The dolphin was sleek and impossibly beautiful. It came closer and closer, until it brushed against Ken's legs. It was his turn to shiver, with a sensual delight that made his entire body tremble.

As they played together, Ken began to touch the dolphin – tentatively at first – until finally, he put his arm over its back and they swam together. The dolphin's head beside Ken's, its eye looking directly into his.

Ken was filled with joy and for weeks he could think of little else. He wanted to be with the dolphin forever – to live with it in the sea or have it come and live with him. Neither was possible. This dolphin was his first true playmate – an equal – and for the next several years, until the dolphins stopped coming, their relationship was one of the most precious in his life.

Several private tutors schooled Ken and his sister. The arrangement suited Ken's father although his mother argued that he should go to a proper school. When Ken was eleven he agreed with his mother out of simple curiosity to know what went on behind the doors of St. Julian's, where the children of the privileged boarded and a few, like him, attended as day students.

He was enrolled in a class with boys his own age. On the first day he walked into the classroom and before he could look around to find a seat the master said, "Aha! Master Kirkby! I see you have now condescended to visit us. Come and stand before the classroom and let us take a good look at you."

Ken walked to the front of the room, holding his head high. A tense silence filled the room as the other students stared at Ken and then at the master.

He sat when he was told to and looking up focused on a triangle the master had chalked on the blackboard. "Master Kirkby," the teacher said. "Do you have any idea what that is?"

"No, Ken said. "It's a drawing of some sort."

"When you refer to teachers you call them sir," the master said.

"Yes, sir."

"Well what kind of a drawing do you think it is?"

"It's an abstract and beyond that I have no idea, sir."

"That is called a theorem. It is Pythagoras' Theorem and it's very important."

"Why is it important, sir?"

"Without knowing geometry and mathematics we couldn't have the world we have."

That struck Ken as being a particularly absurd statement. The world, he thought, has nothing to do with Pythagoras. Fish don't know about Pythagoras and they live their own perfect lives. Only people think it's important, he reasoned.

The master asked a student to come up and demonstrate the theorem, solving the square of the hypotenuse by adding the sum of the squares of the other two sides.

"Now Master Kirkby," the teacher said. "Would you care to come up here and do that?"

Ken went to the front of the board and started to work out the numbers from the opposite end. It couldn't matter which way you did it, the results would be the same.

"No," the master said. "You have to follow it exactly as prescribed in the book. This is how you do it."

"But how are we going to find a new theorem or a new thing if we simply follow what has already been done?" Ken asked.

"Ah!" he said, smiling at the class, as though he were letting them in on some great joke. "And I suppose you propose that you're the one who is going to find these marvellous new things."

"Actually," Ken said, "I am – many of them. I have already found some but they're mine and they're secrets."

"Well, you seem to have some feelings about this."

"Yes, I do."

"Go ahead then – express your understanding of this."

"Yes sir." Ken picked up the chalk and drew two birds. One bird was flying along while the other one lay crumpled at the foot of a brick wall that it had crashed into.

"What precisely does that mean?" the master asked.

"This bird is flying along without thinking about Pythagoras' Theorem and this bird was thinking about Pythagoras' Theorem and flew into a wall."

"I suppose you think you're very funny," the teacher said.

"In my universe I think I'm funny," Ken said. "And I enjoy being funny."

"Is that so?" the teacher said. "And I suppose you think this is very funny."

"No sir, it isn't very funny. It's actually very, very sad."

"Yes," he said, walking to his desk. "Sadder than you think." He wrote something on a piece of paper, folded it and handed it to Ken. "Take that to the headmaster," he said.

Ken left the classroom to the sniggers of the other students and searched for the headmaster's office.

This behaviour about drawing the birds was spawned by the treatment that I got when I walked in there. I was dealt with in a rather stupid way. If there were twelve points in one's life that were important, this incident would be one of my key ones. I've always had somewhere deep inside me a sense of knowing the moment when I am in the moment. To this day I can't explain how that happens but I do know when I'm in it. It had become apparent to me that there were very specific rules for the "good" people – the "nice" people – and those were the people who had lots of money. The poor people lived in a different world. And the rich people were hiring minions such as this teacher to do their bidding. The rich people didn't want to look after their own children – they just shunted them off to boarding schools.

Ken found the office and knocked on the door.

"Come in," a voice called.

Ken walked in and handed the folded note to a woman sitting behind a desk in the small anteroom. She unfolded it, scanned what was written there and looked back up at Ken with a curious half-smile.

She stood, walked around her desk and ushered Ken into the inner office. The headmaster was an unremarkable looking man, with a balding head and a soft belly. He took the note from his secretary and peered at it through wire-rimmed spectacles. Placing the note on his desk he said, "So, this is your first day at St. Julian's and you seem to have managed to turn the place inside out. Everything was peaceful here and was going along just fine. In the village, you have a reputation for being disruptive, and you think you're going to bring that same attitude into this school. Well, I can assure you you're not." And extending the note across the desk to Ken, he said, "This note says 'thrash this boy.' So, I am going to do that in the hope that we will never have to do it again. I want you to understand that you must obey the rules here."

"Take down your pants," the headmaster ordered.

"I beg your pardon?" Ken said.

"I said, take down your pants and bend over that stool," he said, picking up a thin, flexible cane and giving it a few swings. It looked much like a fly-fishing rod but the sections were bound with cord so that when it whistled through the air the tip bent backwards, but when it made contact, the tip curled around the object it was lacerating.

Ken did as he was told and as he bent over the stool he put himself into a sort of dream. "I'm not going to let this affect me," he promised himself. "I'm just not going to allow it."

The blows rained down on his bare buttocks leaving thin, raised welts. Ken felt physical pain but it was as though the pain were being inflicted on someone else. When the headmaster was done, he said, "There. Now I hope we don't have to do this again."

A hush fell over the classroom as Ken entered and sat, his face expressionless.

"Maybe you'd like to come to the blackboard and try again," the master said. "And this time perhaps you will take this matter seriously."

Ken walked to the blackboard, took a piece of chalk and drew an entire flock of birds crashing into a brick wall. He drew one bird flying overhead.

"Ah, so we're still being funny, are we?" the teacher said. "And what do you suppose that means?"

Ken answered, "I think the point of this is that you want to have all the people obeying foolishness so that everyone eventually will be crashing into the wall. The one up here that is flying along – that's me. I'm not crashing into your wall."

The master said nothing. He bent over his desk, wrote another note, folded it and handed it to Ken. "Take this to the headmaster," he said.

Ken knew what to expect this time. But, although the thrashing was harder, he didn't make a sound. When he returned to the classroom he felt a fire burning in his stomach. If this was a war, the school had lost, because anyone who had to resort to violence was already defeated. This place that was supposed to impart higher education really had nothing to do with learning. It thrived on brutality and fear.

Ken was thrashed three times that morning, each time more harshly than the last. Not once did he let one grain of emotion show. By creating his own reality inside his mind, he neutralized the reality of the thrashing. When the pain began, he escaped into his private world.

After the third beating, Ken returned to the classroom and was once again invited to the blackboard at the front of the room.

"No," he said. "I refuse. Why don't you have someone else explain this?"

"Oh!" the master said. Now you're directing the classroom?"

"Well, apparently someone has to, because I think you're a bunch of violent perverts. That's what I think of you. I am here of my own volition. I was not made to come here. All these poor people around me have been made to come. I don't allow people to make me do anything."

The boys in the room became still.

A feeling came over me and I didn't know the word for that feeling. But I knew that I was launched into hell fire and if I lost this one I would lose everything. But I wasn't going to lose it. I didn't care what it meant. Here was the line I had drawn in the sand. There would be no crossing that line.

The master glared at Ken, waved him to sit down and turned his attention to the rest of the class. The instructor was in a foul humour, and the boys quietly went about their work and did as they were told.

At the end of the long day, Ken walked to the foot of the Avenue of Princes and to Francisco's hut perched on the side of the cliff. He told him the story of his first day at school.

"What!?" Francisco shouted.

"There, look," Ken said, pulling down his trousers.

"My God!" Francisco cried. "This is brutality!" and he ranted about the horrors perpetrated by stupid, violent people. But Ken interrupted him asking him not to tell anyone and reluctantly, Francisco agreed.

At home, Ken told no one. This was a private battle between him and the monsters at the school.

Day after day the same performance was repeated. Ken kept score. The other children stayed away from him. Although some might have thought him brave and even admired him, their fear of being associated with him was far greater than their willingness to accept him. Ken did, however, befriend one boy. He was quiet, tall and round with nothing to distinguish him other than his eyes. There was a clear and intense quality about them and when he looked at a person, he rarely blinked, focussing his attention so completely it was as though he was looking into the person's soul. Ken had heard that the boy's grandfather had been Admiral Miklós Horthy von Nagybányaa who served as Hungarian regent from 1920 – 1933. When he and his family escaped the Nazis they made their way to Portugal where they lived in exile.

Ken was drawn to the boy with the strange eyes and they began to talk when they met in the corridors of the school. One day Ken asked him about the beatings. "Do they do this to you?"

"They have," he said.

"And don't you react to it?"

"No. The rules are the rules and you have to obey the rules."

"Even if they're very bad rules?"

"Well, yes. They're the rules."

"I was told that your father was murdered."

"Yes, he was."

"For defying Hitler?"

"Yes."

"Doesn't that tell you something?"

"Yes, it tells me that you get killed for defying the rules."

"I don't mind if I get killed," Ken said.

He thought about that conversation over the next few days and decided that his friend was part of a great human tragedy. He tried to make him understand. "If we lose this we lose it all," he said. "We have to do something."

"Well, maybe you have to. I don't. I don't want to get beaten."

"But they will lose," Ken insisted.

"How are they going to lose?"

Ken let his friend in on his scheme. "We'll drive them crazy," he said. "All we have to do is suffer a little physical pain, which can be dealt with. We'll drive them nuts and eventually they'll do something really silly – go far too far and we'll get them!"

The boy thought about it and agreed that the plan might work. He began being more defiant but his heart wasn't engaged – not the way Ken's was. He had put his life on the line for this battle.

This was my first understanding of us as a species. We're a crisis species. We will put band-aids on things and we will call them fancy names and we will wriggle this way and wriggle that way and put on more and more little band-aids until eventually there's a hemorrhage. Then there's a crisis and then we'll do something about it. I could not have articulated that then, but that was the feeling I had.

Francisco was the only other person with whom Ken shared his strategy. "It's a very dangerous plan," the old man said.

"Yes, but life is very, very dangerous," Ken said. "Look at the fish that we catch and the birds that we shoot. One day we will be killed or we will simply die. So life is very dangerous, isn't it?"

"Yes, it is," Francisco agreed.

"And here at least I'm directing the danger. I want to be the maker of my own danger. But, I will come to you one day and tell you that I have won."

The thrashings grew more brutal, but the harsher his treatment the more Ken knew he was winning. The headmaster was losing control.

Near the end of the term, when Ken had counted 138 beatings, he once more entered the office and this time, instead of standing in front of the big desk, he sat down.

"Don't sit down," the headmaster growled. "I haven't invited you to sit."

"Well, I'm doing it anyway," Ken said, placidly. "And I want to tell you what I think of you. I think you're a little man – a very, very tiny person." Ken held his thumb and forefinger about an inch apart to demonstrate. "The people who have hired you and who have hired all the people here have taken very tiny people who will obey their rules, no matter how ridiculous or horrible those rules are. And you do it because you have no other place in the world to go. This is your last refuge. This is the way you have to be. I think you're evil."

A light flickered in the headmaster's eyes. He sputtered incoherent words as he reached for his cane.

"You cannot inflict pain on me," Ken said. "Not physically. The pain that I feel is in a different place."

The headmaster came at him. Ken pulled down his trousers and lifted his shirt. "Go on then," Ken taunted him.

The man lost control and flailed Ken's back and buttocks until his arm could no longer lift the cane. He threw down his weapon, stormed out of the room and slammed the door. Slowly Ken pulled his clothes back on, feeling the blood soaking into his shirt. This was his moment.

He left the school and walked home. By the time he got there the blood had begun to congeal and each movement caused pain. Ken Sr. had left his office early that day and was at home to greet his son. His smile of welcome faded. You don't look well," he said. "You're white."

"I'm not too well," Ken said.

"What happened?"

Ken moved to take his jacket off, but when his father saw the pain it was causing he put out his hands to help. "What is this?" he asked. The shirt under the jacket was soaked in blood. His face grew white and his lips compressed into a thin line. Gently he put his arms around his son, "What on earth happened?"

Ken told him the story.

His father's lips grew whiter and thinner until they formed a colourless line. When Ken had finished his tale, he said, "We're going to the doctor right now and we're also going to the police. He documented the evidence of the beating with a camera and had charges laid against the headmaster. The man was arrested and left the country within a month.

That was the moment I knew I was politically powerful. The understanding I had of my life changed. It was my first political victory. This is where the steel began to be forged. These things have stayed with me for life, not in any negative or harsh way but as little reminders that we can overcome almost anything if we learn how to do it.

Ken had won the battle but he was also expelled from the school because he could not be seen as having won.

A few weeks later, Louise's brother, James – and his family – arrived from Spain.

The two men talked about their multitude of business interests. They dealt in a vast number of industrial concerns, including mining, road building, steel manufacturing and shipbuilding. They agreed it would be wise to forge an alliance in the event that the business climate became unstable, since Spain and Portugal were ruled by dictatorships, and there was always the chance of trouble in a totalitarian regime. Such forces might be difficult to fight as a single businessman but a larger consortium could be effective in bringing influence to bear on the government. Putting aside their animosity, they shook hands on the agreement that they would come to each other's rescue in the event that trouble should occur.

During his Uncle James' visit, Ken spent more time than usual at Francisco's shack. One day, the old man presented Ken with a big stone he had carried up from the beach. "Draw that stone," he said.

Ken did.

"Well, all you've told me is what I already know about that," Francisco said. "I can see that. You don't need to tell me that. Tell me something about the stone that I can't see."

Ken spent the rest of the day wrestling with the notion of drawing a stone that would tell the old man something he didn't already know. He discarded drawing after drawing, and after hours of work, he presented one to Francisco who nodded in satisfaction. For Ken, it was a mystery – to him it still looked like a stone. But he learned that he could only draw what he could draw. The viewer would either read something into the drawing or not – making it significant was not his job.

When he finished his last drawing he said to Francisco, "You show me how to do things and I make drawings that tell you stories and yet I don't know any stories about you. Are you married? Do you have children? Who are you?"

Francisco told Ken the facts. Yes, he was married and he lived with his wife in the village. He had a son who was doing his military service in one of the colonies in Africa. The only part of his life he was prepared to tell stories about – the only part that made his eyes blaze – was his life as a fisherman. When he was a young man, Portugal had a vast fleet of tall ships that sailed by the hundreds to the Grand Banks where they fished for cod.

Francisco told him it was a rough life. Many fishermen died on the choppy, foggy seas. Once, he was hired on to a whaling ship that sailed to the Arctic to hunt for the huge mammals, in the Baffin Island area. Ken was enthralled with the old man's tales of ice spreading as far as the eyes could see, of huge polar bears on the floes, of Eskimos living in igloos made of blocks of solid snow.

Because he wanted more and more stories, Ken made a bargain with Francisco. In exchange for drawings, the old man would tell him tales of the Arctic.

The exchange continued for many years. Visits with Francisco consisted of gathering food, cooking, eating, drawing, telling stories and then taking hammers and chisels to the beach and continuing the work of building the wall.

But outside of the magical world with Francisco there loomed the threat of being sent to school in England. Community opinion was that a child who was effectively in trouble with the church and the school, who rarely wore shoes and who spoke the language of the peasants was too disruptive of the order of things.

One day, Ken's father addressed the subject. "How do you feel about school in England?" he asked.

"I don't want to do anything of the kind," Ken said.

"What will happen if real pressure is brought to bear on you?"

"I won't go. I just won't. I've had enough of that world and I don't belong to it."

"Well, what do you propose to do for an education – the formal side of it?"

"No one wants to learn more than I do," Ken said. "I'd like to have someone teach me. It can't be hard. Millions of people around the world read and do arithmetic."

He pondered his education for several days and decided that the wisest thing would be to attend art school. When he presented this idea, his father agreed that if his mind was made up to be an artist, then art school was the logical choice.

Rui dismissed the notion, with an elaborate shrug. "Why on earth do you need to go to art school?" he asked. "You're a magnificent, genius primitive hatched out of thin air. Don't mess it up. Just persist in what you are doing."

"Michelangelo had an apprenticeship," Ken argued. "So did da Vinci and lots of others."

"An apprenticeship is one thing," Rui said. "Art school is a completely different matter."

Art school was an affectation, he said. Art schools and the teachers in them tended to parrot whatever had been written in art history books. Teachers had massaged the past repeatedly, with interpretations piled on top of each other. The putty they worked with never hardened – teachers continued kneading it until no one could discern its original shape. The fact is, he said, most of the artists whose work we so admire weren't even producing what they wanted to create. They made art to order, for their patrons – which were the church and the nobility. Art, as taught in the schools, was something between an industry and a passing fad. Rui was adamant – Ken's art should not be touched, changed or influenced by a teacher.

"I don't interfere with how you draw," he said. 'I don't tell you anything. I just watch you and we talk. Your friend, Francisco – it's the same. Your father – it's the same. That's all you need."

Ken was not convinced. His investigations led him to an art school just outside Lisbon, not far from the village. He sent a letter but received no response. He enlisted his father's help in drafting another letter. This time a response came – the school didn't take young students. Ken should apply again when he was eighteen.

In reply, his father packaged up some of his son's drawings and sent them to the school. Their evasive reply seemed to indicate they didn't believe an eleven-year-old boy was the author of the drawings.

Ken Sr. visited the school and after a number of meetings and lunches, Ken was admitted. On his first day, he was surprised to find that the entire institution was dedicated to the study of Pablo Picasso. Students were required to learn about him and his work, and to draw and paint like him.

Ken walked home after the first day thinking, "Is that art school? Is that what it's all about? Why are they teaching me to paint the way someone else paints? I'm not interested in painting like Picasso."

On the second day he said, "This is not what I came here for. I didn't come here to paint like Picasso."

"What's wrong with Picasso?" the teacher asked.

"Personally, I think he can't paint," Ken said.

The teacher's mouth dropped open. "I suppose *you're* going to judge that he can't paint?"

Ken shrugged. "I think he's a man who is full of very negative thoughts and emotions. Look at his paintings – they're brutal! Is this what is going on inside him? Look at the women he paints! Look at how he paints them! He's a misogynist! I do not want to paint like Picasso. Perhaps you should be reminded that Picasso is alive and well and painting and living in France. I came here to learn other things."

"What do you want to know?" the teacher asked.

"I want to know the technical things. I want to know about different materials – how do they work? Once I know how to manipulate the materials, I will decide what is what and no one is going to decide for me. How on earth can anyone teach someone about what is in their souls or what could potentially be there? Not one single human out of all the humans that have ever been will see into my soul, and likewise I will never see into the soul of any other human being. The question is, do they want to look? And are they brave enough? The most dangerous place in the world is the centre of one's self where all the secrets and all the fears lie. I'm prepared to go there even if it shrivels me up like an autumn leaf. That's what it's about to me."

On the third day, Ken refused to do what the teacher asked of him. "Show me how to use different materials." Ken said.

"No. You have to follow the rules."

Ken sighed. "Picasso broke all the bloody rules – don't you understand?"

"Oh – and you're going to break all the rules!"

"Absolutely – I'm going to shatter them and then pick up all the pieces and see what happens when you put them back together again differently – but not as ugly as Picasso."

At the end of the class, Ken packed up his books and pencils and left. His formal art education was finished.

Ken's father made inquiries and found a tutor – John Traynor, an Irishman – who gave lessons in his private school. Ken found the lessons, if not exciting, at least enjoyable and interesting.

Shortly after Ken's uncle's visit, his grandfather, Don Hymie, and grandmother, Victoria, came to stay for several weeks. Victoria was the matriarch of the family and ruled it with the proverbial iron fist. She was a tiny woman with a curved back, a stooped gait and hair that reached the floor when she let it down.

Ken loved to brush his grandmother's hair with her silver-backed tortoiseshell brush. Victoria, in turn, enjoyed nothing more than having her hair combed and the two became friends. Ken was the only one in the family who she never tried to terrorize. She called him a clown. "Tu es un Paeaso." But the word had deeper textures than merely clown. It embodied the village idiot, the King's fool and the savant.

Ken also developed a strong relationship with his grandfather, whose passion was his plants and his orchards. He derived enormous pleasure from grafting fruit trees and he was an avid historian and linguist. When he came to visit, he told Ken, "I am going to be your history teacher."

Every day Ken and Don Hymie walked to the beach to have lunch with Francisco. Class distinctions meant nothing to Don Hymie and that alone was enough to command Ken's love and respect.

At low tide, they would wade out and hunt for shrimps, which they would quickly throw into a pot of boiling water and eat by the handful, accompanied by large pitchers of beer. While they ate bread and shrimp and drank beer, Don Hymie told stories of his family history dating back for hundreds and hundreds of years.

As summer drew to a close that year, his father asked him one day – as was his custom – what he wanted for his birthday.

There was no question in Ken's mind. His grandfather, knowing how much he loved art, had given him a book of paintings that hung in the Prado museum in Madrid. One of those paintings had become an obsession – a landscape dotted with tiny encampments – tiny in relation to the enormous giant wreathed in mist that strode across that landscape. Beasts and people fled from his might. "The Colossus," Don Hymie had explained to him, was painted by Goya, Spain's most famous and revered artist.

"I want to go to The Prado and see 'The Colossus'," Ken said.

"Very well, go get the book and let's discuss it," his father said.

Ken, his father and grandfather pored over the picture. Don Hymie explained, "Goya was so upset by his own people that he painted and drew a great number of images of the Spaniards as being a brutal and disappointing people. Many of his drawings portrayed the people as monsters. The portrait of this giant is a painting that embodies all his feelings."

Ken had no idea what it was about the picture that compelled him but he felt that he had to see it as enormous as it was in life. In the book, it was merely a postcard stuck on the page.

When the day of his birthday dawned, Ken and his father boarded the train from Lisbon to Madrid. Don Hymie had returned to Spain but had arranged to meet them at the station and accompany them to the Prado. As night fell, Ken and his father wandered from coach to coach and came upon two Guardia de Seville, rifles slung over their shoulders and tin hats perched awkwardly on their heads. They were cutting up a watermelon, standing on the shifting platform connecting two of the cars. One of the guards offered Ken a hunk of the melon. He accepted gratefully and sat down on the metal grid, careful to avoid the crack that opened and closed and shifted from side to side. He bit into the fruit, juice squirting from the sides of his mouth and dribbling down his chin. He spat out the seeds, aiming at the steel rails slipping by beneath him.

"I don't know if I'm hitting the rails. I can't see," he said to his father.

His father smiled, "Well, that's what art is about," he said. "It probably takes two hundred years – maybe five hundred years – before we know what the consequences are of our actions. Whether it's an artist or an engineer or a scientist or a philosopher, we will never know at the time. It's for others to judge after we're gone. All we can do is get on with the getting on and do it with a good heart and try very, very hard not to have ill intent in any of it, because the world will certainly help you out in that department. You can make the finest invention you want, and it won't be very long before someone finds a way of turning that tool into a weapon."

"But has there ever been anybody who knows the final consequences of what they have made?"

"No," his father said.

"But do you get an inkling as to the consequences?"

"Yes, you do. We get all kinds of inklings. The problem here is that we are seeking answers – always seeking answers. The problem isn't the answer. The problem is the question. I have a suspicion that if ever once in the lives of humans a perfect question could be asked, you would find the answer beautifully wrapped up in it. The answer is in itself. Ask yourself, for instance, what is the reason for the universe? The universe. What is the purpose of life? Life. Nothing more."

"So – no God?" Ken asked. "No devil?"

"No. I think these are just inventions of an insecure creature."

By the time they arrived at the Prado, Ken was almost trembling with excitement. He glanced quickly at the magnificent works of art, growing more and more impatient to discover "The Colossus" – and growing ever more frustrated when they walked through room after room without finding the object of his obsession.

Finally Ken's father steered them to the office of the director who graciously ushered them in and Ken opened his book, pointing to the painting. "We can't find this," he said.

"Well, come," the director said. "I'll show you exactly where this painting is."

He led the way up two flights of stairs passing through several rooms before coming to a small alcove. There, around the corner and almost hidden from view was "The Colossus."

Ken's face fell. This magnificent painting – this immense picture – was tiny – hardly bigger than the postcard in the book.

"You don't seem to be very happy," the director said.

"No – it's so small."

"Well, how big did you think it was going to be?"

"I thought it would be huge."

"Ah, but it is huge. It's huge in its meaning."

"Yes, I know," Ken said.

"Oh. You do? What do you think it's about?"

"It's about people. It's a portrait of monstrosity."

"Yes it is."

"It wasn't my interpretation," Ken said. "It was my grandfather's, Don Hymie."

"You're a very lucky young man to have a grandfather like Don Hymie. One day, maybe you'll be a great man too. Now, let's go back to my office and talk about this."

They walked back down the stairs to the director's office where they talked about art and the nature of people and the world – a conversation that carried on over a leisurely lunch at a nearby café.

Once again, I had the feeling that this was important. I didn't know what it meant but my tummy told me that all of this stuff was very, very important. The people who surrounded me – the adults and the children – didn't seem the least interested in these things. But if you're not interested in these things then you're in trouble, I thought. You have to be interested. We're going to find the answer to ourselves in these matters. These were the building blocks of a philosophy that eventually led to my being called an arrogant little bastard.

3

Politics and Michelangelo

Barely a year after the new tutor had been installed to round out Ken's education, his uncle James insisted that Ken be sent to England for proper schooling. Ken was puzzled. After all, no one pressured his sister about an education. Nor was there any great argument about his uncle's son, Peter.

What Ken didn't know was that his uncle James had a plan for Ken. The argument about Ken arose most often in discussion about Ken Sr.'s and James' business interests. The quandary both men faced was succession. Who would take over the family business and carry it on into the future? James had been watching his feisty young nephew and saw in him the energy, creativity and sheer nerve it would take to run a business empire. In both families someone had always emerged to take over the business – someone who would fight and move forward against all odds. James had tagged young Ken as the person most suited to do this.

Ken Sr. finally said, "Enough. He is going on the path of his choosing. I think he is one of the people in the world who didn't come with a tabula rasa. He came with something. Some of us seem to do that. I think I did and I think he has too. The interference that occurred in my life was damaging and painful and took a lot of undoing. So no – he's going to go the way he's going to go."

They did, however, continue to talk about business and reaffirmed their agreement to come to each other's assistance if trouble should come either politically or corporately.

Ken continued drawing, fishing and hunting, which had become his latest obsession. On his thirteenth birthday, Ken's father gave him a Portuguese ONA 410 rifle, which became his closest and most intimate companion. He and Francisco shot and collected birds, sometimes accompanied by Francisco's friend, Juaon, who had the homeliest body and the sweetest temperament Ken had ever encountered.

Like Quasimodo, his back presented a large, rounded hump that caused his arms to thrust forward and circle in front of him. Bumps and pockmarks covered his face and body. His nose was bulbous, his lips pendulous and his teeth either missing or crooked. But a light shone in his eyes and Ken made many drawings of him. One day, when he had finished a drawing of Juaon at Rui's house, the architect offered to purchase it.

"I'll give it to you," Ken said.

"No," he said. "You have to learn about artwork. You don't give it away. If you do, it becomes worthless. Things that are given, such as works of art, tend to sit on the shelf for a while and then they go into a bedroom somewhere and before you know it they're in the basement and they become part of the flotsam and jetsam of people's lives. But if you pay a great sum of money for something it goes over the mantel and you hold cocktail parties to boast about your acquisition. That is one side of the art world you're going to have to learn about. How do we attribute value to something in a world that understands very little? Everything is quantified in our world. Therefore, if it has a big number attached to it, it must be of great value."

Ken and Rui agreed on a sum of money that was not too great but that seemed like a great deal to Ken. With great pride he told his father that he had sold a drawing to Rui.

"Did you offer to give it to him?" His father asked.

"Yes, I did and he wouldn't take it," Ken said and repeated what Rui had told him.

Ken Sr. smiled. "Yes, that's probably quite wise," he said.

One day, When Francisco and Ken came out of the shack to go fishing they noticed a young woman walking on the beach. Ken had seen her from time to time walking to or from the hospital where she worked, or climbing down the cliffs to the ocean. On this day, as so often happened, the beach was empty, save for themselves and the marine life that scurried about the rocks. The young woman had not seen the old man and the boy and thinking herself utterly alone, took off her clothes and walked into the water. Ken was mesmerized; she was the most beautiful creature he had ever seen. "Look at that," he whispered to Francisco.

"Yes," he said, as though reading his thoughts, "She is very beautiful. She has a limp, you know."

"What does a limp have to do with anything?"

"It's a long and complicated story – and we should not be interfering here. She thinks she's alone so let's let her be alone."

From that day on she became Ken's passion. He discovered that she was a nursing student and that she had come from a village several miles away. Her family were peasants but she had studied hard because she was determined that she would not become a servant for rich people.

He also became friends with Dawn Coates, a girl who was being tutored at the same small school he attended each day. Her parents were divorced – her mother, American, and her father, English. She was one of the first children he had ever admired. She was strong and direct and seemed fearless. Ken's father was pleased that his son had finally found a friend his own age – and not one he classified a "waiter." He explained, "They're waiting for the old folks to die so that they become the inheritors of the fortunes and of the businesses. But they don't actually do anything. I suppose you could say that old inheritances of old interests and much money are really producing idiots. You'll notice quite often that a person makes a great amount of money and then passes it on to the next generation. The second generation manages to hold on to it and between the third and fifth generation they lose it. Consequently, they have to hire people to look after them – not just servants in the house but servants at all levels. They just become figureheads. Their interests are run by the brains they hire."

"I don't agree with it," he added. "I think it's folly and I don't feel that inheritance is a good idea. So this is what I think we should do. I love you very much. I will give you everything in life that a father can possibly give his son, and I will try as best I can to prepare you to live in this world. But I'm not going to leave you a penny. I don't want you to become a waiter. I want you to live your life full bore.

"Therefore, while I am alive and we have money – and money is something that doesn't necessarily stay; sometimes it's here and sometimes it's gone – I'm going to make a one-time gift to you of some money, which you can do with as you please. I hope it will help you learn about money. Money is a very peculiar thing."

"What am I going to do with this money?" Ken asked.

"Whatever you wish. A gift is a gift and once I give it to you, it's yours. A gift with attachments is no gift at all." The gift was to be equivalent of about two hundred thousand dollars.

"What do you do with *your* money?" Ken asked.

"My money is divided into many areas to cover many needs," he said.

"But what do you do with your own money?"

"Actually, do you know Mr. Ben Sax who comes every second Thursday for dinner? He is my banker and he looks after me and my interests and our money, and I do all my banking through him. He has an office at the Bank of London and South America on the Street of Gold in Lisbon."

"Maybe, I should talk to him about my money."

"I think that would be very wise," his father agreed.

A couple of days later they drove to Lisbon. Mr. Sax's office was imposing and oppressive. The walls were covered with dark studded leather while the furniture was massive and made of wood so dark it was almost black. Sitting behind an enormous desk in the dim room was the diminutive Mr. Sax, who beamed with disarming warmth. Ken's father sat back and let his son present the story of how he had come into the princely sum of two hundred thousand dollars.

"What would you like me to do?" Mr. Sax asked, when Ken was finished.

"I would like you to help me deal with the money," Ken said.

"So you would like me to be the guardian of your money?"

"Yes, I suppose that's it."

"And then what?"

"I don't know. What do you do with money?"

"You can do anything you want," he said. "But if you intend for it to grow, then you invest it, and hopefully, you invest it in wise ways."

"What do you suggest?" Ken asked.

Mr. Sax described several options that seemed very complicated to Ken. "And then," he said, "There is currency trading. You buy one currency against another currency and as it goes up and down you buy and sell, and buy and sell. If you give me a buy-sell order, I will do that. If you study the matter, you will find that the Portuguese escudo against the American dollar seems to vary, on a regular basis, between twenty-eight to thirty escudos to the dollar. If you're buying and selling, you can accumulate quite a lot of money over time."

Ken signed the agreement. As they left the bank, he said to his father, "This currency business sounds very interesting. Do you do it?"

"Oh no," his father said.

"Why don't you?"

"It's immoral."

"What do you mean it's immoral?"

"You're buying currency and selling currency," he said. "You don't make anything. You don't do anything. You're making money for doing nothing and there's something wrong with that."

"Then why did you let me do it?" Ken asked.

"You're an independent soul today," his father replied. "You are a man of your own and now you live in this world as you will. You are welcome under my roof forever and ever. I don't care what crime you commit, you're still my son and you're welcome in my home. But you are free – utterly free to go out in the world."

That day, Ken Sr. also thought it was time to apprise his son of the political situation in the country. He told Ken never to speak of personal topics at home when the servants were present. They might not be quite what they seemed, he explained, and they might be listening. Portugal was under the rule of a dictator. It was a fascist government and that sort of government tends to be paranoid. "They watch anyone who might command power," he said.

He told him that everything one did would be noticed and since Ken had made himself very noticed indeed in Parede, the authorities would come to the conclusion that any views he held must also be the views of his parents. He asked Ken to never talk about politics – not to anyone.

He explained the recent history of the country. In the early 1920s, the king of Portugal and his heir were assassinated but no one was able to form a government and the country descended into chaos. More and more warring factions emerged that fought with each other and demonstrated against each other.

Some of those factions finally approached Antonio Oliveira Salazar who had graduated in law from Coimbra University, in northern Portugal, in 1914, and had become a lecturer in economics there. Initially, he said "no" to ruling the country, explaining that he was a professor not a politician.

Eventually, he did agree and assumed absolute power establishing an anti-democratic, anti-parliamentarian and authoritarian regime that would last four decades. He was regarded as a fascist and seen to be in league with Franco and Spain. He was included in many meetings of the Axis powers and yet he steered Portugal down a middle path during the war.

He was able to learn vast amounts of information from the Axis meetings and passed it on to Churchill before Churchill was even in power. Salazar knew that it was in his best interests to assist the Allies, and perhaps because to all appearances he was aligned with the Axis he had various levels of police and secret police that watched everyone.

Enrique Galvoa, the man who had been instrumental in bringing Salazar to office, became disillusioned as the leader assumed absolute power and ruled with an iron hand. Galvoa made his views known and was eventually arrested and sent to jail in Africa. Imprisonment didn't stop him. He organized the inmates and the jailers and turned the prison into a far more humane place. And although he had always been a hunter, in Africa, he became interested in nature and its preservation.

Through sheer force of personality, he befriended the warden who gave him more and more latitude to come and go – and eventually released him. Galvoa travelled throughout Portuguese Africa including Mozambique, Angola and Guinea. He wrote about the state of the environment and about the plight of creatures that, even then, were endangered. He became well known in Africa and commanded a great deal of respect there. After some years, he took charge of the jail, running it along fairly democratic lines.

Ken's father told him that he had struck up a correspondence with Galvoa despite the fact that in a fascist dictatorship, such a connection was highly dangerous. However, Ken Sr., whether through sheer naiveté or brash self-confidence, had no hesitation in exchanging letters with Galvoa or other left-leaning acquaintances in Europe.

He told his son it was possible to start with the best of intentions but where politics were involved, the situation could quickly get out of hand. A democracy, he said, was probably as close as mankind would ever get to a miracle.

Ken wanted to know how one could have a political system that worked when society, even on the smallest scale, was dysfunctional. He pointed out that even in their own household they had servants, all of them women, most of them young and illiterate, who were paid a pittance. In most households the servants were treated like animals. In a country where this was going on, how could there ever be a fair political system?

"Just between you and I, that is my interest," Ken Sr. Said. "But, you can't go into the street with guns and mobs behind you – it just doesn't work. What we need to do is bring the wages of the people up so they will have something to lose. People who have nothing to lose are the most dangerous people on earth."

He explained that it was because of this reasoning that he paid his staff double the normal salary. "That," he said, "Is actually a very political act because the handful of families who wield power want to keep the populace down so they can control them. Doing what I am doing is an overt political act. "

His father said that he was walking a thin line but if he could get away with what he was doing, he would win. Others would have to follow his lead – they would have to match the salaries he was paying or all the best brains in the country would go to work for him. Once he had the best brains, he would be in a position to start other companies and continue to expand his business interests to the detriment of others. But as his companies grew and he employed more and more people fairly, his ideas would also spread.

"But that's a very slow way of doing things," Ken said. "I want to change things quickly."

"There are no quick fixes," his father said. "Anybody who tells you there are is just selling you snake oil."

Ken had complained to his father several times about the servants. He explained that he couldn't bear being served – that he felt uncomfortable with it. "Why can't we get up and serve ourselves?" he asked. "What's wrong with us making our own beds? What's wrong with us cleaning the house?"

"That's the culture we're in," his father said. "We're not in charge here. This is not our country. We're here as guests and there's a limit to how much we can disrupt this society."

"It sounds a bit like an excuse."

"Partially, it is. But anyone who wants to move things along too quickly is going to destroy the very thing they're trying to do."

He added that he paid their servants the same way he paid his office and factory workers – twice what anyone else paid. He admonished his son once again to be careful with his conversation in earshot of the servants. The Kirkbys were a prominent, well-known and powerful family, he said and it would be foolhardy to think they were not being watched. They had to assume that their servants had already been approached to report on what went on in the house and on what was talked about. "Don't forget," he said. "Everything that you say will be taken as coming out of my mouth and originating from my mind."

Silence fell between them while Ken thought about what his father had said. He asked about his aunt Helen who had just come to visit. She was his mother's older sister – a strikingly beautiful woman, tall with startling green eyes and gleaming, long black hair. She spent most of her time in her bedroom, rarely coming out to talk with anyone but when she did she invariably took a contrary viewpoint. She was late for everything, including meals. Most disturbingly, from Ken's point of view, there was an aura of profound sadness about her. Ken thought he understood a bit about that because although he was blissfully happy most of the time, every now and then, when he looked at the world and the things people did to each other, a feeling of deep, almost overwhelming sorrow would pass through him and linger for some moments.

Ken's father explained that his aunt was a very unhappy woman and apparently, from what his father had learned and read of his mother's family history, there had been at least one suicide in the family's eighteen generations. However, it was something no one talked about. It was considered shameful, he said. Some family members even believed that such deep unhappiness was contagious. "I don't believe it," he told Ken. "I think it's nonsense. But this has been a legend and a belief for so long that it has taken on its own power."

The next day Ken's father introduced him to Francisco, who he called Frank, the Count of Peniche. Frank was six-foot-two, with a perfectly bald shining dome. From the tips of his gleaming shoes to his courtly and gentle manners, he was perfectly polished. He shook Ken's hand and the two of them chatted for a while about Ken's drawings and his adventures on the beach. Then Frank said, "I have brought you something. I gather that my namesake, Francisco, has told you many stories about northern Canada."

"Yes."

"And are you interested in that?"

"Yes – very interested."

"Well, I have a book here, which tells the story of a biologist who went to study snow geese in Ungava Bay and during his time there fell in love with a Cree woman. So this is the story of how all that happened and how they lived their lives. Are you interested in it?"

"Oh, yes."

"Well, if you like it, I also have other books that deal with Canada. I have one book that I think would be very interesting to you. It's the story of a young man who encounters the plains Indians while in search of a stolen black pearl. He lives with the Indians and learns to speak their language. If you like the book I have given you, I will search this one out in my library and bring you that one too."

Reading the book was slow and difficult for Ken, but the subject matter fascinated him so much he persevered. He fell in love with the book about the Canadian North. What the author described fitted perfectly into his dreams of freedom and adventure. When he finished, he asked Frank for more and Frank gave him the book about the quest for the black pearl. Like the first book, this one described exactly how Ken imagined his life could be – a life completely opposite from the tightly structured society he lived in – a life lived on a giant land with huge skies, and rolling hills and herds of buffalo – a life where the hero was the master of his own life and could do whatever he pleased.

Ken still drew every day, but now, most of his drawings were of the beautiful young woman he had seen on the beach. From his memory, he drew, her face, and her body that he had glimpsed just once as she walked naked into the sea.

One day he showed the drawings to Francisco. The old man acknowledged they were very good but why had he made so many of this woman?

"I really like her," Ken said.

"What do you mean when you say you really like her?"

"I can't stop thinking about her."

"That could be a problem," Francisco said.

"Why?"

"In our society I'm on one side of the fence and you're on the other. We're not supposed to be together. Because of your father and his personal views, this has been overcome and we're good friends. But when it comes to an interest in a young woman, your family is not allowed to mix with families of peasant stock."

"No one is going to tell me who I can associate with and who I can't," Ken said.

"But it's more than association," Francisco said. "The feelings you're having right now are leading somewhere and that means that you are falling in love."

"Is that what it is?"

"And you're much too young for that."

The next day, Ken walked to the entrance of the hospital and waited outside. For the first time in his life, he felt fear, and he was intrigued, interested, excited and disappointed in himself for feeling afraid. He had survived more than a hundred beatings from the headmaster at St. Julian's and not once had he felt anything like this. He had come to believe that he lived in a state of grace and fear was something that would never touch him. And yet here he was, his stomach churning.

When he saw the young woman he smiled and gave her the drawing, explaining his love of art and how he had drawn her face from memory. He admitted that he had created many drawings of her and he told her how he had first seen her on the beach. "Yes," she said. "You're helping Francisco build the wall."

"Yes," he said and added that he probably shouldn't tell her but he related how when he had seen her on the beach she had taken her clothes off and gone swimming. The young woman's face flushed deep red. Did he have drawings of that too? Ken admitted he did. Had he shown them to anyone? No –would she like to have them? Yes – and while she waited Ken ran home and rushed back carrying a stack of drawings.

They sat on the steps of the hospital looking at them while Ken marvelled at her tenacity. She could easily have been one of the servants in his house but somehow she had done something that had changed the course of her life. She talked about her family and her village. She told Ken that she was going to do whatever it took to get an education and to have a rewarding career.

Ken told her about his family and she said, "Yes, I know about your family and they probably won't be happy if you're associated with me."

"My worry was that you wouldn't want to associate with me because people have said things about me," Ken said.

She smiled. "Yes, there are all kinds of stories in the village about you."

"Like what?"

"There are stories about you and religion. Apparently, you are a very dangerous person who associates with dangerous people. The priest thinks you're the devil."

"No one in the market will talk to me," Ken said. "Everybody's scared and I'm just a kid. If they're scared of a kid, how solid is their religion and their thinking? Do you go to church?"

"No."

"Do you get into trouble because of that?"

"I don't live at home any more," she said. "I live on my own so I do as I please."

"But what about society?"

"Society doesn't pay any attention."

"How come?"

"Because I'm not notorious and I'm not rich and I'm not in any position for people to notice me."

"So do people have to be rich and notorious to be noticed?"

"Yes, of course. Also, I have a limp."

Ken recalled that Francisco had also pointed out her limp. "Yes, you have the slightest limp – I have a long nose. What does it matter?"

"That's an awkward and difficult subject," she said. "I don't want to talk about it right now."

Miloo became the central focus of his life and as their friendship deepened, Ken confessed that he liked her – but far more than the word implied. He liked her very deeply.

"You can't like me that much," she said. "You come from one world and I come from another and there is no hope that we could ever be more than just passing friends. It would be nothing but trouble for everybody."

Ken felt a familiar rebel anger stirring in him. "Why? Did somebody make a rule?"

"Yes," she said. "Those are the rules."

"But if the rules are bad, do you still accept them?"

"It's everybody," she said. "It's everywhere you turn. That's the way it is."

"Well, I don't accept it."

"You'll get into a lot of trouble."

"I don't care. It seems that all the best things in my life are trouble and I just won't accept it."

Ken's father noted the growing friendship between his son and Miloo. Perhaps thinking to distract him, he asked him one late summer day what he would like for his next birthday. Ken opened his Michelangelo book to the photograph of David. "I want to see that," he said.

"Why that?" his father asked.

"It's probably the most perfect thing I have ever seen. It has only one flaw."

"And what's the flaw?"

"Look at his hand," Ken pointed to the picture. "He's holding a stone in his hand and that's the stone he was putting in a sling to throw at Goliath. Everything else is perfect but this hand is weird. Why would he do that? Why would he make such a strange hand on such a beautiful body?"

"I don't know," his father admitted. "So, that's what you really want to do?"

"Yes. I want to go to Florence."

On the morning of his thirteenth birthday, he and his father boarded the train to Italy. In Florence, they stepped into a line that seemed to stretch to infinity outside the gates of the Accademia delle Belle Arti. Slowly the line inched its way to the spot where the colossal 17-foot statue towered over the crowd. Ken wanted to feast his eyes, but the relentless throng forced him to walk by it after only a passing glance.

As they left the museum, his father asked, "Did you like it?"

"How can you look at something that way?" Ken asked. "I want to spend a lot of time there."

"I'm afraid that's just the way it is," his father said. "You're just one of millions of people who also want to see it."

Ken was adamant. He didn't care about the realities of the situation. He wanted to see the statue of David on his own and he wanted to take all the time in the world to absorb its beauty. He would talk of nothing else and finally his father relented and asked permission to see the director of the museum. They were ushered into his office and Ken explained how his grandfather had given him the book of Michelangelo and how very interested he was in seeing David and how disappointed he was after coming all this way, that he couldn't see the statue properly because there were so many people.

The director smiled. "That's true," he said. "There are quite a lot of people who want to see David."

"But, you can look at it alone," Ken said. "No one comes at night."

"That's quite true," the director admitted. "In fact night time is the best time to see it. The incandescent lights make it look very different."

The director agreed to allow Ken into the museum that night. But first they went out to supper where they discussed Michelangelo's works. The director explained that the art world knew a great deal about Michelangelo because he was a profuse letter writer. The museum had all his writings in safekeeping, even his grocery lists. His letters had allowed historians to determine his relationship to the Pope and to authorities in government.

That night Ken walked through the museum completely alone. Time stopped. He was carried away by the experience – so much so that he could not afterwards describe to his father how he had felt. He only knew that it was as if he had discovered an electrical cord attached to the universe that he was able to plug directly into his soul.

After they had toured Florence, they travelled on to Milan to look at some of the works of Leonardo da Vinci, which Ken thought seemed cold and cruel. He told his father that the Last Supper was an odd painting. "If it's supposed to be the twelve apostles why is one of them a woman?'

"No, they're all men," his father said.

"But look at that," Ken insisted, pointing at the figure leaning away from Jesus on his right hand side, "That doesn't look like a man."

Once again they found themselves talking to a museum director. The director of the church of Santa Maria delle Grazie insisted that all the figures in the painting were men.

"Show me a man who looks like that," Ken said.

"Oh yes, it is – absolutely, it is a man," the director insisted. "There are no women in that picture."

Ken left, wondering why neither the director nor his father could perceive what he saw so plainly.

From Milan, they travelled to Rome where they gazed at Michelangelo's magnificent ceiling in the Sistine Chapel and the other treasures the Vatican museum housed.

I think, in large measure, that is where I started to get the understanding of monumental art. I think it was always in me. That time when I went to Spain to see The Colossus painting that I was so disappointed in – there seemed to be some kind of need to see art on a monumental scale. Seeing David, which is seventeen feet tall – that seemed to be the right size. In order to be able to read I had to see things on a very large scale – so I seemed to need to see art on a very large scale too.

When Don Hymie next came to visit, Ken talked about "The Last Supper" to his grandfather. "The one leaning away from the centre of the table is a woman,"

"Do you think so?" he asked.

"Absolutely. Don't you?"

His grandfather studied the picture gravely. "Yes, actually I do," he said. "But you won't find anyone to support the idea. It has always been assumed that it was all men. I don't think early Christianity was as misogynistic but it certainly developed that way."

Ken's fourteenth birthday failed to follow the usual pattern. His father had not asked him what he wanted nor had he made any plans for an exciting trip. But, on the morning of September 1, 1954, Ken came down to breakfast and found a large beautiful box emblazoned with a crest lying on the table in front of his chair. He hugged his parents, glanced quickly at his birthday card and carefully opened the box. Inside was a large book bound in royal blue Moroccan leather with red and gold trim and gold embossed writing.

He was enchanted before opening it. What precious story could such a book contain? But it was no tale of fact or fiction – inside the volume were the letters of Michelangelo. Ken's mind flashed back to the many conversations he'd had with his father about a recent visit to his grandfather and everything his grandfather had told him, including his premise that true history can only be found in the diaries and letters written by the protagonists – not in the lengthy interpretation of events written after the fact. The book was an exquisite gift, not just because it was beautiful but also because it represented physical proof that his father listened to him with full care and attention.

The book also had great significance because it wasn't the sort of manuscript his father could have picked off a shelf in a bookstore. He had contacted the director of the Accademia delle Belle Arti in Florence and had arranged for a handwriting expert to make perfect copies of Michelangelo's letters. The letters looked identical to the originals – right down to the ink blotches and crossed out words. It was the only book of its kind in the world.

After breakfast, Ken took the book to Rui's house where the architect opened it and silently and slowly leafed through the pages. When he raised his head, tears shone in the corners of his eyes.

"You are the luckiest person," he said when he finally put the book down, "But why are you so fascinated with Michelangelo?"

Ken explained that of all the paintings and drawings and sculptures he had seen, Michelangelo's called to him in a special way. He felt as though they lived inside him and that their lines, colours and forms were engraved on his soul. It wasn't so much that he owned them,; rather it felt as though they possessed him.

What was his favourite work, Rui asked. Was it the *David*?

No, he said, the *David* was pretty – absolutely pretty – too pretty. It was finished. He told Rui about the artist's unfinished sculptures that were stored here and there in Florence away from public view. He had started work on many major pieces that had been partly carved and chiselled out of raw stone and then abandoned in various stages of completion. Some were bare outlines in the stone. For him these pieces represented perfection.

"Why?" Rui asked.

"The *David* whispers to you," Ken explained. "But these unfinished sculptures howl at you. They are so powerful it's as if all the complaints of humanity come through them."

"Do they have mouths?" Rui asked.

"No – they're just blocked out giant pieces of marble. But these are the things that really tear at me."

"These sculptures – they sound primitive," Rui said.

"Well, they are primitive," Ken said but that was precisely their appeal. "I'm primitive. It seems to me that all the feelings I have are terribly primitive. Whenever I encounter the nice, dancing world of all these extravagant nuances and the veneer – the mask – I get my back up. That's how it affects me. The roughness of these sculptures – that's the mastery. He didn't need to finish them. I'm sure he wanted to but for me it's good fortune that he didn't. And they have this power. I have no idea why they are not on view for the public."

The conversation was interrupted abruptly by the jangling of the telephone. Ken had to come home immediately. Don Hymie was very ill. The family was leaving for Spain immediately.

Don Hymie and his family were in residence in their summer home near Madrid in a village called Miraflores where the entire family had gathered. The turmoil in the house disturbed Ken. His refuge was his ailing grandfather's bedchamber where he spent many hours sitting by his side.

On the third day that he kept vigil, his grandfather's shaking began to diminish and in a barely audible whisper he said, "Close the door."

Ken did as he was asked and came back to his grandfather's side. He rearranged the pillows and as he settled the old man back, he noticed that his hands had become still.

"Come close," Don Hymie said, wrapping his arms around his grandson and holding him near. Then he gently pushed Ken back and held him at arm's length. "I want you to listen to your old grandpa," he said. "And I want you to listen very carefully." His eyes, that only an hour before had been hazy and clouded, were wide open and shining.

"Look at me," he said. "I'm going to make a prediction for you and I don't ever want you to forget it. You have to keep it inside you – don't tell it to anyone. You're going to have a very bright and beautiful life. It won't be an easy life but it will shine. The gods favour you. You are one of destiny's creatures."

He gave Ken's shoulders an almost imperceptible squeeze and lay back against the pillows. Ken held his hand, wondering what his grandfather had meant. Were these just the ramblings of a dying man? Did he have a vision? He noticed that the old man smelled different. "Is this how you smell when you're dying?" he wondered. And then the old man's hand became limp and his face changed. Ken listened, but the sound of his grandfather's breathing was no longer present in the room.

He sat by the old man's side while time stopped and his thoughts stilled. Then he wrapped his arms around him and held him close and felt a large weight lift – a shadow disappeared and peace settled on him.

When he left the room to join the others he told them that Don Hymie had died. He left the house and walked aimlessly up and down the streets of Miraflores for hours, feeling as though he was floating just above the cobbles, his mind suspended in a place that thoughts could not penetrate.

When he returned he found his grandmother in the garden. She came to meet him, put her arm through his and walked with him down the street.

"Did you have a good talk with grandpa?"

"I did."

"Well, that's good."

"Why?"

"Grandpa knows things."

Don Hymie's body was taken to Valencia where the funeral took place. An enormous throng of people crowded into the huge cathedral and lined the steps and sidewalks. Everyone came: the powerful and the peasants – and perhaps the peasants grieved more than the ruling elite. Seeing the tears of love and loss and listening to the heartfelt tributes these people paid to his grandfather, Ken thought how strange it was that this outpouring came upon death. How sad it wasn't done while he was still alive.

4

Good-byes

In the early 1950s, Parede and the Avenue of Princes saw an influx of foreign ambassadors. The American ambassador and his son became Ken's new neighbours and the Portuguese ambassador to the United States, who had a son and daughter, bought a summer home nearby.

One day the Portuguese ambassador invited Ken to a garden party with the lure of a special surprise. On the day of the party, Ken dressed in his best clothes and wandered across the lawns where uniformed waiters glided by with trays of iced lemonade, and platters of seafood, and exotic fruits.

When the ambassador found Ken, he took him by the arm and led him across the lawn to where another gentleman was standing, holding a frosty glass. "I want to introduce you," he said. "This is Monsieur Desjardines. He is the Canadian ambassador to Portugal. You're so fascinated with Canada and the Arctic – it's all I hear you talk about – so, here is the man!"

Ken's mind fell into instant turmoil. There was so much he wanted to ask, but before he even began to marshal his thoughts he blurted out, "I want to be a Canadian."

"You want to be a Canadian?" the ambassador smiled.

"Absolutely," Ken said. "I want to be a Canadian."

"What on earth makes you want to be a Canadian? What do you know about Canada?"

"My friend Francisco, who lives on the beach, tells me stories." And he repeated some of Francisco's tales of whaling, and the Arctic, and life with the Eskimos.

"That's where I want to go," he said. "I want to go to the North. I want to be one of those people."

"One of the people who live in the Arctic?"

"Yes. I want to be a Canadian."

"There are many Canadians that live all across the country," the ambassador explained.

"I want to be one of those that live in the North," Ken said.

"Oh! You want to be an Eskimo!"

"Yes!"

"Then I have bad news for you," Monsieur Desjardines said. "They are a different race from you."

"Why should that matter?"

They sipped lemonade together while they talked about Canada and the far north. Ken asked him if he had ever seen an Eskimo and he admitted that he had not. That was odd, Ken thought. How could a Canadian government official never have seen an Eskimo? And how was it that this same government official spoke with a French accent?

The ambassador explained that he was from French Canada, and there was also an English Canada; and Eskimos lived in an area that few Canadians ever travelled to, and Eskimos lived in a place where no one ever travelled. "Canada is very large," he said.

"I know," Ken said. "I have a globe at home and I've seen how big it is."

"The globe can't really show it," he said. "It's the second biggest country in the world and the Eskimos live in the Arctic. There are no roads and you can't get there unless you go by ship or by air; and by ship only in the summer, *if* it's a good summer."

"Well, that's where I'm going," Ken insisted. "I want to be a Canadian." He asked the ambassador if he had ever seen an iceberg. Only in pictures, he said. Ken was astounded. How could a Canadian not have seen an iceberg? In fact, the ambassador continued, he was quite certain that very, very few Canadians had ever seen an iceberg.

"Does everyone walk around with their eyes closed?" Ken asked.

Monsieur Desjardines smiled. "No," he said. The icebergs were very far away from where most Canadians lived. In fact, the distance from Ottawa to the Arctic was as great as the distance from Ottawa to Parede – perhaps greater. And that great distance, he said, was only one small part of Canada.

"That is still the thing I want most in life," Ken said.

"If you became a Canadian what would you do?" the ambassador asked.

"I'd go to the North and go and see these things my friend Francisco has told me about."

"You don't have to be a Canadian to do that. You can just travel to Canada and see it. Why don't you want to live here? It's a beautiful life you have."

Ken admitted that parts of his life were beautiful but there were also parts that were not. He told him how restricted Portuguese society was – how it appeared to be frozen in its history. The future was already mapped out for this country. The rules were set and obedience was expected.

"I don't want to live in a part of the world that is finished."

"So, Canada isn't finished?"

"It sounds to me like an unmade place. How many people live there?"

"Maybe, twenty million."

"In the second largest country in the world, that must mean there is a great distance between people."

Monsieur Desjardines told Ken that many people lived in big cities although most of those, with the exception of Montreal, were a great deal smaller than most European cities. When Ken said that he wanted to know more, the ambassador promised that he would give him some books about Canada. He kept his promise and gave him many volumes over the next several years.

They also talked about Ken's art and he told him that he planned to draw and paint the North. Ken said that he also liked to fish, and when the ambassador admitted that he too liked to fish, Ken promised to take him to meet Francisco.

"I'd love to do that," the ambassador said. "I'm a fanatic. Wherever I go in the world I take every opportunity to go fishing."

Ken and Monsieur Desjardines became good friends and often went fishing with Francisco, especially in July when the marlin congregated in the bay.

Ken continued to see Miloo and when his mother forbade the relationship, he continued to meet her in secret.

The mid-1950s ushered in a tense time for Portugal. Salazar had been in power for a long time and, like many absolute rulers, he was becoming afraid of the younger men coming up in the ranks. One day, after Ken had accompanied his father to his office and they were driving home, Ken Sr. pointed out the increase in police and army patrols on the roads. The outskirts of the village bristled with armed men. Parede's streets, however, were still clear. Because of the predominately foreign population of the seaside town, it was tacitly considered off limits.

When Ken asked Francisco what was going on, the old man shrugged. "The government is in a state of paranoia – again." And that was all he knew about the situation. Ken watched the artillery in the seaside cliffs with new eyes. It had always been there – hidden from view – but now he observed the telltale signs of war preparations. Before the Second World War, Britain and Portugal had built a huge infrastructure of artillery in caves hollowed out of cliffs that towered over the coast. Enormous semicircular steel doors enclosed the guns. On the ridge above the village, which paralleled the coast, larger guns had been buried in the ground. They had remained hidden for years but recently elevators had brought them to the surface and now their massive barrels pointed out to sea, once again.

A public notice, displayed at the local post office, announced that there would be manoeuvres and the guns were to be fired. Ken took up a prime viewing position on the front balcony of their house. From here he could see straight up the Avenue of Princes to the ridge above the village where an enormous cannon barrel pointed west. The first salvo was scheduled for 11 a.m. Ken was ready and at the exact chime of 11, the gun fired with a deafening roar followed by an ominous drone as the shell sped about 150 feet above ground, hurtled over the cliff and plunged into the sea where a giant plume of water erupted like an undersea volcano. When the excitement of the manoeuvres was over, Ken was left with a hollow feeling that bordered on despair.

The idea of moving to Canada became more and more exciting. Oh, to live in a country that was huge, and sparsely populated, and that seemed peaceful. You never heard stories about this sort of thing going on in Canada. I tried to spend even more time with the Canadian ambassador and, given his passion for fishing, it wasn't too difficult.

Miloo was the brightest light in his sky. He didn't know if he was in love with her – he didn't know what "in love" meant. He only knew that some powerful emotion had taken residence inside him that was unlike anything he had ever experienced. It wasn't only lust, although that too played a large part – it was simply that, with Miloo, he found a comfort that was like coming home. Miloo, had a fire inside her that burned as bright as his own. When he was with Miloo, he felt as though there was one other soul on the planet who understood him completely.

Their relationship gradually changed. Miloo told him stories of her life. She explained that her limp – such a minor impediment – was considered significant. In Portugal, only the men were allowed to have flaws. The women had to be perfect.

Ken raged, his anger, as always, flared when he encountered an injustice. They held hands when they walked and sometimes they stopped walking so that they could stand with their arms wrapped around each other. She protested that society would not allow them to be together and yet she searched him out and welcomed the intimacy.

Then one night, when the tide was low and they walked along the beach where the water was still warm from the heat of the sun, she suggested they go for a swim. They took off their clothes and plunged into the still, moonlit pool. Finally they came together in an embrace and Ken was lost – they were both lost in each other.

Over the next two years the political situation in Portugal began to deteriorate rapidly. Secret police, informers and spies were everywhere and no matter how careful you were, someone was watching and talking.

Ken's father was unaware that he had a mole in his own office. He had hired a gem cutter from Antwerp, in Belgium, the world centre of diamond cutting. His background was a bit shady, but he was an expert in his craft and Ken Sr. had not inquired too deeply into his background. Lisbon was the kind of centre that attracted unusual people: the brilliant, the demonic, and the nefarious – they all gravitated to Portugal's magic city.

Because of the attraction Lisbon held for those who drifted on the fringes of society, governments from around the world stationed their undercover operatives there. Spies followed spies, and double agents crossed triple agents, and one followed another in a complicated and often amusing dance. If you knew the city and had even the slightest inkling of what was going on, you could walk into a restaurant and watch one person sitting at a table watching another person and leave shortly after they had left, and then another person from across the room follow both of them and so on.

The Portuguese secret police kept tabs on the entire dance, although they weren't at all secret to the experienced observer. With their identical trench coats and slouching fedoras, they stood out in a crowd as clearly as if they had sported polka-dotted clown suits. But that was the idea – the government was sending a message to the rest of the world that it had lots of secret police, so everyone had better watch their step.

Sadly, ordinary people were also recruited to inform on their friends and neighbours. They were paid based on the quantity and value of the information they passed on, not by salary. The more they informed the more money they received. As a result, many innocent people were ruined. No one knew who the informers were and so people lost trust in even their closest friends.

New Year's Eve, 1956. Thanks to Ken's careful plotting, the Canadian ambassador had invited Ken's family to a party at his home. Ken was more determined than ever to immigrate to Canada and part of his plan involved forging a relationship between his parents and the Canadian ambassador in the hopes it would make them more comfortable with the idea of leaving their home.

When the family arrived at the residence Monsieur Desjardines met them at the door and immediately spirited Ken away. "Come up to my office," he said. "I have something for you."

Shutting the door behind him, Desjardines said, "I have two letters here and two maps. The first is a letter of introduction to a couple who live in British Columbia on Vancouver Island. They have a little cottage on the shore by a stream. It was once known as the Pink River. It's now called Nile Creek. I go there every year to fish and it is the finest sea-run cutthroat trout and salmon fly-fishing in the ocean. This letter will introduce you and here is a map that will tell you how to get there. This second one is to a Mr. Paddy McGelgan. He's a wild, wild Irishman and is the absolute twin of King George. He lives on a lake between Merritt and Kamloops in British Columbia and I fish there every year before I go to Nile Creek. It is, without question, the finest rainbow trout fly-fishing in the world – and I have been almost everywhere."

Desjardines picked up another smaller envelope. "This is a separate matter," he said. "In the event that circumstances should become difficult, this is my contact information. Do you have a special pocket where you put things?"

"No," Ken said.

"Well, keep this on your person – just in case you need to contact me in a special moment."

"What sort of special moment?"

"I think you can guess what I am talking about. Times are difficult and since I'm your friend, I might be of help."

Canada became the main topic of conversation between Ken and his father. Ken had developed a sense of great urgency about leaving. Logically, perhaps, there was no rush, but he had an unsettling sense that something was about to occur and he had learned to trust his feelings.

One day Ken's father was called to the docks on a matter of some urgency. Ken accompanied his father to the wharf where a crowd was blocking the gangplank. One of their number approached Ken's father and swore at him, telling him to leave or there would be big trouble.

"What is the problem?" Ken Sr. asked calmly.

The man spat on the ground, waved his fists and flung a string of curses at him. Suddenly, faster than Ken could think, his father balled his hand into a fist and punched the man in the face so hard that it lifted him off his feet and sent him sprawling to the ground, where he lay immobile.

Ken Sr. turned around and said quite calmly, "Come along."

Ken was rooted to the spot.

His father stepped over the man, turned around again and said, "What are you waiting for? I said I was a pacifist. I didn't say I was perfect."

Ken nodded and stepped gingerly around the man. The other men stepped back, their eyes following the pair as they boarded the ship.

"What are you going to do about this?" Ken asked.

"Do about what?" his father said. "They're trying to send me a message. This is not the first time that I have been approached in this manner. Apparently, something very serious is going on and I'm on the wrong side of the tracks to the business and government community. Obviously, there are troubles and I just want to send a message that I know how to deal with troubles at whatever level they come."

I feel that to some extent my father was quite naïve. For all his immense goodness and super intelligence, I think there were some blind spots there. Politically speaking, I think he was a very naïve man. I don't think he really saw the magnitude of his actions – of how they were affecting people. In a society which was dancing so carefully, he had thrown open the doors in the most polite and gentle way but in a way that challenged the entire structure of a closed society – a society in which the vast majority of people were kept poor to form a cheap labour pool. For a non-political person, he was behaving in the most overtly political way and was a visible threat to the regime. Add this to the present paranoia and it was a recipe for disaster.

On the drive back to Parede, Ken's father pulled the car to the side of the road and they talked about the future. "Your interest in Canada is fascinating. Are these just romantic notions or is there more to it? What is driving this passion?"

Ken explained. "Here I am in this life. You've helped me to be the person I truly am and I am nothing but a pariah to these people. To the nice people around us I am regarded as nothing but trouble. I would like to live in a country where I can be a contributor. Even if I was not helped there, I would at least be given free rein to live. I don't want to live in a country that is dripping with fear. And I don't want to live in a country where I can't be with the woman I love."

"I understand."

"I really want to go there and I get the worst feelings that we're not going to be able to get out of here. I want us to go before the inevitable occurs. Remember when the Mafia tried to set up shop? They got rid of them in ninety days. If they can get rid of them so easily – and of their political enemies – how difficult would it be to get rid of us? A convenient taxi accident? It's amazing how many taxis run into things in Lisbon."

"This would be very hard on your mother," his father said. "Much as I love her, she is completely unprepared. She has always lived in a hothouse world. You and I are the only ones who have actually lived in the real day-to-day world populated by ordinary human beings."

"I'm very, very serious," Ken said. "I don't want to cause anger or trouble or worry but I want to go to Canada. And first, I want to go and see those places that Francisco has told me about. I want to meet Eskimos. I want to see icebergs and polar bears and igloos and the immense land – some of it rolling forever – the biggest place you have ever seen. I want to see the places where the mountains are so old they've worn down and you can feel the ache in their wearing. I want to see the huge glaciers, which calve and break off into chunks as tall as the tallest building and several city blocks long. These are the things that I want to see."

His father regarded him quietly. "It sounds like a lovely idea," he said at last. "And what do you think you would do there?"

"I don't know. I just want to be there. And I hope you won't be angry with me or disappointed or hurt, but that's where I'm going."

"Not at all," he said and squeezed Ken's shoulder. "Good for you. And I notice that you have very skilfully engaged the Canadian ambassador. You seem to get along very well. I like that. You have a natural talent for being with everybody. You have my blessing."

As his father pulled the car back on the road, Ken asked if he could have an emerald from his father's mines – one of the emeralds he regularly gave to his friends.

"Certainly," he said. "I didn't think you were interested in gemstones."

"I'm interested in one gemstone," he said.

"Which one?"

"If you let me see them, I'll pick out the one I'm interested in."

In his father's den, he looked through the collection and chose one. The next day he gave it to Miloo. She put her arms around him and held him tight, shivering and crying against him.

"This is only a minor token of the way I feel about you," Ken said. "I love you beyond words and this is only a symbol of that love."

"I'm so frightened of the feelings I have," she cried.

"I'm going to ask you not to be," Ken said. "Don't be frightened. It's fear that kills us. I've been talking with the Canadian ambassador about going to Canada and I want you to come with me."

"Canada? It sounds so far away. It sounds so dangerous."

"Yes, it is far away, but how could it be any more dangerous than where we are right now? Look at what's going on here. There are more people disappearing every day and everyone is pretending that nothing is happening. No one is doing anything about it. Everyone goes home at night, looking around corners and holding their breath – wondering if they'll get a knock on the door at three in the morning and disappear too. I won't live that way."

"What can you do about it?"

"There are always things you can do if you don't let fear get in the way. If you stop thinking you shut the door on fear. When you start to think about things you get fearful. You just have to have the simplest of plans and stop thinking. Carry it out. For instance, these people who are informing – what on earth are they informing on in a village like this? What could the local people be doing that could possibly be of any danger to anyone? This is corruption beyond the imagination. This is madness. My grandmother told me one of her Spanish sayings – not all those who are in the madhouse are mad and not all those who are out aren't. From what I see, I think that the lunatics are out and they've put us in the asylum."

He took her hand. "Will you come to Canada with me?"

"I'd have to leave my family."

"You and your family don't get along."

"But, they are still my family."

"Would you like to live in a country where we have the freedom and the right to be who we are?"

"Yes, I would."

"Would you like to live with me?"

"Yes."

"Do you love me?"

"Yes."

"Enough to come?"

"Yes."

Later that day Ken talked with Francisco about the deteriorating political situation. Ken admitted that he had plotted a fishing trip – in his mind – where he would take one of the local informers out on the boat, get him thoroughly drunk and toss him overboard to feed the sharks.

"I admit that the idea does have some appeal," Francisco said. "But we won't talk much more about that, will we?"

"Well, not for a while," Kens said grudgingly. "Do you think there are other people who have the same thoughts?"

"Yes," the old man chuckled. "Probably two-thirds of my countrymen have the same thoughts."

"Do you think that things are explosive enough that it could boil up at any minute?"

"There is a fever building," Francisco said. "Whether it's now or a year from now or ten years from now, we can't predict. But there is no question – there is a great wave of dissent showing its head here and there. That's why the government is behaving the way it is. It's hoping to quell the situation."

In all this turmoil, Rui had begun planning Ken's first exhibition. Ken was completely disinterested, but Rui attached great importance to the event. He rented a small museum in Lisbon and had the drawings framed, hanging only one or two in each of the empty, echoing chambers. None of the pictures were to be for sale. Rui sent invitations to the intelligentsia and the elite of Lisbon society. Ken brought only one guest – Miloo – and he was bursting with pride that this peasant girl he loved moved through the crowd with all the grace and charm of one who had been born to mingle with people like this.

On that day Ken was transformed from an urchin demon to a divine being. He was publicly lauded as "a great artist".

Ken listened to the overwhelming praise and thought, "What a bunch of hypocrites! I've been doing this all along. It's known that I make these drawings, but now that they are placed in a certain setting and they're shown by a certain man in the presence of all these people, they have taken on value."

Rather than being elated, he was saddened and angered. These people had no idea whether these drawings had any real beauty or value – they praised them because others did. He had not created them for anyone else's approval; he had drawn them because drawing was something he had to do – like breathing.

Ken's three best friends, Francisco, Rui, and his father, were perplexed by his attitude. Miloo did not understand his feelings, either. "At the age of sixteen you have achieved what most artists work for their whole lives," she said. "And yet it doesn't seem to mean anything to you."

Ken said, "I'm a drawer and a painter, and I simply describe things as I see them. Everything else is by the way."

The exhibition further reinforced his growing need to leave the country. Then another incident occurred that convinced Ken that he and his family could afford to wait no longer. He was walking down the Street of Gold, in Lisbon, on his way to see Ben Sax, his banker, when he stumbled into a street demonstration outside the bank. As he approached the protestors, a convoy of military jeeps roared down the street, the soldiers manning machine guns mounted in the back.

Before Ken had time to absorb and process what he was seeing, one of the machine gunners opened fire on the crowd. While most of the people froze in horror, Ken threw himself to the ground, grabbing the woman closest to him and hauling her down with him. "Get down," he yelled. A second later the machine gun strafed over their heads and a bullet went cleanly through the head of the man who had been standing beside the woman. Blood and brains spattered over the wall above them and the lifeless body slumped to the street.

Ken felt blood roaring in his ears, every nerve in his body vibrating. The jeeps disappeared as quickly as they had come and were followed by a wave of ambulances that removed the dead and injured. When they had departed all that was left to tell of the horror that had taken place were the bloodstains on the cracked pavement and on the old stone walls. The bullets had made small craters in the stone and Ken recalled having seen similar marks elsewhere in the city – bullet holes that were never repaired and that served as reminders of the consequences of disobedience to the regime.

When his legs had stopped shaking and would support him again, he grabbed the woman's arm and pulled her through the bank doors. "Stay here," he told her, and at that moment, police marched down the street arresting everyone they could lay their hands on. Ben Sax, hurrying across the marble floor of the bank, noticed Ken and pushed him toward his office. Several people were gathered there, speaking in hushed tones.

"This is a very bad time," Ben said. "I can't see you right now, but you must stay here until the situation settles down. Don't leave." Ken gratefully sank into a chair while Ben called his father to come and get him when it was safe.

Ken's father drove home by a much longer route than usual.

"We have to get out of here," Ken said once they had left the city behind.

"I agree with you," his father said. "Things in the company are much worse than I thought."

He confessed that his chief accountant, who had been the principal government informer, had also handed sensitive information to rival companies, including his uncle's company. Instead of honouring their agreement, James had used the information to his advantage. Ken Sr.'s business was imploding.

He wasted no more time pondering the future but applied immediately for immigration to Canada for himself and his family. He had acquaintances in Winnipeg and Montreal who were eager for his expertise in their businesses. He used all his contacts – including Ellen Fairclough, the Minister of Citizenship and Immigration in the Diefenbaker Government. Ken Sr.'s application was approved within weeks while Ken's, his mother's, and his sister's crept their way through bureaucratic red tape.

Ken Sr.'s friend, the Count of Peniche, commissioned a private airplane, which would quietly carry Ken's father from a small airport outside Lisbon to England. On the way to the airport on the morning of the flight, Ken felt the hair on the back of his neck bristling. If anything was going to happen, it would be now. Certainly the government wanted his father out of the country but perhaps simply getting rid of him wasn't enough. They might be vengeful and angry enough to kill him.

The bullet he prepared himself for did not come. The Count ushered the family, through a service entrance and out onto the field. There was time for only the quickest goodbye and Ken Sr. was gone.

Within days, Ken and his family moved out of the house on the Avenue of Princes and took up residence in a hotel in Lisbon. The family and servants packed in a whirlwind, taking with them only their most personal possessions. One room in the house was filled with Ken's drawings – thousands and thousands of them stacked on every flat surface. Ken opened the door to the room and surveyed his life's work. He didn't want anyone else to touch them. He couldn't express why. In fact, if pressed he would probably not have been able to articulate his reasons even to himself. He only knew that he had to destroy them.

He dropped the drawings in great armfuls from the window into the garden where he piled them into a deep trench and burned them. When Rui heard what Ken had done he was livid. "What have you done?" he cried. "All this should have been catalogued and put away for the future! This is so important!"

A flash of anger ran through Ken. He had seen society's hypocrisy when a new artist's work was presented in just the right away, with invitations sent to just the right people. It had nothing to do with art – not with his art. For him, burning the drawings was an exorcism – he wasn't just burning drawings, he was burning the attitudes of an entire society, he was about to leave behind.

A few days later, as Ken entered the hotel lobby he found Juoan, the hunchback, waiting for him in the foyer. It was very bad news, he told him. Ken had to come immediately to see Francisco.

Francisco was waiting for him in the shack. "Miloo is dead," he told him.

Ken's breath stopped. "Don't tell me things like that."

"It's true." Francisco explained that she had fallen ill while visiting her family in the north. She paid no attention to her illness, and by the time she returned and went to the hospital, it was too late.

Ken tore out of the shack and ran to the hospital, Francisco following. If he talked to the doctor, surely he would confirm that Miloo was alive. Someone had made a terrible mistake.

The doctor explained that Miloo's appendix had burst and she had died of acute peritonitis.

At that moment, Ken's world ended. He staggered to his feet and opened the door to the corridor. Francisco was waiting for him. He took a few stumbling steps and a nurse rushed up to him. "You bastard," she hissed. "You killed her."

Francisco grabbed Ken's arm and began to push past her.

"What do you mean?" Ken asked.

"She was pregnant!"

Ken's legs wobbled. He turned, braced himself against the wall and groped his way back to the doctor's office. "She was pregnant?" he asked.

"Yes, she was," he said. "But in the very early stages of pregnancy."

"How early?"

"Perhaps a month."

"Was this the cause of her death?"

"Absolutely not."

"How can I be sure of that?"

"You can consult any doctor you wish and he will tell you that. Her pregnancy just happened to coincide with this."

The days and nights blended into one another. Ken wouldn't talk and he couldn't eat or sit still. He could not bear to be inside his own body – a body with an enormous empty, echoing cavern where a heart used to be. He walked, pacing endlessly up and down the beach, on the village streets, and on the sidewalks of Lisbon.

The emptiness of his body lay on him like a massive stone. He could not swallow past the obstruction in his throat. It blocked the emptiness where there used to be a stomach, lungs, kidneys – there was nothing left inside him and since he felt nothing, he thought about ending his own life.

One minute he was numb and then a wrenching sadness swept over him, threatening to drown him in its endless ocean. A minute later white-hot anger engulfed him and flared into a murderous rage.

When the stone moved from his throat long enough to let air through, he talked to Francisco but even that led to despair. He knew that nothing Francisco could say could ever bring her back.

This is a time I am not sure of myself. How to describe this? This is what I have come to. The stories of my life are true. Some of the stories happened to others and were told to me. There are also the stories of what I did, and with the passage of time and tragedy, they have melted together. This emotion, this loss – it has never gone. All I can give now are my impressions of what happened because I think I was completely out of my mind with grief. When I began to emerge a little from this whirlpool of misery I was shocked at the depth of the feelings I had and how dangerous they were.

I so wanted to see her and I so wanted to talk to her family. Francisco did have a power over me and he said that was the worst possible thing for me to do. So, I had to invent a way of being. I actually had to concoct a self that was not affected by this.

His friend Desjardines spent many long hours consoling Ken over his unspeakable loss. The Canadian ambassador was not the only person who tried to comfort him – Rui and Juoan listened and sat or walked with him, too. The love they and Francisco poured out may have been the only thing that prevented him from taking his life.

Desjardines was in regular communication with Ken and his father over the next few months. Ken Sr. had settled in Vancouver and had negotiated a contract with Bartle & Gibson, a large plumbing and heating company. When his family ran into immigration problems, Ken Sr. contacted Ellen Fairclough again and she assured him she would find a way to bring his family to Canada.

Six weeks later, just as Ken was beginning to live in the world again, he found Juoan waiting for him once again at the hotel. "You have to come," he said. "I have very bad news."

Ken's face drained of colour. Was this some cruel joke? Was the past going to play itself out all over again?

"Francisco is dead," Juoan said. "He died from a huge heart attack."

Ken sank into himself. With a feeling of utter helplessness and resignation, he once again took a taxi to Parede, and for the first time he actually entered Francisco's house on the outskirts of the village. He had met Francisco's wife only a handful of times in all the years he had been so close to the old man. She was small with an almost angelic face. Over the next days Ken spent many hours with her, sitting in her presence and reminiscing about the man they had both loved so much.

Juoan and Ken took Francisco's body to the beach and wrapped it in many layers of burlap, sewing them together with netting cord. They placed heavy stones at his feet and laid him in the bottom of the big rowboat. They rowed out to where the shallow water dropped off abruptly – to one of the deepest chasms in the Atlantic Ocean – and there they heaved him over the side: giving his body to the world he had loved most dearly.

When they came back, their muscles aching, they pulled the boat up on the beach and sat on the sand. Slowly people arrived from the village and sat with them, and talked, and told stories of Francisco, until the sun set and the moon rose in the sky.

Ken had never had any doubts about going to Canada but now, long before he stepped on the airplane, he felt as though he had already left. There was nothing in the old world now to hold him or his heart.

While he waited, he moved through the days like an automaton. There seemed no point to getting up in the morning or even to going to bed at night. Hour followed meaningless hour. He lived in two worlds. He invented a persona that greeted the world and protected the heartache inside. As time went on, living two distinct lives became a habit. Few people were allowed inside.

Finally, in late summer, they received permission to go to Canada. Ken said his good-byes to Rui and Juoan. He went to the bank, withdrew a major portion of his money in cash and presented it to Francisco's widow.

He refused to take any money with him. It had become part of the poison of the regime and of that society and so he gave it away – every penny.

The final good-byes were to his uncle. James came to Lisbon to have dinner with his sister and her children the night before they were to leave, and even though there were no last minute recriminations, it was still the most difficult dinner Ken had ever endured. It was all he could do to retain an air of distant civility in the presence of the man who had betrayed his father.

The next day they boarded the Bristol Britannia turbo prop that flew them to Amsterdam. There they refuelled and continued on to Reykjavik and then on to Vancouver. Ken noticed, almost as an afterthought, that he was spending most of his eighteenth birthday suspended in the air – high above the Atlantic, and then high above the vast country that was to be his new home.

As we flew across Canada I began to realize how unbelievably huge the country was. I looked down and it looked like snow and ice and clouds forever. And as we were coming over the mountains I thought, "What a beautiful, beautiful place."

5

Nile Creek, Peter Hope Lake and the Peace Country

Ken's joy at being reunited with his father was tempered by the realization that the towering person he had known had become an old man in the months they had been apart. Ken Sr. drove his family from the airport to an apartment on Barclay Street in the West End of Vancouver: it would be their temporary residence while their permanent home at nearby Comox and Bidwell was being prepared.

They were exhausted from the long trip but Ken Sr.'s enthusiasm wouldn't allow them to rest. "I have to show you something," he insisted and drove them out to Horseshoe Bay. "This is what your new home looks like." he said. There at the mouth of Howe Sound they looked up the inlet to the towering snow-capped coastal mountains. Turning around and negotiating the hill behind the bay they faced west to the low mountains that ran like a spine up Vancouver Island.

The next morning Ken and his father drove to Bartle & Gibson on Annacis Island, where Ken was offered a job as a crane operator. Canada amazed him. It was filled with a multitude of new smells, tastes, and sounds. Every day brought something different to marvel at. One of those was the vast distances between places, even within the city. In Portugal he had been able to walk almost anywhere. In this new place, a driver's license became one of his first priorities.

He talked to everyone he met. Had they ever seen an Eskimo? No one had met one. Canada was the land of the Eskimos and no one had seen one? Were Eskimos just a myth or were Canadians simply blind to their surroundings?

When he passed his driving test, he purchased an old TR2 Triumph that was temperamental but had a ragtop that came down in good weather. More importantly, the car provided distraction – one more weapon to help him fight the pain of loss.

Embracing new adventures helped as well. Armed with his letters of introduction from the Canadian ambassador, Ken made Nile Creek his first destination. Early one morning he drove to the docks at Burrard Inlet, where he boarded the Blackball Ferry that was like a floating version of the Orient Express with ornate chandeliers, curlicue railings and wedding-cake smokestacks. It might have been dropped into the harbour directly from the China Seas. Ken explored the floating palace and then stood on the railing leaning over the side, his eyes growing wider as they passed under the Lions Gate Bridge and chugged into the open waters of Georgia Strait. The sheer immensity of the snow-capped mountains, forested islands and vast ocean staggered him. Gulls swooped by, eagles soared overhead, seals and sea lions dived into the water.

After docking in Nanaimo, Ken drove north on a narrow gravel road, badly rutted and peppered with potholes. The TR2, with its worn shocks, rattled up the road that lay at the bottom of a canyon, its sides covered in giant firs. When he arrived at Nile Creek and found the little cottage he had been directed to, he knocked on the door and handed his letter of introduction to the elderly couple who greeted him.

"We've heard a lot about you," they said. "Monsieur Desjardines wrote to us a number of times; telling us about you, and the wonderful times he had with you in Portugal, and about how you want to be a Canadian."

They took Ken out to the mouth of the creek where the water was so thick with salmon it presented a solid wall.

The next morning they launched a rowboat and rowed out to the kelp beds, that lay several hundred yards from shore. After tying up to the outer rim of the semi-translucent mass, they cast their lures along the edge of the kelp bed. The moment the lure hit the water a fish struck. Then, miraculously the fish leapt into the air, dancing on the water. Listening to the old man's shouted instructions, Ken learned how to handle Pacific salmon. They pulled in one fish after another, each cast of the line producing another salmon. When the big box in the bottom of the boat was almost filled they tossed them back, keeping two for their supper.

Ken spent the rest of the week fishing, and drawing fish – particularly the cutthroat trout that fascinated him even more than the salmon.

His next trip was to the wild country near Kamloops. As he drew close to Merritt the countryside grew arid with rugged rolling hills and tall ponderosa pines, which gradually gave way to a vast grassland covered with scrub.

He drove up the Nicola Valley, drinking in the smell of sage and basking in the golden autumn sun. Bees buzzed lazily, half asleep in the golden fields. Eventually he found the gravel road he was looking for that climbed up and up into the mountains. He drove through the Stump Lake Ranch and past the sign that said, "Peter Hope Fishing Camp". He drove on through mud puddles so deep that the water seeped through the floorboards. When he could drive no farther, he parked and walked across a small creaking bridge to an island with a tiny log cabin wearing fresh golden logs on one side, and old weathered logs on the other.

Ken knocked on the door.

"Come in," a voice yelled.

Ken stepped over the threshold. He recognized Paddy McGelgan from the description the Canadian ambassador had given him. "He looks exactly like King George V".

Ken handed him the letter of introduction.

"So how's the old bastard doing?" the man bawled.

"Last time I saw him he was doing fine."

"Yes he told me all about you – I've got a letter here somewhere. He said you were a fisherman – you love to fish and that's good. There's a lot of fishermen, you know, but there are hardly any anglers. Do you know how to fly-fish?"

"No."

Paddy made it his mission to teach him, and each morning and afternoon for the better part of a week Ken spent several hours alone in the boat struggling with the line until he had mastered the art. Then Paddy showed him how to fish – which he called hunting, not fishing – for the elusive lake trout.

For Ken the experience personified this new country. The trout were like no fish he had ever encountered. They lived in an alien landscape and yet he knew it as though he had been born into it. It was the home inside his heart – a home that had always been there – but that he had come to for the first time.

It is something beyond my ability with words to describe the comfort – it is as though I had travelled the universe, and had walked back into my home and sat down in my own armchair, and breathed a mighty sigh of satisfaction and relief. Out of all of this came an understanding of life through fishing, which sounds odd. The fish is a representative of the illusionary world that we all live in. There is the trout, but the trout is not there – it is only there by the virtue of its shadow. And then you put on your fly line, and you put on a leader, and it gets thinner and thinner until it gets down to something ridiculously thin that maybe has two or three pounds of breaking tension. Then you put on a fly that is the size of two pinheads, and then you cast it out when these trout are swimming by, but not when they're there. Then you let this minuscule thing slip down into the water very slowly – it takes lots of time. And your heart is beating ninety to the minute watching these fish coming by, and you are contemplating the hopelessness of something so minute attracting them, in this water that is so rich with food, because this lake is a food factory. It's utterly hopeless. And then you watch the tip of the fly rod, which is two inches above the water, and you watch the tiny bow and when that bow comes up ever so slightly as though it might not even have happened, you lift your rod up very carefully and all of a sudden that magical shadow is on your minuscule hook. And you have now entered a realm where suddenly the impossible is possible. Walking through that door was a way into this new land.

Paddy McGelgan was wild, grumpy and difficult, but Ken was forever grateful to the man. He had taken enormous care to lead him to the door and give him the tools to walk through it. The moment that Ken saw the magic in fly-fishing and realized that he had to control his own impulses to be successful, he regained control over his life. When he realized the fish he saw in the lake were only shadows, he saw how much in his own life was merely an illusion.

After that trip to Peter Hope Lake he became quieter and observed more. He became more curious. The question "Why?" was constantly in his mind. Why did the immigrants that populated Vancouver constantly refer to the "Old Country" nostalgically, rather than embrace their adopted land? Why did people do what they did and say what they said? There was no answer. Merely asking the question was enough.

Unlike the immigrants who longed for the ways of home, Ken longed to embrace Canada. He had noticed that the country referred to itself as "a nation under the rule of law". What law? What were the laws this country was under? He went to the Queen's Printer and obtained a copy of the constitution, known as the British North America Act.

In the evenings, when Ken arrived home from work, he would sprawl in an armchair and read the document. He found it utterly disarming. It was written in plain English and was generally absent of the "lawyer-ese" that official documents tend to be peppered with. One part that dealt with taxation stated, "There shall be no double taxation". It was that simple.

A few months after arriving in Canada, Ken's mother was diagnosed with breast cancer. It took two operations at the University of British Columbia hospital to eradicate it but she remained profoundly unhappy, and desperately wanted to return home to her friends and family overseas.

To avoid the turmoil at home, Ken spent his free time exploring the city. He took a map of the town and cut it into sections. He wondered through Chinatown, the lower east side, and the British Properties. While he walked, he watched for art galleries but because most of his exploration occurred after work, the few galleries he found were closed. Peering through the windows he saw paintings that were either old English landscapes or stylized soldiers on horseback.

One day while walking up Granville Street he peered into the window of a gallery on the east side near Fourteenth Avenue. He caught his breath. The paintings depicted a rugged, unforgiving landscape drawn with a great economy of brush strokes, each stroke powerful and very sure of its purpose.

"Oh my god," Ken thought. "I am going to have to completely relearn everything. That is it! That is how you paint this country!"

He waited impatiently for the weekend to arrive and on Saturday morning went back to the gallery. The owner explained that The Group of Seven produced these paintings.

Ken explained that he too was a painter. The man shrugged and said, "Ah, the world's full of artists – starving, hopeless artists."

Two weeks later, Ken went back to the gallery with an armful of drawings he had based on the paintings – scenes of the stark northern Ontario and Quebec landscapes. The gallery owner looked at them. "Fine," he said. "They're good drawings but people here don't buy drawings. My recommendation is that you go to art school."

Ken gathered up his work. "I don't think so," he said.

As the weeks passed, he began to wonder if the Arctic and the Arctic people were a myth. He scoured the newspapers for any mention of the North but north, according to the media, was Prince George. Ken searched it out on a map and discovered that Prince George was roughly in the centre of the province. There were many, many miles remaining before you reached the northern edge of British Columbia.

He went to the Dominion Map Company where he obtained maps of the Arctic that he spread out on the dining room table. He was shocked to discover that the Alaska Highway was the only road north and it led to Whitehorse and Fairbanks, not to the eastern Arctic, which was his dreamed-of destination.

He learned that there was also an ice road. In the winter, big semi-trailers drove north on the ice-covered Mackenzie River, to deliver the annual supply of food and goods to the northern settlements as far as the Beaufort Sea. He studied the scale of the maps and plotted the distance with a ruler. To his dismay he discovered that in Vancouver he was just as far from the Arctic as he had been in Lisbon. In fact, it might have been easier to reach the eastern Arctic from Lisbon rather than southern British Columbia.

As a starting point he decided to find employment as far north as he could get. He answered a Coast Eldridge advertisement for a soil tester in the Peace River Country, in northern British Columbia: they were doing research to help determine the best places in the province to build hydroelectric dams.

Ken made an appointment with Doug Elsdun, the personnel manager, who turned him down because he lacked formal education. Ken refused to take no for an answer and haunted the reception room outside Elsdun's office until he capitulated and hired him.

In the early summer of 1959, a week before departing for the North, the new hires met at the company's offices. They were a varied bunch: one was a tall, lean man in his mid-fifties who let everyone know that he was a committed communist; one was an engineering student; and another one was studying music. The boss of the group was a plump, middle-aged man who, when he wasn't puffing on a foul-smelling pipe, had a perpetual grin on his face. Two more sat quietly in a corner, their legs splayed in front of them, their eyes on the ground. The tall lean man introduced himself as John and became Ken's new mentor.

A week later the group met at the Vancouver airport where they boarded an airplane bound for Prince George. John slid into the seat beside Ken and regaled him with stories on the long flight. John, who Ken learned was known as "Long Tall John" had worked in logging camps, construction camps, and canneries most of his life. He told stories well and Ken learned more about the country west of the Rocky Mountains during that flight than he had in all the books he had read.

John told him that half a dozen families who were, in truth, robber barons ran the province. The fishing industry, owned by a handful of people, would simply string nets across rivers, decimate entire runs of salmon, can them, and ship them to Europe. When one river was depleted they moved on to the next. He told him the story of the logging industry – of H.R. MacMillan who founded MacMillan Bloedel, the province's largest logging company. He called H.R. the biggest plundering thief he had ever heard of. He told of the time H.R. called a meeting of the logging companies in British Columbia and convinced them they could get better prices for their lumber if they would send him to England to broker the deal. They agreed and H.R. did indeed get better contracts but every one of them was in his name. When he got back, he owned the logging industry.

At Prince George they transferred to another airplane that flew them north into Peace River country, landing on a rutted dirt runway that had been carved out of the wilderness. The plane bounced and clattered before it came to an abrupt stop that tossed the passengers forward in their seats. Dust obscured the windows and blew into the cabin as the door opened. The pilot kept the engines running while the crew tossed luggage to the ground. When the last man had descended, the plane turned around and roared off, kicked up a fine dust that settled inside eyes, noses and in every fold of clothing.

The men watched, their shoulders hunched against the wind and grit, until the plane disappeared. Around them was an eerie emptiness – nothing but rolling hills and endless stands of trees.

John turned to him. "Welcome to the armpit of hell. There's dust here everywhere. You'll learn about dust like you never even thought about it before. And just wait until it starts to rain cause then it turns into mud. Mud everywhere. Folks around here call it gumbo. And I'm gonna tell you, it's slicker 'n goose shit. You can't walk on it, you can't drive on it, and it sticks to everything. You'll learn about mud. The first thing we're gonna do is get you a pair of really good gum boots and a bucket."

"Why the bucket?" Ken asked.

"Every day you put your gumboots in a bucket of water to try to melt this crap off them."

Ken was digesting this information when John pointed to another dust cloud making its way, erratically, toward them. Out of the swirling cloud a small bus materialized.

"That's our crummy," John said.

The bus was so covered in layer upon layer of dust, mud and grime that it was impossible to make out what kind of bus it was or even what colour it might be. The windows were entirely obscured save for round tattered holes where passengers had swiped off just enough caked-on grunge to allow fleeting glances at the passing scene.

They drove down the dusty dirt road until they turned on to a wider gravel road where the odd truck and car passed – the Alaska Highway.

At the small town of Hudson Hope they picked up bags of mail and supplies and then continued up the valley for about 40 miles, passed through a gate and arrived at an encampment of trailers placed in rows opposite a big common building.

Ken and John tossed their bags into their rooms and familiarized themselves with the camp and the old Dodge Fargo they would share. A box in the back was filled with tools and equipment to gather mineral and dirt samples. A trailer at the foot of Portage Mountain housed a laboratory that tested the samples. Their job was to provide the lab with materials – every sort of material they could pick up, dig up or drill for over a vast terrain. Once they had picked samples from one area, machines excavated deeper and they picked up more samples. They were looking for clay – an enormous amount of clay because it was to form the backbone of the giant dam. The hundreds of millions of tons of clay needed – of just the right sort – could not be trucked into this remote area. It had to be found on site.

Ken was generally left to himself and did pretty much what he pleased. As long as he produced the required number of samples each day, no one bothered with him. He liked the repetitious work because it allowed his mind to wander freely along its own paths. He also had time to draw. When John discovered Ken was an artist, he gave him a drawing board made from a big sheet of plywood on top of which he had taped smooth kitchen Formica.

"Now show me how you draw," John said.

"What would you like me to draw?"

"Anything."

Ken brought John back to his room where he made him sit still while he sketched a portrait. When it was done, John looked. "Jesus Christ! That's amazing!" he said.

"It's just a sketch," Ken said. During the next few days he filled it in. Among the materials he had brought to the camp, was rich, thick silk-screening paper. The soft pencils Ken used etched the paper leaving a silvery shimmer so that when the portrait was finished it looked like a monochromatic painting.

John became his biggest fan, demanding to see every sketch Ken drew. But Ken didn't draw as much as he had hoped to. The countryside, with its soft velvety hills was almost featureless. The only element in that placid landscape to capture his attention was the narrows where the Peace River encountered a high canyon that stretched about ten miles before broadening out again. The river raged through that canyon and no one who had tried to raft it had come out alive.

Day after day, they went out into the dusty fields, measuring the depth and width of various areas, picking up gravel, putting it through sieves and collecting samples of rock and clay. One day blended into the next. The camp was devoid of any sort of formal entertainment. The policy stated, "No Alcohol, No Gambling, No Women!".

The guards inspected every truck that came through the gate, searching for alcohol. And though every vehicle was thoroughly examined, every man had his stash of beer.

One day Ken asked John about this phenomenon. "They inspect every car and every truck that comes through. How do they get the beer?"

"They bring it in by boat for Chrissake!" John said.

Two outfitters, who ran operations some distance up the river, sold beer to the men in camp and made a tidy profit. The outfitters had government contracts to transport people up and down the river in their big freighter canoes and occasionally they hired out as fishing guides. Ken made a deal with one company to be taken on guided fishing trips in exchange for drawings.

Patrick, a tall, handsome Native man was the second outfitter who did contract work for the camp, often taking Ken out to collect samples. He had a striking aquiline nose and high, rugged cheekbones but his most arresting feature was his presence. Every movement was a dance of unself-conscious grace and dignity.

One day while Ken was up river with him, Patrick asked about the drawings. "What do you charge?"

"Mostly I don't," Ken said and explained that as far as he could tell most people in Canada didn't like drawings.

"I like drawings," Patrick said. "What did you charge the other outfitters, if you don't mind me asking?"

"I didn't," Ken said. "I made a deal. I made the drawings in exchange for guided fishing trips up the river."

"I'd like to make that deal too," Patrick said.

"What do you want me to draw?" Ken asked.

Patrick wanted portraits of his younger twin sisters and of his parents.

The best part of that trade was the prospect of spending more time with Patrick. He felt at ease in his regal presence and he found his long silences comforting. White people always seemed to have to fill in conversational gaps with words. Patrick was content to let silences be.

He invited Ken to supper at his home a few miles down the road toward Hudson Hope. Ken approached Patrick's home on a wide drive that swept up a hill, affording a commanding view of Patrick's ranch. The centrepiece was a substantial log building surrounded by a collection of tidy yards and pastures. The fields were fenced and every fence was painted. Sheep, horses and cows were neatly separated, each in their own pasture.

He entered the great room that stretched a full fifty feet, each wall built with massive honey-toned logs. An enormous stone fireplace occupied one end of the room and was topped by a bleached animal skull. An airtight wood stove graced the other end of the room, its heat radiating out into the room. Ken felt instantly at home.

He just had time to take in and admire his surroundings before Patrick introduced his identical twin sisters, Margaret and Jessica. Like Patrick, they had a single long jet-black braid that hung down their backs, almost brushing the tops of their thighs. Their skin glowed gold with a hint of damask rose. They looked at Ken out of huge black eyes that seemed to see right through him into some mysterious depths. When Ken took their hands in greeting he touched skin as soft as eiderdown.

When Ken asked about the skull Patrick explained that it was a buffalo skull nailed there to remind them of their ancestors who had migrated to the Peace River to escape the American Indian wars. A group made of Sioux, Comanche, and Lakota had slipped across the border seeking refuge, convinced that they were about to be exterminated. They continued to travel north until they found a place where the land was largely unpopulated both by white men and by other Indians.

The Peace River was a rich country, he said. He didn't have to hunt much – the moose and deer simply walked across the yard periodically and he shot them for "trespassing". He pointed out the tree in the yard where he hung and dressed the carcasses and he showed him the small log house where he stored the meat. There was an inner log house encased in an outer house. The space between was packed with sawdust. Holes in the walls could be fitted with blocks or screens consisting of four layers of fine mesh that prevented insects from entering. As long as no insect came near the meat it would keep forever.

While he listened to Patrick, sitting comfortably in the big, warm room, Ken realized, with a jolt of joy, that this was the Canada he had been searching for. This was the Canada of the books he had read in Portugal.

This was the Canada of real people and true adventure.

After supper, Patrick asked again if Ken would draw portraits of his sisters and parents. The girls looked at each other in surprise and turned toward their brother who told them that Ken was an artist and he had asked him to do their portraits. The girls looked down in sudden shyness.

"Where are your parents?" Ken asked.

"Our father is dead. He died many years ago in a logging accident near Prince George."

"And your mother?"

"She's dead too. She died from TB, alcohol, and a broken heart."

He handed Ken several photographs of his parents. "Can you work from these?"

"I don't know, I've never done it before," Ken said. "But, I'll try."

He began work on the portraits of the sisters, spending almost every evening at the ranch. When his shift ended, he loaded his drawing supplies into the truck, anticipated the first sight of the tidy ranch over the rise of the hill, and relished the feeling of coming home. For the first time in his life, he felt that there was a place where he belonged.

As the summer grew into fall, the crummy arrived several times a week with new arrivals, and trucks roared into the camp in a steady stream bringing equipment and supplies. New trailers were pulled in and hooked up to create new living quarters. A small town was rapidly taking shape.

Tanker trucks sprayed water on the dirt road day and night in an effort to keep down the dust kicked up by the rumbling flow of traffic. In the heat of late summer the water evaporated almost instantly.

A crew arrived that drilled a tight pattern of holes three feet deep into the rock near the camp, packing it with ninety-seven percent nitro-glycerine. On the day the charge was scheduled to explode, Ken went up river with Patrick. He told his friend that he was uneasy about the charge being laid so close to the camp. Patrick said it was madness, but shrugged philosophically – they were going to do what they were going to do and no one could stop them – certainly not him. He was only an Indian.

While he worked, Patrick asked him about his plans. "Maybe you'd like to stay here," he said.

"Yes, maybe," Ken said. "But first I want to go north."

"You can have a good life here," Patrick said. "I like you a lot and my sisters like you too. If you want to stay with us, you're welcome."

"Thank you for the offer, that's very kind," Ken said.

"Maybe you'd like to marry one of them."

Ken wasn't surprised that Patrick had noticed his attraction to them. They had set up a roller coaster of emotions in his heart. He wanted them, but at the same time, the image of Miloo held steady in front of his eyes and brought on a bitter grief. How could he move forward? How to explain this to Patrick?

A deafening roar that sounded like a thousand thunderclaps crashing down at once interrupted their conversation. The shock reverberated through the earth, setting every tree and leaf trembling.

With some trepidation, they motored back to camp. The row of ten double-wide trailers closest to the blasting site had taken the full brunt of the shock. Windows were blown out, curtains were strewn around the camp and the force had bent the walls inwards.

The rock that should have been pulverized had broken up into jagged boulders weighing at least ten and twenty tons apiece.

One night while Ken was visiting the ranch, and after Patrick and Margaret had gone to bed, he sat down opposite Jessica and began drawing her face in the golden glow of the kerosene lamps.

It was late when he finished. Leaning over his shoulder, she said, "Pretty good. I wish I could do that. Now I want you to do a drawing of me the way I want you to do it."

"What's that?" Ken asked.

"Nude."

He shook his head. "That's not the deal I made with your brother. It didn't have anything to do with nudes and I'm not comfortable with the idea."

"My brother isn't the only one with ideas around here," she said softly. "And neither are you."

Standing in front of him she did something magical with the dress she was wearing. One minute she was clothed and the next she was standing naked in front of him, her head turned slightly away – her body angled toward him. She stood tall and straight like a golden statue, the warm glow of the lamps reflecting off her body. She was more than beautiful – handsome, magnetic, lustrous – a beauty that compelled his complete attention. Ken drew deep, silent breaths, trying to still the turmoil inside him. The everyday Jessica was gone – or perhaps not gone – perhaps she had simply unleashed all the power inside her. She was the most commanding figure he had ever seen.

There was nothing for Ken to do but to take out a fresh sheet of paper and begin drawing. And as so often happened to him in moments of profound significance, showers of unseen icy crystals poured into his stomach. He could not have explained anything that was happening to him in that moment – not intellectually – but emotionally and spiritually he was lost.

He drew, his hand moving at lightning speed. No thought was required – no caution. Something had taken over his soul and the drawing appeared almost of its own accord.

That was the first time I had ever gone into a trance or a state I can only imagine as a trance and when I came out of it, there it was – absolutely perfect and all the while she hadn't moved a muscle, or changed her pose or her expression.

Ken put his pencil down and slowly came back to the room. "Come and take a look," he said.

She stood beside him and silently gazed at the picture. "I wish I could do that," she whispered. Then she placed a hand on his head, "My god, you're soaking," she said. Ken's hair was as wet as if he had come in from a spring shower. His shirt clung to his body in damp folds.

Still gloriously naked, Jessica sat beside him on the couch and told him what it was like to be an Indian. She and her sister had been fortunate. They had escaped much of the pain that so many of her race had lived through. The girls had attended a public school but Patrick had been sent to a residential school and refused to talk about those years.

The Indians had been chased from their land again and again. She expressed no anger or resentment. Her voice remained gentle and soft – that gentleness fanned the flames of Ken's anger. Wars had been fought in Europe over territory and land. Why had the Indians not fought back?

"It's not in our nature to lash out and hurt others," she said. "When we get hurt, we hurt ourselves. It seems to be something that is rooted deeply in our cultural background."

She said that she and Patrick and her sister belonged nowhere. They were not white and yet by Indian standards, they were not natives either. They belonged to no tribe and did not live on a reservation. They were completely free and had no wish to be involved in any part of the political or racial battle. "We've managed to make a very good life for ourselves," she said. "We work together, we are partners and we help each other."

Jessica was describing the life he wished to live. His story was different but it was also the same. He too had no desire to be categorized or pigeonholed. He too wanted to unfold and allow life to happen rather than force any particular direction.

Jessica turned down the lights, leaving one kerosene lamp glowing in the dark. Then she took Ken's hand and led him into her bedroom. Like everything else about her, her room was also unexpected. It was as spare and sparse as her manner. To still his turmoil, Ken forced all his concentration on studying his new surroundings. He slipped under the goose down cover and Jessica lay opposite him, her face cradled in her hand, her eyes unblinking, gazing deeply into his. "I've never slept with a man," she said. "I'll bet you can't say that."

"Actually I can," he said grinning.

"You know what I mean," she smiled back at him.

"Yes, I do."

She waited and when he didn't reach for her, she asked, "Is there something about me? Maybe, you don't like me?"

"No, I like you a lot," he said, thinking that he liked her far too much and that was the cause of this ache that was spreading in his chest. "I think you're a marvellous person."

"If it's not me, then is it what happened to you in Portugal?"

Ken's breath whooshed out of his lungs. "How do you know about Portugal?"

"You talked to Patrick and he told me about it."

"How much did he tell you?"

"That some bad things happened. That the woman you loved died and you blame yourself for it."

Ken looked away.

"You're like my brother," she said. "You won't talk about it, will you?"

"No, I really don't want to talk about it."

"You sure are like my brother. I don't know what it is about you men. You'll talk forever about some things but there are things that neither one of you will talk about. And if you don't start talking about them, you're going to be ghosts, living with ghosts in a ghost world. My brother went to residential school and he won't talk about it. There must have been some kind of hell there because it's something he just won't go near."

Jessica explained how the Indian children had been taken away from their families and forced into residential schools where they were supposed to be assimilated into the white man's world. Ken's heart ached. His experience of school, though not that harsh, had also been cruel.

Jessica turned over on her back. "I'm going to tell you our story, and my story, from the beginning," she said. She began with the mythology of how the world was created and how human beings came to be. The words that rolled off her tongue were as satiny smooth as her skin. She told about her tribe and the Indian wars and how they had come to the place they were today.

When she finished, she told Ken it was now his turn but he couldn't do it – not all the way from the beginning to now. He had no creation myth and no core view. His story was fragmented. He lay on his back, doing his best to describe his story. Her eyes never left him and he felt her soul all around him.

When he grew silent, Jessica moved closer and folded him into her arms. They held each other gently, tenderly, and Ken felt a hunger beyond any ability to interpret and that hunger was matched exactly by a terror of having what he ached for. Very gently, very determinedly, Ken made love to her and some time before dawn they fell asleep. Once during the night Ken woke up. The kerosene lamp was burning low and by its fading light, he looked at her, realizing that everything he was experiencing was beyond any story he had ever told or heard. He was in the middle of a magical spell.

In the morning, when he next opened his eyes Jessica was standing by the bed with a cup of coffee. "Drink this," she said and as he took a sip she kissed him as softly as a butterfly. "Good morning beautiful man who draws beautiful things."

While Jessica made breakfast, Ken walked down the hall into the bathroom. There on the counter beside the sink was a note and on top of the note a mug and a toothbrush. The note read, "This is your toothbrush. This is your cup. Use them at your peril. If you do, you are mine forever". It was signed Jessica, with a heart woven through her name.

It was Ken's undoing. All the control he had exercised vanished. The dam was breached. Such simplicity – such a plain statement – but it contained the power of thunder. Ken wept – great heaving sobs whose noise he drowned in the torrent of the shower's waterfall. When he had gathered together the pieces of himself and dried his face, he came to Jessica in the kitchen, standing at the sink. He wrapped his arms around her. Slowly she turned and nestled into him. The pieces he had stitched together unravelled. Tears cascaded from his eyes, burning a path down his cheeks.

When his sobs began to subside, she pulled back and looked at him. Her eyes were wet. "I wish my brother could do this. This is what I want him to do. You have to get it out," she said. "I am your home. Don't forget it. I am your home."

6

Jessica

Ken spent most of his free time at the ranch. Patrick also took him fishing more often and began to open up to him. One day while they were eating lunch on the riverbank Ken told him about his school experience in Portugal. When he had finished his story he asked Patrick about his time at the residential school.

"It sounds like you were taught by the same bunch of people as me," Patrick said. "But you escaped early. I got away later."

"I'd never heard about residential schools," Ken said. "The school I went to was residential too, but I was one of the very few people who didn't stay there because I lived so close by. And that in itself caused trouble because when you're the odd one out you're like the white bird – you're going to get picked on by all the black birds."

Patrick nodded.

"Is it okay for me to ask you about this? I sense that you really don't want to talk about it and I don't want to go where I'm not invited. But there's obviously something there. Jessica mentioned that it's something you won't talk about."

"It's not something that I won't talk about," Patrick said. "It's something that I haven't found a way of talking about. I don't think there are words to describe what happened there."

"What is it? Is it the same as what I described?"

"No, not at all," and Patrick told Ken the story of the residential schools that began when the government decided to assimilate the Indians into white Canadian society. It handed the responsibility for native education over to the churches; they took the children away from their families and sent them to schools where they were dressed in European clothing and were not allowed to speak their own language. When they did, they were beaten. Their education centred around the Bible with little or no focus on mathematics or science.

"They wanted us to break away from the old ways," he said. "And in the summer when you returned to your family, you were different. That's how "the great divide" began. And there were other things that happened – that were very difficult."

"Like physical punishment?" Ken asked.

"Yes, but of a horrible kind."

"Well, I decided to take them on and use myself as the whipping boy."

"That's one of the things that interests me about your story and about you," Patrick said. "Are you sure you aren't an Indian? That's the kind of thing we do."

"No, it was just a way of achieving a goal I wanted. It was a mixture of vengeance and proving myself smarter. What were the other horrible things that were done to you?"

Patrick looked away. "I really don't want to talk about it."

On his trips with Patrick, Ken discovered a new world, so far removed from the one he had grown up in, it might have been on a different planet.

I began to have the sense that I had left the shadow of my own people and of my own world. I was not in that world and I was not in this world and that has been a familiar place my whole life. In fact when I look at the paintings that I make, they are actually portraits of that. I'm incredibly interested in the places in between. I remember painting an old barn when I was going through the barn phase, as everyone does. I noticed at one point that the barn itself was not it. The barn was there so that I could paint the cracks in it. I began to get the idea that time is short and the journey is long and there is only one way to go in the journey. Imagine a giant sitting on a beach surrounded by huge boulders and he has picked up two of them and he's banging them together. Every time he bangs them together a grain of sand is created. If he goes on for long enough, at some point, there will be a beach. That concept pleased me no end – that there was no quick way of creating a beach. Consequently, there could be no quick way of getting anything. Whatever it is that I was doing was going to take a very long time and that was okay. There was something very pleasing about the fact that it was going to take a very long time. The times in my life when I have been in some form of contentment are when I have been immersed in a project, the end of which I cannot see. And my mind stops worrying or considering what I will do next. I have paddled from one giant project to the next.

He absorbed Patrick's stories and tried to fit them into a logical context. There had to be a reason for the actions the Europeans had taken. One day while they were motoring on the river he asked Patrick, "Why do you think the newcomers tried to deal with the native population this way? The residential schools seem to be a complexly bizarre notion. We know that if you say to someone, 'This is my castle and you can't come in', they're going to bash the door down to gain entrance."

"Yes. It's bizarre," Patrick said.

"When you force people to do anything – well we know what the reaction to that is going to be."

'But they didn't want us in that way," Patrick said. "They needed us to be the victims. Victims are easy to deal with. But I can see down into the future that the ultimate victim will be the entire society. Unless it comes to terms with all of this, we will all be immersed in a nightmare. The descendants of those who did this will become the victims. We will become a place that is poisoned by it all. I see no effort being made to acknowledge it, to understand it, and to deal with it. It's not a matter of compensation and money – although I guarantee you that's where it's going. There will be all kinds of commissions set up, endless bureaucracy, vast sums of money, most of which will be swallowed by the bureaucracy and it will only make the situation worse. The only redress is to not do these things today."

Ken became involved in many of the camp activities. He organized film nights for the workers. When a group of new men arrived, who spoke only Portuguese, Ken became a useful interpreter and when W.A.C. Bennett, the Premier of the province announced a visit to inspect the site, the camp manager tapped Ken for the role of tour guide.

He drove him over the site in the old Dodge Fargo and as they talked, they forged the beginning of a long and cordial relationship. Bennett was so taken with Ken's insights, he encouraged him to join his party. Ken, however, demurred. He had no political ambitions.

Winter came and with it the first snowfall. Unlike the fluffy white flakes Ken had always imagined, this snow was hard and crystalline and squeaked underfoot. Ken bought warm clothing in town and relished the biting touch of cold wind on his face.

With the advent of winter, he made the acquaintance of a Métis man who lived on the opposite side of the Peace River. He was renowned for his dog sled team and for the method he used to obtain his dogs. When one of his bitches came into heat he put her outside. The alpha wolf of the local pack would mate with her and the result was a litter of wolf hybrid pups that were strong and potentially dangerous. Patrick said that if those dogs ever got loose they would form a pack – the most dangerous pack of all – animals acclimatized to man.

Ken barely heard Patrick's concerns over the dogs – he had heard the word "wolf" and his attention was arrested. Wolves?

"Sure," Patrick said. "There are lots of wolves here."

"I haven't seen a wolf," Ken said.

Patrick laughed. "You know you guys over there in Europe read way too much "Little Red Riding Hood". All those stories about wolves are nonsense."

As the temperature dipped lower and lower the Peace River froze, and Patrick explained that the wolf pack travelled on the ice, passing by the camp at least three times a month. Ken began to frequent the river and watch for them. Two months passed without a sighting and then one day he saw the beasts trotting around the bend. He was no more than twenty-five feet away as they loped by.

He reported his sighting to Patrick. "They didn't even stop, or look, or sniff – they just went by."

"I told you so," Patrick said. "They couldn't care less. You don't matter to them – you just don't count."

Wolves weren't the real danger. One man in camp drove a Volkswagen, and as the snow grew deeper and deeper, the snow blowers cleared the road, carving a canyon between towering mounds of snow. One day the man found himself driving behind a moose that was ambling along the road. The man decided to give chase. With no escape possible, the moose trotted faster and faster – until he grew tired and irritated. He turned and charged the car, impaling it on his antlers and flipping the car on its side. The animal went on a rampage and didn't stop until the vehicle was almost crushed, trapping the terrified man inside. Hours later a crew found him shivering and frightened inside the smashed car.

Ken revised his understanding of nature. Wolves? Not a problem. An angry moose – now there was a formidable foe.

As the days grew colder and shorter he began to feel torn between his intense desire to go to the Arctic and his need for Jessica.

To satisfy his first yearning, he went on a mission to find and collect every piece of information he could glean about the far north. He questioned everyone who worked at or passed through the camp including truck drivers, pilots and police officers. One day his search bore fruit. A bush pilot who had landed with a load of goods said he had been to the Arctic but was mystified why anyone would want to go there. "The Arctic is something you have to be careful of," he said.

"Why? Because it will kill me?" Ken asked.

"No, that's not it," he said. "If you go there, it will own you forever. I've flown in Saudi Arabia, in the Amazon – you name it – but I've never been in a place like the Arctic. It gets into you in such a way that it will never leave. It will haunt you. When you're there you can't wait to get out and the minute you're out you can't wait to get back in."

The pilot told him of others in the area who Ken might get in touch with for more information, but tracking them down proved challenging. The world Ken lived in was transitory. People moved in and out of camps weekly, daily, sometimes hourly. No one knew how long they would be in any particular place or where they were going next.

The only people Ken knew who had roots were Patrick and his family. For Ken, who had grown up on the streets of Portugal, a country whose stones were often older than Christ, this was a bewildering human landscape. People moved not to go somewhere, but simply because they were dissatisfied with where they were. They had an itch; they were trying to make as much money as they could, as quickly as they could, so that they could leave and go somewhere else. But they didn't know where they wanted to go or how much money they needed to get there.

The bush pilot told Ken that there was no such place as the Arctic – it was an arbitrary dotted line drawn on a map, by people who had never been there. The Arctic was a hundred thousand million places, he said, with an enormous variety of climates and vast distances between small communities. You might find a few people on the land, he said, but not many. Most of them had been rounded up and put into camps built like villages. The idea of the Eskimo as one homogenous group of people was as big a myth as to say that all Europeans were one race.

Nevertheless, the government had decided that the Eskimos had to be gathered together – regardless of tribe or dialect – and placed in communities, which they would use as a base to go out and trap fur animals for the Hudson's Bay Company. Then they depended on the company for their survival and were, in fact, essentially owned by it. Each Eskimo had been given a number and a letter. Those west of Coppermine River were assigned the letter W and a number. Those East of the area were given an E and a number, and in some cases, those letters and numbers were tattooed on their arms.

Ken was horrified. He repeated to Jessica, Patrick, and Long John what the pilot had told him. John was furious, not at the government, but at Ken and his wild dreams. "You're on a wild goose chase! You're mad!" he shouted. "There's nothing to go to – thousands of square miles of absolutely nothing but ice, wind, and rocks – lots of frozen rocks and no people. I tell you, there are no people there. The place is a bloody, frozen desert. You're made of flesh and blood – you're not a god! What is it with you English and your half-baked need to go to desolate places? As if life isn't difficult enough without going looking for trouble!"

"For someone who's never been to the Arctic you seem to have a helluva lot of knowledge about it," Ken said. "How do you know there's nothing there?"

"I don't need to go there," John said. "I can read. There's a place called "The Barrens" and I imagine it's called that for a good reason, don't you think?" John pulled out a map and pointed to the place. "Read it – it's right there. The Barrens – there's nothing there. When he first looked at the place, one of the explorers wrote in his diary, 'This is the place that God gave to Cain'. All I can see is that the place is going to kill you – not much different from every other Englishman who's gone up there. I can see a small headline in some small newspaper somewhere, 'The Arctic wastes claim another Englishman.'"

"It didn't kill Francisco," Ken argued.

John waved his hand at Ken dismissively. "There's just no point in arguing with you. You're so damn bull-headed."

A knock on the door interrupted them. The janitor came in. He was a refugee who had escaped the communist regime in Czechoslovakia, where he had been a professor of mathematics. His credentials were not recognized in Canada and so he had taken a series of menial jobs. When he discovered that he could use his skill and knowledge of mathematics to become a formidable gambler he had started travelling from camp to camp, where gambling was forbidden but proved to be the major source of entertainment.

Ken asked him to teach him how to gamble. The man refused but said he'd give him a few pointers on the understanding that he would never gamble.

"Why not?" Ken asked.

"That's the deal or there's no deal," the janitor said. He explained that no matter how well Ken learned or how talented he was, he was not a gambler. The same mania he had for the Arctic could easily translate into anything he did – including gambling – and if he gambled seriously, he would likely sell his soul.

"If you want to make a few bucks on the side I can help you," he said. "I can tell you what to do. So here's the deal; I'll tell you when to bet, who to bet on, how much to bet, which games to bet on, and who to stay away from. So, what are you trying to achieve? What's your figure?"

Ken shrugged. "Forty thousand dollars!"

"Forty thousand dollars! That seems pretty definite. What do you want forty thousand dollars for?"

"I have no idea."

"Well, why do you need it?"

"I don't need it."

The man thought about this for a minute. "Are you prepared to promise me that after you've achieved what you want, you'll never ever gamble again?"

"Yes," Ken said, and they shook hands.

He followed his mentor's instructions with great care, and over the next few weeks the money, in grubby tens and twenties, accumulated until he reached his goal of forty thousand dollars.

He stashed the bills in waxed cardboard Sunoco tubes, used for testing concrete samples, and labelled them radioactive.

With temperatures dipping far below freezing and staying there, most outdoor work was curtailed but testing in the lab continued. The engineers had left and John taught Ken how to use a slide rule and how to do most of the routine jobs the trained professionals had done.

One night, as he walked back to his quarters from the lab, he heard a crackling overhead and looked up. The heavens were on fire. Curtains of light undulated across the sky – white, red, electric blue – wave after wave of shimmering light. This was the Aurora Borealis, Francisco had talked about – but who could have imagined it! Ken stood, head back, transfixed, until his neck ached, and then he lay down in a snowdrift, burning the sight on to his retina. It was too beautiful – he had to share it. He jumped into the old Dodge Fargo and drove to Jessica's house.

As he drove up, and cut the rattling old engine, Jessica stepped out on the porch, holding a kerosene lantern.

"Sorry I'm so late," Ken said swinging himself to the ground. "But look – look up!" He pointed to the sky.

In the morning they woke to a crystal cold day. The temperature had dropped to minus thirty-five degrees Fahrenheit. The truck engine refused to turn over and Jessica smiled like the Cheshire cat, refusing to help Ken get it started. "Now you'll never be able to leave," she said. Laughing she disappeared and came back and handed him a bulky package wrapped in brown paper. "Open it. It's for you."

"Let me guess," Ken said.

"You'll never guess. Not ever."

Carefully, he began to open the package. "Not that way," she said impatiently. "Rip the damn thing open!"

Ken tore it open. Inside was a soft leather jacket with fringes and intricate beadwork. "It's beautiful," Ken breathed. "Where did you get it?"

"I made it," she said. "It's moose hide. I shot the moose; I prepared the hide and I did the beadwork. I made it for you. Put it on. I want to see how you look."

He slipped on the heavy leather jacket. "Don't move," she said. "I'll be right back."

When she returned, she was wearing an identical jacket. "What do you think?" she asked, spinning slowly on her toes.

Waves of emotion passed through him. Every time he thought his love could grow no deeper and no larger, he discovered new depths and new breadths of emotion.

"I love you, I love you, I love you," she said, walking closer to him. "I love you. Marry me! Will you marry me?"

A thousand thoughts crowded through his mind and flew away. "Yes," Ken said, and it seemed that some other voice had said it – but it was his voice and yes was the only possible answer his heart could reply.

Jessica flung herself at him and wrapped her arms around him. "Are you serious?" she asked, pulling back and looking searchingly into his eyes.

He tried to say yes but his throat had filled with tears and no words came out. He nodded mutely, and then croaked, "Yes, I will marry you."

They held each other fiercely, tenderly. Patrick came into the room and cleared his throat. "We're getting married," Jessica called out to him.

"We're getting married," she said again, as Margaret came into the kitchen. And then they stood, giant grins on their faces, everyone so pleased and not knowing what to say or do next with all the happiness hovering and whirling through the air.

"Well," Patrick said, "Let's make some fresh coffee."

A few minutes later there was a knock at the door and Long John walked in. "Christ it's cold," he said, hurrying to the stove and holding his hands out to its warmth.

"We're getting married," Jessica said.

"Who's getting married?" he asked, taking the cup of coffee that Jessica held out to him.

"Ken and I. We're getting married."

"Huh! So, what's the punch line?" John asked.

"It's not a joke," Jessica said.

"Well, holy smokes," John said, pulling a kitchen chair close to the stove. "Married, huh? Well, that's one way of keeping this crazy man with his half-baked ideas from killing himself up there in the Arctic wastes."

"What brings you to us on this chilly day?" Patrick asked.

"Well, let's see, where do I begin?" John said, leaning back. "In short, you've been fired," he said, pointing at Ken. " You know all those test reports that we've been doing and that you've been signing? You're not the one who's supposed to be signing them. These things are supposed to be signed by a professional engineer."

"We don't have a professional engineer," Ken pointed out.

"I know," John said. "And I was wondering how long it would take for something like this to happen. Somebody downtown, probably at Hydro, got wind of the fact that somebody other than a professional was putting out these reports and they're not being vetted. Who knows what the politics are, but they passed the word and that's when 'the old proverbial' hit the fan. So, I got a phone call telling me that you're fired and the owner of the company is on his way up. I think he's afraid they'll lose the contract for not following proper protocol."

Ken couldn't wait to get back to the camp. Patrick gave the old Fargo a boost and Ken tore up the driveway with Long John in hot pursuit. He waved at the guard as he passed through the gates and pulled up in front of the manager's office.

"I hear there's some kind of problem in Vancouver," the manager said.

"Yes, I hear I've been fired!" Ken said.

"Shit, I know," the man muttered. "That's all I need!"

"What do you mean it's all you need?"

"Well who's going to organize the movies and who's going to be my translator – we've got more busloads of Portuguese guys coming!"

"Not my problem!" Ken said.

"Grab a coffee and shut the door," the manager said. When he was sure no one could hear, he said, "I'll hire you."

"Sure," Ken said. "That's fine, but let's sort this out first. I'll keep your offer as an ace in the hole."

Later that day a small plane landed at the airstrip, disgorging the owner of the company and his entourage, who commandeered an office and closed the door. Ken slammed the door open and strode into the room. One man jumped to his feet and tried to usher Ken out. "No," he said, shaking the man off. "If this is about me, I'm going to have my say. You don't hire an engineer. You don't have one on the job, but you expect the job to get done. I've learned how to do it. I'm doing it and what's more, ask yourself, is there any single thing wrong in the information provided? Show me one thing that is incorrect – just one! I know you can't. The other question I have, is why am I doing the job of four to five men and getting paid for one? I'm glad I'm fired. It feels good. Have a nice time!"

Ken slammed out of the room, as boldly as he had entered, got in the truck, and drove back to Jessica's house. He was nearing the gate when he spotted the camp manager in his rear view mirror. Ken stopped and waited for him to pull alongside.

"Are you fired?" he asked.

"I haven't a damned clue and I don't care. I'm having a good time."

"Let me know immediately," he said. "I'll get you on the payroll right away."

"How much?" Ken asked.

"What are you making now?"

"That's got nothing to do with it."

"Well what do you want?"

"When I know what I want I'll tell you. Right now I don't want anything."

Late that evening John came to the log house with the news that the entire issue had been smoothed over. He had told the owner that he was the one who had taught Ken how to use a slide rule, and that everything had been done correctly. They had screwed up in head office, not Ken. The camp manager had also spoken on his behalf. In fact, John said, it was a lovefest. "Everyone's in love with you. And the owner of the company looks like a dummy. Of course, he's not – he's a smart guy but he had no idea what was going on. He has a lot of other companies to look after. But this is a big project with a lot of contracts. No one wants to look like an idiot. But, everybody's happy now!"

"Well, isn't that wonderful!" Ken said. "I'm not happy!"

"But it's okay – you're supposed to come back," John said.

"I'm not going anywhere," Ken said. "I've been fired."

"So what do we do?"

"I have no idea. Let them make an offer."

"What do you mean 'make an offer'?"

"Since I'm doing the work of four or five people, I want to be paid accordingly or I'm not going back. So, John, how about you becoming a messenger the other way around? Go back and tell them my story and let them make an offer."

"You little bugger," John grinned. "You're really going to do it, aren't you?"

John drove off and came back the next day with an offer of $450 per month.

Ken shook his head, "No."

John continued to drive back and forth with offers that Ken refused to accept. After two-and-a-half days, Ken said yes to $2,500 per month.

News of Ken's engagement swept through the camp. The manager offered him married accommodation and then asked, "Who's the lucky young lady?"

"Jessica, Patrick's sister. I'll ask her about moving to the management camp and see what she says. I doubt it though – she has a ranch down the road and lots of animals to look after. But I'll ask."

The manager's face flushed red and he looked down and shuffled his feet. "Yes, well, that could be a bit difficult."

"Difficult? Why?"

"It's just that there's a company policy – no Indians in the company management camp."

"Do you mean there are no Indians allowed in the camp?"

"I don't know," the man's face flushed redder. "That's just the policy. It's simply something that's been handed down."

"What bright spark came up with that idea?" Ken asked. "Don't you think it's strange that aboriginal people can't live any damned place they want, given the entire country was theirs in the first place?"

The manager shrugged.

"Tell me this, if you can. How about black people or brownish people or Jews? Can they live in the camp?"

"No policy on that, as far as I know," the man replied. "Why?"

"Just curious."

Despite Ken's state of bliss he had one nagging concern. Would Jessica want to come to the Arctic with him? Should he ask her? When he finally did she laughed, "I can't believe it took you this long. Of course I'll come – right after we get married. You look surprised."

"I am," he said. "I didn't think it was something that interested you."

"Yes it does. It does because it's your big dream. It's been building since you were a child. Every time you talk about it, which happens to be most of the time in case you didn't know, it's as if a light is shining from the inside of you. I've never met anyone else with a big dream."

"It doesn't seem like a big dream to me," Ken said. "I just want to go there and see it all."

"It's more than that," she said. "It's much more than that. This dream is bigger than you."

"What do you mean this dream is bigger than me?"

"It is. It's bigger than you and it's bigger than me and you have no say in it."

"You're beginning to sound like my grandfather in Spain just before he died. You're giving me goose bumps."

Later, when Ken was alone with Patrick he asked him what Jessica meant when she said, things like, "I am your home," or "The dream is bigger than you."

He smiled, "Yup, that sounds like Jessica all right. She's been like that since she was a child, making pronouncements that seem to come from nowhere and are never explained. It's almost as if she's having some sort of separate conversation on some different level at the same time that she's talking with us. Maybe she's living half her life in another dimension – I don't know."

"I find it a bit unnerving at times," Ken said.

"I wouldn't let it trouble you too much," Patrick said. "Even though she can be a bit spooky at times. In another time she probably would have been considered a Shaman or some such special person."

Ken asked Patrick what he thought of his sister marrying a white European. Their family had never intermarried. Would it be an issue?

"No." Patrick said. "Why?"

"I just wondered," Ken said. "It's been on my mind for some time. Is there any reason why your ancestors did not marry Europeans?"

"Not that I know of. It just simply worked out that way. What about your family? Will marrying a non-European be a problem for them?"

"I don't think so," Ken said. "But, I don't really know. I've never talked to them about it and come to think of it, I haven't talked to them for a long time. But I really don't mind one way or the other. This is my business."

Ken and Jessica began to plan their trip to the Arctic. Jessica immersed herself in research. She talked to everyone, especially the bush pilots that she invited to the house, and she began to piece the stories together and gather names of possible contacts. She marked places on the maps that Ken had purchased. The biggest challenge was finding a way to get there. The only road was the Alaska Highway, which led in the opposite direction to where they wanted to go. The only other highway was the Mackenzie River and it was navigable only twice a year: in the depths of winter by truck, or in late summer by boat.

The river was not a simple route. It was a mass of arms and branches interspersed with innumerable islands. The bush pilots warned them, "Don't go down that river. If you want to get lost forever, that's the place to go."

While Ken and Jessica planned, a series of blasts at the camp had moved hundreds of thousands of tons of shale and uncovered what appeared to be dinosaur prints. Experts were summoned who confirmed the find and Ken was put in charge of making impressions. But the weather was too cold for the plaster of Paris to set, so each print had to be covered with a small tent and heated. It was a slow, mind-numbing job and it caused all work to slow to a crawl. But the contract stipulated that if artifacts were found during construction they had to be preserved and must take priority.

More experts came who slowed the work even more. The men grew frustrated as the endless winter dragged on. Tempers flared during the long, long nights and the mood was exacerbated by the endless noise of diesels running 24/7 – fleets of trucks and other enormous pieces of equipment, motors idling to stop them from freezing up – each with its own tempo – creating a cacophony that no one could shut out, not even in their deepest sleep.

Working conditions worsened. Rocks and boulders either heaved up to the surface as frost shifted the roadbed, or fell from cliff faces and damaged vehicles passing below. Injuries and deaths mounted.

Workers paid little attention to danger. One day the operator of a crane with a long boom swung his machine around, not noticing the man walking directly in the path below him. The enormous ball and hook dangling from the end of the boom removed the back of his skull.

Every time someone was killed, work stopped. One cold day a siren sounded at about noon and the first aid medics tore out of the small field hospital and rushed into the lab. "Bring your trucks down," they yelled, pointing to an area of the camp where a large wooden scaffold was being erected.

John and Ken raced down in their pickups. A large part of the scaffold had collapsed and five men had fallen to the rock surface below. The two men who were still clinging to life were placed in the station wagon ambulances and driven to the clinic. One died on the way and the other shortly after arriving. While an investigation took place, Ken and John were given time off. Ken drove to Jessica's house and stayed with her for a week, helping her to plan their wedding.

At the end of the week, he returned to camp, while Jessica, Margaret, and Patrick prepared for a trip to Fort St. John – to engage a Justice of the Peace, and to load the truck with supplies for the reception.

Ken was working at the lab the day Patrick and his sisters set off on the hundred-mile journey to town. He was bent over a specimen when he heard the familiar wail of the siren. Looking up, he saw one of the ambulances heading for the camp's main gate.

He ran to the first aid clinic next door. "What's going on?" he asked.

"There's been an accident on the road," the medic said.

"What sort of accident?"

"A tractor-trailer jackknifed and went off the road."

"Anyone else involved?"

"A pickup truck. There's other help coming from town."

Ken's skin crawled. He forced the bile in his throat back down into his gut and ran back to the lab, yelling through the door to John that he was going to check on Jessica and her family. He cranked up the truck, his heart pounding, an unnameable fear rising in his chest. He put his foot to the floor, the truck careening around potholes and over the rutted washboard road. About thirty miles down the road he saw the flashing lights. He pulled up, got out of the truck and ran to the RCMP car parked at the edge of the road. Below him, at the bottom of the embankment, amid the jagged broken-up pieces of the semi, the pickup burned. Shaking beyond control, Ken ran, stumbling and sliding down the steep slope. The young RCMP officer he had met previously was struggling back up toward him. He held up his hand. "Don't go down there!" he shouted to Ken.

Ken stumbled toward him.

"Don't go down there!" He yelled, again.

The officer grabbed at Ken's shirt. Ken spun away. "Is the pickup blue?" he shouted.

"I don't know." The officer said.

"How many people are in the truck?"

"I don't know."

"How many people in the god damned truck?" Ken screamed.

"Three, I think."

"What do you mean, you think?"

"Don't go down there, the officer pleaded. "Please don't go down there."

Ken ran down; tripped, fell, rolled, picked himself up and scrambled down. He stopped when he hit the wall of heat bursting from the truck. The flames were dying; the truck was gutted. But what he saw was a vision he would spend the rest of his life trying to erase from his mind – a scene that would come to him in nightmares over and over, until sleep meant nothing but reliving the carnage – pieces of charred bodies inside the truck – one of them still wearing a piece of fringed and beaded leather jacket.

I have spent so much of my life trying to contain these feelings – to deal with these things. For a person of that age I had seen far too much death. I was born to it – born in it. Anyone looking at me – coming from the right side of the tracks, from a privileged family – anyone who would imagine the sort of life a person like that would have would be completely off the mark. So, I have to deal with these feelings very severely because I can't make the pictures go away. They don't go away. I'm a very disciplined soul and have been able to deal with so many things in my life through sheer, brute will power. But when it comes to Miloo and this, those images just will not go away. They dwell in me.

Ken stood beside the truck, unable to move, his eyes taking in a sight that no human should see; his eyes seeing things that no man who loved should ever look at. Something inside him melted – hot lava overflowing from some place in his chest, spilling out, like life oozing through his pores. "Why can I have everything in life except what is most precious to me?" Did he cry it out loud? Did he think it?

He rushed to the truck – tried to wrench the door open – his palms blistered with fire – he felt no pain. The RCMP officer pulled him away. He fought while the officer wrestled him to the ground. Others arrived, and more hands pulled him away. Arms wrapped around him. He was numb; he was raging; he was shaking uncontrollably.

People pulled him back up the steep slope and bundled him into the back seat of the police cruiser, wrapping him in layers of blankets. Nothing could stop his limbs shivering. Blackness crept in on the edges of his vision, and he felt as though he had dropped into the bottom of a deep, dark well. It was all a dream that he would awaken from. But, no – there would be no awakening. He was caught in a nightmare, and he had no control – none. His mind, body, and soul splintered. He could feel the jagged edges of what used to be Ken, and he was helpless to piece them back together again.

At some point he felt the cruiser move. Then it stopped and he heard voices, and saw Long John's face hovering over his. At the camp, the officer took him to the clinic where they treated the burns on his hands and released him into John's custody, with orders that he was not to be left alone. But late that night, after John had dozed off, Ken staggered out to his truck and drove to the ranch. He entered Jessica's room and lay down in her bed. His fingers touched the sheets; he inhaled the sweet odour of her and tried to blot out the picture of the body in the truck. He pictured his Jessica – his beautiful magnificent Jessica – his love.

He lay on the bed, staring at the guns on the wall. And he fought the biggest battle of his life. Eventually he fell asleep, only to be embraced by the nightmare of reliving the day over and over again.

When he opened his eyes, he looked up at a woman with a large, round face who was sitting on the edge of the bed. Her eyes were swollen and red. "I'm no longer here," Ken thought. "I've been transported somewhere."

"It's okay," the woman said. "I'm Jessica's auntie." And she began weeping. Then she lay down beside Ken, and they lay together drifting in and out of dreams. The stove had long gone out, but neither of them noticed the cold.

Hours or minutes passed. Ken had no sense of time. He heard a door creak open and footsteps clumping through the house. Then Long John appeared in the doorway.

"Leave him alone," the woman said. "He's better here than anywhere else. He can stay here as long as he likes. He can stay here forever."

Ken remained in the house for several days before going back to camp. He moved like a robot, automatically performing his duties. When he had arrived at the camp, he had weighed one hundred forty-five pounds and had quickly filled out to one hundred ninety pounds. In a few short months, he shrunk to his former weight. He couldn't eat. He retched even when he tried to drink water. He carried the vision of the truck – and the charred bodies inside it – everywhere he went.

He worked as many hours a day as his body could bear and slept only when he was too exhausted to keep his eyes open. His dreams were haunted by the vision of the crushed and burning pickup truck. Long John, the camp manager, the Portuguese workers, and almost everyone else in camp, tried to console him. But Ken was like a feral animal; he preferred to crawl into his room, shut the door, and nurse his wounds in private.

The only person he talked to was Jessica's auntie, who had taken up temporary residence at the ranch. It felt like home to him and he desperately wanted to stay but knew that he would find no lasting peace there. On his final visit, he took one of Jessica's rifles, a pup tent, and an assortment of camping gear.

His real solace was packing, unpacking, and repacking his gear into a large rucksack, in preparation for his trip to the Arctic. Trying to make the backpack light enough to shoulder, and yet contain all the items he would need for a journey of about a year, became an all-consuming task. Ken neatly solved the problem of bringing enough drawing materials by packing several rolls of adding machine tape, which were small enough to fit into the lab's metal cylinders where they would stay dry. He rigged up a system of unrolling the paper and re-rolling the used end over a small wooden stick, to keep it compact and orderly. The only other drawing tools he packed were a large quantity of ordinary HB pencils, and a pocket knife donated by one of the Portuguese men "to sharpen the pencils."

He gave his notice in June, packed the gear he couldn't take with him – including the money rolled in the tubes with the radioactive stickers – and shipped it all to his parents, in Vancouver. He enclosed a long letter, describing camp life and his plans for his trip, omitting all mention of Jessica or her family.

7

The Tundra

Ken left the camp in mid-June, flying to Fort St. John with one of the bush pilots Jessica had spoken with. She had left a long list of contacts and information that revealed there was more activity in the far north than Ken had imagined. Mining companies were staking claims, the Geographic Survey of Canada was mapping the land, and aboriginal and non-aboriginal people were living in various camps scattered here and there. The bush pilots were the highway that linked these settlements.

From Fort St. John, Ken flew with another bush pilot to a camp on the Mackenzie River, not far from Yellowknife, where he started making drawings – on his adding machine paper – of the native people, known as "Slavies".

Within the week, he hitched rides with other pilots, working his way up the MacKenize River to Great Bear Lake. Looking down from the air, he began to have a sense of the immensity of the landscape. Although his imagination had conjured up images of vast, unpopulated, snow-covered fields stretching to the horizon nothing could have prepared him for the immeasurable tapestry of trees, rocks, and snow. There was no night, and there were no icebergs or polar bears – this was not the land of Francisco's stories. This was a land covered in scrub trees, tiny plants, patches of early summer snow, and moss that released black swarms of mosquitoes if you stepped on it. From the air, the land looked like a lace tablecloth, stretching to infinity in all directions.

For Ken, emerging out of the wreckage of his dreams and the broken remains of his heart, it was the perfect landscape to begin to rebuild his life. Wherever a small, single or two-engine plane dropped him off, he would gaze around in wonderment and try to capture his impressions in tiny drawings.

The Aboriginals he met were divided into four groups: the Slavies, the Dog Ribs, the Yellowknives, and a variety of unnamed others. Ken asked them questions about their origins but received no answers. He began to understand that asking questions was considered rude and he consciously made a decision to become a quiet observer.

By listening, he learned that these people wondered if perhaps he was a government agent. Why else would he be asking so many questions? Whenever they gave information, their children were taken from them so the less said the better. Most of the children had already been gathered up and sent to residential schools and the people were divided on the issue. Some thought that the white man's schooling would give their children the best chance at a future in this new world; others wanted to keep their children with them, to live as they had always done, on the land. None of them wanted to lose members of their family.

Sunlight streamed down day and night over this "in-between" land, caught between the Taiga and the Tundra – a land that didn't quite know what it wanted to be.

Ken flew to Coppermine, just inside the Arctic Circle, and then travelled to a camp in nearby Bloody Falls; named for the 1771 massacre that took place here when the Indians ambushed the Eskimos while they slept in their tents.

Samuel Hearn – likely the first white explorer to come to the Coppermine River – had recorded the dates, of his arrival and of the bloody battle he witnessed, on a riverside boulder. Ken looked at the boulder until the dates were engraved on his mind. The boulder marked his entrance to the North.

Ken watched the people pulling enormous fish out of the river by the camp. It didn't seem to matter what kind of bait they used – all they had to do was drop a line in the water and they had a fish.

After a couple of days in camp he asked if someone could take him across to the eastern shore of the river, where a small hill in the otherwise flat landscape would give him a good view. Many people refused to take him. Finally, one man grudgingly acquiesced and paddled him across.

On the other side, he heaved his pack on his back and trudged toward the hill. The ground was hard, covered with tiny low plants and flowers, and dotted with prickly shrubs. The few trees were stunted willows. From the top of the hill, he looked toward an infinitely distant horizon. An undulating landscape spread before him but what filled his vision was the great bowl of blue sky, unbroken into eternity.

Ken drank in the vast emptiness, letting it fill his senses. As his eyes scanned the immense land they fell on another rise some distance away – or perhaps it was close. He had no orientation points to tell him how close or near a thing was. No trees, no buildings, no foreground objects to give him a point of reference.

On the rise, he saw a group of people. Perhaps, these were the Eskimos who roamed the land – the people he had heard about. He approached the people and then stopped, his senses reeling. Yes, they were people – but not in the conventional sense at all. This was a group of stone people – stark, lonely and majestic stone people.

Ken circled around the stone people, which he later learned were called Inuksuit. Around and around he walked, occasionally reaching out a hand to touch them in a dazed kind of wonderment and awe. For the first time in many weeks, his spirit began to lift.

I thought I was quite a well-informed person on a variety of subjects, given that in my upbringing, acquiring general knowledge was considered important. General knowledge led you to being a generalist and it's the generalists that run the world so you want to have vast amounts of knowledge in a variety of areas. So, you learn about the pyramids and the sphinx and Stonehenge and Easter Island and all of that. But here were these strange human-like figures made of stone that I had never heard of – and at that point, I started to come out of my stupor. These figures got a hold of me. This was something that captured my attention in a major way.

He set up his tent some distance from them, thinking perhaps they were sacred symbols and while he struggled with his tent, he kept glancing at the stone men, reluctant to look away even for a moment lest he lose the magic. With his little tent tamed, and his camp set up on the windy plain, he dug out one of his rolls of paper – from the depths of his backpack – and began drawing. He rolled the paper farther after each drawing and began another. He couldn't stop; he was infused with the same energy he had felt when he first began drawing, in Portugal, as a young boy.

When his stomach let him know he was hungry, he walked down to the river and caught a fish. Cooking was a challenge because there was so little wood of any kind to burn. He had learned to start a fire with dried moss and then add bits of shrubbery to get an intense blaze that lasted mere minutes. He usually managed to cook one side of the fish over the flame. Then he had to start a fresh fire to cook the other side. In time, he learned to eat and enjoy raw fish because it was so much simpler.

While camped near the Inuksuit for several days, making drawing after drawing, he noticed a group of people setting up camp some distance from him near the river. The people on the west side of the river didn't acknowledge these people on the east side, and they in turn did not speak to the people on the west bank. Ken concluded that these were Eskimos, the people he had been searching for.

The Eskimos paid no attention to Ken and he did not try to make contact. Instead, he continued to draw, fish and cook his meals. He was consciously becoming a silent person and the deeper he fell into the stillness, the greater the solace he found.

One day a woman with a deeply lined and weathered face carried some fish and bannock on a flat stone to Ken's tent, placed it on the ground and walked back to her camp. Ken ate gratefully. "How shall I respond?" he wondered.

He walked to the river to wash the stone, marvelling at its polished smoothness and its almost soapy texture. When it was clean, he walked to their camp and placed it near their tents. For the next several days, the old woman came to his tent once each day bearing food on the same stone and each day Ken ate the meal, washed the stone and returned it.

One day Ken went to the river and caught several fish, cleaned them, and brought them to their camp. Exchanges of food occurred more frequently over the next few days, and then one day there was a look, a gesture, a nod, and Ken moved his tent to the Eskimo's camp.

They never made contact with his eyes but looked past him to some distant point on the horizon. One day he broke his silence and told them his name and where he came from. They smiled and spoke a language that wasn't quite guttural and yet it seemed to come from the back of the throat.

One middle-aged man looked Ken's way and said in English, "We are what you call Eskimos but our real name is Inuit."

The old woman who had first approached Ken's camp gave the man a quick glance and he fell silent.

The days passed in a quiet routine, but with the absence of night Ken's conventional sense of time gradually faded. One time he woke up from a deep sleep, his elbows and knees jammed uncomfortably against his possessions. Feeling cramped he laid his things out on the ground and rested on his stomach, gazing at the vegetation just below his chin. He could have been in an airplane looking down at the jungles of the Amazon. Lulled by the stillness, he began to wonder about his life.

Here I was in this place that I had dreamed about so much. Part of me was incredibly captivated and very excited. But part of me was chained to darkness. Although I had been able to sleep better, there was still a horrible fear. My dream world contained the horrible image that would not go away. I wondered if I would ever come to a time in my life when the exquisite and the extraordinary and magnificent would not be chained up to this horrible darkness. And I remembered that I was very young, but so far, this is how my life seemed to have been. And I wondered if this was a phase that I had to go through. Or was it something that everyone had to experience? Is this just the way life is? If that's true, what do you do about it? How do you live a good life if this is the way life is? Is it possible to separate things and put them in different compartments and not allow them to touch each other? How do you keep these things apart and is it a good idea to do that? I imagined the horrible darkness to be a virus that had to be put away in quarantine so that it would not infect everything else. Perhaps I could visit it now and then – feed it enough to keep it satisfied but not enough so that it could procreate.

While these ideas tumbled through his head, he became aware that he had customers for his unintentional flea market. Among the possessions he had laid out on the ground was his roll of drawing paper, partially unravelled to reveal tiny images of the Inuksuit.

The old woman smiled and giggled as she pored over them. Ken showed her how the rolled-up paper mechanism worked and she rolled it farther and farther back, studying each drawing carefully and nodding her head, smiling occasionally.

When she was finished, she rolled the paper back to the most recent ones, pointed to one of the stone structures and said, "Inukshuk" in a voice like a soft and flowing melody.

She repeated the word and pointed to him. "Inukshuk," Ken said, disappointed in his own harsh voice that turned the melody of the word into a plain, guttural statement. She smiled and nodded. She pointed to a picture with two stone structures, pointed to one, then the other and held up two fingers, "Inuksuit!"

"Inuksuit," Ken said.

She pointed to herself. "Inuk."

"Inuk," Ken said.

The old woman pointed to herself and the man and held up two fingers. "Inuit."

"Inuit," Ken repeated.

She smiled and nodded her head. A couple of other people from the camp came and joined the group, smiling. Ken was full of curiosity and questions. Were all these people related? There were eight in the camp – were they a family? But he had promised himself: no questions. Don't speak unless you are invited to.

One of the people brought a stone, holding meat sliced almost paper thin. It was partly cooked, but the inside was red and raw. The food was passed around. Ken took a sliver and bit into it – a mild and delicious flavour and a texture that melted in the mouth like cotton candy.

The old woman pointed to the meat. "Tuktu!"

"I wonder what Tuktu is," Ken thought. He repeated the word and everyone smiled. "Eeeee," they said in approval.

As he ate the meat, he noticed the man who spoke a bit of English looking intently at the 30/30 rifle that had once belonged to Jessica. Ken picked it up, pulled the lever down to open the breach, and handed it to him. The man smiled, revealing yellowed, uneven teeth. He examined it, turned it over in his hands, pulled the lever back and aimed it at various points on the tundra. Finally, he put it down beside him. When the women left and walked back to their tents, the man leaned close to Ken and asked, "How much ammunition do you have?"

He reached into his backpack and pulled out what he had: two boxes containing 500 rounds each. The man raised his eyebrows and nodded, then reached into his pocket and pulled out a smaller bullet. "Do you have any of these?" he asked.

The bullet was an extra long .22 "No," Ken said. "I don't. Is this what you use?'

The man nodded.

"What do you shoot with it?'

"Everything," he said.

Impossible, Ken thought. "Caribou?" he asked. "Polar bears?"

The man nodded and shifted his attention to one of the maps that was spread out on the ground. He pointed to a spot on the map near the village of Coppermine and only a few miles from the ocean. Ken nodded and suddenly realized that the open water that was so close to the camp was the Northwest Passage, that almost mythical stretch of water that Europeans had searched for and died trying to find – that precious piece of ocean that so few men had ever laid eyes on.

Ken scrambled to his feet, grabbed his roll of drawing paper, and climbed the next rise and from there, he saw it – the silver gray waters, sparkling like diamonds in the sun. "I'm looking at what people searched for, for hundreds of years, and couldn't find!" he thought. Overcome with wonder, he sat and began to draw the vision in front of him, making heavy black lines to represent the ocean. As he drew, he wondered about the European explorers. Surely they must have found the Inuksuit. Wouldn't they have wondered who built them? And wouldn't they have concluded that whoever built these things could steer them to the Northwest Passage? Or were these Europeans so arrogant that they believed anyone who lived here was a savage and couldn't possibly tell them anything or help them in any way?

When he walked back down the rise to his tent, he found the man still examining the rifle. "Do you want to shoot it?" Ken asked.

He nodded.

They walked some distance from the camp and when they came to a small valley with a few sandbanks, the man stopped and lowered himself to the ground. Ken sat beside him. The man took several bullets out of one of the boxes and filled the breach. Then he raised the rifle to his shoulder, pointing and aiming here and there. "What are you going to shoot?" Ken asked.

"Siksik," he said.

Ken waited, staring out at the tundra, listening to the silence. Suddenly, the man rose, picked up a stone, and flung it at one of the sandbanks. A fat ground squirrel popped up chattering, "Siksik, siksik".

As other heads emerged out of hidden burrows, the man raised the rifle, squinted through the sight, and pulled the trigger. Sound exploded into the stillness, and an animal toppled. The man shot four more times and four more siksik fell.

Satisfied, the man lowered the rifle, picked up the animals and walked back to camp, where he presented them to the old woman. She nodded and smiled, laying them out in a row and then producing a half-moon shaped object made of iron. Pointing to it she said, "Ulu."

"Ulu," Ken repeated.

Deftly, she skinned the animals with the homemade knife and cut them into sections. Another woman shuffled over carrying a large pot into which they placed the meat.

And everything was unspoken. This was a world in which each person knew what to do. You didn't; have to chatter about it. It seemed you only talked if there was something really important that needed to be said. There was something very appealing about that. I wondered how much of what we talked about was utter nonsense.

Ken asked the hunter about the silence.

"No, we don't talk much," he said.

"How did you learn English?" Ken asked.

"Hospital."

"Hospital?"

"TB. I was in the hospital."

After a long silence he said. "Good rifle."

Ken nodded.

"Too expensive," he said. "The bullets – too expensive."

"Twenty-twos are cheaper?"

"Yes."

"Where do you get them?"

"It's very hard to get them."

"Do they sell them in the village across the river?"

"Yes."

"So why don't we go over there?"

The man didn't answer.

"I can go over there," Ken suggested.

"Good idea," the man said.

"Would you like me to go over there?"

"Yes."

"How do I cross the river?"

The man walked to a clump of willows, growing waist high on the riverbank, where a big freighter canoe was hidden. Ken shouldered his backpack, tucked a wad of money into his pocket, and climbed into the canoe. The current carried them swiftly downriver. The man steered with the tiller and his paddle, angling them toward the opposite shore. On the bank, they pulled the canoe ashore and dragged it into another clump of willows. Ken shouldered his pack and walked into town.

The village was a ramshackle collection of caribou hide tents, canvas tents, and buildings cobbled together from the flotsam and jetsam of camp life. Towering over this evil-smelling collection of hovels was a white church with a tall steeple, gleaming in the sun. Ken walked down the centre of the muddy main street. As he walked, people stopped and stared. A bell tinkled as he opened the door of the Hudson's Bay Company store. As his eyes adjusted slowly to the gloom he made out an eclectic collection of goods that included tea, animal traps, jars of molasses, tubs of lard, sacks of flour and sugar, and bolts of cloth, but no rifles or ammunition. While his eyes roamed over the shelves, a door at the back of the store opened and a burly man entered and shuffled behind the counter.

"Good morning," Ken said.

"Can I help you?" the man asked.

"I hope so," Ken replied. "Do you have any drawing paper?"

"Drawing paper? What kind of drawing paper?"

"Paper that you make drawings on."

"No, we don't have any."

"Do you have any tobacco?"

"Yes, I have tobacco." He pointed to a shelf where tobacco was packaged in large tins. Ken placed four tins on the wooden counter.

"Do you have rolling papers?"

The man pointed again and while Ken searched his mind for other things the people might need the storekeeper asked, "Why do you want drawing paper?"

"I'm an artist."

"And just where might you be from?"

"I might be from a whole bunch of places but mostly I'm from Portugal."

"Portugal. That's pretty far away."

"Yes, I guess it is."

"If you don't mind my asking, how did you get here?"

"I walked here."

"You just walked here."

Ken nodded, still searching his mind. "How do you make bannock?" he asked.

The storekeeper gave him a list of ingredients that Ken collected. He recalled how much the people liked tea and added several large packages of orange pekoe to the stack he was building on the counter. Finally, he asked, "Do you have any ammunition?" and showed him a 30/30 shell.

"Nope. Don't have any of those right now."

"But you do get them?"

"Yes, occasionally, but it's not a very popular bullet around here."

Ken showed him the .22 extra long. "Do you have any of these?"

"Yeah, we got those," and from the room at the back of the store he produced two boxes of shells, each containing 500 rounds.

"Do you have more?"

"More? What do you propose to do – start a revolution? And how do you propose to pay for all this?"

"With money," Ken said, reaching into his pocket and pulling out a wad of bills. "How much?"

The storekeeper opened a ledger and painstakingly detailed every dollar, penny, and inventory number. Ken peeled off the bills, handed them to the man, and placed the items in his backpack.

Back at camp Ken distributed the tobacco, paper, tea, flour, and other goods. From the bottom of the pack he pulled out four boxes of .22 extra long shells and presented them to the hunter. At that moment, he sensed a shift.

A couple of days later they struck camp, packed their belongings into the canoe, and motored to the mouth of the river, where it flowed into the Northwest Passage. From there they headed east. Several hours later they stopped where about 15 people were camped. While they set up their tents, Ken heard the word Kabluna spoken several times.

"What does this word 'Kabluna' mean?" Ken asked his friend.

"It means white man."

"So I am a Kabluna."

"Yes and if there were two, they would be Kablunat." Then he chuckled.

"You think something is funny?"

"Yes. You know what the word really means? It means 'eyebrows over belly button.'"

"Huh?"

"White man is hairy, noisy, rude, always in a hurry, falling over, nothing but trouble."

Ken laughed, thinking how wise he had been to go into this world quietly.

When the hunter picked up his rifle and left the camp, Ken followed, crossing the tundra until they came to a stream flowing out of a shallow lake. There they sat and waited. After what seemed like hours the hunter tensed. Ken scanned the horizon and noticed an almost indiscernible movement – tiny specks that slowly resolved themselves into a small herd of caribou moving toward them. When they were within twenty yards the man lifted the .22, aimed, and shot. Five explosions followed in rapid succession and five caribou fell, each with blood pouring out of a small, lethal hole behind its ear.

The man laid down his rifle, took his knife out of his pocket, and smoothly slit their throats, while Ken pulled their heads down to spill the blood.

Back at the camp, the others converged on the carcasses, gutting, cleaning, and skinning the animals expertly, taking care to waste nothing.

The old woman showed Ken how to take a piece of liver, place it in his mouth and cut it off with an ulu. He swallowed appreciatively while the old woman nodded approval. Later that day the people moved their camp to the edge of the shallow lake. When they were settled, Ken made sketches and drawings of the people in the camp. He started with the old woman, placing her weathered face in the foreground of and slightly to the side of an Inukshuk. When he was finished, he touched her hand and gave her the drawing. Her face broke into a big, gap-toothed smile. She showed it to the others who also nodded and smiled, and shyly pointed at themselves and him. The old woman determined who would have their portrait drawn next and directed them to him. Taking a cue from Ken's earlier gesture, she gently touched his hand when she wanted his attention.

After he had completed several drawings, he indicated that he would do more the next day and handed the paper and pencil to the nearest person.

He walked along the shore of the shallow lake until he arrived at a stream, where a large boulder stood with a big flat stone balanced on top and on top of that a smooth, round reddish stone. Around him were other stone arrangements that were man made yet not in the shape of people as the Inuksuit had been. What did it mean? What did any of it mean? Nothing that Ken had encountered in the Arctic matched up with the pictures in his imagination.

He had conjured a land of ice and snow but what he had found was a bare, flat land of rocks and pebbles with the occasional patch of rapidly melting snow. The land stretched to the horizon in every direction – a thin brown and green ribbon under the immense dome of an enormous sky. The sun burned in that sky, without ever dipping below the horizon, with a light so intense it almost seared his eyes. The wind blew without stopping – a hot wind that might have come from the shores of Africa.

Staring at the flat ribbon of land, Ken's eyelids drooped and closed. He lay back on the moss and slept. When he woke, he felt more rested than he had in many weeks. The sun had moved a long distance across the sky. The wind had died and the clouds of black flies and mosquitoes had subsided. The world was still with a silence like a thick, suffocating blanket – silent colours, silent sky, silent land – everything silent except Ken's thoughts.

As he strained his ears to capture something, anything, he noticed a strange hissing emanating from inside his body. As he concentrated on it, it grew until it was a roaring waterfall in his head. He wondered if something had happened to him. Perhaps the landscape was not as silent as he thought it was. Perhaps he was going deaf.

He rolled over, picked up two small stones and banged them together. They made a satisfying clicking noise. He was not deaf. He banged them together more rapidly and the roaring sound began to diminish. When he stopped the noise once again filled his head.

When he sat up he saw the old woman and the man sitting a short distance away observing him. When they saw that he had noticed them, they came to sit beside him. The man said, "My mother says you are a very quiet Kabluna."

"Maybe all Kablunat are quiet," he said.

The man translated for his mother and said, "She says that all other Kablunat that she has known are noisy. They talk a lot."

"Maybe I don't have much to say," he replied. "Maybe I don't know very much."

When Ken questioned the old woman about the Inuksuit she told him a story that began a long, long time ago when there were very few human beings. They travelled over the vast land in small family groups, following the herds of caribou that were the source of their food, their tents, their clothing, and their utensils. They could not afford to deplete their energy by chasing the food. Instead, they made stone human beings and called them Inukshuk, which means, like a person or acting in the place of a person.

The people placed the Inuksuit in V-shaped formations. The caribou with their poor eyesight, thought the Inuksuit were hunters and so it required only a very few people to herd them into a trap. The closer they came to the end of the V, the closer together the Inuksuit were placed.

At the point of the V, hunters hid behind boulders while women and children lay on the ground beside the Inuksuit. As the caribou approached, the women and children jumped up, waved their arms, and danced about, to give the appearance of many, many hunters. The caribou would then stampede to the end of the V, which was usually at the junction of a lake and a river. When the caribou plunged into the lake, the hunters hidden behind the boulders would jump into their kayaks and paddle after them, spearing them in the water. Then they would haul them back to shore where the entire family, even the children, would clean and gut the animals.

Inuksuit also took on many other shapes, the old woman said. The one on the river's edge where they were sitting was a fishing Inukshuk. She knew this because it was topped with a smooth stone taken from the riverbed. It indicted that the fishing was good here. Other shapes had other meanings and the configurations of Inuksuit had meaning also.

To my mind, what I was hearing sounded like language but they didn't write the language on a piece of paper – they wrote it directly on the land. And I was beginning to get the picture of absolute practicality. Here you could live with minimum technology if you knew how. To think that you could direct an entire way of life by putting a few stones together just so, so that other people coming would be able to read the significance of these things. The degree of sophistication of this began to seep into me and I realized there was much to learn here. And this way of life was like the people were – inscrutable and so subtle that unless you slowed right down to their pace and took every little detail in, it would appear to be the bleakest place on earth. In fact, it's probably one of the most populous places on earth in plants, animals, birds, and insects. Wherever you turned there were insects, including the billions and billions of blackflies and mosquitoes.

Ever since the old woman's son had refused to go to the store in Coppermine, Ken had sensed a certain tension when they referred to the Kablunat. He believed that he had won enough trust that he could ask about it, but he had also noticed that no one asked direct questions or spoke about themselves. When the hunter translated for his mother he didn't use words such as "I" or "me". Instead, he said "one" as in "One wonders ..." The language was composed of indirect statements and wonderment.

Ken said that he wondered about their reluctance to have contact with the people in the town and the old woman countered with, "What is Kabluna looking for?"

He told the story of Francisco and how he had learned about the Arctic and how he had wanted to come to this place all his life.

"Yes, but what is Kabluna looking for?" she asked.

"I'm looking for the beautiful things that I heard about in the old man's stories."

"Does Kabluna work for the government of the Kablunat?"

"No."

"Who does Kabluna work for?"

"I don't work for anyone."

"But all the Kablunat work for the government."

Ken explained that he was an artist and that he told stories by drawing and painting them and in his world that was a recognized profession.

"Is Kabluna running away?" she asked.

"Why would I be running away?"

"Kablunat either work for the government or they're running away."

In the silence Ken thought that in part she was right. He was running from the nightmares. "I'm running *to* something," he said. "But right now I have a big noise in my ears and in my head."

The old woman smiled. "Kablunat can sometimes hear their own noise." She explained that the noise was the sound of his blood rushing through his ears and that a number of Kablunat had gone crazy in the north and had had to be tied up and taken away. Silence – real profound silence – could break a man.

When they returned to camp new arrivals were setting up their tent. The family consisted of an older woman, a young couple, two children aged about five or six, and a baby that the woman carried in a big hood on her upper back. The new family wore white clothes patterned with an intricate design of beads. Flaps in front and back were inlaid seamlessly with different coloured hides.

This was marvellously intriguing. Everything I looked at now took on an ever-increasing significance. Because this was such a vast place I noticed the smallest of things. I was in a place where all the things I was used to – buildings, trees, cars, noises – were completely absent. Even the land itself was a nonentity. It was a place of sky. I was in a state of sensory deprivation and at the same time, in a place of sensory overload. I was feeling emotionally disturbed at times and I thought that was because of the recent tragedy in my life but added to that was the combination of deprivation and overload. The story the old woman had told about people going crazy made sense. Unless you had a compelling desire and reason to be in this world, you would simply fall apart here. I was so thankful for the upbringing I'd had, particularly with Francisco – somehow it had prepared me for this kind of life.

The old woman gave Ken the paper and pencil he had left at the camp and motioned him to make more drawings, especially of the children. As he flipped through the roll to find fresh paper, he noticed that someone had made a series of remarkable drawings of groups of people hunting or fishing. There was no horizon line and no other object to give them a sense of place but their simple clarity told a story that was understandable to any culture in the world.

When Ken looked up from the roll he noticed that the children had taken their clothes off and were swimming and playing in the water of the shallow lake. Everyone else in the camp quickly joined them.

Ken stood on the edge of the lake, fully dressed. A little boy ran out of the water, tugged at Ken's sleeve and called out a word several times. "What does this word mean?" he shouted to the hunter who was splashing in the lake.

"It means uncle," he called back, explaining that every young male is uncle and every man who is old is grandfather. Everybody is related on that level, he said. And there were words in the language that asked, when you greeted each other, "Are we related?" The laws and rules of the people were actually taboos and if you were related to someone, it was forbidden to hurt them – that was the biggest taboo.

With the child's urging, Ken shyly took his clothes off and dipped his foot into water as warm as his body temperature. He plunged in, bemused by the idea of swimming in the Arctic, the land of cold and ice. As he stroked through the water he asked the hunter about the tattoos that covered the bodies of the two old women. He said that before Kablunat began to rule the Arctic, tattoos were a sign of great beauty. Some people had their faces tattooed as well as their bodies and many of the tattoos had significance. Now, most of the people no longer lived on the land and tattoos seemed to be offensive to Kablunat.

"What do you mean the people don't live on the land any more?" Ken asked.

"Everybody has been rounded up and put into villages," the man said, and swam away.

When they had finished bathing and were lying on the ground letting the warm wind dry their skin he asked about people being rounded up. The old woman asked again, "Kabluna does not work for the government?'

"No,"

"Does Kabluna think he might one day work for the government?"

"No."

She told the story, parts of which Ken had heard before. The government of the Kablunat called the people Eskimos and they rounded them all up and put them in fabricated villages. Then they took their children away from them and sent them to residential schools, usually in the south. Terrible things happened there but those things were not talked about.

The Kablunat could not speak Inuktitut nor did they have any interest in learning it. So, instead of calling the people by their names each one was given a letter – E for east and W for west depending on where they lived – and a number. In the residential schools the children were not allowed to speak their native language. They were taught religion, reading and writing. When the children went back to their homes at holiday times, they no longer paid respect to their elders and looked down on their parents and grandparents. That, the old woman said, was the destruction of their society – a deliberate, systematic and well-thought-out tearing down of their way of life.

Ken swallowed down his outrage and anger. These people were on the run, trying to live in the way they always had. But there was no real escape and they too were caught up in the vortex of a new world. If they didn't co-operate with the Kablunat their children would be taken from them, and they wanted the bullets, flour, lard, and other things sold by the Hudson's Bay Company. They were living in a dilemma, trying to be true to their way of life in a world that would no longer allow it.

The old woman had told her story with no trace of resentment or anger. If this had occurred in Europe they would be at war. How could they swim and play with carefree abandon, while all the while, storm clouds were gathering on the horizon?

When they were dry and sun-warmed, they dressed, retrieved sacks and rudimentary bone spears from their tents and walked along the river to a place where rocks created a barrier that forced the water to rush through in one narrow torrent.

The river was teeming with enormous Arctic Char covered in shiny iridescent green scales. The men took turns standing in the river at the mouth of the rushing water, deftly spearing the fish as they hurtled through the chasm one by one.

On shore, Ken's friend took out a sharp knife and slit open the belly of one of the big fish exposing a white strip of pure fat. He peeled it off, put the end in his mouth and cut it off with his ulu. He passed Ken a piece of the precious fat that melted deliciously on one's tongue.

Ken became mesmerized by the minutiae of Inuit life. Everything they did was alien to his previous experience. He watched one of the men make a drum from the hide of a young caribou. Only the skin of a young animal would do, the man explained. It was shaved clean, soaked with water and spread out in the hot sun where it bleached white. It was then stretched over several pieces of wood that had also been soaked, bent to make a circle and bound together with strips of leather. The skin was sewn on to the hoop and left out in the sun again, this time to shrink.

Watching the process, Ken understood how important each piece of wood was to these people. Where he came from people would have used just one piece of wood to form the hoop. Here, the circle was made of many small pieces of wood. Trees didn't grow on the tundra. There might be the occasional knee-high shrub and very rarely, willows that grew waist high in protected gullies. Every scrap of wood was hoarded and used with care and precision.

The Inuit had to obtain additional wood from the south where the sub-Arctic Indians lived. The old woman told Ken that there had been an uneasy truce between the Indians and the Inuit, which was often not honoured. Raids and massacres had taken place for years.

When the woman told stories through her son, she often said words that she asked Ken to repeat. When he learned a new Inuktitut word, she smiled and when he began to put words together to form a sentence, she beamed. It was the most difficult language he had ever learned, but then the people were like no others he had ever encountered. They didn't make eye contact when they spoke and they had no word for me, mine or I.

Raising your voice, particularly to children, was taboo. Children were expected to learn by the example others set. They ate when they were hungry, slept when they were tired, and played when they wanted to. Adult displeasure was shown in the smallest facial expressions – the wrinkling of a nose or a slightly raised eyebrow.

One day a young man named John joined the camp. He was about sixteen years old and he spoke excellent English. He told Ken that he was on holiday from the residential school in the south but he had decided not to return. They had cut off his hair and had beaten him for speaking his language. The old woman was his grandmother, and John told Ken that she and others were trying to get their children back. But this was not easy. While they needed to be stationary so that they could be contacted, they also needed to keep moving so that the authorities could not locate them and take more of their children away.

They were fugitives in their own land. Every few days they moved east but because the sun never set Ken had no stars to guide him and no directional signposts. His maps were useless. The lines on the paper bore no resemblance to the landmarks he encountered – and it struck him that bringing maps to their land might actually be an insult.

One day when the women had been gathering dry willow twigs to make a fire, Ken crumpled up the maps and placed them under the sticks. The women smiled gently and inclined their heads. When his watch stopped he removed it from his wrist, placed it in a crevice between the stones of an Inukshuk and felt pleased with the symbolism: a dead time machine from a foolish age nestled in the embrace of an ancient stone figure.

The maps and the watch had been the thinnest of threads connecting him to another world and now those threads were severed. He had no idea where he was or what time it might be. He was in the care of kind, knowledgeable souls and that was all he needed to know.

One morning John took him to the old woman's tent to be presented with a pair of boots made from caribou hide. "Kamik," she said.

"Kamik," Ken repeated.

The boots were lined with the skin of a glaucous gull, with the feathers pointing downward to give the foot an easy entry and to keep the boot on the foot. When Ken stepped into them he noticed they were still wet, and would mould themselves to the shape and size of his feet as they dried. The sole of the boot was made from thick caribou hide with a half-inch of the bristly hair attached. He could feel every nuance of the ground he stepped on and yet his feet were perfectly cushioned.

"How do you make these boots?" Ken wanted to know. This time his curiosity was rewarded. The old woman taught him the entire process; from shooting the animal, to skinning it, preparing the hide, saving the parts, and creating the tools needed to make them. She took a bone from the wing of the gull and shattered a part of it to produce a needle, so sharp that to touch it to the skin would draw blood. In the wider end of the bone she drilled a hole using a small bow, the string of which she threaded through her teeth. And although it was a large needle that made a sizeable hole, she skilfully overlapped the skins to make the boots watertight. The process, like everything else the people did, was a slow, careful one. The Arctic was an inhospitable land; one mistake no matter how small, could mean the difference between life and death.

When the old woman saw that Ken was genuinely interested, she taught him things that Inuit men would never learn. He was even invited to witness a young woman of the clan giving birth.

Ken began to see a pattern in their travels. Their journeys took them up rivers and then back down again toward the sea in a zigzag path that led gradually east. The Inuksuit too had a pattern: they were predominantly built along the rivers and the seashore. The farther inland they went, the smaller the Inuksuit; although no matter how small they were, from a distance they all appeared immense.

In some places, boulders that weighed many tons had been lifted off the ground and placed on a tripod of smaller stones. Inuksuit were then built on top of the boulder. When Ken asked who had created them, the old woman said, the Tunit – who were giants with children's minds that had lived on the land a very long time ago – made them. This was before the time of the Inuit and before the time of the Dorset – who had also preceded the Inuit.

Was the woman's story true? Perhaps. The Inuit didn't use the word "no" or the phrase "I don't know." Ken had no better explanation – yet, without at least the technology of the pyramid builders there could be no way to erect something so massive.

As they continued to move east, they entered their own territory. Through the most subtle hints and innuendos Ken realized that the old woman had plans for him. He was a young person – a Kabluna perhaps – but a young man. John explained to Ken that although he was Kabluna he also was becoming Inuk. To be Inuk is to live on the land in the way of the Inuit. Colour or race didn't matter. It was a spirit and an attitude that made you one of the people.

As they travelled, the sun began to dip briefly below the land and the world fell into a short twilight. Often, when the sun had just disappeared, a green flash would explode across the horizon – an intense band that wrapped itself around the sky and feathered out into the stars. Sometimes, in that brief period of semi-darkness, Ken would sit on the tundra and gaze out at the ribbon of land on the horizon, and as he looked, the horizon would curl up and up around him and form a bowl, with the sky hovering above. The Arctic was a land of mirages, dreams, visions, and possibilities. When the sun set, it rose again only inches from the same spot where it had disappeared. East and west had no meaning – they were simply directions that Europeans had drawn on a map – and maps meant nothing here.

One day, John Asked Ken why he was here. Once again, Ken recited the story of the tales Fransisco had told him as a child and how they had led him here.

"But, what is it you want?" John asked.

"I want to go everywhere," Ken replied. "I want to see everything. I want to know everything."

"Where is everywhere? Where is everything?" John asked.

Ken pointed to a small rise. "I want to go over there."

"There is no over there," John said.

"Of course there is over there."

"No, that's the problem with you Kablunat. You don't understand the universe. You don't understand these basic things."

John pulled Ken across the tundra. "I'll show you what I mean," he said. They walked a bit farther and stopped. "Where are you?" John asked.

"I'm here," Ken said.

John nodded, grabbed Ken by the arm again and walked about a hundred yards farther. "Where are you?"

"I'm here."

"There you are. There is no over there."

Ken's mind reeled and his world rocked on its foundations. John was telling him that reality was only real right now and only where you are. He was falling through a door that had been opened in his mind, and he was falling through it into a place with no bottom.

His world was linear. He played chess on a flat board placed on a table. John's world was a cube, and his people played chess in three dimensions. The world he lived in now was merely the surface of the earth. The above and the below were equally important and valid.

The next day Ken followed a line of Inuksuit until he had long lost sight of the camp, searching for a vantage point from which he could incorporate the entire grouping into a drawing. Where the land met the sky, he noticed a misty line stretching as far as he could see in both directions. The line gradually broadened as the smoky haze grew. Then spirals emerged from the fog, like lazy tornados spinning into the sky, growing and then disappearing. The line moved, grew, and rippled.

As the line drew nearer, it resolved itself into caribou – so many that counting them, or even estimating their numbers, would have been futile. Caribou covered the land. Ken could not outrun them, and he had nowhere to hide. He stood where he was as their thunder grew, until the herd engulfed him. They passed around him, parting as though he were a natural obstacle in their path. Their large hooves, with two dangling front pads and single dew pad, clicked past him. They browsed the lichen as they walked, fermenting it in their stomachs and scenting the air with the gasses their stomachs passed off.

When Ken realized he was perfectly safe, he sank to the ground and watched the world through a forest of millions of moving legs. When he stood again, he let the river of caribou carry him back to camp.

He abandoned his vow of calm and waiting silence, jabbering excitedly about his experience. The people laughed. While Ken had been walking with the caribou they had been harvesting the beasts. The caribou herds were life sustenance and life itself. In the years when the big herds changed their routes and did not arrive, the people faced starvation. In the North, people relied on the caribou and seals. Some people were seal people. Ken's people were caribou people.

When the last of the caribou had passed, they dragged the fresh carcasses to several large piles of rocks that they lifted to reveal deep pits lined with more rocks. They lowered the meat into the pits and replaced the rocks. The main danger to their food reserves was marauding wolverines. By caching their meat under rocks too heavy for the wolverines to move, they guaranteed a food supply for the season to come.

The days changed. The shiny green bearberry that covered the tundra turned blood red and when Ken gazed across the land he saw a river of crimson. One morning the snow geese flew across in the hundreds of thousands. When they settled on the land a down blanket covered the scarlet sea.

The days grew shorter and the temperature dipped dramatically. Ken shivered in his sleeping bag and the old woman gave him two caribou hides – one to put under his bag and one to cover it. He developed a new understanding of the word "cold". Cold was not simply a word here – it was a palpable, physical thing, which assaulted every sense – it was the god that controlled the land.

A few days after giving him the caribou hides, the old woman presented him with a caribou parka lined with Arctic fox. Through her son, she explained that this was to be worn without undergarments, next to the skin. The parka was light, soft and astonishingly warm.

They continued to travel east until they came to a lake dotted with a number of small islands, where they had left sleigh dogs that had whelped in early summer. The animals were wild, ferocious, and pugnacious. They took them back to the mainland where they pegged them to the ground, placing the lead dog at the front of the pack. Once a day someone tossed a frozen fish to each dog, which it consumed ravenously. The dogs were born to pull sleighs and once in the traces would run across the ice until they dropped from exhaustion.

With the dogs in tow, they continued trekking to the place the old woman called home. She was a Netsielik, People of the Seal. Her husband, who had died of TB, was People of the Caribou. TB had become epidemic among the Inuit. Several people in the group had severe coughs and often spit up bloody phlegm.

Snow began to stream across the land, blowing from the west in a million little rivulets. The temperature, already chillingly cold, continued to drop. The old woman gave Ken a pair of trousers made from caribou hide and sewed a wolverine hide along the edge of the hood of Ken's parka. To the amusement of the Inuit, Ken sat on the frozen tundra in his new clothes, watching the snow dance across the land. He felt fortunate. He was living his childhood dreams. This was the Arctic he had envisioned – the land of Francisco's stories.

He thought back to his grandfather's dying words, "You're going to have a very bright and beautiful life. It won't be an easy life but it will shine. The gods favour you. You are one of destiny's creatures".

He thought about the deceased people he had loved so much: Miloo, Francisco, Jessica – and felt their presence deep inside him, as he sat among the rivers of crystal snow. He felt a black weight lift from him, and he closed his eyes, focusing on lightness. When he opened them he saw the old woman watching him from the slit of her tent.

Later that day she told him to move into the large tent that she shared with her son and about a dozen others. When he entered, she told him to take off his parka. Another woman beat it with a long bone, to release the snow crystals and keep it dry.

That night everyone curled up naked under layers of caribou hides, with Ken given the best spot in the middle. He quickly grew accustomed to life in the tent.

I started to get an understanding of hunter people and how very, very different they are in every way – in language, in thought, and in behaviour. I felt completely at home. I suspected – and to this day, I suspect – that I was born a hunter/gatherer, into a sedentary society. No wonder I wriggled and wrestled and didn't fit. Here, I had no cravings or needs or thoughts of my southern life. I had the sense that I was descending back to a beginning somewhere. I was living with people of a hunter/gatherer culture who had lived this way for a great amount of time. I felt that I had been given an opportunity that I should not squander. We fantasize in movies and comics about having a time machine and being able to travel to another time – I was actually doing that and it was happening in a way that I had never envisioned. We can't understand things unless we're in them and although I didn't have a true grasp of what was happening to me, I was marching backwards in time, probably back to the cave. That idea appealed to me –and the farther back I went, the easier I was with my history and myself.

They entered one of the most challenging seasons of the year – the transition between summer and winter. They could not travel on the rivers, by canoe, because they were frozen and they could not travel on the rivers, by dog sled, because they were not frozen solid enough to bear the weight. It was too cold and windy to walk but there was not enough snow for the sleds to move across the tundra. So, they waited inside their tents, the women sewing and telling stories, the men shaping tools in long, deep silence. Day dissolved into night and night back again into day.

Ken noticed the tiny carvings on even the simplest soapstone utensils the Inuit used, like the Kudliks or seal oil lamps. No artist Ken had encountered had achieved such a degree of elegant simplicity. They captured the very essence of the creature they depicted. "Could I learn to draw that way?" Ken wondered. "This is something new – this is something I have never seen before."

All the carvings, with the exception of some monstrous humanoid-looking creatures, were of animals the people used for food. The old woman explained that the odd creatures were spirits and she told him about a world populated by good and evil and shape-shifting spirits. They made ivory carvings of them less than an inch high that they placed around the tent and that were used by angacock or shamans. The angacock was one of the secret parts of their lives that had survived the influx of Europeans, with all their technology and scientific understanding of the universe. Ken learned to ask questions that led him to a deeper understanding of a world where his previous knowledge didn't fit. He was a child again, watching, and listening, and writing new information on a blank slate.

The old woman told teaching stories as harsh as the landscape. Each story was retold many times, always in the same way. These stories were repeated from generation to generation, telling of the consequences of jealousy and possessiveness and other undesirable traits. When the stories ended, silence wrapped itself around the small community. Time lost meaning. No one felt the need to speak.

8

A Different World

One morning, John invited Ken to go seal hunting and led him to a small gully where several sleds were hidden under the snow. John pulled out the smallest of them, which consisted of two long wooden runners with slats tied down by strips of walrus hide.

When the Inuit could get metal, they inserted it in the bottom of the runners. In either case, they dug up humus from under the Arctic moss and urinated on it to make a friable mud, which they rubbed on the runners. The mud froze instantly. Then they used a plane to level out the humus until it was as smooth as glass. The result was an interface of ice on ice that allowed the sleighs to travel quickly, smoothly, and silently.

John picked a team of dogs and tied each to the traces individually in a fan shape that would glide safely over thin ice. John had considerable trouble handling the animals and an older man gave him a hand, beating and kicking the dogs viciously to bring them into line. "This is not what you think it is," the old woman said to Ken. "These animals are bred to be wild, vicious, and mean. But they have the stamina inside. Don't view what you see with your conditioned eyes. It's different up here."

With the dogs sorted out, they glided away, the animals pulling eagerly. They came to a shallow depression where uncountable numbers of yellow bones lay in the white snow. There they waited until they saw a stirring at the edge of the sea. Before the seals could escape into deep water, John lifted his rifle and fired a quick round of shots, killing four of the animals. They tied them to the sled and rode back to camp where they were greeted with great joy. Not only was fresh seal meat a treat, the oil would keep the lamps lit for many days.

As the days grew colder, Ken learned that it took an immense amount of food just to stay alive. They ate like animals. They thought about food all the time and devoured as much as their bodies could consume, but regardless how much meat and fat they ate, maintaining weight was a struggle.

When they had wolfed down an enormous meal, dipped liberally in fat, they would lie back in their tents, burping their appreciation; and for several hours, while their bodies burned the fuel, Ken could feel his temperature soar. The days and nights blended one into another, and long periods of quiet contemplation were interspersed with intense bouts of hunting. Ken learned to breathe differently. Taking in great gulps of the frigid air would have burned his lungs, so he inhaled slowly and measurably through his nostrils, calculating each breath.

One day another group of people arrived at their camp with several dog teams. Among them was a boy in his early teens. He too had recently come from a residential school and was sullen and spoke to no one. The group brought word that the caribou had not come their way and they were here to join Ken's group and hopefully share in what they had. Ken's group agreed to travel together and to share their abundance. They planned to move further east, to where they hoped to find enough seals and walrus to provide meat for the long winter.

One day before setting out, the troubled youth was particularly disrespectful to one of the elders and was quietly chastised. He walked away from the camp and had gone only a short distance before several people went in search of him. No one could survive long in this cold. The wind began to howl picking up ice crystals and blowing them across the land and the searchers hurried back to the tents. Within minutes the world was white; taking even one step outside the tent was certain death.

They waited in silence and Ken found himself feeling both disconcerted and exhilarated by their patience and lack of anxiety. He was unsettled because he had lost all sense of reference and elated because each moment was perfect. He was alive in the now and nothing else mattered. The long hours of silence gave Ken only one point of focus – himself. He was meeting himself for the first time and the self he was meeting was neither good nor evil – he just was – and Ken embraced that self with his mind and heart, quietly blessing every event that had led him on this journey to this place.

The white storm lasted for several days and when it ended, the people left their tents to resume the search. There was no sign of the dogs, just small mounds of snow scattered around the tents. When the people nudged the mounds, the dogs emerged from their igloos, shaking the snow off and wagging their tails furiously. They untethered several of them to assist in the search, and their acute sense of smell led them to another mound of snow under which they found the frozen boy.

There was no crying or wailing. They wrapped him in caribou hide and with great effort moved rocks, that the wind had swept bare, to form an oval. Gently, they placed the boy in the oval, placing some of his possessions with him. Then they walked away. They had eaten animals all their lives; in death, they completed the circle and returned their bodies to the beasts.

The days grew shorter and the sunsets became a spectacle that Ken tried in vain to draw. The colours that flared across the sky were every hue he had ever seen: blue, blood red, lemon yellow, pink, orange ... he believed that if he tried to capture those sunsets on canvas, no one would believe that they were real.

The old woman explained that the colours were caused by wildfires in the south, in the boreal forest. When the wind was just right, the smoke dispersed to the north and created a prism. Ken didn't care about the explanation – he wanted only to immerse himself in his senses, which he feared would never be acute enough to fully absorb the glory around him.

When the sun had set, the Northern Lights took centre stage and put on a show that dwarfed even the sunsets. One night, Ken lay on his back in the snow looking up at the black dome directly overhead, from which colours poured like paint flowing from an overturned bucket. But this paint was purple, and gold, and blue, and rippled, and moved, and danced, across the sky.

The old woman found him lying in the snow, his arms stretched up and his hands reaching for the silken shawls of colour.

She smiled. A gentle intimacy had grown between them. She had adopted him and he now "belonged" to her, not in any possessive way, but in a way that let him know that he was part of her home. She told him that the Northern Lights were the spirits of her ancestors and that they were dancing for them because they were happy. Then she took his hand and tugged until he scrambled to his feet. Ken still did not fully understand that beyond a certain point, the feeling of cold disappeared, and drowsiness settled in until a body froze.

Travelling in the winter was easier and faster than it had been in the summer, when they had had to follow the intricate jigsaw puzzle of rivers and lakes with pieces of the puzzle missing. In this season their route was direct and the dogs pulled willingly and tirelessly. They travelled at a steady pace, broken only when the dog handlers had to stop and untangle the animals from the traces.

The days grew shorter, the sun plunging abruptly below the horizon after only a few hours of daylight. They travelled in the dark, but a dark unlike any Ken had experienced. The stars filled the sky with light that was reflected and multiplied by the crystals of snow and ice on the ground. True darkness only descended when clouds covered the sky, and then it was so dark that nothing was visible. Even a sliver of moon created a light so bright it was almost daylight – a hauntingly blue daylight that created a dreamscape of snow. When they stopped, they would hastily pitch a tent with everyone crowding inside to eat and sleep. Then they would pack up the tent and continue to move east.

One bright day, after gazing at the intense whiteness, Ken felt a pain burn his eyes – a pain of pure agony. "Snow blindness", the old woman said. Ken closed his eyes, his lids like coarse sandpaper scraping against his eyeballs. Opening them was worse. The woman tied a piece of soft hide over his eyes and all he could do was bear the agony and wait. For days, he travelled as a blind man, in pain and nauseated from the gentle rocking of the sleigh. When the pain eased, he took off the hide, and the old woman gave him a pair of goggles with a small slit, explaining that he would have to carve them to fit his face. He carved with great care so they barely touched his skin. Close contact would freeze them to his pores.

They had been travelling a long time, when a golden glow appeared on the horizon. As they drew nearer, the golden fire resolved into a large group of igloos. The dogs heralded their approach, and people streamed out of the igloos to welcome them. The first questions were about food. The caribou had not crossed their path this season. Did the new people have caribou? Yes, they had much caribou and it would be shared.

A feast was prepared for the newcomers, who entered the largest igloo in the centre of the village. In the anteroom, they took off their parkas and beat them vigorously before entering the main room, where layers of caribou hides were spread on ice benches that circled the room. Kidney shaped seal oil lamps provided warmth and light. When they had eaten and told stories, people dispersed to their own igloos. Ken and his people crawled under many layers of hides and slept. The old woman had told the people that Ken was a quiet Kabluna. "He is a friend," she had said. "He is now Inuk."

The next morning while the men built igloos, Ken pulled out his roll of sketch paper and drew them, as they searched for the right sort of snow by poking deep into it with a knife or a long sharpened piece of bone. When they found the right spot, they drew a circle and began cutting out uniform chunks of hard-packed snow, beginning at what would become the entrance. They lifted the blocks into place, bevelling the edges, and chinking the spaces between with loose snow.

Ken was invited to accompany the men on the next hunt. For the Inuit, hunting is the essence of life. The animals must be revered and not offended. Kablunat don't understand this, the old woman told him, but Ken was now Inuk – no longer a Kablunat. She convinced the hunters that Ken was an exception. They set off onto the frozen sea that was covered with a thin layer of transparent ice that moved in front of the sled teams like a rubbery wave. Underneath them, thousands of air bubbles bounced and rolled.

When they spotted a seal in the water beneath them they searched for the beast's breathing hole and waited. When the seal was forced up to gasp for air one of the men heaved a long spear and the water stained crimson.

More people arrived at the igloo settlement. Ken would often sit on the tundra, gazing at a starlit horizon of shadowed white, and suddenly out of the vast emptiness, a sleigh would appear. The tundra's gentle undulations hid people, much like the Sahara's dunes hid the Bedouins who would seem to appear as if by magic.

The old woman had overcome her suspicions that Ken was a government agent. He had listened to her stories and had begun to absorb the Inuit understanding of the universe. But, he had not talked about himself, and he didn't tell his story until she repeated her request three times. Finally, over several days and nights he told her about his life. The people who listened peppered him with questions. What was Spain? Where was it? What was Europe? He answered their questions thoughtfully, but only alluded to the pain and loss he had suffered, not because he didn't trust them to understand but because he didn't trust himself to speak.

When he was finished, the old woman leaned back as though she had eaten a large meal and had had her fill. She said nothing, but Ken felt a new sense of intimacy, and when he began to call her grandmother, she smiled with pleasure.

She included him in all the camp's activities, encouraging him to break the rules and to ask as many questions as he liked.

"What is your interest in me?" he asked.

"The future tells about the future," she said.

He said that he was afraid that when the day came for him to leave he would cause pain.

"The future will take care of itself," she said.

She asked him to tell his story over and over again; until she learned it in the same way she had learned her own stories. He told her that the two women he had loved came alive every night in his dreams, and he lived the tragedies over and over again in tortuous detail – and he was afraid to enter into a relationship again.

She explained that death was all around; in the killing of the food, and in the deaths of the people – it was always only a step away. "Yes, it's difficult," she said. "But you do the difficult anyway."

She repeated that he was now Inuk – no longer a foreign man.

"But my skin is a different colour," he said. "And I'm taller with a different shaped body."

It was of no consequence, she said. Inuk meant to live in the way of the people. One of the challenges the Inuit faced was intermarriage. The taboo on marrying a relative was as strong as the ban on fighting with family. And yet, in this vast and sparsely populated land, locating a spouse you were not related to was often difficult. Ken, as a young single man who lived in the way of the people was most welcome in the community.

In the long silences of the eternal night, Ken examined each new concept. He had hardly noticed that the sun no longer rose in the sky. There was so much to understand that the cycle of day and night seemed insignificant.

One day the dogs heralded the arrival of a new family. They staggered into camp with barely enough dogs to pull the sleighs. The animals' ribs stood out through their fur, and they lay down exhausted, their eyes glazed. The people had to be helped from their sleds. Inside the big igloo, they explained that they had come from far away and had left most of their people behind. They had not found caribou this season and had run out of food. They had no seal oil for heat. They were dying.

One young man's toes were badly frostbitten. The elders determined that they would have to be removed to prevent gangrene, a common condition in the North where blood circulation to the extremities slowed.

There was no hospital – not even a doctor. The old woman said she would select the person to perform the operation, but the young man said he would do it himself.

The old woman stopped Ken as he turned to leave. "No," she said. "Kabluna wants to go everywhere and experience everything. This is part of everything."

The young man honed a knife and with immense concentration and deliberation, selected the correct place to amputate the toes. One by one, he sawed through flesh, sinew, and bone. He did not complain, cry, or moan, taking the same impassive, measured care that he would if he had been skinning an animal.

It shocked me. How can someone do that in that way and not fall into paroxysms of agony? And I knew I had something to learn. I had to investigate what pain was and how it was dealt with. I knew these people were not superhuman but their understanding of humanness was very different from mine and it probably came from eons of living in that environment.

These things set me on a very different track in my own head. They led me to deal with our concepts of possible/impossible, difficult/not difficult and so on. Nature is neither good nor bad. Nature is neither kind nor unkind. Nature simply is. Possible and impossible are things of the imagination – just as the pain is in our imagination. And seeing as we don't know enough to make these judgments, we shouldn't even consider worrying about them. If there is something in you to be done that is powerful then you set about doing it and you take out all the imaginings of the dark monsters you might meet on the road ahead. They may, in fact, never materialize. These concepts were the golden door through which I walked toward a completely different understanding, an understanding that has made it much more difficult for me to live in our culture.

A council was held to decide the fate of those who had been left behind to starve to death. Four dog sleighs were loaded with food, blankets, and other necessities, and when it seemed that Ken was to be left behind, the old woman intervened. "He goes," she said.

They navigated by starlight, without pause, stretching themselves past their limits, and using every ounce of energy they had.

They arrived at a grim scene. Some people had died, and many others were close to death. The interiors of the igloos had become glazed with ice from melting snow, shutting out the air and becoming frigid tombs. Seal oil for heat had run out many days before.

The men produced oil and lit the lamps; they covered people with blankets and distributed food. They also made decisions about who to take and who to leave behind. Those who were near death would not be rescued.

The return journey was long and arduous. Clouds obscured the star map, and they often lost their way. When they finally returned, eager hands carried the ill people into warm igloos.

With the increase in population, the hunters spread out over the land in search of food. Walruses had been sighted, and the old woman insisted that Ken be included in the hunt. Walruses were considered the most dangerous creatures in the Arctic – more treacherous than polar bears. Their tusks were deadly weapons, and the beasts had to be confronted on the ice because they could snap a kayak in two, as though it were a matchstick.

Several hours from camp they found the animals. The hunters fired rounds from their small bore rifles into the hide of one of the brutes, wounding it severely. Then one of the men raised his spear and dealt the death blow. With blood staining the ice, they skinned its thick hide and cut the meat up, for the trip back to camp.

They feasted that night, dining on the nut-flavoured flesh, generously larded with blubber. The big igloo was crowded with bodies and warmed by the soft glow of seal oil lamps. As the bodies grew sated and heat built up, grandmother called for a drummer and as the rhythm reverberated off the igloo's walls, she began to chant a song about a place called Nunavut. Ken allowed himself to be lulled into a deep trancelike state. The drumbeats resonated and echoed inside him. The others sat with eyes half closed, swaying gently to the beat.

When the drumming ended and the old woman's song died, Ken pulled himself to his feet and walked out into the cold night. The Northern Lights undulated across the glittering dome of the sky, and soon he became aware that grandmother had followed him, her arms tucked inside her long fur sleeves. She laid one rough, brown hand on his arm.

"The ancestors are dancing," she said.

"The Inuit ancestors?"

"Yours too," she said. "Those you have loved – they are dancing for you. It is good for one to let go – to let the dead go on their way, or one will not be in a good mood. And they will not be in a good mood, and they will not dance for one."

"But they *are* dancing," Ken said.

She squeezed his arm. "Maybe some are missing. The dead must be allowed to go. One should not hunger for them and impede their journey. One should not get in their way, or they will not be in a good mood and we will not be in a good mood."

The lights faded and the old woman made a shrill, sharp sound and clapped her hands. The lights began to dance again. She made the same sound again, and the lights intensified. Watching them, Ken was filled with an immense sense of gratitude. Whatever troubles and pains lived in his heart, they were surely minor compared to the tribulations of these people who were now his family.

He was intensely aware of being in this place of his childhood dreams, a spectator to events he could never have imagined – and the thought pleased and distressed him in almost equal proportions. The power of the sky, and the land, and the creatures it contained, intoxicated him. He was in awe of the people's acceptance and understanding, of their history and their predicament. He admired their determination not to succumb to the power of a distant government, which at best, was ambivalent toward them, and at worst, considered them a nuisance that needed to be eliminated. They were wards of the state, little more than children in the government's eyes, forbidden to live freely in their own world – not allowed to live in the white world, and caught in a limbo of no hope and no future.

How did he fit in? Was being a spectator his only role? Was he destined to record the life of these people on impossibly small ribbons of adding machine tape?

What was emerging in his drawings and in his mind was a portrait of heaven and a sketch of hell, something so knotted that to unravel the bonds seemed an impossible task.

He had never before been merely a watcher. He had always participated fully in his life. But what could he do? He was a novice to this way of life and depended on the goodwill of these people who were little more than refugees.

Speaking carefully, in the language he was beginning to master, he asked her, "Why are you showing me all the ways of your people?"

"For reasons," she said, "For reasons."

"And what about the song in the igloo," he asked. "What is Nunavut?"

The old woman clapped her hands and the Northern Lights brightened. "The ancestors are happy when they know we are watching them dance."

One day, with the young people gathered around her, she sang the song of Nunavut again, and then told a tale called "The Story of Nunavut". The word means *our land* she said but it also means more. Nunavut means our land and all that it encompasses – including all of the stories from the beginning.

Nunavut was a creation story of the people and the animals. It was the story of how the people lived in the old days and about the good and evil spirits and monsters. It was the story of how the Kablunat came and brought good things like tools and rifles, and bad things like the diseases that killed the people – and that were still devastating the population. The story told how some people who were ill were taken to hospitals in the south. Some, who were deemed criminals by the Kablunat, were sent to jails in the south. Others were sent to places much further north, where the hunting was bad, and they starved to death. All of this took place for reasons only the Kablunat could fathom.

There was no anger in the story. At its core, was a shouldering of all responsibility. The Inuit believed that they had done something evil to bring about this fate.

The old woman's story ended with provocative questions about the future. How could the Inuit show the Kablunat that they were human beings with valuable ideas and ways? How could they help the Kablunaut regard them as equals? How could they win the Kablunat's respect?

The longer she spoke, the more beautifully her ancient wrinkled face glowed in the soft light of the seal oil lamps. Ken had met people who were considered illustrious by Western society, but sitting and listening, spellbound, in that igloo he was sure that he was in the presence of true greatness.

She concluded her story by saying, "Perhaps, it would be a good idea if we could have Isumataq."

John translated. "Isumataq means many things. "It can mean very big or it can mean the boss, but if you put all the meanings together, the big one is, 'an object or a person in whose presence wisdom might reveal itself.'"

This electrified me. This went very deep inside: the idea that wisdom was not something that one had, that wisdom was something that existed and one must allow it to show itself as opposed to having ego involved. That I am wise and I am great? No. Wisdom is great, and it must show itself, but it can only do so if one is prepared to allow that to happen. How interesting. Here was a thinking that had occurred before with the peoples who lived in the deserts of the east. A sky god had been invented and he would only reveal himself through you; he wasn't something that simply existed. It was your behaviour and your way that allowed that god to exist. That god could be good or evil but that was dependent on your behaviour. That way of thinking eventually became written down as the Old Testament. There had surely never been a connection between those people and the Inuit and yet here was an original seminal idea being spoken by a woman in a completely different time and space and place. All these things were like jolts hitting me. Here I was living with an ancient people that were speaking to me directly. This was not something being told to me by a teacher or a relative. I was getting the original story and it affected me very profoundly.

When the old woman finished her story, silence enveloped the igloo like a down blanket. Quietly, Ken stood and walked outside. The sky was filled with as many stars as Ken's mind was filled with thoughts. In one instant, his life had changed. Knowingly or not, the old women had answered his question about his role in this place, and in the lives of the Inuit.

She joined him, and he linked his arm through hers. Together they stood gazing at the sky. Icy crystals of thought invaded his heart, while an avalanche of ideas roared through his mind.

This was that crystal moment when everything that had happened before made sense. I now had a clear purpose. I had gone to the Arctic because of the stories that had been told to me in that cave in Portugal, but now, I felt an urgency to gather as much information as possible – and to disseminate it. It was clear to me how brilliantly I had been prepared. From this moment on, I was no longer pursuing childhood dreams. I had a white-hot fire burning inside me.

One day, the sun reappeared over the horizon and Ken felt as though he was awakening from a dream. For a seemingly endless amount of time, he had lived in darkness, listening to stories and legends, and the line between waking and dreaming had blurred. And now the sun – a cause for celebration – a reason for feasting!

Feasting also served to remind them of their great good fortune. They had food, warmth, and clothing. Even more important, others had been helped and they were grateful to have been able to help them. The young man who had amputated his toes had survived, and that was even further cause for thanksgiving.

As the days grew longer, the polar bears came out of hibernation. One had been spotted nearby and men quickly prepared for the hunt. Once again, grandmother prevailed upon the hunters to include Ken. When the dogs picked up the scent they were released from their traces, and the men followed their high-pitched howling.

When the dogs found their quarry they surrounded it, darting in close, and then running back, staying out of reach of its lethal claws. Finally, overheated and exhausted, the bear collapsed. The hunters fired at the downed body until it lay still in a pool of blood, and then they began the enormous task of skinning and butchering it. The oldest hunter stood back. "In my day, that's not how we hunted bears," he said. "When we hunted, it was one man with a spear and one bear with his claws. No

Kabluna would have the balls to do that."

Ken promised himself that he would prove to this man that he was no ordinary Kabluna.

As the long spring progressed, grandmother invited Ken and a handful of other people to come with her on trips whose purpose seemed to be nothing more than to give Ken an opportunity to meet more of her people. Some were doing well, others were hungry, and ill, and barely eking out a living from the land. They took very few provisions, relying on the land to feed them. Every day, death ran beside the dog sleds. Ken had never been so acutely aware of life and of the very thin line that divided it from death. If he died, the event would have little more significance than the death of a tuktu.

The Inuit had patience beyond anything he had seen. When hunting seals they would stand motionless above a breathing hole for hours. Their success depended entirely on the element of surprise.

He pondered his purpose here and came back, again and again, to the idea of Isumataq. If he was to make a mark in this life it was intimately tied up with Isumataq and Nunavut.

My endless questioning – what is it all about anyway? – led me farther and farther away from the absolutes of my world, which had become very hollow, thin, and meaningless. The greatest thing was to question, and to wonder. It led me to the realization that we have no answers, that if we can only wonder, we will then become a much less invasive and dangerous lot. And, I was learning all this from a people who lived in a dimension where this could be understood. Had I not come to this place, I wouldn't have had any of these feelings and understandings, and I would be just one more hopeless creature that lives in that hopeless world. At the time, of course, I didn't realize how much I was changing.

The ice began to break up, producing leads, or long rivers. One day Ken noticed a seal basking in the sun beside one of these leads. Suddenly, a long black and white snout broke the surface and just as quickly disappeared. As Ken watched, the huge snout broke the surface again; an enormous mouth opened, enveloped the seal and disappeared again. A moment later, a giant black and white body flashed through the air and then slipped back beneath the water.

When he recounted this scene and his amazement at this new creature, perhaps a monster, the people laughed. He had encountered an Orca and would surely meet many more.

At another lead, he encountered narwhals, the Arctic whales distinguished by a single long tusk protruding from their upper left jaw. The group had camped near the lead, waiting for the creatures to appear. Three days passed while the hunters sat and watched. On the third day, one of the men sat up and glanced around. The others picked up their spears and moved closer. Again, they waited. Then, it appeared as if unicorns broke through the water. As quick as a breath, the hunters speared one of the giant creatures.

The days lengthened and they travelled, the sleighs flying over the smooth, hard packed crystallized snow. The sleds were packed with seal and walrus meat, enough for their own needs and for those they might encounter who had not fared well over the winter.

The farther east they travelled, the fewer people they found on the land. The hunting had been bad, and the people had taken refuge in the sparse settlements that lined the western shore of Hudson's Bay. At places like Baker Lake, and Rankin Inlet, they were given small, square prefabricated houses that were barged in during the summer months. They had shelter, and they could buy white bread and cereal at the Hudson's Bay store. But, their children were taken from them and sent to residential schools in the south. Losing their children was the price they paid for food and shelter.

Ken told the old woman that he wanted to visit one of the settlements. She refused. He asked again, many times, and each time she said no, the manager of the Hudson's Bay Company and the Anglican and Catholic priests, were much too interested in knowing who was still on the land. The priests were rivals – each trying to secure the most converts – because each young Inuit was sent to either the Anglican or Catholic school in the south, where they were subsidized by the government. The more students each church enrolled, the higher the government subsidy they received.

The old woman's reluctance increased Ken's determination to approach one of the towns. He would do what he had done in Coppermine, he said – tell the people that he was an artist wandering around the Arctic. The old woman explained that his visit to Coppermine would have been noticed, and recorded, and the information would likely have been passed on to other settlements.

John wanted to visit one of the towns as well, and he helped Ken develop a scheme. The next time they knew they were close to one of the settlements, they would tell the others that they were going on a hunt. They began to go out together frequently so that this would not arouse suspicion. By the time they were near Baker Lake, no one raised any objections when Ken and John set out, ostensibly to hunt seals.

They travelled in a direct line, but when they got close, John started driving the dog team in elaborate figure eights and circles, ending with a wide circle that crossed through the final figure eight. They topped a small rise, from which they could see the small assortment of huts straggling unevenly along both sides of an ice road. John settled down to wait, while Ken walked down the rise in his kamiks, leaving no mark on the crust of fine, wind-driven snow. The town slept under the light of the half-moon and the stars. He watched for teams of dogs, pegged outside, that might be disturbed and set off an alarm. He walked down the road between the dilapidated shacks made of tin and tarpaper. Near the end of the short road were more substantial buildings; one was likely the RCMP station and the other the Hudson's Bay Store. Just past them were two churches – the only buildings that were at all imposing.

Baker Lake could have been a ghost town, yet two hundred people lived there. The thin vapour steaming off the roofs of the buildings was the only sign of warmth and life.

His curiosity satisfied, he turned and walked back. Climbing the rise to meet John, he was overcome with euphoria. He had entered the enemy camp and had gotten away with it. John's big ear-to-ear smile signalled his own elation. Silently, they pushed off on the sleigh, making figure eights that intersected the tracks they had already left. Then John turned the sled on a diagonal path away from the camp. Ken caught John's eye and they started laughing uncontrollably, tears rolling from their eyes, and freezing on their cheeks.

Gasping, Ken asked, "Where are we going?"

"I don't know," John said, and that set them off again, howling at the moon and the stars.

Finally, breathing raggedly, he said they were going seal hunting. If anyone from the town should find tracks, unravel them and follow them, they would not find their camp.

They arrived back in the morning with the carcasses of two seals. The old woman said nothing, and asked no questions, but her penetrating look told Ken that she knew about the trip.

John and Ken became friends, travelling together for the next two years across the Arctic and coming back to camp periodically to rest and tell stories – and then to set off again on another journey.

When John was past the age that the Kablunat would take him, and send him to school, he and Ken visited Baker Lake again. Ken said that he was an affluent European artist, recording the life of the animals in the Arctic, and John was his guide. They also visited Rankin Inlet, farther to the south.

Word was broadcast across the Arctic about a European artist travelling with a native guide. At the Rankin Inlet Hudson's Bay Store, Ken asked the manager if he had adding machine paper and showed him some of his thousands of drawings. The man shook his head. They didn't sell adding machine paper, he said, though they had an adding machine at the store. There wasn't much call for that sort of thing. Ken began to peel bills off his wad of money to pay for the flour, lard, and other staples for the camp. He had not touched the stash since he had purchased goods at Coppermine. The thickness of the money roll convinced the manager to part with several rolls of his adding machine tape.

"And I suppose you're just passing through?" the manager asked, repeating back the words Ken had spoken in Coppermine.

"Yes," Ken answered, "Just passing through. "Wonderful place – wonderful people – wonderful time – thanks a lot."

"Let's go," Ken said to John, as he emerged from the store. They walked quickly down the main road out of town. Glancing over their shoulders, they noticed two men following them. Ken stopped, grabbed John's arm, and turned around. They walked back to the Hudson's Bay store.

He told the manager there was someone with a dog team, just outside of town, who seemed to be lost. "Just trying to be helpful," he said, hoping to put anyone off their trail.

They walked out of town, in the opposite direction, away from camp. When they were out of sight and sound of the town they stopped, scanning the horizon. When they were sure they were not being followed, they continued walking. When Ken turned toward camp, John shook his head. He had taken the precaution of telling grandmother to move camp. They veered slightly from their course and eventually arrived at the new campsite.

One day, John and Ken rode on a boat to Baffin Island, a land of ancient rounded hills that had migrated north from the equator before men walked the earth – a land that had once been the cradle of life.

Ken felt a profound need to see more and more, hoping that one day he would encounter a place in the Arctic where the people were happy and were living as they had before they encountered the white man's civilization. The groups they met had adapted to the new culture that had invaded their land, and used the new tools the Europeans had brought, but most were living a life of meagre subsistence. He never discovered the place he was searching for.

Near the top of the Pannertung Fjord, where there had once been a thriving whaling station, until the European hunters had decimated the beasts, they saw a group of Inuit, hauling the freshly-killed carcass of one of the behemoths on their kayaks, the boats lashed together. Slowly, and with great effort, they paddled the whale back to shore.

Another day, they encountered the hunter who had challenged Ken with the polar bear kill. Ken goaded him, respectfully but insistently, until he capitulated and they set off to hunt a polar bear, in the traditional way. The hunter became prey, allowing the bear to track and corner him against a wall of sea ice where he wedged the end of his spear into the ground and at the last possible moment, looking directly into the eyes of death, drove it home. If the hunter had failed, Ken would have been the bear's next prey and although he had proved that he was unafraid, he also regretted the hunt. He had somehow overstepped a line of civility in that culture.

Once they came upon a group of people who were very ill. Some had already died, and more were very close to death. A Métis man who was ill had come from the south to their camp, to trade with them. They looked after him and healed him before letting him go. But soon after he left, they fell ill with fevers so high they rolled in the snow and ice to cool their bodies. Their temperatures climbed until the lining of their brains swelled and killed them. Their plight was unthinkable, and all John and Ken could do was watch their painful deaths, and listen to their silent screams. Ken shook uncontrollably – then time stopped. He and John may have been there hours or days – he had no idea. Eventually they moved on, with the grim images of people suffering and resigned to death, engraved on their minds.

After many months, John and Ken once again returned to camp. The old woman always asked to hear the tales of their adventures, over and over again. When Ken told about the horrible disease they had encountered and the dying people, she nodded. "This is the way it is," she said. "Yes, it is terrible, but this is the way it is."

That night, while they feasted, other grandmothers joined them, and Ken and John told the stories of their travels again, by the warmth of the seal oil lamps. When they finished, grandmother sat down on the floor in front of Ken and said, "In our mind, you are Inuk. You are learning our language and eating our food and you are a part of us. Our wish is that you will stay with us. But if you are not going to stay and marry one of us – and you say you have to go back to your world – then it is our wish that you tell the people in your world the things that you have seen – all of the things that you have seen."

Ken pondered her words. The moment had a feeling of immense importance. "I will try to do that," he said. "But you have to understand that I am just a man who draws drawings and paints paintings, and in my world I am not a very important person."

"Look at me," she said.

Surprised by such rare directness, Ken looked into her eyes, which gazed unflinchingly into his. "I'm going to tell you a story that you have already heard. Put your hands here," she said, touching her arms.

Ken placed his hands on her arms, and she put her hands on his shoulders. Then, in her language, she spoke the words that he had heard his grandfather say minutes before he died. "Don't concern yourself with what is normal in life – with the possible and the impossible. You are one who shines in this world, and the rules will be different for you."

My blood ran cold, and I broke out in goose bumps. It had been a big moment in my life when my grandfather told me that. How could she have known that? Much later, in reflecting, I realized that she had been very clever. She asked many times about my grandparents, and, like a good fortune teller, she extracted all the information and handed it back to me. But, at the time this happened, it really affected me. And, given all my experiences of the place, it had significance far greater in that moment than it did as time passed. But, all of this affected me profoundly. The time came for me to leave. I wanted to go, and I did not want to go. I thought, "I could live here". But there were other parts of me that wanted so much more. Now, I was equipped with vast knowledge of something and I wondered how many people had actually experienced something like this – and as an artist, I had subject matter that was absolutely stunning. And so, I decided that I would leave. And the only time I saw emotions out in the open there was when I left. And whatever happened there never stopped. It has gone on, and on, and on, in my soul – and it seems to have fortified this madness for the Arctic and the Arctic people.

Ken Kirkby Sr. with his children, Louise and Ken, in Portugal

Photo: Gadi Hoz

Portuguese Consul General Antonio Tanger Correia, second from left, introducing Ken to a party at the Portuguese Consul General's office

Toronto Mayor David Crombie speaks at the opening of the Columbus Centre's Joseph D. Carrier Gallery

Ken Kirkby, Joseph D. Carrier and Rocco Pannese at The Columbus Centre Gallery, which became the Joseph D. Carrier Gallery

Ken with Flora McDonald, a minister in Brian Mulroney's cabinet, at the Columbus Centre

Ken shaking hands with Premier Peterson at Anton Cetin's Reception Dinner (Artist of the Year 1986), November 14, 1997

Photo: Roberto Lissia

Ken's first brushstroke of Isumataq

Ken Kirkby with the painting that hangs in the Yellowknife Airport

Ken in the studio with Isumataq in progress

Ken with an inukshuk near Baker Lake

Ken in a caribou parka on an island in Hudson's Bay

Joan Scottie and her daughter, Hilu, at Ferguson Lake in what is now Nunavut

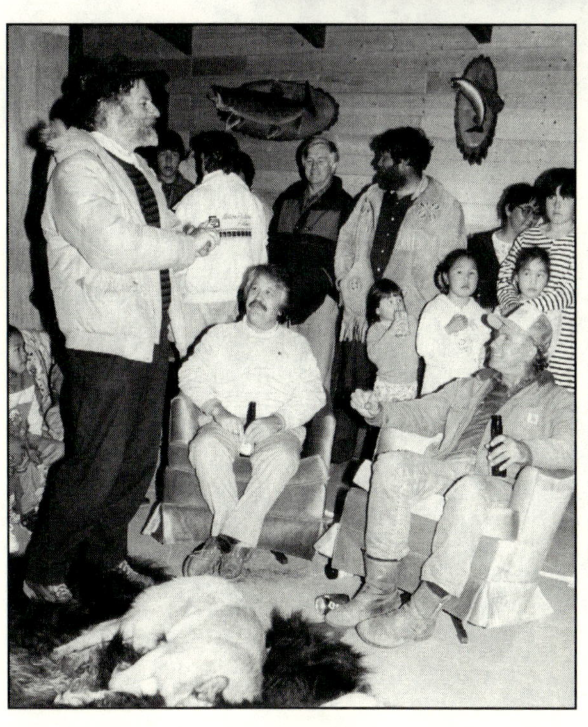

Ken talking to business managers in the Arctic at Ferguson Lake Lodge, strategizing on bringing tourists to the Arctic

Ken Kirkby, Joe Clark and Jean Chretien at the unveiling of Isumataq in Parliament

Ken with Brian Mulroney, after the unveiling of Isumataq in Parliament

Ken Kirkby presents an original oil painting to the Right Honourable Prime Minister Kim Campbell

Ken with Honourable John Fraser, Speaker of the House, receiving the Confederation medal in Parliament

9

An Artist in Vancouver

Ken packed his meagre belongings, wrapping his rolls of drawings in sealskin to protect them from cold and damp. He left the north as he had arrived, more than five years earlier, hitching rides on bush planes, boats, and rickety trucks until he arrived in northern Manitoba. He travelled across Manitoba, Saskatchewan, and Alberta until, in the fall of 1965, he arrived at the Vancouver airport, in a small bush plane.

He called his parents from the airport, his first contact with them in five years. They walked past him three times before they recognized the young man with the full black beard, long black hair, and a body heavy with muscle.

In his parent's apartment, in the West End, the deafening noise kept him awake at night. The food was insipid, and the ways of the people strange.

He rented a small apartment in the West End, and got a job with Gordon Spratt, the former chief engineer of Coast Eldridge, who had formed his own company. But Ken's focus was on painting. However, when he unwrapped the sealskin from his rolls of tape he discovered that his thousands and thousands of drawings were ruined. In the heat, fat had oozed out from his inexpertly prepared sealskin, staining the drawings and making them useful only as rough references for his paintings.

Regardless, he painted in a frenzy of excitement. He painted the Inuit hunting, preparing meals and making tools. He painted every scene engraved on his mind, from the minutiae of daily life to the vast emptiness of the landscape. When he took his paintings to art dealers, they shrugged and turned away. He told his stories to the owners and was met with bottomless indifference.

He grew increasingly angry and annoyed with the Vancouver art scene and sent photographs of the paintings to galleries across Canada. Not one offered to show them.

He tried to give them to the galleries, and still they didn't want them. Finally, he stopped. "Maybe it's me. Maybe I have to learn how to paint this place."

One day, while poking through an antique shop, he found a book titled *The Group of Seven* and as he leafed through it, he reacquainted himself with their vision of Canada. With the Group of Seven paintings as a template, he taught himself to paint again, working only on southern landscapes. He took several to the owner of The Golden Key Gallery who placed one in the window and sold it within two days. More sold during the next few months, but then the gallery owner sold his business and Ken was once again without an outlet.

Still, he persisted and one day, while sketching the bent shapes of driftwood, in the dunes near the airport, it occurred to him that he could make a profit from the abundance of wood on the beach. He purchased a pickup truck and two chain saws, cut up the wood, wrapped velvet ribbons around the most attractive pieces, and attached a card with his telephone number. He left the wood on the front steps of the city's grand homes and within days, the orders came in. While he delivered and stacked the firewood, he told the homeowners his stories of the Arctic, and when they asked about his paintings, he would display the canvases he carried in the cab of his truck. The Arctic paintings didn't sell but the southern landscapes were a hit.

He taught himself to become a storyteller, rehearsing every anecdote he had, practising his tone, volume, order of words and, most importantly, his choice of words. Where was the power of the story?

His clients listened, but showed little interest, so he made a list of every service club in the city. Would they like a guest speaker at their next meeting? Yes, they would like to hear about the Arctic, and so, Ken did the rounds. Each audience contained a handful of people who showed mild interest – the rest were bored, and often antagonistic. Sometimes he was heckled, and a red tide of anger would creep up from his chest to flush his neck and cheeks. Once someone shouted that he, and the rest of the people there, resented an immigrant telling Canadians how to live in their country and run their lives.

"That is hardly what I am doing," Ken retorted. "I intend no disrespect. I am simply here bringing information from a faraway place."

His words dropped like ragged bits of paper to lie discarded on the floor. Perhaps his stories were so outside the experience of most Canadians that they seemed like tall tales – unlikely and unbelievable. There had to be a better way to tell people about the Arctic but what was it?

His father told him that he was involving himself in matters that were none of his business. He was not a citizen of Canada and until he was, he should keep his opinions to himself. He responded that he was only doing what he had learned at his father's knee, in Portugal. He reminded his father that Ken Sr. had not been a citizen of Portugal and yet he had become deeply involved in the affairs of that country and had worked hard to help the people. The Inuit were human beings in great distress, he said, and he was trying to help.

His mother pleaded with him not to go into politics.

"I'm not in politics. I'm simply trying to help some wonderful people who were very kind to me".

Ken applied for his Canadian citizenship and checked the mail daily for the summons to appear, before the court. He studied Canadian history and absorbed reams of information about the country.

Often, he had to put his books aside. Since returning from the Arctic, he had begun to suffer debilitating headaches. The pain would continue for days and was often accompanied by nausea.

When the headaches were at their worst, even the faintest amount of light was like a sword penetrating his brain, and he spent hours lying in a darkened room. He also contracted a cold that never seemed to leave him, but periodically faded into the background and then reappeared even worse than before. He finally visited the family doctor, who diagnosed migraines, the same condition his grandmother had suffered from.

"Very little is understood about migraines," he said. They can be mild or extremely severe and totally unbearable."

Ken told the doctor he was an artist, and his biggest fear was losing his eyesight. When a migraine attacked in full force, his vision blurred and almost disappeared.

There was no remedy, the doctor said. He suggested that Ken record his attacks and avoid the situations that triggered them. His cold was easier to cure. He had severe tonsillitis and within days underwent surgery at the Georgia Medical Clinic.

While he had been in the Arctic, his mother and father had purchased five acres in the Fraser Valley, near Mission, that he agreed to clear for them. Since there was valuable timber on the land, Ken partnered with a local logger, and together they set up a sawmill operation that attracted other businessmen. One of them advised Ken that buying and selling land was the best way to make a fortune in British Columbia.

Ken took the man's advice. If he was going to have any success helping the Inuit it would take money, and he began to buy land in the Fraser Valley, often for no more than one thousand dollars an acre.

While he worked in the valley, he was summoned to citizenship court and presented himself at the Vancouver courthouse. He sat in the judge's chambers, answering questions with such fluency and passion that the judge invited him to share a cup of tea. As they talked Ken told her his story – how he had listened to Francisco's tales of the Arctic, and had travelled there, and lived there with the Inuit.

"I have a concern," he said. "I spent some years there with those people, and I found things that were beautiful beyond description, and I found things for which words have not been invented because they were so horrible. And I seem to have no luck in telling those stories to people in southern Canada and I wonder what that's about. The minute you talk about the North, people seem to get annoyed, and when you mention the aboriginal people there seems to be trouble on the horizon."

"A lot of mistakes have been made," she said. "And there's a lot of fixing to do."

"But, that's one of the things I would like to help to do," Ken said. "But, I'm afraid it's going to be perceived as the newcomer messing around in something that's none of his business. In fact, I've already been told so."

"I think you're a fine candidate to get into the middle of it and do what you have to do. I'm very glad to have met you and congratulations on becoming a Canadian. I have every confidence you will benefit the country."

To celebrate his new exalted status as a Canadian citizen, Ken went to Nile Creek to fish for salmon. He unloaded his boat from the back of his pickup and pushed off into the ocean. At Northwest Bay, he tied up to a kelp bed, rocking up and down with the long seaweeds. He cast his line, but his mind was not on fishing, so he stowed his gear and let his thoughts coalesce, as he watched the waving fronds of kelp moving gently in the current.

Sitting in the dinghy, tied to the silky kelp, he pondered the strange twists his life had taken. It seemed to him, that no matter where in Canada one was, government took place far away. It had started in England, and although the job of governing had gradually been turned over to Canadians, it was still as distant in the minds of the citizens as Ottawa was from the farthest eastern, western and northern regions of the land. People appeared to wait for instructions from some distant place. Was this because Canada had only recently emerged from colonial status?

The clash appeared to be not between two nationalities, the English and the French, but between two diverse cultures – that of city people who had been swallowed up by bureaucracy, and that of country folk, such as farmers, loggers, miners, and fishermen, who were the real risk takers. Ken still had a great deal to learn about his new home but of one thing he was sure, telling people his stories about the Arctic pushed them away. Until he knew how to approach them properly, it was best to keep quiet. But, to accomplish what he had in mind he would need a lot of money, and in Canada, the words money and art were rarely spoken in the same sentence.

What parent in this new world would want their offspring to marry an artist – someone who was probably a combination of self-indulgent, unbalanced, insecure, a daydreamer and quite possibly effeminate? A creature who lived in an attic somewhere with the dust and spiders, and who could not fight his way out of a paper bag if his life depended on it? This, to my mind, was the prevailing idea of an artist and everyone believed it – the art-

ists, agents, dealers and the public. I wondered about this. How did this come to be? My understanding of an artist was completely different.

It struck me that there was a point in fairly recent history when we changed from being artisans to becoming the modern idea of the artist. That moment came with the death of van Gogh. He had played a major role in getting the world to look at new forms of art, which had much to do with the impressionist movement. I had read considerably on it. Van Gogh sold just one painting in his lifetime. I think in large part he was too busy, he was moving things ahead and I think he had a vision that very much included the future – and that idea excited me a lot. What is art? It isn't just something pretty. Art is something that changes the world and it can only be done one piece at a time.

My understanding of art, relative to my new country, was forged at this moment. Art and politics were inextricably entwined. Van Gogh had a most peculiar and unhealthy relationship with his brother, Theo. They corresponded every day so we have an immense pool of information. Van Gogh wasn't mad at all. He was very ill and became sicker as he grew older. I think he had many things wrong with him, including epilepsy. After he cut off his ear, and eventually shot himself and took three days to die, a friend of Theo's, a well-known journalist in Paris, asked if he could see some of the correspondence. Theo agreed. After the fellow researched a goodly amount of it, he asked if he could write some articles. Theo agreed – and those articles created damnation for the artists of today, because van Gogh was presented as a madman and a victim. It so hit the sensibility of France that he became the grand, tragic figure, and the model for how all artists would be viewed in the eye and the mind of the public. And because the world in those days looked to Paris for matters artistic, the story spread like quicksilver. To my mind, that was the birth of the modern perception of the artist.

Ken compared the "artist as victim" mythos with the Renaissance view of artists, when people like him commanded the attention of kings, queens, princes and Popes. Pleased with the clarity of his thoughts, he picked up his fishing rod and got back to the business at hand, promising himself that if he did nothing else in his life he would never join that anaemic club of modern day artists. He would be an artist in the tradition of the Italian Renaissance. If he were to follow in anyone's footsteps, it would be in those of Michelangelo. He would be a warrior artist.

To burn off some of the restless energy that possessed him since returning home, he began to play tennis, at the courts in Stanley Park, where he met Helen Michaelchuck, a local teacher. He also studied real estate investing, which seemed to him like a false-fronted building in an old black and white western movie. It was an empty concept set up to make money – no value traded hands. No service was purchased. But, he wanted at least two or three million dollars to tell the story of the Arctic across the country, and real estate was a quick money-maker.

While he studied, he periodically found himself distracted by the thought of the one art gallery in Vancouver he had not approached with his paintings – the Alex Fraser Gallery. Stories of Alex Fraser, and his treatment of artists in his London and Vancouver galleries, had circulated through the art community for years. Ken was angry with himself. He was rarely afraid of anyone and had met no one in Canada yet who had intimidated him. Alex Fraser's reputation did.

He had heard that the man was irascible – so what? He had heard he was powerful. Was it in his power to judge his work? What if he found it wanting?

The only thing worse than his fear was the prospect of his disappointment in himself if he refused to face it, so one day he screwed up his courage, loaded his truck with paintings, and drove to 41st Avenue near Boulevard in Kerrisdale.

He walked into the gallery, where an attractive middle-aged woman asked if she could help him.

"Yes, I'm here to see Mr. Fraser if he's about."

"Mr. Fraser doesn't see people without an appointment."

"Oh, that's a shame. I'm here and I have some paintings. Please, can you ask if he'll see me?"

She smiled and walked into a back room. A few minutes later, a small man with slicked-back hair and icy, blue-green eyes walked out. He was dressed in a perfectly fitted gray pinstriped suit, with knife pleats in the trousers and shoes that shone like mirrors.

Exhaling a great puff of smoke, he lowered himself into a big armchair, and placed two packages of Players unfiltered cigarettes and an ashtray on the little gate-legged table beside it. Taking a fresh cigarette from one of the packages, he lit it from the one in his yellowed fingers, and crushed the stub in the ashtray.

Turning to the woman who had followed him out of the back room he called, "Doreen! Doreen, I want you to tell the young man about manners. Ask him does he understand the meaning of manners?"

"Mr. Fraser would like to know if you understand the meaning of manners," she said, turning to Ken.

"Indeed I do," Ken said. "And I apologize for coming in without an appointment but I was nervous and I managed to screw up all my courage to come in – and here I am."

"Doreen! Doreen, tell him he is quite right to be nervous in approaching me. Ask him what it is that he wants."

"I have some paintings and would like to show them to Mr. Fraser."

"Tell the young man that I can't bloody see his paintings, anywhere. Where are his paintings?"

"I have them in my pickup truck."

"Well I can't see them in his damn pickup truck!"

"Mr. Fraser would like you to bring them in, because he can't see them in your pickup truck" Doreen said.

Ken hurried out to the truck and brought in about a dozen canvases.

"Doreen! Doreen, tell the young man to place them on the floor all around the gallery."

Ken spread them out – paintings of the mountains, the seashore, the grasslands around Peter Hope Lake, and several of the Arctic. When he was done, Fraser stared at them intently and silently, for many long minutes, moving back and forth across the room and lighting one cigarette from the stub of another.

"Doreen! Doreen," he finally said. "Tell the young man to pull out that painting there, and that one there, and those two over there. Tell him they're rubbish."

Ken gathered up the Arctic paintings, leaving the rest on the floor.

"Now as for the rest of them, they have some possibilities. Ask the young man what he wants for them."

"That's one of the reasons I'm here," Ken said. "To ask what I should charge for them."

Fraser's head spun around, and he looked directly at Ken for the first time. "If you bloody well don't know what you want in this life, then you damn well won't get it."

He turned to Doreen. "Ask the young man what he wants for them."

"A hundred and fifty dollars apiece," Ken said.

"The young man doesn't think much of himself does he? Doreen! Doreen, do the mathematics on it, and make out a cheque and give it to the young man."

Doreen punched numbers into the adding machine, wrote out a cheque and handed it to Alex Fraser. "There you go, young fellow," he said passing it to Ken. "What is your name?"

"Ken Kirkby."

"That's a nice sounding name."

"Is it okay if we write my name on the cheque?"

"You can write anything you want on the bloody cheque. I couldn't care less. Now, I want you to listen to me. You might make a fine artist one day. You're a hell of a technician. Where did you study?"

"I studied all by myself."

"Really? So you're one of these primitives that hatched right out of the stone."

"I am."

"Is that so? We must talk about that. Now, I want you to come back soon."

"Yes sir."

Ken walked out of the gallery triumphant. He had actually sold some paintings in this new country! The amount of money didn't matter – he had sold his paintings – and not just to anyone – to the legendary Alex Fraser! And no one he knew actually sold paintings – they gave them to galleries on consignment!

He threw himself into his painting with renewed enthusiasm. Alex Fraser had called his Arctic paintings rubbish, but he was too pleased with his success to dwell on one small disappointment.

Ken painted, but as the weeks passed his trepidation returned. What if Fraser rejected him next time? One day, the telephone rang. He recognized Doreen's voice. "Mr. Kirkby, Mr. Fraser would like to have a word with you."

"Do you bloody know the English language?" Fraser shouted down the line.

"I dare say I do."

"I don't bloody think so. Tell me, what does the word soon mean?"

"I guess it's all relative."

"Don't get smart with me. When I say soon, I mean soon."

"Yes but is that two hours? Two minutes? Two weeks?"

"I told you, don't get smart with me. Do you have any paintings?"

"I do."

"Well what the bloody hell are they doing there? They're no good there! You've got to bring them here."

"All right, I'll bring them."

"Now."

"I was going to shower…"

"That stuff doesn't matter. Get in your bloody truck and bring me your paintings."

Ken hung up, picked up a stack of paintings, including a couple of Arctic canvases, and drove to the gallery. Once again, he propped the paintings against the walls while Fraser went into a reverie. Thirty minutes passed. "That one and that one," pointing his finger at the Arctic landscapes, "They're rubbish. I told you already. Don't you listen? They're rubbish."

"Well what's bad about them?"

"They're just rubbish. It's plain to see. I suppose you're one of those who's in love with that bunch of idiots called, the Group of Seven. They're rubbish too, you know."

"I think they're marvellous," Ken said.

"Well that shows you how weak your mind is. What do you want for these?"

"I suppose a hundred and fifty dollars each."

Fraser shook his head and sighed. "We have to do a lot of work on you, don't we? Doreen! Doreen, make the man a cheque for five hundred dollars each."

Ken flushed. Five hundred dollars each!

Doreen passed the cheque to Fraser who handed it to Ken pointing at the top line. "You see? Your name is written on it. You like your name written on it, don't you? Apparently, you don't like having to write your own name. Now, just so that we understand, come back soon. Do you understand?"

"Exactly how long is soon?"

"Soon."

"Two weeks?"

"No. Soon."

Ken drove home, thrilled at his success and completely at sea, trying to understand this very strange man who appeared to have become his patron.

He had dinner that night with Helen who told him he had no idea how lucky he was. "I've never heard of anyone selling a painting. This is amazing!"

"Yes, I guess it is."

"No, you don't get it," she said. "I don't think it's been done."

"Oh I'm sure it's been done."

"No. I really don't think it's been done."

He continued to paint with growing passion and a couple of weeks after his visit he called the gallery. Was it all right to bring some more paintings over?

"Of course it's okay," Fraser said. "Let's see what you can do when you're in a hurry."

Fraser gazed intently at the paintings spread around the room. "That's better," he said. "I like that much better. And I see you didn't bring any rubbish with you. There isn't a painting there that's rubbish. Congratulations! A person who can paint beautifully and do it fast is a painter. You're going to be a hell of a painter. Twenty years ago, I said I wouldn't take on another artist. You people are exhausting – you suck the life out of a man. But I'm going to break that rule – I'm going to take you on. And I'm going to educate you from the beginning to the end. You're very lucky, you know. You don't know how lucky you are to have me. Now we have to transact some business. Follow me."

Ken trailed into the back room after him. The furniture consisted of one high stool, where Fraser sat down – everything else in the room was carefully arranged to be within arm's reach. He opened the cupboard behind him, from which he extracted an unopened bottle of bonded stock rye whiskey. Unscrewing the top with one hand, he turned the latch on the little window above his head with the other, pushed it open, and tossed the cap through it. Then he reached to the side, and turned on the tap of the small bar sink, and filled a pitcher with water. Lastly, he opened another cupboard, lifted down two tumblers, poured a goodly measure of whiskey into both, and splashed water into the glasses.

"This is how you and I are going to do business," he said. "We're going to drink."

'In the middle of the day?" Ken asked.

"What's that got to do with anything? We're going to drink."

"Why do we have to drink?" Ken eyed the whiskey with revulsion. "My guess is it's to do with, 'get a man drunk and you'll find out who he is.'"

"Who told you that?"

"My father."

"I'd like to meet your father." He took a large swallow. "So, tell me about yourself."

Ken told his story, while he watched Fraser drink until the bottle was empty. He drank a bottle every day, he said, and he was as proud of that as the fact that he was a one match a day man. He struck a match in the morning to light his first cigarette, and every subsequent cigarette, for the rest of the day, was lit from the stub of the last. "It takes discipline to do that."

"I want you to come to the gallery two or three days a week. I want to hear your story. I want you to tell me your feelings, your thoughts, your understanding of the universe – everything. I want to listen to you. I want to hear you."

For several weeks, Ken visited and talked, while Fraser downed a bottle of rye and smoked an eternal chain of cigarettes. "You have a passion that is white-hot and I love it," he said. "We have all these artists around, and they're all limp. I want to see a man with a paintbrush in one hand and a sword in the other. That's you."

One day, Ken asked Fraser why he never saw the paintings he sold to him. "Where do you put them?"

"I've sold them."

"All of them?"

Yes, all of them."

"Oh my gosh. Well, that's terrific."

"You look surprised."

"I am."

"That's not a very nice thing to say to me. Of course, they're sold. So, bring me some more. Go and paint."

"There's a limit to my speed."

"I'm sure there is and I want to find it. I suspect the faster you paint the better you get. You're thinking too much. Don't think. Painting isn't about thinking. This is not an intellectual exercise. The best bloody thing would be to get some farmers off the prairies and put a paintbrush in their hands and let them paint. Painting is for barbarians, not for intellectuals."

A few weeks later, Fraser said, "We're going to have an exhibit. Now paint away, and keep bringing them."

Shortly before the day of the exhibit, Ken delivered more paintings. His hands shook as he pocketed the cheque.

"Why are you so agitated?" Fraser asked.

"I'm nervous," Ken admitted.

"What are you nervous about?"

"What if the paintings don't sell?"

"I beg your pardon?"

"What if they don't sell?"

Fraser sat up on his stool. "You know, I've been insulted in my life but I've never been insulted so badly. Now you take that back."

"Well, what did I say?"

"Of course they'll bloody sell. The question is, to whom are we going to sell them? Would you prefer to sell them to the dentist across the street or to the man who picks up the rubbish? Or would you like to sell them to the Queen Mother?"

"Given a choice…"

"Of course, there's a choice."

"I'd like to sell them to the Queen Mother."

"Good boy," Fraser beamed. "Of course, you would. But you wouldn't have known that unless I'd said it, would you?"

"Well, I wouldn't have thought of it."

"You've got to think of a lot of things." He tapped his fingers against his glass. "Nervous, are you? Doreen! Doreen, call her Majesty."

Doreen dialled the telephone, spoke into it briefly and passed it to Fraser. Ken didn't remember a single word of the conversation he heard but there was no doubt in his mind that Fraser was indeed talking to the Queen Mother, and selling her four paintings. He put the receiver down. "Doreen, Doreen…" She dialled someone else, and then someone else, and then another person, and at the end of an hour, all but two of the paintings were sold. Fraser smiled with satisfaction. "Chunky Woodward. Have you heard of Woodward's Department Store? C.N. Woodward – he's the owner. I want you to meet him. Doreen! Doreen, get Chunky on the phone!"

"Chunky! It's Alex! I'm at the gallery. I have someone here I want you to meet… No… Right now… Okay."

He turned to Ken. "You and this man are going to be very good friends. You've burbled about this Peter Hope Lake that you go to. That's up at the edge of the Douglas Lake Ranch."

Ken nodded. "I've seen the name."

"It's the largest working ranch there is – a genuine ranch. Nothing to do with pickup trucks. It's a cowboy ranch and it's everything that I've heard you talk about. You love fishing, and you love hunting. You love the outdoors. You love that country. This is the man that owns the Douglas Lake Ranch."

Minutes later, a shiny, silver-gray Aston Martin pulled up outside the gallery and a tall, lean, dignified looking gentleman with graying hair got out and strode into the gallery.

Alex shook his hand and waved his arm at several of Ken's paintings propped up against the walls of the gallery. "This young fellow here paints these paintings. Chunky, I want you to have a couple of them. I recommend them strongly."

After completing the transaction, they had lunch, and by the time the bill arrived, Ken had an invitation to the ranch. "Do you feel better now?" Fraser asked. "And do I have your permission now to have an exhibit? Are you still nervous?"

"Yes, yes, and no. But all of this is quite mystifying."

"You'll see," Fraser said. "In time you'll learn."

"But, why do we want to have a show when all the paintings are sold?"

"We're not having a show. We're having an exhibit."

"What's the difference?"

"There's a huge difference. A show is something thin and tinny – something that ordinary people would do. We aren't ordinary, are we? We're going to do the extraordinary. You should already know that. A show is a modern thing that implies show, tell, and sale. I'm talking about an exhibit, and by exhibit I mean displaying something that nobody can have."

"But won't people be put out when they come and there's nothing to buy?"

"I certainly hope so. That's the main reason for having an exhibition. People want what they can't have. And it's not just a matter of them being sold, but of who has purchased them and that they were left out of the picture – so to speak. You see, when you're selling something that nobody needs, you don't leave it up to the gods. You have to engineer matters – which is what we're doing."

"You're the first genuine primitive I've encountered. I'd sworn off taking on any more people but you interest me. You're unschooled in the extreme – so much so, you don't know that the way you're painting isn't supposed to work. But, you don't know that and it so happens that what you're doing does work – it works beautifully. But beyond all that, anyone who goes into the business of selling firewood so he can sell paintings is worth looking into, don't you think? Besides, you were becoming an interesting nuisance. God knows what you'll get up to next."

Ken asked him about his Arctic paintings. What was it about them that he didn't like?

Fraser didn't answer. Paint more, he said. Paint more paintings of the southern landscapes that he could exhibit in galleries in Kelowna and Calgary.

On the evening of the exhibit, Fraser monopolized him: taking him by the arm, steering him around the room, and introducing him to the guests. Some complained that all the paintings bore red sold stickers.

Fraser assured them that as soon as a painting was available they would be contacted to come and view it.

"Just one?"

"Yes. Just one. He's not a machine – he's a painter."

"But what if I don't like it?"

"Not a problem. Your name will be placed on the bottom of the list and another person will be called."

Doreen followed them, carrying a small notebook in which she entered orders. When the evening wound down, Fraser told Ken's parents that they should be proud of their son – he was potentially brilliant and would go far. "But don't tell him that," he said in a bellowing aside. "His head is already swelled quite enough."

Later that night, while having dinner with Helen, he opened the envelope Fraser had slipped into his pocket. Inside was a note full of praise for his work. At the bottom was a postscript. "Your Arctic paintings will have to wait a while. You aren't ready to paint them yet and your public is not ready to receive them."

"Do you realize how lucky you are?" Helen asked when he showed her the note.

"I think so. I think I was born lucky." Or perhaps it was something more than luck. His grandfather and the old grandmother had predicted that power would come to him – that life would be kind to him and open many doors for him. Perhaps they had seen something in him that he had not.

The next morning, Fraser called. "Come and see me at noon – I have an idea," and he hung up.

At noon, Ken walked into the gallery. "There's something I want you to do for me," Fraser said. "I want you to go to auctions for me. I'll give you a list of paintings for each auction, and I will put a price on each of the pictures I'm interested in. But you have to agree not to go a penny over the amount I say. And I'll give you cash. I don't want to do this by cheque."

"Why me?" Ken asked. "Why don't you do it?"

"Because as soon as I enter one of these auctions and start bidding the jig is up, and the prices are up too. I'm too bloody well-known for my own good. You understand?"

"I think so. Where are these auctions?"

"All over the bloody place – Winnipeg, Victoria, Vancouver, Regina – all over."

"Sure. I'll be happy to try that, but you know that while I'm doing that I won't be painting."

"Don't worry about that," Fraser said.

"I'm not worried. I just don't want you to get in a huff about not having enough paintings."

"I said don't worry. I'll make it worth your while."

"That's not what I mean. I'm happy to do it for you in return for what you're doing for me. And I don't want any money for it."

"You don't want any money! Well, I never – a man who doesn't want money. So what do you want?"

"I just don't want you to get upset when my painting production falls off because I'm doing other things for you."

"Of course, I'll be upset at your lack of paintings. Why wouldn't I be?"

"But that's not reasonable!"

"It's quite reasonable in light of how you present yourself – as the one apart – the one to whom the rules don't apply – the one who walked in here without an appointment. There isn't a painter in the country that would dare do that. And, your shenanigans in the Peace River Country – and your wanderings in the Arctic – as if you owned the bloody place. You put yourself forward, with a quiet aloofness, as the man who can do everything and anything, so I'm sure it won't be any kind of a trick for you to be in two places at the same time, doing two different things at the same time."

"Well," Ken said. "That's not how I see myself."

"Fine. But I'm only telling you how you portray yourself."

"If I was who you say I am, I'd be able to get my Arctic paintings and stories out to the public, and I can't."

"Your Arctic paintings are the only tentative part of you. You haven't come to terms with that subject. You're unsure and it shows. Everything else you paint is clear, simple, strong and sure-footed. But don't be concerned. In good time, all of this will look after itself. With your confidence and your bloody single-mindedness, you'll work your way through it. But right now, you're not there and I will neither show them nor recommend them. In that area you have a long way to go."

That evening, he related the conversation to Helen.

She laughed. "Don't tell me you're surprised. You have an ego as big as the world. You're full of yourself. The long and short of it is that you're arrogant. Alex is right. You wander into a place, you give it the once-over and all of a sudden, you're going to fix everything, you're in control, and you'll take care of it. That's what it looks like from the outside."

"It does?"

"Yes, it does. And what do you have in mind anyway? Where are you heading with all this?"

He told her about his life with the Inuit, and how profoundly it had affected him. He wanted to make a difference in these people's lives.

She suggested these were matters for the government to take care of.

"Jesus H. Christ!" Ken said. "Here we go again. What the hell do you think a government is – some sort of amorphous blob that exists out there completely independent of citizens? Who the hell is government?"

"It's this big thing out there that runs everything."

"And what do you think it's made of? Do you think it just fell out of the sky, and bounced around for awhile, and then settled down and became government?"

"But you're just the little guy."

He threw his fork down on his plate. "I cannot abide the term – 'the little guy'. Talk about setting oneself up to be nothing more than a victim. Here comes the steamroller! Everybody lie down and have it roll over you. No, thank you. I propose to find a way of doing something about it, and if it takes me the rest of my life to do it, I'm going to do it – and that's the course I'm on."

"Well," Helen sniffed. "A lot of people would call that arrogant. Who the hell do you think you are?"

"I think I am someone with ideas, and the ability to think my way through a situation. And I think it's up to me to use all my gifts to the fullest, and do what I can."

"To what end?"

"To do my part in a grander scheme. If I don't then I'm just a fraud. I'm just using up the oxygen, wearing out the sidewalk, consuming stuff, and returning nothing. What is the point of being human? I'm doing my part, and apparently, I'm expected to do yours too – and everybody else's."

"My God! You really believe this stuff, don't you?"

"It's not a matter of believing it. I don't care about believing. It's a matter of being that. If you hand your power over to someone else, then it's only a matter of time until you end up with another in a long line of despots. If you don't take on your responsibilities, you end up with a dictator running stuff."

Helen shrugged. "Fine, if you say so." She cleared away the supper dishes.

Helen was angry. Since they had decided to share an apartment, she had brought up the subject of marriage a couple of times. Ken didn't want to marry her – or anyone else. He argued with Helen that, in the old days, people who detested each other stayed together, and lived unhappy lives. Today, people had freedom, and they should take advantage of it. People had the romantic notion that marriage was an elaborate wedding and a honeymoon that continued forever. It never did.

He did not allow himself to recall how very close he had come to marrying Jessica, and that if he could, he would do it in a heartbeat.

10

Success – and a Son

A couple of days after the exhibition, Ken jumped into his new Austin Healey and boarded the Victoria ferry to attend his first art auction. He returned with every painting Fraser had wanted.

"I have an idea," he said to the beaming Fraser who was examining one of the paintings.

"I hope so," he replied distractedly.

"I would like to get into the auction business with you."

"Is that so? And how do you propose to do that?"

"I propose a fifty/fifty deal. I'll put up half the money and I'll do all the running around – going to the auctions and so on."

"And who does the choosing of the works to be acquired?"

"You do, of course."

"It's a deal," he said, holding out his hand, his eyes still concentrated on the painting. "When do you want to start?"

"Right now."

"Good. I think you'll find that you just made a very wise decision and I think you will find that I'm a very nice fellow to let you make it."

Fraser kept Ken working day and night. He also taught him the art business and passed on his unique understanding of human nature. He explained old money versus new money and how it worked – how, generally, you didn't sell paintings to old money because those families had their walls full of paintings. The exception was the nobility who were always acquiring art that would eventually find its way into museums and national galleries.

New money bought art – new money thought it could buy anything, including happiness. When people with new money met people like he and Ken, they would hear the word "no", and that word was like a finger untying the bow of their big, shiny, packaged perfect life. If they thought they couldn't have something, they wanted it and would stop at nothing to get it. "And that," Fraser said, "is why we have exhibits where you can't buy anything. Other galleries don't seem to understand this but it's very simple. All you have to do is invite the right people and drive them out of their minds. You can have all the money you want."

They weren't really in the business of selling paintings, he said, they were retailing stories. "And you are one of those creatures who has stories pouring out of him, one after the other, and if I didn't turn off the switch, you'd go on, and on, and on, until you wore a hole in the ground. And that's wonderful, but now you have to learn how to hone those stories so that they don't make the stones yawn. Tell it all beautifully, but get to the point. You have a habit of going around in circles. If there's a very long way around it, you'll find it."

One morning, the telephone woke Ken out of a deep sleep.

"Are you painting?"

"I was sleeping."

"Sleeping? Hell, you'll have an eternity to sleep. You should be painting. But never mind; come to the gallery at noon. I have something for you. And bring burgers and fries."

When Ken arrived, Fraser ushered him into the back room and extracted a crumpled brown paper bag from the bottom shelf of his framing table.

"Open it." he said.

Inside were dozens of rolls of bills.

"Count it," Fraser said.

"Why should I count it?"

"I want to see the look on your face."

The bills totalled fifty-four thousand dollars. "How on earth did you manage this?" Ken asked.

"Remember the painting of the cattle that we got for eighteen hundred dollars?" It fetched twenty-nine thousand pounds sterling in London. And that was just the start."

Fraser poured a tumbler of rye, while they went over an Edmonton auction catalogue and discussed Ken's next exhibition at the Hamilton Gallery, in Kelowna.

"Will all the paintings in the Hamilton Gallery be sold beforehand?" Ken asked.

"Of course," Fraser said. "Why do you ask?"

"I'd very much like to sell a painting to Mr. Bennett."

"Which Mr. Bennett?"

"The Premier."

"Why do you want Mr. Bennett to buy one of your paintings?"

Ken told him how they'd met, in the Peace River country. "And I thought that since Kelowna was his home town, it would be an opportunity to see him again. And maybe I'll give him a painting."

"Give him a painting? Bloody hell you will! You don't give paintings to anyone – not ever and not under any circumstances. Do you understand?"

"Why?"

"A painting that is given is all but worthless. It'll be up in the attic or down in the basement before you know it. A painting must always be well paid for and it will be up above the mantel quicker than you can snap your fingers – and it will stay there. And another thing you need to know – you never give wealth a gift. It's one of the 'middle classes' really bad habits."

When Ken walked into the gallery in Kelowna, Jack Hamilton took him into the back office and handed him an envelope. "I see you keep very fancy company," he said.

Ken tore it open. The premier had written that he would be delighted to visit the gallery the next morning at eight.

At seven-fifty, Jack staggered down the steps from the apartment above the gallery, in his rumpled pyjamas, unlocked the front door to let Ken in, and shuffled back up the stairs. At eight sharp, a chauffeur driven car pulled up, and Bennett stepped out. He gave Ken a hearty handshake, sat down at a small table near the front of the gallery and asked to hear stories of the Arctic. "I thought you were just going up there for a month or two, but you seem to have gotten yourself lost up there."

"In a way, I did," Ken replied. "It's a long story."

"I want to hear it."

He told the Premier about his adventures and the atrocious conditions the people lived with. He talked about the famine and the disease, and the autocratic rule of the church, the RCMP, and the Hudson's Bay Company. When he finished, he asked if there was anything the Premier could do to help the people up there.

Bennett stood. "Let's see your paintings," he said.

They walked through the gallery.

"What do the red dots signify?" Bennett asked.

"It means they're sold."

"It looks like they're all sold."

"Yes, they are."

"You must be doing very well."

"Yes I am – I'm very lucky."

"I'd say there's more than luck involved. I know nothing about art but I do like what you're doing, especially that one," pointing to a landscape of rolling grasslands. "I'd be interested in owning that one."

"I'm sorry," Ken said. "I'm afraid the entire exhibit was sold before it got here."

He led him into the back office where three paintings leaned against the wall. "These are not sold," he said.

Bennett pointed to one of the high plateau on the Douglas Lake Ranch. "I like that one. Where is that?"

"The Douglas Lake Ranch."

"How did you arrange to get into the Douglas Lake Ranch?"

"I know Chunky Woodward, and he gave me permission to roam around his land and paint."

"You don't waste time getting acquainted with just the right people, do you? Does Mr. Woodward own one of your paintings?"

"Yes sir – he owns several."

"How much is that one?"

"Eight hundred dollars."

"Good, I'll have that one. I'll ask my wife to come down and pick out a frame, and she'll arrange for the payment." He looked around. "Are you the only one running the gallery? Where is everyone?"

"Well sir, I think when they heard you were coming, they all ran for cover."

Bennett roared. "Well, there's nothing like being popular. Now, about the question of the Northwest Territories." He explained that the Yukon and the Territories were federal responsibilities. The provinces had no say or influence in their governance. In fact, his own experience with the federal government was one long drawn-out set of disappointments. "If they don't pay attention and are not willing to listen to the needs of British Columbians, I can imagine what their response would be to the people of the far north who are out of sight and out of mind."

"I don't have to imagine," Ken said. "I was there and I saw – it was nothing short of unconscionable."

"You need to get into politics and work from the inside, and bring your concerns to the public at large that way."

"As I see it, I am in politics. However, you've made it clear that short of a Prime Minister with a majority government, an elected politician doesn't stand a chance of getting this idea of mine done. I wonder – when conditions are extreme and it's a matter of conscience, does one always have to obey all the rules, all the time? If we did, we would never have achieved democracy in the first place."

Bennett smiled. "I must say, on occasion, I have asked myself the same question. But, I have to tell you, it does one good to see a young person passionately interested in the affairs of the nation."

"But, my concern is the Inuit and the conditions they live under."

"That's all part of the fabric, isn't it? And I have every confidence that you'll find a way of getting your voice heard."

"I wish I had your confidence. I can't imagine how I can possibly help those people."

"If I had one piece of advice for you it would be legislation by exhaustion – the last man standing wins. If you persist, and you never leave it alone, you'll wear everybody out, and you'll get your way."

"But, by then, there won't be any of them left."

"So, where are the Arctic paintings?"

"I can't find any gallery willing to show them."

"I'm sure you will. And, remember what I said to you at the Peace River camp. You would make a fine member of our party. You're a natural-born politician. We'd love to have you involved in our party. Keep in touch."

A few months later, Ken finally agreed to marry Helen and in the summer of 1967, she flew to Toronto – where her family organized the wedding – while Ken followed in the car. The ceremony was elaborate and fussy, but the honeymoon in Montreal, which was hosting the World Exposition that year, was idyllic. They drove back across the country and took the ferry to Nile Creek, where they fished and lolled in the sun.

Back in Vancouver, Ken poured his energy into real estate investing. While others agonized over the market and analyzed each piece of property, Ken dropped the question into his brain, as though he was delivering it to a receptionist in a large office tower – trusting her to take it to the correct department, where the experts would figure it out.

He scouted the Fraser Valley and visited the land planning offices in communities from Richmond to Abbotsford, telling the administrators and clerks that he was looking for land as an investment. He was flooded by calls from real estate agents and came to terms with three of them. If they could bring him the sort of deals he was looking for, they would make two commissions – one from a sale to him and one from the resale. In return, they passed along all the information they came across.

On his next trip to Peter Hope Lake, he met the new owners, Jules Bloom, his wife Joey – and their brood of children. The peace of the country stole over him, and the cares of his life in the city fell away. In the frenzy of making land deals, painting, and attending auctions, he had almost forgotten his primary mission – to help the people of the Arctic. He needed this place more than ever, and asked Jules if he might build a small log cabin on the property and pay an annual rent. They drew a design sketch even before shaking hands on the deal.

A day later, they cut up an old dead tree to make the piers for the foundation. When Ken inspected the logs he noticed a rotted section in the centre of one, cleaned it out and placed a metal cylinder, containing a roll of large bills totalling one hundred fifty thousand dollars, inside – planning to add to the cache until it totalled half a million.

Hoping to help his son deal with his newfound wealth, Ken Sr. introduced him to a man who had recently started a new mortgage and trust company. He looked after the financial affairs of several professional athletes and successful businessmen, and Ken was impressed with the program he put together for him. He hired his father to oversee his new financial manager and rented an office for him in the trust company's building. Ken did as his advisor recommended, putting most of his cash into short-term mortgages at favourable rates, and became known to local bankers as a young man with a Midas touch. The arrangement gave him more time to paint, attend auctions, and fish at Peter Hope Lake.

He began a new series of Arctic paintings that were more sure-footed than any he had done previously, and he was beginning to feel a sense of momentum, when Helen visited him at his father's office, shut the door and announced, "I'm pregnant."

Impossible, Ken thought. They had an agreement that there would be no children – he had been adamant that children would never fit into his plans. And, Helen had been taking birth control pills. This was no accident. This was betrayal and manipulation. He suggested an abortion. Helen said no. Over the next few weeks and months he experienced moments of elation – a child – how wonderful! But, when he considered his commitment to the Arctic, his mood plummeted.

When he sank into his black hole he went to Peter Hope Lake, where he found solace as he sat in the grasslands beside an enormous boulder overlooking the lake.

One day, while he was in the office with his father, looking over his statements, he determined that he had enough money to do what he wanted. It was time to get out of real estate and to cash in his investments. His father advised him to extricate himself slowly. Ken agreed and left his father to get on with the job.

Michael was born on May 23, 1974 and Ken, despite his earlier anger and deep misgivings, fell instantly in love. Michael was his son – a new baby and a new being. His life would never be the same again. Helen, however, fell into a deep postnatal depression. Ken wanted to fix it and only succeeded in driving Helen deeper into her misery. In his desperation to return their lives to normalcy, he bought her a shiny new Mercedes. When he saw the smile on her face, he broached the idea of a larger home. He wanted a studio away from the noise and activity of the family. They found a small blueberry farm on Fourth Road, in Richmond. The farmhouse was one of the oldest homes in the area that was still in good repair. Ken sealed off the ground floor and, with a quiet space of his own, became very productive.

He was working on an Arctic painting when a local teacher, a former colleague of Helen's, called and asked if he would speak to her Grade 4 students about painting.

"Painting," Ken thought. "How do you talk about painting? Painting is something you do and something you absorb. If he was going to talk to children he had to be honest. Children had the best bullshit meters in the world. Yes, he would talk to them, but he would tell stories, and the gorier the better.

When he entered the classroom, he sat on the teacher's desk, his feet dangling, and told stories about the Arctic. The children listened raptly.

He received another speaking request, and then another, and another. He accepted all of them. His talks were a training ground for what was to come. Fraser had been right. ""We're not selling paintings; we're selling stories."

He spoke to classrooms of elementary students and to older students in high schools. One time he began with, "Before we get going I want to tell you, just so that no fraud is committed here – I never went to school."

The children gasped.

"It's kind of weird, isn't it – that I've been asked to come and talk to you but I didn't go to school? Now, make of that what you will. I'm not suggesting that you don't get a formal education, but I am suggesting that there are those of us who probably fare better if we don't."

He shared his thoughts on education – what it is and what it is not. He wove his ideas into stories of the Arctic, stories of politics, and stories of old mythology. His stories posed questions. "Why do we think things are right and why do we think other things are wrong? Where did we get all this stuff? Who wrote it down? Who says it's true?"

His speaking invitations multiplied, until he could accept no more. He met with the principal of one school that had made a request, and said, "I want to speak to the whole school. Give me your auditorium. This is a performance, and I don't want forty-five minutes – I want the entire afternoon."

He asked that the banners in the auditorium be taken down, all the lights turned off, and the windows curtained. He asked for one microphone, with a long cord, and a spotlight on centre stage. There would be no adults in the auditorium, although teachers could position themselves out of sight where they could hear. The children were to come in and sit on the floor. When they were seated, the room would be plunged into total darkness, and the children would sit for three minutes in silence, before he walked on the stage.

"Are you out of your mind?" the principal said. "These aren't children – they're little animals! It will be chaos! You obviously don't understand children!"

"I probably do," Ken said. "I was one once and I probably still am."

"It can't be done."

"Fine. I live in a world where apparently everything can't be done. Have you ever tried this?"

"No."

"Then, you're educating children and giving them advice based on things you've never done. That's one hell of a way of going about things. Well, that's my offer – take it or leave it."

"But, why do you want to do it this way?'

"Because. I want it to be something compelling and different. What you do here is mechanistic, rote, and boring. If you want children to get something out of something, you have to at least put something forward and given that they are the most important people on earth, we should try harder. You're bringing me here for a reason. I'm prepared to take responsibility."

Reluctantly, the principal agreed to Ken's terms. Before the performance, Ken asked himself what he wanted to achieve. That question led to others. What are stories really? How many are there? Are they all a rehashing of a single story – or a mere handful of stories? What was the first novel? What was the first story ever told, and why was it told?

He'd read the stories of the Bible. He was captivated by the Arthurian legends. Why were they so compelling? Generation after generation had fallen under their spell. They called to something deep inside the human soul. Why these stories? Why did music touch that same place? He concluded that they were basic, archetypal tales that touched sensitive places – places of magic. People needed a magical hero. They wanted to know there was someone or something special in the world. Ken connected the genius with the idiot, the clown, and the magician. This event would be about magic.

On the appointed day, the children filed into the auditorium and sat down. When they were settled, the lights went out, and only the red exit signs over the doors cast a faint glow in the blackness. Ken waited in the wings. The silence became a buzz that grew louder and louder. When it had reached a near chaotic level, he walked onto the stage, guided by the faint shine of the metallic microphone. At a pre-arranged signal, the solitary spotlight flashed on. The children fixed their gaze on a man with black hair and beard, dressed completely in black, including his cowboy boots. The auditorium hushed.

He lowered himself to the floor, in the circle of light, and removed one boot, placing it carefully to the side. He pulled off his sock and draped it gently over the boot. Then, he pulled a very large knife out of his pocket. The light danced off the blade. Slowly, and deliberately, he began to saw at his toes.

"This story is about gangrene," he said. "A friend of mine cut off his toes to save his life." He told five stories that afternoon, each grimmer than the previous. The children didn't move.

When he finished, the silence was as absolute as the darkness. "When somebody gives a gift, it works very well when somebody then gives a gift in return," Ken said "I've come here today. I've asked for nothing. I don't get paid for doing this. I didn't ask to be paid for doing this. You're here to be educated, and one of the key things I want to pass on to you today is to consider others always. So, you might want to contribute something to me. Here's what I'm asking for: I've told you stories, now it's your turn to tell me stories."

A faint rustling arose in the room – a tension that was almost a physical presence. When it had become almost unbearable, a voice spoke from the back of the room.

"I can't hear you," Ken said.

The boy tried again.

"I can't hear you. Come up front, so that I can make out what you're saying."

A tall skinny boy picked his way through the sea of bodies to the stage. Ken held out his hand and pulled him up into the spotlight. "Who are you?" Ken asked. "Who are you inside? Don't tell me the ordinary stuff – I want to hear the real stuff."

Another child hopped up onto the stage – and then another, and another. Ken was overwhelmed. The children poured out their hearts to him. He was a magic man – a man who wanted to know about them, and a man who listened to their secrets and their fears.

The bell marked the end of the school day, and not a single child left the room. The teachers came, and still no one moved. When the parents arrived, the lights were turned on and the children ushered out. Like the Pied Piper, Ken led a trail of children into the parking lot, where they continued to talk.

Ken was elated. He had touched the children where they lived.

Helen told him he was a devil – he was upsetting the whole modus operandi of the school system.

"And it needs to be upset," he said.

Ken pondered what had occurred that afternoon. One night, he woke from a deep sleep with the thought that this could be the most effective political tool for disseminating his message. No one would suspect children of political motives – they were too young to vote. But children are compelling. How many parents could deny their children?

He gave more presentations – each one a more polished performance. At the end of one talk, he said, I'm here. I've asked for nothing – except for one thing. I don't want money and I'm not interested in your applause. I'm interested in your help. Save the energy of your applause, and use it to help. The price of what I have done today is that you write a letter to your Prime Minister, telling him what you think of what you heard today. You might want to consider that for a nation to be great it must know every corner of itself. All the people need to meet each other. All the people need to know each other. People need to be silent until they've met each other, so that they don't go around saying stupid things about people they have never met, or places they have never seen."

The school was the training ground for them to become citizens, he said. The running of the country was their responsibly. Government was not something far away. It was their job, and this was the time to practise.

It worked. Parents began to pay attention. Ken cut down on his sleep hours. When he made time for his family, he and Helen argued about Michael. She was too protective, he said. She disagreed, and their confrontations intensified.

11

Death and Rebirth

Ken worked feverishly on his new series of paintings of the North. Unlike his previous Arctic paintings, there were no scenic panoramas of the tundra – these paintings told a story that began with the grasslands of Peter Hope Lake, then moved up to northern British Columbia, and finally to the Arctic itself. When he was finished, he gathered up the twenty-eight canvases and took them to Alex Fraser, where he laid them out around the walls of the gallery.

"I want to force the issue, with these paintings, in this country," he said. "And don't tell me they're rubbish – tell me what it is about them that you don't like."

"There isn't anything about them that I don't like," Fraser said. "They're absolutely wonderful."

Ken stared at him. "Five minutes ago they were rubbish!"

"That wasn't five minutes ago," he said. "That was several years ago. These paintings are highly developed and very good."

"Good! Great! Then help me put on an exhibit. I don't care about the money. I want to get this idea out."

"You're wasting your time."

"Hell, there's no point in just telling me I'm wasting my time, or it's rubbish, or it's lovely – that doesn't mean anything to me. Why won't it fly here?"

"Look, what is the number one topic of conversation here – at the grocery store, at the bank, at the water cooler – everywhere? What is the number one topic of Canadian conversation?"

"Hockey," Ken said.

"No it isn't," Fraser said. "Not by a long shot."

"Okay – then what?"

"The weather. And listen, because I'm going to give you a doorway into understanding. Why are people talking about the weather all the time? Here, people say it rains all the time. Well, it doesn't – it rains some of the time, and people think it rains all the time. People are hungering for the place they came from – it's wonderful where they came from. Well, if it's so bloody wonderful where they came from, what the hell are they doing here? There is a deep hunger to have the sunshine of their former homes, and of their great-grandparents' former homes. There are these stories that persist about how wonderful life was, and how sunny it was, and how warm it was. But, with the exception of this little coastal strip, this is a very cold country. You're trying to give paintings of vast, distant places that are freezing cold, to Canadians. Why would anyone, with the psyche I've described, even think of buying one? They won't even come out to look at them."

"Well, Jesus!"

"Go ahead – break my argument."

"What else about these paintings then?

"One word – pretty. The Canadian art scene is almost non-existent, but what passes for imagery in the public mind at large is pretty. Doreen! Doreen! Bring some magazines!"

Fraser grabbed the top one, from the stack Doreen delivered, and opened it at random. He turned two pages and pointed. "Look – here's an ad – it's perfect. Isn't that a pretty photograph? Do you notice that it has a white, sandy beach, a scantily clad couple, and palm trees? People work very, very hard to make money, so they can save some up and go to that place – and it's very pretty. That's what is in their minds. You and I are the children and grandchildren of peasants, and we have their tastes."

Fraser reached into his pack of cigarettes, pulled out a fresh one, and lit it from the butt that had almost burned down to his fingertips.

"It's taken Europe an eon to get to its appreciation of art. You're expecting too much, too quickly."

"But, if we don't push we won't get anywhere," Ken said.

"It's not just a matter of pushing the public. We have to find individuals who will get behind this. It's not just good old Alex and Ken who are going to go and foist this on the country. It's a much bigger story."

Ken left the gallery deep in thought. Yes, there was truth in what Fraser had said but it wasn't the whole truth. Canada was ready for his paintings. The Group of Seven was proof. Fraser thought they were rubbish too. If he wanted to tell his story through his paintings, it wouldn't be with Alex Fraser by his side.

Unexpectedly, Ken received a letter from his Aunt Vicki in Madrid. She had taken the photographs he had sent her, of his latest paintings, and shown them to a popular gallery owner who wanted to exhibit them.

He tapped the note against his desk, read it again, and picked up a pen. He wrote a letter to Mr. McEachern, the Minister of Foreign Affairs, describing his good fortune in coming to Canada, and telling him how he had arrived in this country. He wrote about his art and said that he wished to go back to Europe for an exhibition in Madrid.

He sent the letter by registered post and, to his surprise, received a prompt and lengthy reply, expressing great interest in his story and his upcoming exhibit. How could he help? Mr. McEachern asked. And could he see some of his work?

Ken crated the twenty-eight paintings and sent them by special delivery to Ottawa.

Two days later, Mr. McEachern telephoned. "This is absolutely marvellous! We have your paintings spread all over the place! There must be a really wonderful story behind all this."

"There is," Ken said.

"Maybe, you could write it all down and tell me."

"Well sir, if you would spare me a few moments, I will fly to Ottawa and tell you the story."

"Fine."

"Then I'll see you shortly."

He flew to the capital the following day and took a cab to Parliament.

As he stepped out of the cab, he felt a shiver run up his spine. This was it! This was the seat of power. This was his country, and these buildings were his. He climbed up the steps and walked in, his heels clicking satisfyingly on the stone floor. The echoing hall was almost deserted – only a few people walked about, intent on their business. A receptionist sat behind an oversized desk in the centre of the hall.

"I want to see Mr. McEachern, the Minister of Foreign Affairs," Ken said.

Mr. McEachern's secretary led him up several flights of broad stairs and into a suite of offices, where Ken's paintings leaned against the walls. McEachern burst into the room and grasped Ken's hand. "Marvellous – absolutely marvellous. But, I'm curious why you've come through the Ministry of Foreign Affairs. This is a matter of art."

"Is it?" Ken asked. "I think it's something quite different. I was a man born into a place on the earth where he didn't belong and, by good fortune and some help, he found the country that fits. I'm the luckiest man you will ever look at, because I found my place on the planet – and that's my passion – it's not money, or fame, or any of that. To find the place to be, and then to be who you are in that place, is everything. This country is my passion, and I wish to return to where I came from and show my country off. That's why I wrote to Foreign Affairs and that's why I want your help. There's also the matter of some difficulties from the past – politically."

"Yes, I gathered that," McEachern replied. "You've had quite a life – I've looked into you. What would you like me to do to help?"

"I would like to accept the invitation of the gallery in Madrid, and I would like to go there with the blessing of my country. I would like a letter from you, indicating that I am going there as a Canadian, with all of the goodwill and blessings of my country, as well as its protection."

"Yes. What else?"

"I would like to have the Canadian ambassador available to me to help me tell this story, and to make contacts in Madrid. I don't want to use my family's contacts. I want to come in, brand new and fresh, without being in the shadow of my family's name."

"Right," McEachern smiled. "Our ambassador in Madrid, is Monsieur Bolin, and I'm quite sure we can make him available to you at any time you wish. I like this – I like this a lot. Your family in Europe – I gather they are involved in industry? They're certainly very well-to-do. Are you expecting any money from the Canadian government?"

"I don't want a penny," Ken said. "Thanks for asking, but if you offered financial support I wouldn't accept it. I don't think we should expect government to do that sort of thing. If we are moved by a passion for something, we should get on with the job and do it. I would prefer that government money be allocated to looking into the matter of the people in the Arctic – these are desperate matters."

"You have an agenda, don't you?"

"Yes. But, it won't involve you. I'm not asking for your support in that matter. I want your support around the work I am doing to publicize the stories of the Arctic, so that people at large will have an understanding. There's no point in going to government and saying, 'Go fix that.' It has to be willed in the heart of the public."

"So, you're a strategist and a politician."

"No, I'm just an ordinary man who has an idea... it's a very strong idea and I'm pursuing it."

"I'm going to see to it that you have all the things you've asked for. I'm delighted to help."

Ken accepted the gallery's invitation. Spain was changing. Franco had aged, and now wanted to return Spain to the deposed royal family – who had lived near the Kirkbys, in Portugal. Ken had grown up with the Crown Prince, Juan Carlos, who was to take the reins of power.

On a blustery day in early 1975, Ken kissed Helen and Michael goodbye and boarded the plane for Madrid. When he arrived, he was met by his Uncle James and Aunt Vicki, as well as the Canadian ambassador and two aides. He introduced himself to Monsieur Bolin and made introductions to his aunt and uncle.

At his uncle's apartment, across the street from the old Royal Palace, Monsieur Bolin asked, "What is it that we can do for you?"

"I want to meet the one person who it's impossible to meet," Ken said. "I'm trying to make a statement. I don't know how familiar you are with Spanish art history, but it was Goya who painted the soul of his country. More than any other artist, he portrayed the psyche and reality of Spain. He was very close to the Queen, who reportedly is the Naked Maja in his famous painting. Consequently, he was arrested, and if not for people in very high office, he would have lost his head. Well, he was also very close to the Duchess of Alba and she was very beautiful, intelligent, articulate, and powerful. I know that the monarchy has been suspended – but not really. I want to meet the woman who is now the Duchess of Alba, whether it's official or not."

"Ask me for an appointment with her majesty Queen Elizabeth and I can arrange it," Bolin said. "But, you're asking for the impossible! You can't meet her!"

"You asked me what I want," Ken said. "That's what I want."

"Do you make a habit of these sorts of requests?"

"I do. The only places I'm interested in going are the places where one can't go. And, I am only interested in doing what apparently one can't do. I can't see any other point for living."

"I see. I'll have to think about that. It's not an easy one. Nobody else will do?"

"No – nobody else will do."

"As you may know, Juan Carlos is now going to come to the throne. Maybe that would be more appropriate."

"No. I want to say something to the Spanish psyche. If I can meet this woman – if this Eskimo can meet her – that is magic."

A few days later, Bolin introduced Ken to Franco's daughter, Isabelle, who was a close friend of the Duchess, and she arranged a meeting at the Duchess' country house.

The elderly Duchess was immaculately dressed in a crisp wool suit, carrying herself with an authority backed by a thousand years of history. Ken presented her with a small painting – the original sketch, drawn on adding machine paper, was taped to the back. He told her the story and said, "I brought this from the Arctic – from my new country. I wanted so much to meet you, and I appreciate so much that you agreed to see me. I would like you to have this, as a gift from me and from this special place. I have also come to invite you to an exhibit of similar works, which have never been seen before. I want these paintings to be exhibited in Europe – in the place where I heard the stories that led me to the Arctic. I would like the Spanish people to know about the story, and if they can meet you, I'm quite sure that the Spanish people will pay attention. I am just a painter, but you have the history of Spain in your veins. As the Duchess of Alba was to Goya, perhaps the Duchess of Alba can be to me."

"I'd be delighted," she said. "What do we do?"

"If you would come to the exhibit, you would honour me greatly, and I would be indebted to you forever."

"I accept," she said.

There are no secrets in Madrid. The media flooded Ken with requests for interviews. The day before the exhibit, he helped hang the paintings; only one in each room of the gallery. Opening night resembled a Hollywood premier. People gathered in the street and, when a chauffeur driven limousine drew up to the curb, the media descended. Ken parted the crowd and opened the door, guiding the Duchess into the gallery. The crowd inside fell back as though God himself had made an entrance.

Ken led her through the rooms, telling the stories of the Canadian North. She nodded, smiled, listened attentively, and left as quickly as she had come. Forty-five minutes later every painting wore a sold sticker.

Ken extended his stay, in order to accept all the invitations he was besieged with. He had been in Madrid for six weeks, when his father called. "You must come home right away."

"What happened?"

"Just, come home immediately. It looks like the trust company has gone under."

He flew home the next day and took a cab directly to his father's apartment, where he found him more agitated than Ken had ever known him to be. "This is real trouble," he said. "We tried to get into the office and it's locked – the locks have been changed and nobody is there."

In his own office, he discovered several key files missing. He arranged a meeting with other clients of the trust company. There were rumours. Some said the company principal had moved to the Fraser Valley, where he had set up an Arabian horse farm and purchased a Rolls-Royce. Others said he had simply vanished without a trace.

Ken called the RCMP commercial crime division and drove to the station with his father. The officer explained that the department was aware of the issue. "It's a complicated mess," he said. "We're going to have to investigate you and your activities, the same as everyone else."

The police found many of the missing files but not a trace of the company president and CEO. Rumours continued to circulate. One claimed that the head of the trust company had had nothing to do with the missing funds. It was Ken Kirkby. He was crazy, and smart, and out of the country when disaster struck. He was the one who had masterminded the plot. The media ran with it and reporters parked their cars and vans in front of his house waiting for one glimpse – to take just one picture with a telephoto lens. Two professional hockey players, convinced that Ken had taken their money, filed a lawsuit. The judge threw it out of court. Ken threw himself into the investigation, working with the police day after day to piece together what had happened.

The RCMP interviewed the victims of the fraud and examined the documents. Sorting through his own papers became a full time job, and there were many times he gave up all hope of making sense of them.

His greater despair was the loss of his friends. Even Alex Fraser refused to take his calls. He kept his despondency under control by concentrating on the job at hand, but as he began to sift through the masses of paperwork he realized he was now burdened with a crushing debt.

At night, Ken escaped to his studio, but even painting couldn't stave off the reality of the disaster. He had built up a reservoir of money, and he had honed his skill at storytelling for the sake of making the Arctic paintings – for the sake of telling the story of the Inuit. His dream lay broken on the studio floor.

Lawsuits were filed against him. He owed money, and people owed him money. There were times Ken sat at the dining room table, papers spread around him wondering, "How do I handle all this? What do I do with this? How do I even begin?"

He began by studying Canada's legal system, spending all of his spare time in the courtrooms or wandering down the court halls. He watched as people stood in front of the bench, staring at the floor and mumbling in reply to the judge's questions. When his day came, he would project his voice to the far corners of the room and hold his head high. He would not be intimidated. Win or lose, he would do it with poise.

His marriage was another casualty of his financial ruin. Helen packed her things and took Michael to Toronto to live with her parents. After the taxi pulled away, Ken walked through the empty house, listening to the echo of his footsteps.

Ken went to Peter Hope Lake to plan his courtroom strategy. He was not guilty – he had done nothing wrong. The owner of the trust company had borrowed against his property and had used Ken's money as collateral to borrow more money – the fault was clear. He would fight his battles himself.

The Bank of British Columbia sued for $300,000 that Ken owed on various real estate transactions, money the trust company had told him had been paid. But even though the company's annual reports had been falsified, they had passed the Securities Commission scrutiny. Ken made a note, "The government has been negligent." He circled the words in red, making them the centre of his strategy.

He retrieved the money he had hidden in the cabin at Peter Hope Lake and made a list of every person he owed. His assets totalled seven million two hundred thousand. With the assets allocated against his debts, he was still short half a million. The four hundred and fifty thousand he had cached almost made up the shortfall. Instead of millions in assets and savings to be used to further his goals of helping the Inuit, he was faced with a massive shortfall.

When the trial date arrived, Ken strode into the courtroom. On one side of the aisle at a long table sat two plaintiffs and five lawyers. On the other side, Ken settled himself in a chair, placing his briefcase on the floor beside him.

The judge walked in, declared the court in session, and surveyed the group in front of him. "Mr. Kirkby," he said. "Where is your lawyer?'

"Your honour, I don't have one," Ken said. "I'm going to be my own lawyer."

"That's very foolhardy."

"Given the state of my circumstances, not only financially, but in all ways, I feel that I'm in a position where I have to fight this battle myself," Ken said.

"I have to caution you," the judge said. "This is not a minor issue."

"I'm aware of that, your honour."

"I'm advising you strongly that we should postpone this until you get a lawyer."

"May I explain to you why I don't want a lawyer?"

Ken said that the lawyers who had supposedly been protecting him had, in fact, not done so. The government, that was supposed to protect his interests had not. He understood the essence of the law, even though he might not know the jargon of the legal profession, and he had more confidence in himself than in anyone else. He understood the consequences and was prepared for them. "If it goes poorly for me, you won't hear me complain."

"I appreciate your analysis," the judge said. "But I think you're wrong and I insist that you get a lawyer."

"Your honour, you can't insist that I get a lawyer."

The judge leaned forward. "Are you preaching the law to me?"

"No, your honour."

"You fancy yourself as a lawyer?"

"No, I don't. But it's not possible to force me to have a lawyer. It's my right as a citizen to defend myself without counsel."

"I told you – don't preach the law to me."

"Your honour, I assure you, I'm not preaching the law to you or to anyone else. I am not a preacher."

"If you keep on this tack, I'm going to find you in contempt of court."

"So be it, your honour. It is my understanding that I have the right to do what I have set out to do."

"I told you if you keep on that tack, I'll find you in contempt and right now you are in contempt of court! Doesn't that frighten you?"

"No your honour, it doesn't. I came from a place where people pointed guns at each other and illiterates held people hostage, a country where life became cheap – where there was dictatorship and revolution. I was in the middle of that, and I wasn't frightened. So, the one place on this planet where a man or a woman does not need to be frightened is in a Canadian courtroom. So, no, I am not frightened and I am very surprised that you would suggest that I should be."

The courtroom buzzed. The judge banged his gavel on the desk and ordered Ken and the plaintiffs to meet him in his chambers. As they crowded in, one of the lawyers whispered to Ken, "Just apologize to the judge, and I'm sure everything will be all right."

Turning his back to him, Ken said, "I just want to reiterate, for all to hear, that I've spent my life trying to shed myself of fear. It is my predominant ambition, and I will not be ruled by fear. Do as you please with me, but I promise you that I will not be fearful. That is my case and I will not apologize. So, you can do any damn thing you want."

The judge stood with his back to the room. When he turned, his face was split by a smile. "Mr. Kirkby, you are right. You're annoying, but you're right. Let's just go back out there and get on with the job."

"But, your honour," Ken said. "It seems that I am in contempt of court. Either one is or one isn't."

"Yes, that's correct."

"So, which is it?"

"You're not going to be in contempt of court."

"I'd like you to say that in the courtroom."

The judge nodded. Back in the courtroom, he said, "Sometimes in life, things get the better of us. I can only imagine what it must be like for Mr. Kirkby who has just had a rather tough time of late. It should also be understood that the court is under intense pressure – the backlog is building and building and what we are trying to do is move things along. But as Mr. Kirkby has reminded us, he does have the right to represent himself, and we will allow him his rights."

The case dragged on for months. When it was finally his turn to defend himself, he said, "The people in this courtroom shouldn't actually be fighting each other. This court case is not appropriate. The securities division of the Attorney General's department is largely at fault here, and it is they who should be answering these questions. It is they who are the overseers of these theoretically audited statements. These documents are frauds, and everything we're talking about begins there."

Ken's despair receded, replaced by the certainty of his rightness and resourcefulness. His creativity was not limited to painting. It was a talent he could wield anywhere, like a magic wand.

The judge said that he legally owed the money, but he also did not owe it – and delayed his ruling. At subsequent sessions, lawyers brought their students to study the case and often gave free advice during the breaks.

The bank foreclosed on his house. Ken didn't care. Helen called and urged him to declare bankruptcy. Ken refused. Let them take what they wanted. He had done nothing wrong.

One day a man called, introducing himself as Ron Gruber. "I've been trying to meet you for years," he said. Gruber carved decoys, many of which had made their way into Ken's extensive collection. "Our paths have crossed many times," he said. "But somehow we've never met. Now, unfortunately, we have to meet under circumstances that aren't the best. I work for a credit company, and I have to cancel and pick up your gas card. I'm awfully sorry to do this."

"That's fine," Ken said. "You're just doing your job. Come over now."

They talked, while consuming an entire bottle of Scotch, and became friends for life. Ron and his wife lived in a big house near Jericho Beach, that had separate living quarters on the ground floor. When Ken told him he had just lost his house, Ron suggested he move into their ground floor suite, and a few days later, Ken loaded his possessions into his truck and drove to Jericho Beach.

Revenue Canada sent a letter demanding a large sum of money in back taxes on his real estate investments. Because he had never taken the money, but only reinvested it, it had never been taxed. Ken put the letter on his bureau. Another letter arrived and then another, until he had accumulated seventeen progressively threatening tax notices. The final one informed him he was being sued. Ken took the notices to his accountant who was as puzzled as Ken. Each one demanded a different sum of money.

When they went to court, the lawyer for Revenue Canada made his statement. The judge turned to Ken. "Guilty or not guilty?"

"Not guilty," Ken said. "Impossibly and completely not guilty."

"How so?"

"Your honour, if I may be allowed to approach the bench and present you with the situation in writing. But, before I do that, may I ask you a question in order to help clarify the situation?"

"What if one were walking down the street," he asked, "and came across a car lot, and spotted a car he fancied, and wanted to buy it, and the salesman didn't know how much it cost? And what if he went to his sales manager and the manager, also, didn't know how much it cost? And what if he went to the owner of the car lot and the owner didn't know how much the car cost – would one be able to conclude a satisfactory transaction?"

"Clearly not," the judge said.

"This would appear to be the same situation," Ken said, handing the demand letters to the judge. "There are seventeen different notices here, which are completely confusing. There is no way, even according to the accountants I am acquainted with, to make head or tail of it. Every single one has a different figure on it: that makes no sense at all."

The judge studied the demands, his frown deepening.

"As far as I'm concerned, I don't owe the money," Ken said.

"I think you're absolutely correct," the judge said. "This is disgraceful." And he threw the case out of court.

He faced more plaintiffs, and reporters continued to ask for interviews. One day, standing on the steps of the courthouse, he criticized the government officials, including lawyers and accountants who refused to step forward. "As far as I'm concerned, I want to know if this is willful blindness or worse." Ken said.

He poured his excess energy into painting. If the galleries wouldn't touch him, he'd sell the canvases himself and do it in the way that everyone else sold things in North America – on the payment plan. If someone was willing to pay at least ten dollars a month, he could have a painting. He told anyone who would listen about his paintings being offered on the "installment plan" and began to do a brisk trade.

Revenue Canada served him another notice for a single and very large figure of money. Once again, he let the letters accumulate until the government took him to court. The same judge presided. Ken asked permission, once again, to approach the bench. "I need to know, is Revenue Canada the law or is it, like the rest of us, subject to the law?" he asked.

"No, it is not the law," the judge said.

"Therefore, is it subject to the law of the land?"

"Yes, it is."

"Please your honour, if you would read these notices. The language used says that Revenue Canada is the law and says what it is going to do – but that is only allowed by you."

The judge read the letters. "You're right," he said. "This is pretty clear." And he threw the case out of court.

Ken refused to stop fighting – but he soon had a different battle to confront. His father was diagnosed with throat cancer and refused an operation to remove the growth. He also said no to radiation and chemotherapy. Ken spent more time with him, taking him fishing, and sitting with him whenever he could, but part of him seemed to have already left the world behind.

One of the hardest things Ken had to bear during those weeks and months was the absence of his son, and when he had a few free days, he flew to Toronto. Helen picked him up and immediately whisked him to a party where he met Marsha, a petite woman, in a long, black velvet skirt, with piercing brown eyes.

With Helen's permission, he met her again, and they became friends, talking for hours about shared thoughts, philosophies, and idealisms. They became lovers and embarked on a long distance relationship that saw one or the other of them flying across the country every couple of months.

Returning from one of his frequent trips, he found another bill from Revenue Canada, for a much smaller sum than the original, but still far too much. Bills and final notices from other creditors were stacked on his desk. He, finally, admitted defeat and declared bankruptcy.

A few weeks later, Ken's father died, with his family by his side. Ken sat on the edge of his father's bed, watching his heart giving out, thinking back to the time he had perched on the edge of his grandfather's bed – two men he had loved – two powerful men – both gone – both with him still.

He was exhausted. While Ron carved his decoys, Ken poured his heart out to him. He was worn. He was interested only in an early discharge from bankruptcy. The court documents stated that the collapse of the trust company was not his doing and that, in fact, he was instrumental in starting the police investigation into the company's wrongdoing. The courts set an early date for his bankruptcy discharge and Ken began to relax.

One morning, Ken woke to the jarring voice of the announcer as the radio alarm went off. He lay on his back, eyes closed. Suddenly, his eyes flew open. He listened, first to the weather. The weather was recorded in numbers. Then the stock market report – the stock market was reported in numbers. Then the traffic report – the traffic jams were estimated in numbers. Everything was numbers. He made connections. How could he not have seen it before? "Wait a minute! I've been trying to get politics and art and philosophy out to the public using the wrong language. It's numbers! We live in a society that quantifies everything!"

His years of trying to tell his story, his frustration, his aggravation – it was nothing – of no consequence! He had the answer. All he had to do was paint the world's largest portrait – and it would be a portrait, not a painting.

In our society, a portrait is of a person or creature, usually a human creature. The Inuit see their land as mother and father. Therefore, if I paint this giant picture of their land – what I see as the centrepiece of their life – I will be painting their mother and their father. Thus it is a portrait and not a painting – not a landscape.

He visualized the project and a smile spread across his face.

So where does this idea go? This project will have to be done in the style of a grand opera, laced with liberal doses of the magician and the combined spirits of Michelangelo, P.T. Barnum, and Flo Ziegfeld. It will have to be done in magnificent, outrageous, and annoying magnitude. If I were to do that here in Vancouver, would it work? It became very clear to me that the answer was no. When you get here, there is no here. Vancouver is a figment – it does not exist. Where would I do it then? And another moment of utter clarity came to me – Toronto of course – downtown Canada. That is where the head offices are, all the key families, all the key money, all the key power and all the banks. Toronto is where the decisions are made. Ottawa is just another figment. Ottawa and Vancouver get their orders from Toronto. Why on earth hadn't I figured all this out a long time ago?

Before leaving for Toronto, Ken's bankruptcy was discharged. His discharge stated that he had been attempting to earn money, for years, to spend on projects that would bring attention to the plight of the Inuit. The money was specifically a means to an end. The discharge went on to say that the causes for his bankruptcy were out of his hands.

He left the courtroom free of the cloud that had shadowed his life for five years. In 1980 he sold his belongings and moved to Toronto, where he rented the top floor of an old house in "little Italy" on Blackthorne Avenue near St. Clair. Marsha introduced him to Henri Amar, who had a framing shop in Vaughn, on the northern border of Toronto, and who could stretch canvases for him. One day, while they were working together, Henri asked Ken to go into business with him and help him with sales.

Ken declined. He was busy painting and re-establishing a rapport with his son. Saturdays belonged to Michael who was now nine years old. They took long meandering walks, during which they talked about every imaginable subject and built a strong relationship based on the confidences they shared.

The other six days of the week, Ken painted and sold his paintings to the public on the installment plan and occasionally took long, thoughtful walks around the city. During one of those treks he found himself on the shores of Lake Ontario, looking back at the city skyline, a hodgepodge of steel and glass monoliths. The tallest of the shiny rectangles was a white slab of stone. He walked toward it until he arrived at an imposing plaza. In the marble floored lobby he approached the reception desk.

"Who owns this building?" he asked.

"Olympia and York," the woman told him.

"Who owns Olympia and York?"

"The Reichmann family."

Ken thanked the woman, and wandered around the lobby, gazing at the marble walls that rose three stories high. The smaller walls were hung with tapestries. A menorah occupied the largest wall.

When he next saw Henri, he mentioned his visit to First Canadian Place and the large bare wall. It was the perfect place for a painting, he said – a painting of the Arctic.

"They don't buy paintings," Henri said.

"What do you mean they don't buy paintings?"

"Just that – they don't buy paintings. Did you see any paintings there?"

"No. I saw a giant menorah on the eastern wall."

"That's right – and on the other walls you saw tapestries. Everyone has tried to sell them paintings. They don't buy paintings."

"Why don't they buy paintings?"

Henri shrugged.

Ken researched the Reichmanns, coming up with scant information. They were Orthodox Jews who originally came from Eastern Europe and for a time had lived in Valencia, his mother's home.

When they immigrated to Canada, and settled in Toronto, they founded a tile company and then became real estate developers. Their flagship building was First Canadian Place, the tallest building in the Commonwealth. Ken talked about them and gnawed on the information he had like a dog on a marrow bone.

"Forget about them and come into business with me," Henri said. "Why try to sell paintings to people who don't buy paintings?"

Ken finally looked at the books, which revealed that the frame factory was struggling to stay alive.

"You can buy half," Henri offered.

"Why would I buy half of a sinking ship?" Ken asked. But, he agreed to become a partner. Perhaps, it would be a good idea to be seen as a businessman instead of an artist. He might be viewed with more respect and given more credibility. He would buy his half with orders for frames. Henri agreed to build Ken a studio across the top of the factory.

Within six months, Ken had paid off the fifteen thousand dollars he owed and moved into his new studio where he began work on two large Arctic paintings – one for First Canadian Place, measuring sixteen by sixteen feet, and one measuring slightly less, for the new international airport planned for Yellowknife.

Marsha said, "You have no money and you're going to create two giant paintings that no one wants to buy. It makes no sense!"

It made sense to him, even though he had no explanation to give. He had learned to listen to his inner voice, and it was telling him to paint the canvases. Nobody's doubts could stop him. He was going to show the world!

The new studio was too small for the massive paintings and so were all the conventional canvases. He joined four lengthened panels with invisible seams by bevelling the wood, squeezing the stretchers together with clamps and creating knife-edges that melded together. Through painstaking experimentation with a torque wrench, Vise-Grips and a canvas stretcher he created a unique design that produced perfect tension on every square inch of canvas. When the tension was perfect, he hosed the canvas down to shrink it. One of his first canvases exploded, and one flew off spinning like a propeller, but he finally got it right and made a sixteen by sixteen and a twelve by fourteen foot canvas.

He was still mystified by his inability to sell paintings of the Arctic. One day, while he was driving on Steeles Road near the Allen Expressway a question leapt into his mind. "If you were limited to one image – one object from all your experiences in the Arctic, and that was all you were allowed to portray, what would it be?"

Inukshuk!

Ken was stopped at a red light. The light turned green, and he sat frozen behind the wheel. Car horns honked behind him. The sound penetrated as though through a thick fog.

"My God! How obtuse have I been? The obvious is so hard to see. The Inukshuk – the quintessential image – the one thing that speaks to the way of life of those people in the far north!"

In a daze, he drove to a nearby park. "The Inukshuk. Can I actually verbalize what it represents? If one can imagine an ancient people, very small numbers, a few families at a time travelling great distances across the land – a very difficult land – and coming upon these directional markers indicating where to go. But from all that I have gleaned, they were there before the Inuit came. I heard the elders say that the Tunit – who were giants with children's minds – built the very large ones, which were a different shape. Most of the Inuksuit were small – they were probably hunting devices. The Inuksuit are a language written on the land."

The Inuksuit are everything.

He drove back to the studio and started painting Arctic scenes dominated by the Inuksuit. For the first time people began to look at the Arctic paintings with interest. One day, he overheard a conversation between Henri and a customer, in the frame factory below his studio on the mezzanine.

"I think Kirkby's a nice guy but I think it's bullshit. I don't think Canada has any of these things. I think he's invented this as a marketing ploy."

Interesting. He asked questions, and confirmed that people thought he was an excellent promoter who had invented stories, of a faraway place, that were designed to bring attention to him and his work.

To overcome this doubt and scepticism, I realized I was going to have to pull off something on an absolutely massive scale. Scale played a role in it. If I was going to be seen as a promoter – fine – let's go with it. Let's not fight it. People want the artist to be peculiar. So I decided, fine, I'm going to play this to the hilt. I am going to be a social engineer. As Stalin said, "The engineer of human souls".

The painting for First Canadian Place built and built in his mind until his vision seemed almost real. He knew that one day the image would explode from his mind onto canvas and when it did, it would be perfect.

12

A Triumph

Henri scoffed at his plans. Where would he sell these huge paintings and furthermore, given he had never sold his smaller Arctic paintings, what made him think the public would find the larger ones any more palatable? Marsha agreed with Henri and suggested that Ken stick to normal paintings.

Ken was certain of his inner voice. One day, Rocco Pannese, a short, round man with an infectious smile, walked into the framing factory. Rocco was involved in the Columbus Centre on Lawrence Avenue – a large Italian-Canadian meeting place – part of which he was trying to turn into an art gallery.

Ken was most interested, and Rocco toured him through the centre, a beautifully designed building that housed tennis courts, sports halls, a library, and recreational facilities. The centre had been conceived by the second generation Italians who had prospered in their parents' adopted country. The building was their gift to the city. Unfortunately, when the children of the original founders took over the management of the Columbus Centre, they created an unwieldy bureaucracy.

Ken told Rocco about his interest in the Arctic and his plan for two immense Arctic paintings.

"But the Reichmanns don't buy paintings," Rocco said.

Ken threw up his hands. "What the hell is all this about? How does anyone know they don't buy paintings? Who started saying that and who repeated it – over and over – until it became an established fact? I'm going to create a painting for them."

Ken caught himself and took a breath. He asked how he could help with the gallery. Who had had the original vision for the Columbus Centre and was he still alive?

Joseph D. Carrier, Rocco said, and yes, he was alive.

"Do you know him?

"Yes."

"Can you get hold of him?"

"Yes."

"Can we meet him then?"

"Why?"

"To tell him that his great vision has been shat upon from a great height."

"I'm not sure that's a good idea."

"I think it's a very good idea. We'll tell him that and then we'll tell him about your vision – your dream. You are pursuing those same visions and ideas that started this centre and the job is not yet finished."

Rocco reluctantly made the appointment. Mr. Carrier was a bright, charming man in his eighties with snowy hair and a trim white moustache.

Ken told him how wonderful his idea had been, but the vision had somehow been diluted. Rocco was the one to revive the vision, he said, with an idea that was in keeping with the original dream. "A key element that is missing is a major art gallery – a gallery that will bring in works from other countries as well as showcasing the work of Canadian artists. It will put the finishing touch on this magnificent place."

"I like that idea," Carrier said. "How odd that we didn't think of that at the time."

"Yes, it's interesting that you didn't. When you think of it, Michelangelo, da Vinci, Raphael, and so many other great artists were all Italians. If you go to Italy, great architecture and great art are everywhere."

Carrier pondered the proposal for a couple of days. "I love the idea," he said when they met again. "Sometimes we have to be woken up from our slumber. You're right – our job isn't done yet. We will have a major gallery. I've spoken to my friends and it's true, the new generation is not exactly on track."

Rocco and Ken must design the gallery, he said, keeping in mind that it had to be the finest in the city. Then, he asked Ken about his paintings and listened attentively to his story. "Does anyone care about the Arctic?" he asked.

"I do," Ken said. "I want to tell that story. I want to tell people what's happening there."

"And what is happening there?"

Ken told him, describing the horrendous conditions the Inuit endured, both physical and spiritual.

"It sounds like hell," he said.

"Yes, hell mixed with heaven."

"And what do you propose to do about it?"

"Tell the world."

"And what good will that do?"

"It will rob them of their innocence and they will have no excuse."

"Is that what you have done to me?"

"Yes it is. Now – what are you going to do with what I have told you?"

"You were brought up by a very old people, weren't you? This sort of passion doesn't come from this generation."

"I was. I was raised in an ancient place by somewhat ancient people."

"So, what do you propose I do?"

"I propose you find out whether I am telling you the truth."

As he and Rocco left, Ken turned and said, "By the way, I think the gallery should be called The Joseph D. Carrier Gallery."

Carrier smiled. "Of course."

Once work on the gallery began, Ken and Carrier met frequently. When Carrier discovered that Ken's paternal grandmother, Constanze Inocente, was from Genoa, he declared that the connection made Ken Italian, and a member of the community. With Carrier's urging, Ken joined the Canadian Italian Business and Professional Association, a dynamic and diverse group that included doctors, lawyers, carpenters, and bricklayers.

As opening night of the Carrier Gallery approached, Ken suggested a show of his Arctic paintings, on a massive scale.

"You haven't sold any and you want to start off with a huge explosion? Rocco asked. "What if it fails?"

"You're sounding like my mother. What if…"

"I love the idea, but what a risk!"

"When you jump off a cliff, make sure you do it head first. Be honourable. Do it big."

What about the cost?" Rocco asked. "Who will pay for it?"

"All we have to do is commit to the vision and the rest will follow."

Ken rented the warehouse next door to the framing factory, a space large enough for his Arctic paintings. He painted the ceiling black, the walls white, and the floor battleship gray. Then, he went to work on the giant paintings. Rocco focussed on the show. They needed a sponsor, Ken said. The show had to be unique. Canadians didn't care about the Arctic so everything about it had to be special.

"If Canadians don't care, why are we doing this?" Rocco asked.

"Because this story has to be told," Ken said, explaining that the entire saga had begun on a beach in Portugal. And that's when it struck him – Portugal would be their sponsor.

He wrote a letter to Dr. Antonio Tanger Correia, the Portuguese Consul General.

Correia called. "Mr. Kirkby. As if you had to explain yourself! What a delight to get your letter. We must have lunch!"

They met for a lunch that extended into dinner. Ken explained that he wanted the invitations for the exhibition to come from the Portuguese people, meaning the Consul General and the Portuguese Ambassador to Canada. "I'm not asking for money," he said. "I simply want you to issue the invitations."

Correia agreed and suggested that David Crombie, the mayor of Toronto, also join them as a sponsor.

"But what is the underlying reason for this?" he asked. "Why do you want the Portuguese government to do this?"

"I love Portugal and I love the people," Ken said. "Unfortunate circumstances caused us to leave, but the good times were still the good times. The people are still wonderful, and the country is still beautiful: but underneath all that, if a government officially does the inviting, every embassy, and every consulate, has to react. Consequently, the Canadians have to react, and what I wish to do is split the atom in such a way as to cause a chain reaction – one that forces my government to pay attention because of the force of will of others."

"So – you are a politician," the ambassador said.

"No, not really," he said. "I am a strategist."

Ken was preparing for the exhibit when Ehor Boyanowsky, a professor of criminology at Simon Fraser University, called. Ken had met him at Peter Hope Lake and through his urging had joined the Steelhead Society of Canada.

Ehor had bad news. The Caroline Mines, in the Coquihalla area, had for many years been storing arsenic and cyanide, used for processing metals, in tailing ponds behind large dams. Flying over those ponds, members of the Steelhead Society had noticed cracks in the structures. Letters, to both the mining company and the government, had been studiously ignored. A recent heavy snow pack and a sudden melt, combined with torrential spring rains, had destroyed the dams; spilling toxic chemicals into the Coquihalla River, renowned for its steelhead trout. All life in the river had been destroyed.

"Please help," Ehor pleaded.

"What can I do?"

"Could you do a major drawing of a steelhead, and a fisherman, and a river? We need a very special painting."

Ken covered a wood panel with many coats of gesso, alternating horizontal with vertical layers. Then, he drew a pencil through the gesso, creating an almost three-dimensional and lifelike effect. He completed "The Return of the Wild One" in twenty-four hours, then bought a plane ticket and flew it to Vancouver, where Ehor met him at the airport.

A printing house volunteered to reproduce the painting and run off hundreds of copies at no charge. The society had hired a team of lawyers while its members manned the telephones, repeating the story of the tragedy to the media.

Ten days later, Ken flew back to Toronto and, two days after that, moved his things into Marsha's apartment. She supported him without question, yet she questioned everything he did. The subject of his finances was constantly on her mind. What did he intend to do with his life? Why do everything on such a large scale – such an unaffordable scale?

Ask Walt Disney why he did things on a large scale, Ken suggested. Or she could ask the Rolling Stones or the Maple Leaf hockey team. "Those people who paint pretty little pictures in their little studios aren't going to amount to a fart in a windstorm. If I'm going to do things, then they're going to be done in a way that is commensurate with the power of my ideas. I'm going to do my ideas justice. If it mangles me in the process, so be it. But to live other than as who I am, and the way I am, is simply to be living in a matchbox – and eventually becoming mentally unwell. If doing it my way isn't suitable, you tell me."

"What is driving this?" she asked one day. "There's something behind this and I'm missing it!"

No, he said, she wasn't missing anything. He had told her so much, but never about his life in the Arctic or his passion for the land and its people. When he told her the story she gaped at him. Why had he never spoken to her of this – this most important and pivotal story of his life?

"It's been so difficult for me," he said. "The pictures that are in my soul and in my mind of what happened in the Arctic – the things that happened to me and to those who I so love and respect – they won't leave me alone. These pictures sear me. To talk about it is difficult and painful. It's also unbelievably frustrating, because at the end of the conversation I've put people off and they invariably say, 'Who the fuck do you think you are! How do you think you can fix this?' At the end of it all, it amounts to little more than entertainment, and I have never had any tolerance for using the misery of others for someone else's entertainment."

"I wish I had known all of this before. It would have explained so much."

"Well, that's me and that's where I'm going."

"At any cost?"

"Any cost."

"On a scale of things, where do I fit in relative to the Arctic?"

"Painting and the Arctic are number one, two, and three – you're four."

"I've never met anyone like you before. I think you have delusions of grandeur."

"Relative to who? Relative to the average soul walking the earth – constrained, thin-lipped, pinch-souled, angry and utterly neutralized? Compared to one of those, do I have delusions of grandeur? If you want to call it that, okay. You can call it what you want – it doesn't make any difference. The fact is, that before I die, I will accomplish what I'm after. As Francisco said in Portugal, 'when you're dying, hell is not having lived the life that was yours to live'. That has never left me. I hear it every day and I'm going to live that life I was meant to live, no matter what."

The show at the Columbus Centre grew in scope. Marsha and Rocco were alternately enthusiastic and appalled at the size of the project. Joseph Carrier on the other hand, came to Ken's studio, periodically, and smiled and nodded approval at everything he saw.

That there was still no money to stage the show brought Rocco to the edge of nervous exhaustion. Ken's reassurances did not fill him with encouragement. "If you're willing to get on this vehicle with me, I'm going to take you for a ride like you've never had – and I will bring you back. You might be bruised but you won't be dead."

Ken outlined a poster campaign to take place in three phases. The posters were to be museum quality: so beautiful that people would rip them off walls in order to take them home and frame them. Invitations, under the auspices of the Portuguese Embassy, were to be printed on the finest paper.

"I don't have any money!" Rocco cried.

"Neither do I," Ken said. "And you have more money than I do."

He refused to compromise. He bartered paintings. He found a printer who agreed to run off fifteen thousand posters, in three lots of five thousand each, and he hired young people to put them up strategically – in Rosedale where the old money lived, and in the financial district downtown. He had flyers printed and distributed to thousands of homes in the city.

He scanned the Toronto Star and the Globe and Mail until he found a journalist with a style he liked. "I have a story of a young boy who grew up on a beach in Portugal, and one day he woke up and he was in the Arctic," he told her. "The story is much better than Sir John Franklin's."

Sharon Singer listened and wrote in her stenographer's pad for seven hours. Then she called her editor. "I think I have a story you're going to love."

The article started a landslide. Other newspapers called, and a CBC crew arrived at the studio. The broadcast caught the eye of Gary McLaren – an amiable, articulate man – whose popular talk show was aired every Sunday morning from Kitchener-Waterloo. He arrived at Ken's studio one day with a cameraman, who filmed while the two men talked.

Two weeks after the show aired, Gary asked for a follow-up. Both shows were so popular that segments with Ken became regular features of the show.

The media coverage drew the attention of a tall, quiet businessman named Irving Shakter, who began to drop into the studio once every couple of weeks to watch Ken paint and to listen to his stories.

"There's something awfully big going on inside of you," he said when they met.

"What makes you think that?" Ken asked.

"I have a sense for it," Irving said. "I used to play hockey, and I could anticipate where the puck was. I was a very good hockey player. I have the same feeling about you as I had about where that puck would be."

"I want to help you," he said one day over lunch.

"I'd appreciate all the help I can get," Ken said. "There hasn't been a helluva a lot of it at this point."

"Yes, so I gather."

Virgil Pires, a tall Portuguese man, became another frequent visitor. "You come from my country," he said when he introduced himself. "You're almost Portuguese. I love what is in the papers and on TV. You talk about my country with so much love.

"I wasn't born in Portugal," Ken said. "But I think that part of my soul is Portuguese."

The collection of paintings for the show grew, most of them featuring an Inukshuk standing sentinel over the stark Arctic landscape. Irving and Virgil visited almost daily, moving the paintings around, discussing the merits of each one, and arguing about who should purchase which. Virgil liked to say proudly, "He's Portuguese, you know."

Irving argued, "Portuguese, my ass. He's no more Portuguese than I am. He's a mongrel – Danish, Irish, Spanish, French, Italian, Jewish grandmothers, Christian grandfathers – grew up in Portugal – I tell you, he's a mongrel!"

"Oh no!" Virgil protested. "This is brilliant! This is magnificent! It was written in heaven! This man has a place in heaven!"

Ken painted, working in a world he was entering for the first time. These visions of the Arctic had been bottled up inside him for years, and a great dam had burst open, spilling out a Niagara of creativity. The faster he painted, the more powerful the pictures.

The week before the show, Irving and Virgil began to choose the paintings they wanted, arguing good-naturedly over several of them. "You can't have them all," Ken said. "You can only have twenty paintings!"

"Between us or each?" Virgil asked.

Were they serious? Ken wondered, beginning to feel excited. "Each," Ken said.

He had completed ninety-six canvases. Virgil and Irving fell on them with the glee of schoolboys who had just been told they could choose a dozen of any sort of candy in the store. They argued, talked, and wrangled possessively over one or two of the larger paintings, until each had a pile of twenty. "How much?" they wanted to know.

Ken forced his voice to remain calm. He studied each painting and methodically wrote the price on a slip of paper. The forty canvases totalled eighty-five thousand dollars.

Neither man flinched. Instead, they insisted on a celebration, and over a bottle of good wine, Ken explained that their paintings would be part of the exhibit – and he recalled one of Alex Fraser's pieces of advice. "Make sure they can see the sold stickers from two blocks away."

The next day, he purchased dozens of the type of red stickers lawyers used as seals at the bottoms of contracts. All those years he had tried to sell just one painting of the far north – now he had sold forty in two hours – to two men out of several billion men on the planet.

He decided to keep Rocco, who was teetering on the verge of a nervous breakdown every time he saw the bills coming in from caterers, florists, and the liquor store, in suspense.

When he told Marsha he had sold some paintings, she asked, "How did you do it?"

"I told my stories about the Arctic and why I was doing this."

"I hope that one day you will be able to sell a painting without having to tell a story."

"Why?" Ken asked, feeling both shocked and curious by the statement.

"Paintings are supposed to speak to you quietly," she said. "You shouldn't be a used car salesman."

"Everything is a story," he said, biting down on his anger. "It's the only thing we have. Every culture on earth has had only one thing – stories. You love the movies, you love novels, you love magazine articles – they're all stories. What's wrong with paintings being stories? Do you think van Gogh and Michelangelo and da Vinci and Picasso would be known today if it wasn't for stories?"

Marsha opened her mouth and he waved his hand at her. "No – don't go into this. We're not going any farther with this."

The night before the opening, he paid a team of young people to spray paint bright yellow Inuksuit on the streets leading to the Columbus Centre and, finally, after he'd painted late into the night for eight months, the day of the exhibition dawned. "I hope there isn't a traffic jam," he said to Rocco, while laughing and praying there would be. Four or five hundred visitors would make the show a triumph.

He arrived at the gallery early to oversee the hanging of the paintings, fuelling himself on black coffee and adrenaline. At about eleven o'clock a well-dressed couple walked into the gallery. The couple complimented Ken on his work, purchased nine paintings and left as quietly as they had come. Ken's excitement mounted.

At seven-thirty, just before the doors opened, Ken put big red stickers on the sold paintings, taking quiet delight in watching Rocco's jaw drop. The Portuguese Ambassador and Consul General were among the first to arrive. The Italian contingent followed on their heels. Mayor David Crombie was next and then the Federal Minister of Culture. Delegations from various foreign consulates and embassies arrived along with Toronto's glitterati. By eight o'clock, the police had arrived to direct the traffic, and Ken's prayed-for car jam stretched down every artery leading to the gallery.

With the gallery jammed, Rocco called the crowd to order and introduced Dr. Antonio Tanger Correia who began his speech with, "A man came to my office and told me that he loved my country and he loved my countrymen. How could a man not fall in love with that? He may not have Portuguese blood in his veins, but I can tell you that his soul is one hundred percent Portuguese".

The Portuguese Ambassador spoke next, then the Mayor, and then Lily Munroe, the Minister of Culture. It was while Ken was standing beside the improvised podium that he noticed the video cameras from both major Canadian networks, as well as several local stations.

Red stickers continued to sprout on the walls until all ninety-six paintings were sold. As the evening progressed Rocco's face became almost as red as the sold signs. "We're safe!" he whispered to Ken.

"You were never not safe," he said. "I'm the guy paying – why were you so worried?"

When the last of the guests departed, Ken led a couple dozen of his guests, including his son, Michael, to the restaurant downstairs. While the others ate, he answered their questions. After all this time they finally wanted to know about the Arctic. They cared. They were interested. They listened.

Finally, he had the stage for telling his stories – how it had all happened, why it had happened, where it had come from, and what was driving it. He didn't waste one second eating. He poured out his heart.

Later that night, he and Marsha walked into their house and sank exhausted on the couch. "How do you feel?" she asked.

"I don't even know where to begin," he said. "I feel ecstatic. I feel profoundly moved. I feel feelings that I don't have words for, in combinations that I have never imagined. If you could travel the biggest roller coaster in the world… at a million miles an hour… it would not equal what I feel. I'm going to need time to sort out what I feel… but right now I don't want to sort it out… I just want to feel it."

"I would sure like to know what's driving you," she said. "What is this thing? It's amazing! How did you know it would work?"

"I didn't even think about. It's not something to think about – it's something to do. We think ourselves out of doing things. We scare ourselves. If it feels good in my gut – if I get a hundred billion little ice crystals falling there, that's all there is to it – it's right – and I haven't a clue why. In time maybe I'll try to explain it to you but if I tried to do that now, I feel I would disintegrate into a trillion particles and blow away like a wisp of smoke. I am so close to the edge, I don't dare go any farther."

The next morning, he found Rocco standing in the middle of the gallery gazing around at the red stickers with an enormous grin on his face.

"There are all kinds of people here," he said, grabbing Ken's arm. "They want to talk to you, and I told them to go down to the restaurant."

The tables were filled with media people, and Ken spent the morning answering questions. When the last of the journalists left, Rocco handed him an envelope that had arrived in the morning mail. The address was written in old-fashioned curlicue script and inside was a card and a note from Salvador Grimaldi, a landscape architect, congratulating him on the event and on his magnificent paintings. "I would appreciate a call," the note said. "I would love to meet you. We have crossed paths many times although we have never met. Please call."

Ken dialled the number and they met at the gallery later that day. Salvador Grimaldi sparkled – his eyes twinkled, his smile stretched across his cheeks and he bounced when he walked. He was like a boiling kettle, bubbling over with life.

He explained that he had once done aerial surveys of the Arctic and had flown across the land many times. On occasion, he had noticed groups of people travelling across the land. He had been told that they were Eskimos on the move, and a white man who had gone native was travelling with them.

"That was you!" Salvador exclaimed. "And I've wondered about you for years. And here you are with all these Inuksuit. This is the first time I've heard anybody in the southern part of this country talk about them or describe them, and here you have a world full of them. I just had to meet you!"

They talked all afternoon. Ken told Salvador about his ambition to get his message out to the public, and Salvador told him about his work as a landscape architect. The Reichmann family was one of his largest clients.

"The Reichmanns?" Ken asked.

"Yes," Salvador nodded.

"Would you mind if we returned to the subject of the Reichmanns another time?" Ken asked, arranging to meet him again in a couple of days. He wanted time to consider how to use this information and to plan his next steps.

In the morning, while he was working on the Reichmann painting and pondered Salvador's relationship with the family, Henri banged into the studio shouting, "I've had enough! I'm selling the company!"

Rocco suggested that Ken buy him out and hire someone to run the framing studio for him. He introduced him to Diane Lyle, a young woman in her twenties who had grown up on a farm and wanted to make a name for herself in the city. Ken agreed with Rocco. She was just the sort of enthusiastic, no-nonsense, ambitious person who could make the business thrive. Ken met with his lawyer, David Freeman, drew up the papers and purchased the framing company for fifteen thousand dollars.

The media continued to be fascinated by him, the way an audience is mesmerized by a performer who embarrasses himself inadvertently, on a talk show. Ken had stepped so far outside the boundaries, had put on a show so over the top, right down to the Inuksuit painted on the streets, that the media haunted his studio just to see what would happen next. Ken continued to feed them quotable lines that seemed to come effortlessly to his lips, but that he had, in fact, been practising for months and years.

But, tidbits wouldn't feed them forever. Eventually they would want to stop nibbling and indulge in another meal – and the next banquet would have to be bigger and better than the last.

He met Salvador Grimaldi for lunch again at Boccacio Restaurant, in the Columbus Centre, and once again the architect came bounding into the room, perfectly dressed in understated, expensive clothing, his eyes sparkling, and his smile spreading goodwill around the room. Ken had a plan.

He told him that his next project had to be an even larger success than the last, and described the two immense paintings he was currently working on: one was a sixteen by sixteen foot canvas, featuring an Inukshuk set against an enormous white cloud, that was intended for the Reichmanns.

Why the Reichmanns? Salvador asked.

"They are a very prominent family which the media and the public have become very interested in," Ken said. "They're secretive and almost impossible to approach. I've been studying them, and the information is very sparse. I know they spent time in Valencia after leaving Eastern Europe, and then they spent time in Morocco, and then from Morocco they moved to Toronto: they started a tile business that immediately turned into a raging success. Then, they went into high-end real estate development, in which they have achieved even greater success. They are an intriguing family – and just what I need. I need a Lorenzo de Medici."

"I want to get to a place where other people cannot go. I want to sell a painting to a man who doesn't buy paintings and see it hung in the foyer of the tallest building in the British Commonwealth – and have that become a media event – even though they don't like the media, that is what I am after. What do you know about the Reichmanns that you feel comfortable passing on to me? I get the idea you're pretty close to them."

Salvador allowed that he was close to Albert Reichmann, who preferred to be called Mr. Albert. He had done his corporate landscaping and was currently working on his personal property. "He's a prince," Salvador said. "A merchant prince. He is a man of many talents, and I find it interesting that you would have, instinctively, known that.'

Ken took Salvador to the studio to see the Reichmann and Yellowknife Airport paintings, in progress. When he unlocked the door and switched on the bank of lights, Salvador froze. The larger painting was nearing completion while the other was only half finished. Even in their incomplete state they overwhelmed the senses. While Salvador filled his eyes, Ken fetched a couple of glasses and poured wine. He handed a glass to Salvador and they sat, gazing at the canvases and talking about the Arctic. Although Salvador had explored that vast land mostly from the air, he had also touched down in remote settlements enough times to have formed an opinion, of the way the Inuit lived and were treated. He agreed with Ken that they were being brutalized. He also agreed that trying to get people to pay attention to things so far distant was a near impossible task.

The Reichmanns were a good choice of patron, Salvador said. "I like the way you think and I like the way you do things. You're exactly what this town needs – this constipated town needs an artist with balls to shake the joint up. Leave it with me – I'm going to talk to Mr. Albert."

Ken painted day and night, sometimes fainting from exhaustion. With the exception of Diane, everyone made demands on his time. She was doing well with the framing shop but her real fascination was with Ken and his stories, and she became his willing assistant, always happy to do more for him. So, just before he had to fly to Vancouver again, he suggested that while he was gone she should blow up all the articles from the newspapers to poster size, frame them, and cover the walls of the shop with them.

Ehor Boyanowski picked him up at the airport and brought him to his home in Deep Cove. There, he crawled into bed and slept for twenty hours. When he woke, Ehor brought him up to date on the Steelhead Society's battle with the mining company. They had turned the issue over to the fledgling Sierra Legal Defence Fund, which was pressing the government, and the company, to undertake the expensive remedial work of restoring the river they had polluted.

Other environmental issues were equally pressing. At James Bay, the Quebec Government planned to build an enormous hydroelectric project, called Big Whale, that was drawing loud protests from both the Inuit and the Cree population. The proposed dam would flood a vast area of land, destroying the several million caribou that migrated through it each year – the largest herd in the world. The damming of such an immense amount of water would also cause a concentration of mercury as well as a significant climatic change. On the West Coast, the British Columbia government proposed to allow Alcan to extend its hydroelectric power generating facility at Kitimat, another important wilderness area.

The leadership of the Steelhead Society asked the membership to spearhead a coalition of groups that would bring media attention to the fact that these massive projects were intended to generate many billions of dollars by selling electricity to the United States. The membership approved the project, and Ken began work on a painting that would be the centrepiece of posters and pamphlets. The slogan, "Stewardship from Sea to Sea to Sea" hung over a pale blue sky with a distant horizon, a thin band of water, and in the foreground, enormous rocks anchoring a majestic Inukshuk. Matthew Cooncome, the Grand Chief of the Cree, welcomed the support and called on other First Nations across the country to join forces.

An early supporter of the project was Yvonne Chounard, the founder of the Patagonia Company, who purchased Ken's original painting, for a very large sum of money – that went directly into the war chest.

13

The Dream of Nunavut

Back in Toronto, he pondered the persistent problem of disseminating his Arctic message – and he recalled his insight on the morning his alarm clock woke him – and he suddenly realized that all news was numbers.

I'd learned that in North America everything is quantified. Everything is numbers. That's how people talk to each other. So never mind talking about art – never mind talking about politics. Let's see what happens if we think about all of this just in terms of numbers. So, given that everything has to be bigger and bigger – like the Reichmann venture that I knew in my guts was going to happen – then after that huge painting, then what? Where do I go then?

I let my mind wander, and I didn't try to rein it in. Quantification – a giant painting – super giant! No – super, super giant! How about on the scale of the Sistine Chapel ceiling? Yes, that was right. And what would it be of? Well, a portrait of the Arctic. How about a portrait of the Northwest Passage? The arrogance of Europeans, who wouldn't even stop for two minutes to question the people who built the Inuksuit – people who would have told them where to find the passage – those Europeans who had to go and find it all by themselves. They didn't wear fur clothes and they weren't savages so they must have been superior, yet they all killed themselves – a cost of so many lives and huge sums of money and they didn't find the Northwest Passage. Okay – portrait of the Northwest Passage. And yes – a portrait – that's what it would be. For the Inuit, the land is mother and the sky is father, so, I am painting a portrait of the mother and the father. And, of course, the people in the south will say, "No, it's a landscape!" and we can get into a rhubarb about it, and I can use that and point out they're goddammed ignorant. They don't even know the reason behind this painting, where it comes from or on whose behalf it's being painted. I could see all sorts of things taking shape here.

Where would it go? Obviously it would be too big to sell, and there would be no point putting it in a church because there was no church big enough. Besides, no one goes to church any more. Where to put it? People aren't religious. Where do people go? Wait! Canadians are religious! Hockey is their religion! Hockey arenas are right across the country. Hockey is Canada's reli-

gion. A painting that goes in hockey arenas, that is toured across the country from one end to the other, telling the story.

Then a whole flood of ideas and memories came into my mind crystal clear. Grandmother doing her dance and her song in the winter – becoming mesmerized and overcome by heat and emotion – going outside and the Northern Lights roaring overhead – and she came out and stood beside me and put her arm in mine and told me that those were the spirits of her ancestors dancing. And she sensed the difficulties I was having over the loss of the two women that I had loved so profoundly. She had said, "It's a good thing to let them go and dance".

During her song and her story, there had been the need of an Isumataq – a person or an object in whose presence wisdom might show itself. The painting would be called Isumataq. And the dream driving all of this was Nunavut.

That was the moment in which the whole thing exploded in one clear vision. It must have been working quietly in my brain all this time and now here it was – all together. Now it poured out and it all came together like a jigsaw puzzle – every piece moved into its proper slot.

Covered in sweat, Ken's body shook with nervous energy. His whole being thrilled and he felt himself to be outside his body – completely outside space and time. The vision was so clear, so compelling, that it possessed him. He knew it would come to own him – night and day – and he didn't care. He gave himself up to it. He paced back and forth, details of Isumataq whirling in his mind and dropping into place like numbers on a slot machine.

He drove home that night with a new excitement coursing through him. When he told Marsha he was going to create a giant painting on the scale of the Sistine Chapel, she smiled and shook her head. In the morning he told Diane who began to plan a studio renovation to accommodate such an enormous painting. While they were hunched over the sketch, Salvador appeared in the doorway, a bottle of brandy in his hand, and a smile on his face.

"I have the equipment, the idea, the staff, and the availability of rock. How would you like a giant Inukshuk in your studio?"

Three days later, Salvador pulled up in a new Saab, followed by a flatbed truck – groaning under the weight of massive blocks of granite – and two extended cab pickups loaded with burly men. At two in the morning, after hours of heavy labour, a seven-foot tall Inukshuk towered over the studio. Salvador waved his arm at it like a magician wielding a wand. "There. Is it to your liking?"

"It's perfect," Ken said.

Salvador's next project was an Inukshuk at the Columbus Centre! Dragging Ken and Joseph Carrier to the lobby, he gestured grandly, "This is where the Inukshuk will stand. And you'll need to make a very large painting for that wall."

Carrier agreed. "I think you're right – a large painting right there. I think you should get going and paint it."

Then, he took Ken's arm and steered him into a corner of the gallery. "You're going to need some money," he said.

"We did pretty well at the show."

"The way you go about things, there isn't enough money in the world."

Ken laughed. "You're probably right."

"If you made a million dollars a month, you'd be short four hundred thousand. So I'll tell you what I'm going to do. I'm going to pay you twenty-five hundred a month for this painting and for several other big ones. I know for sure there's never going to be enough money, but this way, at least you'll have something when things get crazy."

That day he received an invitation from the Italian Canadian Business and Professional Association requesting his services as a speaker at their next quarterly meeting. How many people could he expect at the dinner? He asked Rocco. At least eight hundred, Rocco said and he could expect them to be from every possible walk of life. He could expect workingmen and professionals and politicians. Jean Chrétien, the leader of the opposition, sometimes came to these events.

Here it was at last, his opportunity to say everything he had wanted to say and not to schoolchildren this time. He might be met with resounding indifference – or perhaps he would be able to touch them.

On the evening of the event, he sat at the head table on a raised dais, surveying a packed room. When the emcee introduced him, he stood, his blood pumping with adrenaline and caffeine, and launched into his story of the Arctic. Words poured out of him, and he dimly registered the fact that not one person was talking or looking away. A sea of faces stared up at him. The silence was absolute. Ken was outside his body again – outside time and space. He was possessed, as he had been by the vision of Isumataq. Whatever it was that took over his mind and body, he willingly surrendered to it.

When he came to the end, he thanked his audience for allowing him to speak and for giving him their time and attention. "If anybody should ask you, what was it that I was going on about, please tell them that these stories were the stories of a grandmother who told me to tell them to you."

The hall exploded. The audience leapt to its feet, clapping, whistling, and stamping its feet. Dazed, Ken stumbled to his chair.

"You're supposed to acknowledge them," Marsha said.

Dazed, Ken stood and waved, and a fresh salvo of applause thundered off the walls. Ken shivered. "You're soaking wet," Marsha whispered. Your hair – your clothes – you're completely wet!"

While Ken wiped his forehead, the Emcee quieted the crowd and announced that there would be a question and answer period. Ken made his way back to the lectern, thinking how odd it was that these hundreds of people who were watching him were sitting dry and comfortable in their seats while he was as wet as though he had just come in out of a torrential rainfall.

A young woman, who had been taking notes, rose and asked to hear more about the grandmothers. Ken answered her query in detail. When she was finished, she nodded to the young man beside her who stood, pushed a mop of hair off his broad forehead, and said, "Sir, don't you think that it's inappropriate to be telling other people's stories? I find it very strange that you would be telling these stories of Native people from the North. What's it to you?"

A chorus of boos reverberated in the hall. Ken hushed them to allow the young man to speak. "These Inuk – um – Inukshuks…"

"Actually," Ken said. "Inukshuk is one and Inuksuit is plural."

"Well these things – don't you think that using these things from other people's cultures is wrong-headed? Don't you think that's cultural appropriation?"

He continued, shouting through a hailstorm of catcalls. "Who's paying you to do this?"

"No one is paying me," Ken said. "This is what I want to do."

"Why?"

"I fell in love with these people in the Arctic called Inuit. They taught me a million things. They gave me a grand education, and they have been a blessing in my life. I fell in love with them and their land, and they asked me to give the stories of them and their world to you."

"Why don't they do it?"

"If you knew the story, I don't think you would ask that question. You're one of those ninety-nine percent of Canadians who don't know their own backyard, and you can't be a nation unless you know your own backyard. So, I'm trying to bring you stories in the old oral tradition – stories from afar, so that you know."

"Well, about these grandmothers – why are you so fascinated with them?"

"Who wouldn't be? They are the carriers of the past. If you want to know how things were, the grandmothers are going to tell you. It's called an oral tradition and we are cursed by not having one. We sit and watch television or listen to the radio – that's nothing. When you hear human beings tell you a story, of their lives in antiquity, that has power. So, I do two very old-fashioned things: I'm a cave painter, only I'm painting on canvas – and I'm attempting to be a storyteller."

"So, do you do everything the grandmothers tell you to do?"

"Absolutely," Ken said. "Don't you?"

At the end of the evening, Ken tried to find the young man again, but the press of the crowd overwhelmed him. He accepted congratulations, smiled, and shook hands as he fought his way to the exit and the cool air of the parking lot. He was achingly tired – more tired than he had ever been in his life. Marsha steered him to the car. "What the hell happened to you?" she asked. "Where did that talk come from? You were on fire! This is not the you that I know."

"I have no idea what I said."

"But you must know!"

"No – and it troubles me. I have no idea what the hell I said."

"What do you mean?"

"Just what I told you. Was it beautiful? Was it powerful? Was it strong?"

"More than that. But, what do you mean when you say you don't know what you said?"

"I'm telling you, I don't know what I said. I must have been in some sort of trance."

"You mean you were possessed?"

'I have no idea."

He fell into bed, closed his eyes, and felt a wave of contentment sweep over him. When he woke at eleven o'clock in the morning he felt an urge to laugh out loud. He had expended so much time and energy, to make money to do exactly what he had accomplished the night before – without spending a single penny.

When Ken arrived at his studio about an hour later, he walked into a party. "I've never seen you do anything like that before," Diane said.

"That's because I haven't done anything like that before." He turned to Rocco. "Can either of you remember anything I said?"

"Yes," Rocco said. "Why?"

"Because I can't."

"You're joking."

"I'm serious. I haven't a clue what I said."

When the party dispersed, Ken started making dozens of small sketches for Isumataq that he laid out in various configurations on the floor of his studio until he had what he wanted. With Diane's help, he stretched four small canvases that together measured twelve feet long by one foot high and served as a scale model for the much larger painting. He covered the canvases with coats of gesso, layering the primer horizontally first and then vertically. He drew the scene, in pencil, on the canvas with so much detail and depth it resembled a painting in shades of gray.

He drew three more sketches, each the same size, with nuances of mood and tone. The fourth was the definitive one. But, when he stepped back and looked at it he realized it was too small to scale up to the larger painting. He needed a bigger model, with more detail.

He had more canvases made that together measured twenty-five feet, eight inches long by two feet high. By anyone's standard, this was an immense painting: by Ken's yardstick, it was a miniature. However, the size was ideal, as it allowed him to sketch in every detail and nuance he wanted to convey.

He worked eighteen hours a day, but time had ceased to have meaning. He physically barricaded the studio to discourage visitors. Several weeks later, when the large model was complete, he started to calculate what it would take to paint a portrait that was twelve feet high one hundred fifty-two feet long. He estimated that he would need thirty-eight panels twelve feet high by four feet long, butted seamlessly together.

He had immense issues to deal with. First, he had to find a supplier who could stretch canvases of that size. He also had to keep Rocco supplied with paintings, and he had to complete them on time. And, he had to finish the Reichmann and Yellowknife Airport paintings. In addition, he was once again doing presentations at schools. Common sense told him to say no to those requests, yet he felt an obligation to talk to the children – to fire their minds with dreams. Although he should have been tired, he was bursting with energy. It was as though the furnace of his heart was being stoked with a fuel that burned endlessly – a fuel more potent than food, drink or rest.

He could find no one who would stretch the canvases. Those he approached thought he was mad. He talked to the company that supplied their framing material, explaining that he needed stretchers double kiln dried so they wouldn't warp. They also had to be bevelled so that when the panels came together the seams would disappear.

Ken wanted all the materials he used to be made in Canada. It wasn't possible. No one in Canada made canvas, so he ordered several rolls from Brazil, each roll weighing hundreds of pounds. He also had to import brushes.

With leftover canvas from the Reichmann painting, he and Diane stretched the first panel using the device he had invented that was a combination of canvas stretching pliers, Vise-Grips, and a torque wrench. Every part of the canvas had to be stretched to precisely the same tension.

The canvas was perfect when he could lay it on the floor, toss a coin on it ,and have it bounce off like a bullet. If it wasn't right he started over again – and he began afresh many times.

Keeping in mind his insight about quantifying the painting, he made a precise list of every item he needed. How much glue would he need? How much gesso for four coats on each of thirty-eight panels? How much paint?

Ken met with Mr. Stevenson, of Stevenson and Company paint manufacturers, "I think I'm going to need two tons of paint," Ken said.

"What the hell are you going to do with two tons of paint?" Stevenson asked.

"I need to explain this so it makes some sense to you. I'm going to paint the world's largest portrait."

"Really? With two tons of paint? It's going to be some awfully big giants you're going to paint."

"No – no giants. There are no people in my painting."

"How can it be a portrait if there are no people?"

"It's going to be land, sky, sea, icebergs, and Inuksuit."

"That's a landscape."

"Not according to the Inuit."

"The Inuit? Who are the Inuit?"

"Eskimos to you."

"You mean the Eskimos aren't Eskimos?"

"No – and they never were."

When Ken had finished explaining, Stevenson leaned back, his hands behind his head. "That's one helluva story," he said.

"And that's why I need two tons of paint," Ken said.

What kind of stretcher was going to hold two tons? Stevenson asked. And how was he going to stretch it? And why two tons? How had he arrived at that figure?

Ken told him about the two canvases that were now finished and drying in his studio. They were large. He had an idea what it took to paint large canvases.

But why did he insist on doing things on such a large scale?

"Have you ever noticed that the art scene in Canada is made up of victims that do things in a victim size, who then expect that something grand is going to happen?" Ken asked. "That's not me. I don't know how to do that, and I couldn't sell a painting for a thousand dollars to someone with a mortgage and two kids and a station wagon. I don't know how to do those things. If it isn't done on this scale I just don't seem to be very good."

Stevenson rubbed his chin. "You may want to check your calculations. How do you know it's two tons?"

"I don't. I wanted to get your attention. Do I have it?"

"Yes, you definitely do. But, this quantity of paint is going to cost you a fortune. How are you going to pay for it?"

"With money. What else?"

"Do you have the money to do that?"

"If I put in an order, I'll pay you."

"Over what period of time do you need this paint?"

"Five years, three months and twelve days."

"That precise, is it?"

Ken smiled. "From the Irishness in your look, I'd guess that you don't believe me. You think we're in some pub, in some little village in Ireland, and we're spouting off after we've got ourselves two-thirds cut. I suggest you come to my studio and take a look for yourself."

Stevenson was waiting for him outside the door the next morning. Ken opened it and flicked the light switch. Stevenson took one step forward and stopped, his eyes sweeping the room. "Holy Mother of Mary! Jesus!" he breathed.

Ken leaned back and whispered to Diane, "Get a pad of foolscap paper and a clipboard. Drive a nail in the wall here and hang it up, with a pencil, and every time someone comes in, write down the first comments they make – with the date and the name. Let's keep track of how this hits people."

Stevenson tried to estimate how much paint Ken would need. For such quantities he would need the paint in tubs. Ken shook his head. Tubs of old paint formed a skin that reminded him of custard and he couldn't bear the sight of it. He wanted the paint in the factory's largest tubes. And what would he do with such enormous quantities of empty tubes? That also was not a problem. He would place several eight-foot-tall Plexiglas cylinders in his studio. Every discarded tube and used brush would be tossed into the tubes and the tubes themselves would be part of a travelling exhibition – part of the quantification process.

"Everyone is trying to mystify art," he said. "I'm trying to demystify it. I want people to understand. This art jargon is all about people being self-important. I don't need to be self-important. I *am* important. I want people to understand what we as painters do – or at least what this painter does."

How much would two tons of paint cost? Stevenson had no idea. He had never sold paint by the ton.

"Think about it," Ken said. "Keep in mind that by the time we're halfway through this, this will be the most famous project in the world."

"You're confident of that, are you?"

"Of course I am. Do you think I'm leaving it to the gods to figure this out? This is an engineering process. My uncle was Machiavelli."

"You sound more like a warrior than a painter."

"I was born in a war. It comes naturally to me. In this hand I have a paintbrush and in this hand I have a sword. I'm good with both. I enjoy both. You choose. Remember, you make the paint, I make the magic."

"You think highly of yourself."

"Yes. There are three things that are consistent: gravity, human stupidity and my high opinion of myself."

During the next week, Stevenson called daily, not so much for more specifics to help him with his quotation as for details of Ken's story. On each call, he said the price would probably come down a bit more.

Ken began to add up the costs, and the fact was Isumataq was going to cost a fortune. He enlisted Diane's and Marsha's help in a campaign to raise corporate funds. They composed and mailed dozens of letters. While waiting for replies, Ken concentrated on publicity. There had been an initial flurry of stories in the press, but the media had moved on to newer sensations. Even the raft of articles in the local papers had only been read by a small percentage of the city's population. Even Stevenson, who sold paint to artists, had been completely unaware of the show at the Columbus Centre and prior to Ken's visit, he had been unfamiliar with his name.

He called his old friend Gary McLaren, at CTV, whose Sunday Morning show he had appeared on so many times. He explained the immensity of Isumataq and that he wanted its evolution recorded. When the painting was done, the public would have a behind the scenes look at the making of it in four television segments.

Gary enthusiastically fell in with Ken's proposal and arrived at the studio with his cameraman, Bailey, who filmed while Ken told stories and worked with giant hoses, compressors, nails, and staple guns.

"This is amazing," Gary said one day in the parking lot, during a break in the shooting. "I don't think anyone has ever done this – shown what it's like to be on the inside of an artist's head."

"I've never seen this done before either," Ken said. "And I don't have a clue what the hell I'm doing, but it's being done on a giant scale, which is not the way things are usually done. You're inside this particular scenario, and I think it's the proper approach to the whole concept of art." Then he pointed to First Canadian Place, the tallest office building they could make out on the hazy Toronto skyline.

"See that office building? You can imagine everything that goes on inside that building. That's what I do."

"Hang on a second," Gary said. "Bailey! Grab the camera! Get this on tape!"

Ken started again. "See that office building there? That's First Canadian Place, the tallest office building in the Commonwealth, if it is still the British Commonwealth. Everything that goes on in there, I do. I'm the dreamer, manufacturer, salesman, sales agent, packager, shipper, accountant, banker – everything. And people talk about businessmen and artists as if they were two distinctly separate creatures. I'm the only true entrepreneur – whatever the hell that is. I'm the only true one, because I do it all right from the beginning to the end. Every job is my job."

The next time Salvador dropped by, Ken told him about his publicity campaign. What if the same crew that had erected the Inukshuk in his studio put together a number of Inuksuit, drilled them all and took them apart? Then, in the dead of night, erected them here and there in the city so that the next morning there they would be – mysteriously having arrived out of nowhere.

Salvador thought it was a marvellous plan, but his reason for the visit was to arrange a meeting with Albert Reichmann. It had to be planned several months in advance, but it could be done.

At last! Ken stipulated that the meeting take place at the Reichmann home on an afternoon when Salvador and his crew were working in the garden. "And this is what I want you to say: 'Mr. Albert, there's the man in the garden – the man I told you about. He's been sent.' Just use those words."

"Why would I say that?" Salvador asked.

"Because that's what I want you to say."

"Why?"

"I don't want to tell you."

"What do you mean?"

"I promise I'll tell you when the meeting is over, but those are the words that have to be used."

"Give me some idea about why those particular words."

"Right now I can't, but I just know that those are the right words. They're magic words. Merlin put them in my ear."

Salvador promised to say the exact words, but as Ken got up to continue painting and looked back at him, smiling enigmatically, he admitted to himself that he had no idea whether he would say those words – or indeed, what he would say or do.

The fundraising campaign was a flop. Most of the corporations sent no reply and the two that came were gracious refusals. "Send more letters," Ken said.

"But they're not working," Diane protested.

"It doesn't matter. Send more anyway!"

The Canadian Cancer Society sent a letter asking for his help in their own fundraising campaign. Would he donate a painting of an Inukshuk for a raffle? He and the Premier of Ontario, David Peterson, would pick the winner at a large media event. Ken saw an opportunity for more publicity and cheerfully said yes.

On the last day of the campaign, he met with Peterson, an affable, witty man who was also an art lover. He told Ken that he and his wife had attended his show at the Columbus Centre, but by the time they had arrived every painting was sold.

Ken invited him to his studio for a private showing – and a guarantee that some paintings there would not have a sold sticker. A few days later, Peterson and his wife arrived and lingered in the studio, taking in the large paintings and the sketches of Isumataq. They picked out a canvas and, while Diane and Peterson's wife selected a frame, Ken and the Premier talked and traded stories.

While Ken prepared the stretchers for Isumataq, he continued painting canvases that he sold through the gallery at the Columbus Centre, or that he bartered – in one case for a used Ford station wagon.

While he worked, an image of an Inukshuk standing in front of a Canadian flag began to haunt him. He made a few small pencil sketches and then very rapidly about twenty oil sketches. Using the best of them as models he painted a forty by sixty inch canvas: the Inukshuk towering in front of a Canadian flag unfurling in the wind. He hung the finished painting on the wall of his studio and asked Diane to record peoples' reactions on first seeing it. Generally they gasped, sometimes adding an expletive, "Holy cow!"

When the painting was dry, Diane placed it in a simple, narrow black frame and Ken took it to the gallery to show to Rocco. "Oh my God!" he said. "Where the hell did you come up with that idea?"

"It's been circling around in my mind," he said and asked Rocco to place it in the most prominent spot in the gallery, not just where visitors could see it, but where it would also catch the eye of passing pedestrians and motorists.

"I don't know," Rocco said. "This might get a reaction from the public."

"Well, yes," Ken said. "What the hell do you think this is all about anyway?"

Ken had the painting professionally photographed, made a set of glossy eight by ten prints and sent one to the postmaster general, John Fraser – along with a handwritten letter suggesting the image for a Canadian stamp. Ken had met Fraser several times in Vancouver and had taken an instant liking to him. His sense of humour was matchless, his passion for Canada was real, and his honour was impeccable – and in Ken's experience that was something rare in a politician. He was also an avid fly-fisherman.

John Fraser replied with great enthusiasm. It was a terrific idea, he wrote, explaining he had heard snippets of Ken's Arctic story. This was the sort of thing he welcomed, he said, people bringing ideas into the bureaucracy.

However, he had underestimated the power of that bureaucracy which, unlike John Fraser, did not welcome ideas, and the idea of using Ken's image on a stamp died. Soon after, on September 17, 1984, John Fraser was appointed Minister of Fisheries and had no time or authority to follow up.

Rocco hung the painting but not where Ken wanted it, so Ken brought in an easel and placed it front and centre in the gallery. What he had not anticipated was the reaction of the public. Nothing he had done previously had raised such a ruckus. People were outraged. How dare this painter take the sacred symbol of the Canadian flag and desecrate it so blatantly for financial gain!

The media fell on the story and Ken found himself besieged. Rocco was horrified. Ken laughed. "Finally, I have a reaction!" he crowed.

People called the local radio stations to complain. "It's shameful!" they said. "It's inappropriate!"

Ken called the talk shows and offered to go on the air, not to rebut the callers so much as to take them to task. Diane and Rocco urged him to run from the confrontation. Ken said he would meet it head on with a paintbrush in one hand and a sword in the other. Only Joseph Carrier was pleased. "You go, young man," he said with his impish smile.

Ken drew his line in the sand with the first caller on the first talk show, who accused him of using patriotism and being a scoundrel.

"If you're going to quote others," he said, "At least have the decency to get it right. The quote is, 'Patriotism is the last refuge of a scoundrel'. Now, you remember that so you can impress the folks down at the janitorial company where you no doubt work."

Another caller accused him of wrapping himself in the flag. "Who do you think you are – an American?"

"The last time I looked it was the Canadian flag, not the American flag" he said. "So why don't you do yourself and all of us a favour and buy yourself some glasses?"

Another said, "It's disgraceful – absolutely disgraceful – using the flag. It's a sacred thing. No one should be allowed to do this! You should be charged! And that thing you put in front of the flag – it's disgraceful. What is it? A pile of rocks?"

"That thing you call a pile of rocks actually has a name," Ken replied. "And it's Canadian. It's called an Inukshuk. Can you say Inukshuk? Come on. Say it! Do you know that even if you were to offer me a million dollars, I wouldn't sell it to you? And do you know why I wouldn't sell it to you? Because you're an ignoramus – an idiot!"

Another caller: "I'm a patriot and I love my country and I think your painting is shameful."

"Sir," Ken sneered into the mike. "From the sound of your voice and the echoing chatter, there is no doubt that what passes for a brain in you is actually prefabricated crap. If you had a brain, you would know the meaning of love and patriotism. Let me enlighten you. Maybe you'll even learn something. 'Love' means using the time and the energy of your life to help others. 'Patriotism' is about working every day and night relentlessly for the protection and the betterment of your own country, no matter what the personal cost."

The caller tried to interrupt.

"Shut up!" Ken barked. "I'm not finished. So far as patriotism goes, you haven't even been to the Arctic, have you? No, of course not. It's forty percent of our country. There is much for us to learn there. We are not a country five thousand miles long and a hundred miles deep butted up against the American border. We were born in the Arctic. We are an Arctic nation. North is our dream. You have not gone there, and you have not seen the people, yet you have the unmitigated gall to call this radio station and pollute the Canadian airwaves with your ignorant bullshit."

With each new talk show, Ken became more abrasive. Rocco took the painting down. Ken put it back. The public grew angrier. Letters to the editor in the local papers were full of vitriol. The infamous painting became the office buzz around the water cooler.

Then when the fire was truly raging, Ken put it out. He began his next radio interview with questions. "Why has no one asked me why I painted this? Why has no one asked me what it means? Why has no one asked me why I'm so angry and frustrated at all these people who are calling in with such nasty comments – people who haven't been to the Arctic and who haven't understood any part of it, yet are prepared to go on at great lengths, making absolutely nonsensical comments without the slightest bit of information? Is there anyone out there who could ask me these questions? And is there anyone out there who could call in – who has been there – and tell me their impressions of that place? I defy anyone to go to that giant place – the largest part of the second largest country in the world – and not be utterly captivated by that land and those people. And don't think you can call up and pretend you've been there and bullshit me, because you can't."

One person called and asked what it was about the Arctic and its people that made him so passionate.

Ken explained, "It is the most beautiful place I've ever seen, populated by the most wonderful and intriguing human beings I have ever met. And, these people have been brutalized for a century and a half without the apparent knowledge of ninety-nine percent of the population. I think it's time for a messenger. I think it's time for voices to speak about what is happening up there. How would you feel if the authorities came along and rounded you up, took you out of your house, and took your children away from you – cutting their hair off until it was just stubble? How would you feel if those authorities sent them far, far away to a school? The order came from your federal government to assimilate these people – these savages – to tell their children that they were bad, and that everything about them was bad and evil, and they had to be instructed by force. The government, who was paying the bill with your money, contracted the two main churches in the country to run these schools. There are parts of this country where this story is well-known but the eyes are averted. Those children were brutalized in unthinkable ways – not just verbally and spiritually but also physically, and in many ways used for the sexual gratification of a bunch of perverts. If this happened to your family, wouldn't you want someone to care? Wouldn't you want someone to raise a stink? Wouldn't you want someone to help? That's all I'm trying to do. Apparently, to my surprise, it seems this painting was the two by four needed to apply to the side of your head to get you to pay attention. My job is to announce to you what has gone on and what continues to go on. I'm robbing you of your innocence. I'm not going to give you the chance to say, 'If only I had known'. Now you know. What are you going to do about it?"

The mood of the public changed. People began calling to agree with him. Battle lines were drawn and half – or perhaps even the magic fifty-one percent – agreed with him.

Ken spent an hour or more each day, at the Columbus Centre, talking to people who lined up to see the painting and talk to the artist. Thousands of people came – far more than had attended his opening night.

Ken finished each of his stories with a plea for help. He urged people not to simply believe his stories, but to investigate and make up their own minds. And if they discovered that what he said was true, let the government know how they felt. This was what democracy was about – and he was appalled at how lightly most people took the democracy they lived in. "No one that is born here really takes it seriously," he told them. "Do you know how many rivers of blood were spilled to have what we have here? How can we pretend to be this thing that we say we are when you can't bother to inform yourselves about what goes on in your own country? How can you be a nation without knowing what goes on in your own backyard?"

Ken received a phone call from Wayne Morrison, the executive director of the Friends of Canadian Broadcasting and the stepson of Northrop Frye. Could they meet, he asked? Ken invited him to the studio.

Wayne was a dapper and polished gentleman who expressed fascination with the furor caused by the flag painting. The CBC was about to suffer large financial cuts, which would seriously endanger its existence, he said, and he wanted Ken's help. He wanted to reproduce the flag painting in full page magazine advertisements with Ken standing beside it holding a paintbrush with the quote, "I haven't been this mad in twenty years." Below that would be the story of the CBC cutbacks.

Ken said yes, but he was not prepared to use the painting. He would create another similar one instead. When Diane asked why, he said, "I'm going to give it to Canada and I don't want it reproduced. It's going to go to the country pure."

"You're going to give it away? Good lord, we don't have enough money to do what we're doing and you're going to give paintings away! Why are you going to give something to the government? They already take too much!"

"I didn't say I was going to give it to the government, I'm going to give it to Canada."

"And when are you going to do that?"

"I have no idea. But one day I'll do it and in the meantime that painting is going to hang on the wall."

Ken sketched out a large Inukshuk in the foreground of the new canvas with several smaller Inuksuit dwindling toward the horizon where the Canadian flag formed the backdrop. As he worked he decided to create twelve similar paintings – each one a flag painting, each with a symbol of the Arctic in the foreground and each forty by sixty inches.

When the painting for the CBC was completed, Averill Lehan, a noted photographer, set up in the studio and shot brilliant large transparencies. Wayne Morrison gave the painting the title, "Yearning to Belong". "All of Canada is yearning to belong," he explained. "And we can't seem to find a way of holding hands at these great distances."

Diane was indignant that Ken had given the painting to the Friends of Canadian Broadcasting rather than charge for it. "How can you keep giving paintings away?" she demanded.

"I'm not really giving them away," he said. "These are special causes. There is a value, but it's not in money. It's a different value. And I'm going to keep doing it so stop pestering me."

A large team of designers and advertising people had become involved in the campaign for the CBC and they asked Ken if Inuksuit really existed. "You're a promoter – did you invent this thing?'

"Why don't you folks just find out for yourselves and take the time to go up there and look?" he suggested. "Go to the Arctic."

Until someone proved otherwise, he claimed the Inukshuk was the oldest man-made thing on the continent, the Canadian flag, by contrast, was one of the newest and it was a grand omen that Canadians had finally made something for themselves. Everything else in Canada had been given to the country. "We need these things that we have made for ourselves," he said. "Years ago when I went to Parliament to see the Minister of Foreign Affairs about a show in Spain, I noticed there was no hallmark on the building. All great buildings in Europe bear a hallmark, but when I looked around in Ottawa, everything I saw came from somewhere else. There was very little that was actually Canadian – born in this country. I think this image of the Inukshuk is perfect to go on a shield at the very entrance of Parliament. I would like that to happen after I find a way to give the first flag painting to Parliament."

Diane grew increasingly frustrated by the flood of rejections from the corporations she had approached for the funding of Isumataq. "I can't stand it," she said. "We keep sending out letters asking for support and not one single one comes back positive. They're all negative! There are stacks and stacks of them – why do you even want me to keep them?"

"I don't know," he said. "Just put them away somewhere – I have a feeling."

But Diane continued to fret, and Ken walked down to his favourite park to sit on a bench and watch the city ducks paddling toward him as they searched for handouts. "What's good about these negative responses?" he asked himself. While he waited for an answer he observed the ducks and thought about Diane. Like so many people she abhorred rejection. The word "rejection" captivated him and a phrase sprang to mind: "The world's most rejected man". He imagined a media campaign: "Come and meet the world's most rejected man!" It was bound to succeed. The first three pages of any newspaper were full of tragedies and disasters. The world's most rejected man was a grand tragedy.

He walked back. "We're going to turn this into a game," he said. "Rather than hoping for a positive result, we'll up the ante. We'll send out more letters – hire someone to help you. Their job will be to send out letters – that's all. And we'll pray that we don't get any positive responses. We want rejections. We're going to get filing cabinets and fill them with rejection letters and prove that I am truly the world's most rejected man and then we'll send out a press release and have a huge media event."

Diane sighed.

One day, Ken was introduced to Keith Sharp who had come to Canada from northern England to explore the Arctic. He too had fallen in love with a dream of the Arctic. He arrived in Halifax as a tourist and made his way north, where he met and married an Inuk woman and had several children with her. Through him, Ken learned that several committees had been struck by the Inuit to promote the idea of creating their own territory called Nunavut – the Nunavut of the grandmother's song! While the idea heartened Ken immensely, and conjured the story the grandmother had told, it also discouraged him when he discovered that not a single member of the press knew about it. His contacts in government were also ignorant of an idea called Nunavut.

Ken vowed that Isumataq would have one purpose and one only – to promote the creation of Nunavut. His job was to raise public awareness and bring attention to that forgotten part of the country. Whatever was required – if he had to stage a three-ring circus to get attention, he would do it. He would be relentless.

"Relentless" – he tasted the word on his tongue and found it oddly pleasing. It suited him so perfectly that he painted the word in foot-high letters on the white wall of his studio. Then he added words in a rainbow of colours: "Don't forget to be relentless. Never quit!" As he painted he recalled the words uttered by Bill Bennett more than twenty years ago in the Peace River country: "If I could give you some advice young man, it would be legislation by exhaustion. The last one standing wins".

He also pondered the idea of trying to tell a story to people through a painting. A painting was visual – how could he make it speak in a different language – one that was louder than words? What he needed was a pictorial description so that people would understand. A big painting might move them emotionally but if people could see that painting reproduced in a beautiful brochure that contained other images as well, it would have far more power.

He called Jay Mandarino, who belonged to the young professionals group whose members had been purchasing many of his paintings. Jay's ambition was to make his company the most award-winning printing firm in the country and his office walls were already papered with awards. Ken explained to him that he wanted the world's largest, fanciest, most beautiful, most expensive brochure.

Jay and his design team sketched ideas. Ken looked at each and shook his head – none of them moved him emotionally. He bought a stack of magazines and tore out advertisements for the most luxurious and most highly prized items in the world: Rolls Royce automobiles, Bulgari jewellery, Dior furs. He examined the ads carefully. None moved him.

He came to the conclusion that what he wanted had never been done but slowly the germ of an idea took root in his mind. The brochure would be very long, very large and creamy white. In fact, the brochure would be all about white. The centrefold would be a giant reproduction of Isumataq that would have been photographed in sections and seamlessly married to form one giant image. Jay's design team came to the studio where they studied the model of Isumataq set against the white walls. Ken saw the light of understanding dawning in their eyes and after many more sketches, they showed him a design he liked.

"How many of these do you want?" Jay asked.

"Five thousand."

"Five thousand! Do you have any idea how much that is going to cost?"

Jay pointed out that the paper he had chosen was custom and the onion skin was the most expensive available. Then there was the cost of embossing an Inukshuk on the onion skin. "Not one item here is a stock item," he said.

Ken nodded. "That's it exactly. That's perfect!"

"You're looking at a whacking pile of money."

"Of course."

"How do you propose to pay for it?"

"I haven't a clue."

Jay sat down with his calculator. "Ninety thousand dollars," he said when he finally lifted his head.

Ken made deals. Jay gave him a list of every manufacturer involved in the production of the brochure, starting with Coast Paper in Vancouver.

Ken called and told the story of Isumataq. He offered a painting for the paper, clinching the deal by telling them that everyone involved in the project would very likely win an award and be exposed in some way to massive media coverage. He also threw in some dubious oratory that was so over the top that many people laughed. "Don't worry about this moment," he said. "One day you'll be in paradise with me." If they snickered behind his back, he didn't care because by the time he was done he had bartered for every service he needed – ninety thousand dollars worth. His friends called the money he had used to pay for the brochure "Ken dollars" and it was a term that stuck.

Elias Vanvakis, another of the young professionals who was a successful insurance broker, commissioned a small pencil drawing of an Inukshuk.

"I'll give it to you," Ken said.

"No, I want to buy it."

"Why would you want to buy it?"

"You're painting the largest Inukshuk – I want the smallest," he said.

Ken pocketed the five hundred dollars Elias offered and drew an Inukshuk, which he handed to him. A few weeks later, on Ken's forty-fifth birthday, Elias presented him with a small jeweller's box. Inside was a small gold pin, a perfect replica of the pencil drawing.

Ken pinned it to his shirt. Minutes later he was struck by an idea. A larger version of the pin was exactly what the front cover of the brochure needed – but not in gold paint of even gold leaf – a pure gold Inukshuk.

The pin inspired yet another idea. The nation's highest honour for its citizens was The Order of Canada. He wanted something even more prestigious – an honour that was almost impossible to receive – The Order of the Inukshuk. He ordered a dozen more from the jeweller who had designed it.

Whenever someone asked about the pin, he smiled and inferred that it was special and only a chosen few would ever have the honour of receiving one. To Rocco he said, "Anyone who buys a ten thousand dollar painting, gets one."

Ken was invited to the Columbus Centre again to give the keynote speech at a dinner honouring Premier Peterson. At the end of the speech he was to give him a painting of an Inukshuk. But instead of doing a simple presentation, he told the story of the Order of the Inukshuk – that the pin was the result of a visionary flood of alcohol consumed in the land of the midnight sun on June 21, the longest day of the year. He explained that they were almost impossible to get and only a few very special people would ever be aware of The Order of the Inukshuk. "They come to certain people who are magic," he said. "They come to people like me. Everyone else has to fight for them."

Eight hundred people listened and chuckled while the Premier threw his head back and laughed. When he stepped on to the stage to receive his painting, Ken said, "Now – about those magic people who understand the words patriotism and love – that they mean utter selflessness. I'm pinning this golden Inukshuk on Mr. Peterson's lapel because he has now joined the order of magic people."

Flashes lit up the room, journalists scribbled frantically and within days Inukshuk paintings walked out of the door of the gallery and, much to Ken's relief, money poured in. In spite of his deals for "Ken dollars" the Isumataq project was costing almost half a million dollars a year.

Ken continued to tell people his Arctic stories as he worked, but now he had a name to give to that land – Nunavut! He urged everyone to talk to the media. "This is like going on a giant walk and attracting people from each village," he said. "It's a forever and forever journey until every soul on earth is on board with this idea. This is a great long walk toward this thing called Nunavut."

Averill Lehan, who was photographing Ken's paintings, told him that if he ever went back to the Arctic, he would like to come along, to photograph the North. Roberto Lissia, an Italian journalist who had moved to Canada, also expressed an interest in seeing the Arctic and finally, Gary McLaren said that he too would like to make the trip. When Egidio Coccimilio, a movie sound technician, heard of a possible expedition to the Arctic he also asked to come along, so he could begin filming a documentary.

During one of his shooting sessions with Gary, Ken confided in him that the real and only purpose of Isumataq was to focus attention on Nunavut in a way that was completely apolitical while also being one hundred percent political. "I'm going to present myself as the man who is going to change the shape of the nation," he said. "But no one will meet me. I'm invisible. I'm magic. And when it's all over there will be a giant flash of blue light and I'll be gone."

He also told Gary about "the world's most rejected man". The media would be all over this story, he said, but Gary could tell it first.

The Kitchener-Waterloo station filmed a half hour show dedicated to Ken working in his studio, while he talked with Gary about corporate Canada's rejection of him – and why he had been appealing for funds.

A couple of weeks before the show aired, Diane faxed every radio and television station and every newspaper in Toronto inviting them to meet "the world's most rejected man".

The media lined up at his studio and Ken gave interviews four hours a day every day for a week. The following week he devoted equal time to journalists from Europe and Japan.

Like everything Ken did, he approached television interviews his way. When he was told not to look at the camera, he addressed himself directly to the lens, because he was not so much interested in talking to the interviewer as he was to the public. But despite his increasing exposure he still had a long way to go to achieve fame or notoriety. When he was asked to buy exhibition space for Toronto's first Art Expo he declined, but offered to exhibit two paintings – the flag painting and a twelve by fourteen foot Inukshuk painting – and accompany them, to answer questions and meet the public.

"I'm getting more media coverage than all the other artists in Toronto put together," Ken said. "This will attract people to the exhibit."

"Just who do you think you are?" they asked.

"Do you want the deal or don't you?" he replied.

Ken spent a week at the Toronto Convention Centre and his prediction proved correct – he was the big draw. He shook thousands of hands and talked to an enormous number of people.

14

Back to the Arctic

After a year of hard labour that gave Ken's hands countless blisters and made his wrists so sore he had trouble sleeping at night, he finished stretching all thirty-eight canvases for Isumataq. With Diane's help he erected the panels two feet out from the concrete wall of the studio, each panel held in place by a cross beam. The white panels stretched one hundred fifty-two feet across the white wall. Ken cleared almost everything out of the studio except for the Reichmann painting, which he placed against the wall behind the canvases, and the Yellowknife Airport painting, which he placed on the opposite wall.

For Ken, the studio became a sacred space, where he swore that if he listened hard enough he could hear angels singing. The door from the framing shop opened behind the thirty-eight panels with an immediate view to the only other thing in the room: the giant Inukshuk.

Now that the canvases were erected, Ken contemplated the complete work for the first time and what he saw almost overwhelmed him. The scope of the work he had set for himself was nearly inconceivable to grasp.

First, there was the immense challenge of scaling up the model. One at a time he took a salient feature from the smaller painting and measured from one end to the other on both canvases, making dots with comments to remind himself of what the marks meant. Every two inches had to be measured and marked – horizontally and vertically.

It was the most laborious job he had ever done in his life and he could only work at it for three or four hours each day. His concentration disintegrated if he tried to stay with the work longer than that and he would begin to make mistakes. Each morning the work began again, making point, point, point and points. It was an exercise in patience that at times came close to driving him mad. But it had to be done.

One day, when he had reached his limit, he sat back with a beer and contemplated his work. Endless though it seemed he felt satisfied and happy. It was actually happening. It had been a mere idea – and here it was – it was real.

Then it occurred to him. How was he going to paint the damn thing? He'd already had trouble with the sky in his last two large paintings, that were only a fraction of this size. He had to paint wet on wet. How was he going to do that? Come summer, the paint was going to dry fast, and he had to paint the sky in one complete episode. There would be no stopping. One hundred fifty-two feet of sky! He had a maximum of two hours that he could let the paint sit until it became too tacky. He had two hours before he had to keep adding paint, so that in the end there would be no seam. If he added wet paint to dry, he would end up with a shiny line where the two paints had joined, and he would have countless seams, knitted together like a Frankenstein's monster. Those seams would destroy the painting.

There was only one solution. Above the gallery, where his original studio had been, Ken placed a cot and two large alarm clocks and then had a shower installed that he would need to use frequently. The paint he used was full of lead, zinc, and other heavy metals and although he washed frequently throughout the day, it wouldn't eliminate all risk. Heavy metals settled in the fatty tissues and once there could not be eradicated from the body. In fact, Marsha convinced him to visit a doctor for a full checkup and a battery of tests. The doctor gave him a clean bill of health – so clean, she was frankly surprised when he told her he was not only a smoker, but also a man with an uncommon fondness for good Scotch and red wine.

While the plumber installed a shower, Ken enlisted the help of the window manufacturing company next door to design a moveable scaffold for painting Isumataq. They built it out of aluminum and made it height adjustable as well as portable.

Diane had instructions to bring in one media person a day and, except for rare occasions, he made sure the interviews took place at the studio, where he would perch on a stool in front of his canvas while the reporter sat in one of two comfortable easy chairs beside him.

When he appeared on talk shows, he made sure he caught the cameraman's eye. He had noticed that the cameramen determined airtime and since they seemed irresistibly drawn to dark graphics, he began wearing black pants and turtleneck sweaters. In panel discussions, he took over almost by default – what could people who had never been there say about the Arctic? He remembered the lessons he had learned early in his life about creating drama: don't be directed. You are the director. It's your story – you run the movie.

Finally, Salvador told him that Mr. Albert Reichmann was prepared to meet him on the following Tuesday, at his home, after work.

"What did you tell him?" Ken asked.

"I haven't told him very much," Salvador said. "I said 'There is a messenger. There is a man that has been sent: he needs to see you, and you need to see him.'"

He arrived at the Reichmann home early and joined Salvador in the garden. A short while later, a tall man came to the kitchen door. Salvador greeted him and the two men talked quietly together for a few minutes. Then Salvador pointed, and Ken heard him say, "This is the man I told you about. He is the man who has been sent."

Albert waved Ken toward him. "If you've been sent, you'd better come in."

Ken shook his hand and entered the kitchen.

"Who sent you?" Albert asked.

"It isn't a who; it's a what. An idea sent me and the idea starts with one human being asking another human being for one hour of his life to listen to a story, and the story is of a man you may have some familiarity with. His name is Lorenzo de Medici. Are you familiar with him?"

"Yes I am."

"I want one hour of your life."

Albert sat at the kitchen table, quiet and composed. Even his eyes were still. His hands rested motionlessly on the tabletop, his fingers curled comfortably inward.

Ken sat, took off his watch, and placed it on the table where he could see the time ticking away. He told Albert his understanding of Lorenzo de Medici's life. He drifted away on his words, just as he had when he had made his speech at the Columbus Centre. He lost himself in the intensity of the moment – rushing down the white water of ideas like a kayaker tumbling down a raging river.

"There are parts of that story I wasn't familiar with," Albert said, when Ken had finished. "Where did you get your information?"

He told Albert about his birthday trip to Florence to see the statue of *David* and how on another birthday his father had given him a beautifully bound book of Michelangelo's letters to Popes, kings and princes. The letters, he told him, described his relationship to the Medicis in his own words.

"So you are an artist?"

"I am a painter. Michelangelo was a sculptor who was made to paint. I am a politician who is made to paint. I have a job to do, and I have a mission to carry out that has to do with the people of the Arctic and the soul of a nation. We in Canada wander around very confused as to our identity. Our subjects of conversation are the weather, Quebec, and our identity. I have found the soul of this nation, and in the process, I found many wonderful stories and many wonderful symbols. At the same time, I discovered hell on earth – hell is what is happening to those people. I have been asked by the grandmothers to please tell the world about this. The first thing I want to do is tell you about it."

"Why would you want to tell me about it?"

"In Michelangelo's time there were Popes, queens, and princes. There were people who could sponsor great ideas. Now that's all gone – the

Popes, the princes, the kings, and the queens. They don't engage themselves any more. In my time, I am left not only with dreaming the dream and turning the dream into a concrete reality, and finding a stage to put it on for your consideration, but I am also obliged to do everything you do in your First Canadian Place. I dream it all, I make it all, I market it all, I sell it all, I politic it, I wrap it, I ship it – I'm the accountant, the legal expert – I am everything. I am the ultimate entrepreneur."

A faint smile passed over Albert's face. "So, what is it that I am to do with all of this?"

"It's up to me to create my own Lorenzo de Medici," Ken said. "That is what I have come here for and I have chosen you."

Albert leaned back and roared with laughter. "You have more brass!" he said. "Do you make it a habit to walk into people's kitchens, and into people's lives, and tell stories like this?"

"Yes, I do."

"You do?"

"Yes."

"How do you do it?"

"I don't know, but here we are."

"These grandmothers – this is a very interesting story. Tell me more."

Ken told him his story of the Arctic and what the grandmothers had asked him to do.

Albert let the silence fill the room. "Who are you?" he finally asked.

"Depending on which culture one is speaking to – I am who I am."

"What can I do to help?"

"I have a painting of the heart of the Arctic. It is of something called an Inukshuk. It's sixteen feet by sixteen feet. In order for me to accomplish my job, I need you to buy that painting. It's not so much that I want you to buy it – I need you to buy it, and for an immense sum of money. I have not come here to ask you for money for nothing. I have come here to offer to you, the work that I do – the money is for this painting *and* for much more than this painting. Essentially, it's for everything. If I can tell this story through the world's largest portrait, and get the attention of this country – show the beauty of the soul of our nation, and at the same time, tell about the hell of what is going on, perhaps we can wake the people up so that changes can take place. I don't call myself an artist. I call myself a painter, because if I don't make something that changes the hearts and minds of my species, I have only made intriguing and, perhaps, interesting and beautiful objects. This dream will come into being with your help. How things come to be is never by a single hand and never by a single soul. Only the thing that created this world possesses that ability. You are Lorenzo, to me."

"How much do you want for this painting?" Albert asked.

"More than has ever been paid for a painting in this country," Ken said. "And the figure will never be discussed beyond you and me."

"Why would you want to do that? I would think that you'd want the world to know."

"I do. But I want the world to know it differently. Imagine the talk. 'How did this cowboy-boot wearing character walk into your life when you can't be gotten close to? How did he solicit your help?' No matter how great the sum of money is, if we don't talk about it, it will become mythology and it will become even greater."

"You're almost a social engineer," Albert said.

"I was well taught," Ken said. "My father, who was a saintly man, was actually that."

"All right. How much is the figure?"

Ken told him a massive sum – one that was indeed larger than any that had ever been paid for a painting in Canada. "And every penny will go into Isumataq, and we will deal with the money in such a way that it does and does not exist."

"That sounds a lot like magic."

"It's not a lot *like* magic. It *is* magic. We are engaged in creating a perception of magic."

"I'll do it." Albert said.

Ken leaned across the table, picked up his watch, and put it back on his wrist. "Now, would you like to see it?" he asked.

"Yes, I would like to see it."

"Come with me to the studio, and I'll show it to you."

"Fine. Let's go."

They drove to the studio in Ken's old green station wagon. Inside, the space was empty, the framing studio locked. Ken took him in, placed him in front of the giant painting of an enormous Inukshuk against a blinding white background, and left him alone for twenty minutes. When he came back, he found him still standing where he had left him, dwarfed by the painting and – by the white canvas stretching across the room.

Albert turned. "You're going to use this money for making this giant project – is it this one?" he asked pointing to the canvases.

"Yes, it is. It's going to be called Isumataq. In the Inuit language, Isumataq means an object or a person in whose presence wisdom might show itself. It is my profound prayer that, for a few seconds or for an entire minute, it will enter into the heart and mind of the nation. I hope that it won't be intellectual – this is visceral. I'm not interested in the intellect. I am speaking strictly to the soul."

"What makes you think that this reluctant nation will accept it?"

"Because it doesn't really have an option."

"Oh?"

"No – it is written."
"It is written? Who wrote it?"
"God wrote it and he spoke it through the mouth of an Inuk grandmother."
The room filled with silence. "I'm very happy that you work for good," Albert said at last. "You could be dangerous."
On the drive back Albert asked, "Where do you propose the painting I just purchased be hung?'
"There's only one possible place that it could go and that's in your First Canadian Place."
"Very well."
"I was told that you don't buy paintings, and I find it very wonderful that you bought this one."
Albert smiled. "No, it is not our tradition to buy paintings."
"Yes, I'm aware of that."
"You seem to know a lot about us."
"One day, if we get to know each other, and I hope that we do, I have many, many other stories to tell you. And, I'm sure that you have many stories to tell me, if you choose to."
"So – First Canadian Place. I can't picture where."
"I can."
"You can?"
"Yes, I can. I have wandered through that building many times, and I know exactly where it should go."
"Very well, I'll ask Leon, one of my right hand people, to give you a call, and we'll set up a date, and walk around, and see what is possible."
Ken drove back to the studio alone; filled with a deep, solid, quiet joy. It was almost as though Albert Reichmann's serenity had spread into his body as well. He had no inclination to tell anyone about his triumph. He felt like a Michelangelo who had created his own Pope and his own Lorenzo de Medici. He knew that this time he had not played with magic or played at being a magician. This time real magic had been at work.
How could he describe what had just happened? And if he tried, he had enough past evidence to tell him he would only cause distress – not joy. Marsha would think he was mad. How could he describe to her the taste of an orange… when she had never seen one or held one in her hand?
A few days later, Ken, Leon, and Albert met in the lobby of First Canadian Place.
"Which wall?" Albert asked.
Ken pointed to the Menorah.
"How interesting," Albert said. "A man walks into my life, gets me to buy a painting, wanders around in my building, and then tells me where he wants it; and it's on that wall."

"I mean no disrespect, whatsoever," Ken said. "I know the symbol well. But that is the wall."

Albert exchanged a few words with Leon and then nodded. The painting would go on that wall. Then Ken and Leon tackled the problem of hanging the massive painting on a marble wall. The maintenance staff concluded they would have to drill into the ceiling beams and suspend the painting from thin stainless steel wires.

They hung the painting after business hours. Ken invited the media. He had the panels delivered to the lobby where he bolted them together. Salvador and his staff came along to help. Many members of the young professionals group also arrived on the scene. The media asked how much the painting had sold for. "No comment," Ken said.

"Was it a lot of money?"

"No comment."

"How did you contact Mr. Reichmann?"

"No comment."

"You're an artist," one of them said. "How do you know how to do all these other things? Artists don't know how to be entrepreneurs. Who helps you?"

"That's a big question," Ken said. "It's a spiritual matter. I don't wish to discuss it."

"What do you mean it's a spiritual matter?"

"Just that. I get my knowledge, inspiration, and advice from a higher authority and beyond that, I don't want to discuss it. But, I will say one thing – my advisor is Mr. Albert Reichmann."

"Yes," Albert said, when a reporter asked. "I am honoured to be Mr. Kirkby's advisor. He is doing wonderful work."

Those few words gave Ken the credibility he'd been looking for. He had achieved what his father had always had – the power to command respect and attention wherever he went.

Later that night, when he was one of the last to leave, he paused to look at the painting that he had envisioned hanging in that space so many times. It looked exactly as he had imagined. It was in perfect proportion to the immense lobby. It wasn't until one walked closer to it that one felt the full impact of its size.

His greatest debt was to Salvador, who had arranged the meeting, but when he told him that he wanted to give him several paintings, he refused. Ken painted several canvases regardless and delivered them to his home.

Before getting back to the task of Isumataq, Ken returned to the Arctic. Keith Sharp, the burly Englishman, had moved to a parcel of land near Rankin Inlet and extended an invitation. Ken included Michael as well as Averill the photographer, and Roberto and Egidio, the filmmakers, in his entourage; in mid-July, the somewhat motley crew – loaded down with film gear, anoraks, and sleeping bags boarded a plane from Toronto to Winnipeg.

They made a connection to Churchill, Manitoba with five stops along the way. Roxy Penny, the long-legged chief attendant, bombarded Ken with questions. Where were they going? What were they doing in the Arctic? How long would they be there?

Approaching Rankin Inlet, Ken was in familiar territory; as they prepared to land, the clouds parted and a pool of sun poured over the little town, bathing it in spun gold. Ken, who had recently taken up photography, with the same single-minded zeal he applied to all his projects, snapped photos with one of half a dozen cameras he had brought.

A flood of emotions passed through him. It had been twenty years since he had left the Arctic. His anticipation and joy were softened by homesickness for a place where he was; and for a life he had once lived.

As they disembarked, Roxy handed Ken two plastic shopping bags containing hundreds of tiny airplane-sized bottles of liquor. "It's dry up here," she said. The Inuit had voted for prohibition, which had inevitably created great profits for bootleggers.

When they had corralled their equipment and luggage, they boarded a Twin Otter, with fat tundra tires, that would take them due west, for about a hundred sixty miles, to the shores of Ferguson Lake, where Keith Sharp was building a lodge. The plane skimmed low over the land; a tangle of rivers snaking through gray-green scrub, strewn with myriad lakes, dazzling like diamonds in the sun. Breaking up the dark and light shadows were millions of wildflowers; splashed across the land as though a mad artist had flung giant brushfuls of paint on an enormous living canvas.

He gazed down at a nostalgically familiar landscape. Rainbows, like tiny dust storms, danced everywhere – they arced and crossed each other, and in one case made a complete circle like a whirlpool. Although the rainbows told of small, violent weather systems that could come together to form a gigantic storm, viewed from the sky they created a scene of unutterable beauty.

Michael gazed out of the porthole, spellbound, and for the first time Ken told his son his stories of the Arctic. Finally, the plane began circling lower and landed jarringly on the tussock and boulder strewn ground.

With the engines still running, the pilot heaved gear and luggage onto the ground. Ken, Michael, Roberto, Egidio, and Averill jumped down and watched the plane take off again with a roar of engines. Almost imperceptibly, the airplane lifted – and skimmed the tundra until it disappeared into the horizon. They were left standing in the middle of the vast tundra – in the midst of silence.

Ken noticed a large Inukshuk about a hundred yards off and something moving beside it. A man was coming towards them – a large man.

When he was within speaking distance he said, “My name Franco Barbagallo. I from Italy. I follow you, yes?”

“Who the hell are you?” Ken asked.

“I’m a photojournalist. I follow you, yes? I make you famous.”

“Really? You’re sure of that?”

“Yes. People in Europe want to know about you.”

“What people? How do you know about me? How do you know about this?”

“I am watching. There is media in Europe and I think your story very interesting. I need to know your story. I follow you.”

“I am not running a cult and I’m not looking for followers,” Ken said.

“Bad plan! Bad attitude! I tell your story.”

“How?” Ken asked. “Through pictures?”

“Yes – pictures and Italian words.”

“And then what?”

“Then German words.”

“You speak German?”

“No – I have translator. And, I tell story in English, and French, and Portuguese. You grow up in Portugal, yes?”

“Yes.”

“Okay – I write in Portuguese.”

“How about Greek?”

“Yes, Greek too.”

“How about Russian?”

“Yes, Russian too.”

“Fine,” he said. The Arctic had always presented him with the unexpected – why should anything have changed in the last twenty years?

An hour passed, and a sudden roar of engines announced the arrival of a Honda all-terrain quad heading a small procession of all-terrain vehicles. Riding the lead machine was Keith Sharp, sporting a luxuriant growth of facial hair and weighing in at about three hundred pounds. Their landing site was surrounded by water, so they and their gear had to be transferred into boats and then onto another set of quads on the far shore. Keith and his crew flung the luggage into the trailers they were towing and set off over the rise

Ken asked Keith about the Italian photojournalist.

“He’s been here for about four days,” Keith said.

“He has? What for?”

“Waiting for you.”

“Waiting for me? He says he’s going to follow me around.”

“Apparently so.”

“He says he’s going to make me famous.”

“Make you famous? Make you infamous, maybe. All this man will talk about is you and the Arctic. As if there aren't a lot of people already here; what is it about you?"

"My good looks and great intelligence – can't you see it?"

The lodge was a lodge more in theory than in fact. Several buildings were strewn around the area fronting a pretty lake with a dock, where a Beaver float plane bobbed on the waves. One large building appeared to be complete; another long, low structure had been framed and resembled the skeleton of a motel. A couple of other small, rudimentary structures dotted the property here and there.

Keith ushered them into the large building, which was the central focus of the lodge. The main room was an enormous living and dining room with a muskox rug complete with head and horns splayed across the floor and several sixty-pound Arctic lake trout mounted on the walls. Despite the fact that there were no trees on the tundra, an ancient wood stove graced one wall of the room. An antique kitchen stove hugged another wall; beyond that was a full kitchen with gleaming stainless steel appliances.

A tour of the grounds included one of the small outbuildings where Keith flung open the door and announced, "These are my quarters!" The tiny two room hut accommodated himself, his wife, and their seven children. The last building on the tour was the framed motel. The floor was strewn with insulation, nails, screws, and lumber. "Just throw your stuff down here," Keith said. While the men sorted out their sleeping arrangements, he left and came back with an armload of caribou hides.

Ken was already well known in the Arctic, Keith told him. "Your campaign in the south has made its way up here in a big way."

"What do the people know?" Ken asked.

"The coverage here on radio and television is constant. No one has ever come forward like you have – unelected and unpaid. You have people watching to see what happens next. Not everybody's happy about it."

When the Hudson's Bay Company had begun to lose its influence, it had closed most of its outposts and the former managers had opened independent businesses. About nine of them had become very powerful and controlled most of the commerce and politics. They knew the local language and customs, and many were married to Inuk women. "They're not going to want anyone coming in disturbing the status quo," Keith said. "Any time now, you can expect a plane; one or two of them will be coming in to check out what's going on and to find out why you're not staying in town. I'm just trying to give you a heads up."

"Well, we're just here on a fishing trip," Ken said.

Keith laughed. "Right! Fishing for what?"

"I'm here to take my son fishing and hunting and I want to take photographs."

Keith nodded. "Well, that's something I want to talk to you about. I can help you and I want you to help me." His room bookings for the following year, when the lodge would be completed, were with Americans and a handful of Europeans – not a single Canadian on the reservation list. "You seem to have a great capacity for publicity and getting media attention, and I'd like you to help me. In return, you can come and stay here, have the use of airplanes – anything you want. But I need you to help me to get people to come."

Ken thought about the problem and suggested a slide show in his studio with multiple projectors. He enlisted the help of Averill and Roberto; they commandeered Tergey, the young Norwegian pilot who worked for the lodge.

As Keith had predicted it wasn't long before they heard the sound of an approaching float plane that glided to a landing on the lake. It pulled up to the dock and two men stepped out. They shook hands and asked Ken what he was doing at the lodge. "Fishing with my son," he said, and excused himself, explaining that it had been a long trip and they were tired.

They crawled into their sleeping bags, pulled caribou hides over them, and drifted blissfully off to sleep. Too soon, a hand shaking his arm woke him. "There's someone I want you to meet," Keith said.

Joan Scottie, a reserved and beautiful Inuk woman, had been born about two miles down Ferguson Lake. "Joan has been a friend for years," Keith said. "She's here to help us finish building the lodge. She is the most capable human being you will ever encounter. There isn't anything she can't do. She was born in an igloo and is a computer expert. She is also the finest hunter and fisher you will ever meet."

Joan was also a photography buff. She took Ken to her hut near Keith's home and showed him a collection of photographs. Her Scot and Inuk, father, Basil Scottie, who was almost totally deaf and dumb, glared fiercely at the camera. Another photo showed her family, two men, and seven women, standing formally in a row, dressed in bleached white hides with intricate designs.

"I think I have been where these pictures were taken," Ken said, studying them. "But I can't be sure."

"Yes," she said. "They were taken near here and you were there."

"How do you know?"

"I heard."

"Who told you?"

"Old folks."

"I had an incredible experience – a horrible experience that never left me. It was somewhere in this region – a lot of people died."

"Yes, I know."

"How do you know?"

"I heard."

"I don't know where it was but it was out on the land."

"I know the place," she said. "I can take you to it."

"You can?"

"But before we do that, I would like you to see the place where I was born. Would you like to come with me?"

They roared down the lake in one of the lodge boats and drew up on a beach several miles down the lake. The derelict buildings near the shore had been uninhabited for years. Anthropologists would have concluded that whoever had lived there had left in haste. Outboard motors littered the beach, while tools and artifacts lay scattered in the various buildings. Walking past the buildings and peering inside was like visiting a museum. Inside one of the shacks, Joan said, "I've never come back. I haven't been here since I left when I was very young."

Inside that falling-down building, her story poured out like water tumbling through a burst dam. At the time when the caribou had failed to come, and when the white man's disease had set in, her father had taken heroic steps to save his people. He separated most of the families and isolated them in camps far away from each other, effectively putting them into quarantine. He managed to save most of the mothers and children of the men who had died and took responsibility for the survivors, as was the Inuk tradition. For the rest of his life he was the husband to five women and father to all their children.

The authorities said he had loose morals, but he was such a powerful man that they didn't challenge him. The fantastic stories about him were true, Joan said. A tundra grizzly wandered into camp looking for food, while her father was having a nap one afternoon. He woke up and, unable to locate his rifle, walked up to the bear – that had raised itself menacingly on its hind legs – stuck his knife in its belly, and jerked it up through the flesh. Hours later, when a second bear ambled into the camp, he disembowelled that one too. There were many other such stories about him. They were not legends – they were true. When he died, the authorities transported his wives and children to the settlement at Baker Lake, eighty miles to the north.

Later that day she took him back to her hut and told him that her child, Hilu, was eleven years old and lived in Baker Lake with her grandmother. "She has never been here."

"Would you like Hilu to come here and see the place you were born?" Ken asked.

"Yes, I would," she said.

The next morning Joan brought her daughter from Baker Lake. She wore a full-length parka, white with a hint of Arctic sky blue, the fur collar framing a flawless face with eyes that sparkled in the light. Twelve-year-old Michael stared at her, his jaw slack. A minute later, he and Hilu walked away together, chattering rapidly.

"Come," Joan said. "I want to show you this place where your story happened."

They flew over a network of small lakes, which connected rivers and tundra where muskoxen and caribou fed, following the massive Kazan River, which flowed near Yathkid Lake. On a promontory known as Cairn Point, they spotted a massive Inukshuk at least fourteen feet tall. Past that, the Kazan River wound north. After about forty minutes, Joan tapped Tergey on the shoulder and pointed, "Down there. This is the place."

Tergey banked down, where the river picked up speed before it dropped away in a series of giant cascades, tumbling over massive boulders into a deep gorge. Tergey circled over the river again, then put the plane down, and taxied into a small bay where he threw out a boat anchor.

Ken and Joan walked away from the river and crested a low rise where a giant Inukshuk, resembling two humans embracing, stood guard. Ken circled the stone monument, observing how it changed from different angles as though the figures were locked in an eternal dance. He began snapping pictures. When he stepped back to take a wide-angle shot, he stumbled. Looking down, he noticed a human skull bleached white by the sun and wind. He was standing inside a rectangle outlined by stones. Inside were more bones. Past the grave he was standing in were more graves, and past those more. Some contained complete skeletons; some only scattered bones. Some contained the fragile bones of children and infants.

Joan said, "This is the place."

But it couldn't be the place. Not this place. He didn't remember a river. She must be confusing his story with someone else's. There must have been other places where people had died during that harsh winter when the illness struck and the caribou hadn't come.

"May I photograph this?" he asked her.

She nodded, and he filled many rolls of film with images of the stone graves. "Tell me the story of this place," he said, joining her on the rock where she was sitting.

"You were here," she said. "You're the one who can tell me the story."

He shook his head. "I wasn't here. And how can you know this?"

"I just know it."

"No – there has to be more to it than that."

He had a hollow feeling in his stomach. Had he forgotten? Had he been in such an altered state that he could not remember all that had occurred?

"It was winter," Joan said. "It was dark. The river was frozen, so of course there was no river. Why don't you tell me the story completely from the beginning to the end."

"It's not a story I like to think about. And it's not really one I like to talk about."

"I understand. But I think this story has infected you so much it is like a rage in you. Maybe you should get it out."

"But what if it's the fuel that's making me do all this? Do I really want it out?"

He told her that he had been travelling with a group of Inuit and they had received word that another group of people was in desperate need. They packed sleds with provisions and travelled across the tundra to help them. Some that they found were starving; some had already died. They left behind the ones who could not be saved and brought the others back to their camp where they nurtured them back to health.

As they continued to travel, they met more groups of people who were dying. The disease brought by the white man was having devastating effects among the Inuit who had been isolated for countless centuries. Even a common cold was murderous. The Inuit would explode in a fever – a fever so bad they would roll naked in the freezing snow – a fever that would inflame the meningeal membrane covering the brain and crush it.

Ken told Joan that he and his friend had gone to one village and watched helplessly as everyone around them died, until only they were left alive. He told her that he had little memory of that time. He was in a state where time seemed to stop and all he felt was deep internal agony. And, something else – something very powerful happened that changed his life. When they left, he was a different person.

He told her that the pain he had suffered previously in his life, had laid a foundation that this unspeakable occurrence sat on like a giant object that nothing could erode. "How could this happen in a country like this?" he had asked himself. "How could this be? How could there be no help?"

What made it worse was that the government had no interest in doing anything for these people. The Europeans had called this place "Terra Nullius" – land belonging to no one – as if the people who existed here didn't matter.

Joan listened while she watched the caribou grazing on the opposite side of the river. "Why do you live in Toronto?" she asked. "Why don't you live here? Why don't you paint here?"

"For many years, I tried to do what I am doing in Vancouver and I failed," Ken said. "The reason I failed was that I was too far away from downtown Canada. I need to be in Toronto where all the power and the politics and the money are, and where all the decisions are made."

"Don't you think you could do it better from here?"

"No, I don't – or I would be here. Unless we get people in the south to understand this we will not be successful – they are ninety-nine percent of the population and they live for the most part in big cities."

"Do you like it there?"

"No. It's not where my heart wants to be but it is where I have to be."

"I was in Toronto once. I married Hilu's father and he was from Ottawa, so I've been to Ottawa too."

"What happened?"

"I don't know how you people can live in a place like that. It's soulless. It's like people living in caves up in the air. It's just not human. How is it that someone who isn't born here, who doesn't live here, and only spent a few years here, can love this place and these people so much?"

"I don't know," Ken said. "I don't know how that happened. We can have a lot of ideas and we can say a lot of things, but the reality is that we don't know these things. We don't know the first thing about love – we haven't a clue. We have all sorts of feelings and all sorts of passions. We call it love and hate, but that's just a lazy way of expressing something we know nothing about. I think love is something that is lived. It doesn't have very much to do with the other person although we focus the idea on one person. I think it's a life lived in a particular way. It encompasses all the things that are in that life and it depends on how that life is lived, whether the invitation to love will be heard and accepted. I don't think there is any language, including Inuktitut, that truly expresses what that's all about. The only conclusion I can come to is the one I've given you."

Joan let a long silence hang between them. Ken finally asked her again, how she knew this was the place where he had witnessed so much death. "It's not just you knowing," he said. "There's something more concrete to it. This is a specific place where a specific thing happened."

"I know this is the place because my mother knew these people and knows their story and she knows about you," Joan said. "This was the time of my grandmother, and my grandmother knew you. My grandmother found you very interesting. They called you the quiet Kabluna – the mysterious white man who had the capacity of silence. That's how I know about you."

"Would it be possible to visit them in Baker Lake?" Ken asked.

"Yes."

"Could we visit now?"

"They're away."

"Away?"

"Visiting."

"Family and friends?"

"Yes – very far away."

"So we can't go and see them?"

"No."

"Do you think one day I could meet them?"

"Yes."

"When would that be?"

"Now you're talking like a Kabluna," she said.

Ken nodded, and drifted back into the silence.

"You're very interested in Nunavut," she said.

"I am."

"Why?"

"If Nunavut comes into being and you have destiny in your own hands, wouldn't that be good?"

"I suppose."

"But obviously, it would be good. You don't seem very excited about it."

"The land has been here forever. We have been here forever. Whether we are here for a long time in the future or not, the land will be here. Everything is changing so quickly that we probably won't be here. But even if we are, what difference will it make what you call it, if the same people who are running it now are running it then?"

"What makes you think they would be running it?"

"Of course they would be running it. They run everything, and they have been doing that since they came here."

"But you are the most capable, the most adaptable humans I have ever met. If there is any group of humans who can run their own affairs, it's you."

"Will you come and live here then?"

"I'll come and visit. But my life's work is to tell stories to many, many people."

"Maybe when you have finished telling the stories."

"I can't see that far – I don't know."

"Maybe your soul would be happier if you lived here."

Ken smiled, "I wouldn't doubt that."

The next day, Ken and Michael explored Ferguson Lake. Scattered on the banks were several herds of muskoxen. They had been in decline for a long time but recently the trend had reversed, and the herds had begun to grow at the astounding rate of about twenty-two percent each year. They were docile creatures, but they were also powerful with long, curving pointed horns. Although they often false charged, one time in a hundred they would mount a real offensive and if they managed to overrun their victim, they would tear them to shreds.

The presence of the boat didn't frighten them, and even when Ken pulled into shore, they ignored them. As they approached the herd, one large male began pawing the dirt. After a few snorts he butted his head on the ground, announcing that he was about to charge. They had no hope of outrunning the beast and there was no place to hide. They stood still; convinced they were pulling in their last breaths. Then, from a pounding gallop, the big male abruptly pulled to a dead stop mere inches from where they stood – lather foaming out of his nostrils and mouth. With a huge snort, he liberally sprayed them with all the lather he had built up, turned majestically, and trotted back to the pair of cows he had left behind.

On shaking legs, Ken and Michael walked back to the lake where they washed themselves off, got back into the boat, and motored farther up the lake. They made several more stops, once to become acquainted with ptarmigans – birds about the size of chickens that were so tame they could be picked up with ease.

While they were catching and releasing ptarmigans, Ken noticed that the big rocks surrounding them formed giant circles. He was familiar with tent circles but these were much larger and there were many more of them. They counted more than forty. What were they? What did they signify and who had built them?

When they got back to camp they told Keith about the circles. He was curious enough to radio a helicopter flying in the area and hire it to take them over the stone formations. Ken and the photographers took dozens of pictures. They counted eighty-six circles that no one could explain. A few were 12-feet across but most were as large as thirty and forty feet in diameter with some even bigger than that.

More guests arrived a few days later, in several float planes and helicopters, from Rankin Inlet and landed at the lodge. Several influential Inuit and two of the current "bosses" of the Arctic were among the guests Keith had invited to gather around the lodge's big table and plan the best way to attract tourists to the Arctic. Ken suggested they invest heavily in tourism and be prepared to take a loss for up to five years while promoting the idea of an Arctic adventure to southern Canadians. Again, he offered to create slide shows and give talks in his studio; he suggested they talk to the local airlines about discount rates and packages.

On the night before they left, the camp chef prepared a feast of caribou, muskoxen, grayling, Arctic char, and lake trout. As they lay in their sleeping bags that night, Michael said, "I hope we can come back here soon."

"So do I," Ken said. "And I'll bet we can arrange it."

"I hope so."

15

The Arctic and Portugal

Ken went back to work with a renewed sense of purpose. The enormously expensive brochures he had ordered, were almost ready to go to press. He stopped them. He had returned with many powerful images that he wanted to include in the brochure. He also wanted to include a photograph of himself in a parka – standing in front of his painting of the Canadian flag.

Two weeks later the first brochures came off the press. They were everything Ken had hoped for. Jay at CJ Graphics suggested the brochures would look even more impressive if they were boxed. "Excellent!" Ken said and the boxes were ordered. More money? Ken had long ago stopped keeping track of expenses.

He sent beautifully boxed brochures to each Member of Parliament, to the Prime Minister, and to the Speaker of the House. Almost every member thanked and congratulated him. Diane filed the letters, and every two weeks Ken sent out a progress report. More letters arrived; some included invitations to Ottawa.

The general thrust of these letters I was sending – and they had a slight edge to them – was our progress on bringing the North into the Canadian psyche. It was a bit along the lines of "In the absence of Her Majesty, the Queen, I Ken Kirkby do hereby etc. etc." I was pointing out to them that we were being more active and successful than they were. For all of their departments, and money, and power, apparently, they couldn't get shit done. We were reporting that we were accomplishing a great deal. I was building major inroads. I was not partisan. I would talk to anyone who was elected and had a position. I had become a de facto political figure – unpaid and unelected. This went along seamlessly and no one ever stopped to question, "Who the hell is this guy anyway?"

Writing letters was one of Ken's small measures of relief over the tedious days of drawing Isumataq, two square inches at a time. There were days he wanted to sit down and scream, but he continued the painstaking process until he finally completed the task – nine months after he had started.

When Premier David Peterson called asking him to help organize an exhibition in the legislature, Ken stipulated the date for a year in the future – when he would be finished painting the sky of Isumataq.

His scaffold was built, ladders leaned against the walls, tubes of paint – by the carton – were stacked in the studio, and alarm clocks ticked beside his narrow cot. He was ready to begin painting.

I felt very, very much that things had now solidified. This was now a fact, and for the first time in this entire campaign, I actually knew that I was going to make it – not only the painting, but also my fight for Nunavut. This was it. It was now only a matter of physical labour to complete the vision. There was a different feeling now. The desperation was gone, and there was only a huge engine driving me. Now, there was only confidence. Now, I had access to politicians, business people, media – an infrastructure so massive and on such a personal level that I would be able to get this story through and by hook or by crook it would come into being.

It occurred to him is his newfound euphoria – "We need to celebrate!" He announced the "First Brushstroke" party and invitations went out in the shape of artist's palettes that hit the desk of every media contact in the city. Every couple of days a new invitation in a different colour, embossed with an Inukshuk, went into the mail. He called Keith and told him to fill a plane with choice Arctic food. Bob Engels, the North's most famous bush pilot, volunteered to fly the northern contingent to Toronto. On an evening in early September 1986, Ken climbed up on a ladder, from which he made a speech to a roomful of people, and then splashed a giant brushstroke across the towering, white canvas.

Then he settled into a routine that was to last for almost a year. He painted the sky for several hours, slept for two hours, went back to work, and then slept for two hours. As he painted he had a sense that this was what he was meant to do – to paint on this scale. Every other painting seemed too small – even the giant canvas that hung at First Canadian Place was undersized. How could he ever go back to painting something on a lesser scale? What he really wanted to do was buy Saskatchewan and paint it from helicopters.

One day a woman, wrapped in a fur coat, swished in on stiletto heels. She glanced around the studio and waved her arm at some paintings leaning against the far wall. "I'll have that one, and that one, and that one."

"Madam," Ken said from his perch on the scaffold. "I don't know who you are. I suspect you know who I am or you think you do. I would invite you to go outside, take a walk around, come back in, and say – 'Good morning!'"

She took a step back. "Well! I have never been spoken to that way before!"

Ken waved his hand. "Go on! Go. Shoo... Shoo."

She stalked out, and returned ten minutes later. "Good morning," she said.

"That's so much better."

"I want that," she said pointing to one of the paintings.

"Yes, I heard you," Ken said. "Everybody wants. It's like the song lyrics, 'You can't always get what you want, but if you try, sometimes, you get what you need.' There's something very important in those lyrics and I suggest you think about them and maybe learn something from them."

She narrowed her eyes. "Who the hell do you think you are, talking to me this way?"

"You know very well who I am," Ken said. "The question is – Who the hell do you think you are?"

"I want…"

"Well you can't have three – you can only have one."

He needed the money but he didn't care. He was angry. This woman had taken him right back to his childhood – to the righteous rich people who wouldn't let him play with their children – to the people who thought they were better than anyone else just because they had money – to the people who looked down on people like Miloo.

"But I want…"

"I know what you want. I heard you. You can have one – choose one."

She picked one up. "And have it framed," she said.

"I'm not a framer. You'll have to talk to Diane Lyle in the framing shop and I'm sure she'll look after you."

"And have it delivered," she said.

"I'm neither a framer nor a delivery boy – I'm a painter."

"Just send the bill."

"I've had bad experiences with sending bills. What leaves the studio is paid for."

"I just have bills sent."

"I'm sure you do and I'm sure they wait. I'm not a waiter – I'm a painter."

She strode out and came back with a yellow-uniformed chauffeur leading a tiny Pomeranian on a faux gem-encrusted leash. In her hand she waved a cheque book. "How much?"

"Ten thousand dollars."

"Ten thousand dollars?"

"Yes, ten thousand dollars."

"Well, we're going to have to deal."

"I don't make deals."

"Everybody makes deals."

"Everybody but me – I'm unique."

"I'll give you…"

"You'll give me jack. Every time you argue about the price it goes up five hundred dollars."

"Well, just a minute."

"Five hundred dollars. The price is now ten-five."

"That's ridiculous. I'll give you nine."

Ken shrugged. "Eleven thousand dollars."

"That's ridicu..."

"Eleven thousand five hundred."

"Okay. I'll give you a cheque for ten thousand."

"No you won't. Eleven-five. I told you, those are the terms. You're on my territory, my terms, my talent, my everything. All you have is money."

She glared at him, opened her cheque book and wrote out a cheque for eleven thousand five hundred dollars.

Diane framed and shipped the painting. He suspected that as soon as the woman hung it, she threw a cocktail party, inviting all her friends to come and admire her new acquisition, and to hear the scandalous story of how mortifyingly she had been insulted by the artist – because within days, a parade of chauffeur-driven cars began to arrive. The women who emerged from these cars were desperate to purchase a painting and endure the same astonishing insults. His attitude was the attraction, and he gave them what they wanted in bucketfuls. In only a few weeks, he sold about four hundred thousand dollars worth of paintings – more than he ever had before in one short span of time.

When Ken ran out of paintings at the studio, the women descended on the Carrier Gallery; when it sold out, they placed orders. The longer the waiting list, the more anxious they were to acquire a painting. Finally, he had to tell the women that the list was at least two years long.

When he was alone, he painted in a sort of reverie. The hard work had been done. Isumataq had been painted on the canvas of his mind. All that was left was to put paint on real canvas. In this dreamlike state, he let his mind wander, and again and again it came back to Nunavut. Now that government committees were discussing it and holding meetings, he pondered the political intricacies of this thing he had helped to set in motion.

What will happen? How will it come about? How will the whole thing come together? This will be the largest land claim in human history – everything from the Coppermine River to the North Pole and down to the borders of Labrador. It's one of the biggest chunks of the second-biggest country in the world, inhabited by tiny groups of people scattered across the land. On a human to square mile basis, it's probably the least populated place on earth. I suppose there would have to be a referendum. Would it be for all the people in Canada or would it be for the people living in the Northwest Territories? All of the Northwest Territories? Part of the Northwest Territories? And if there is a referendum and it passes, then what? This could open up a Pandora's Box. *Look at French and English Canada and what a scenario that is. Here, we're going to separate the Arctic – this could be dangerous territory*

– or it could be the ultimate blessing. So let's say Nunavut splits – well, it's still Canada, just a new territory. What would happen to the Inuit of Arctic Quebec – they won't go along with separating – not for a second. So they'll be left out. How would the Cree feel about this? How would the Montagnais and the Innu feel? Wouldn't they want to have a referendum too? This could be complicated.

His musings left him intensely excited. First, there was the fact that so few people knew or cared about the North – and then there were all of these possible ramifications!

The longer he worked on Isumataq, the more he felt that the painting had a life of its own, and he was merely its handmaiden, helping to breathe vitality into it. Marsha brought him food, as did several friends. Egidio was working out a schedule for the filming of Isumataq that included several trips to the Arctic – two during the summer, a couple in the winter, and one in spring. He was worried about the costs. He had filed applications with Telefilm Canada but had had no reply.

They shot some footage in the studio and flew in Keith, Roxy and several of the airline people who serviced the Arctic. During the party following a day of filming, Ken made an arrangement to donate the Yellowknife Airport painting to Canadian North airlines; who would give it to the Friends of the Prince of Wales Northern Heritage Centre in Yellowknife; who would, in turn, give it to the airport on permanent loan. In return, Ken was to receive free air travel anywhere in Canada for the rest of his life.

During all the activity, Ken still managed to continue painting the sky. If anything suffered, it was his sleep. But when winter set in, the cooler temperatures kept the paint wet longer. He also turned the thermostat down to just above freezing, which meant he could sometimes go as long as five hours without painting.

One day, as he was warming his chilled hands, a man walked into his studio who introduced himself as the head of a large financial company with offices in downtown Toronto. "I want a very big painting for my foyer," he said.

"Why?" Ken asked. "Why do you want a big painting for your foyer?"

"That's a peculiar question," he said.

"I think it's a most logical question."

"Well, it's what you put in a foyer."

Ken climbed down from the scaffold. "Do you want a large painting for your foyer because Mr. Albert Reichmann has one?"

"That's probably where it began. It's a very impressive painting."

"Yes, it is, thank you."

"I would like something of that power and size, for my company."

"First, you have to have a place to put it," Ken said. "It may work there, or not – it all depends on the environment. I suspect that you haven't thought your way through it – and I'm not trying to be rude, or difficult. Usually, when people come in and ask for something that's completely outside their understanding, they, probably, aren't asking for the right thing. I'd like to suggest that I come down and make a presentation to your company, on what I think you're looking for."

"You think so?"

"Yes. You don't seem sure about why you want it, and you're not sure about the environment it will be in. I suspect that no matter what I paint you won't be happy. Painting what is in someone else's mind is almost impossible. So, would you do me the courtesy of letting me come down and make a presentation, and see if that is what you want?"

"Certainly."

A few weeks later, Ken walked into the formidable skyscraper in downtown Toronto and gave the board members his analysis. They wanted a large painting for the foyer. Fine – he could supply that, but it wouldn't be as large as the Reichmann painting. And, it would be the first of several canvases. A smaller one would hang in the boardroom, and several others would hang throughout the premises. The preliminary sketches and drawings would be framed and hung as well. The paintings would tell a story that would be repeated in a booklet. A six-minute film would also tell the story, and it would play on a large screen television in the reception area. When a client arrived for a meeting, he would sit and watch the movie.

"Now, they have something interesting," Ken said. "This is something they have not anticipated seeing, and they realize that you are a lot more than just what you do. When you meet the client, you tour them around and show them all the works, and then you sit down and get down to business. By now, they realize that you are interesting people. You have things going on other than making money. When your business is concluded you hand the client a copy of the book – signed by me and your CEO – as something to take away and remind them of the meeting."

Ken suggested they take a holiday during the month of August and turn their offices over to him. When they returned the space would be transformed – not just because the paintings would be hung. What good were paintings if the background didn't complement them? He proposed changing the furniture to set off his work and painting the walls in appropriate colours. Everything had to work – it had to be of a piece.

The cost, he said, was irrelevant – the accountants would write the whole thing off. He thanked them, told them he had to return to his painting, and left. During the next few days several of the board members visited his studio. A couple of weeks later they accepted his fee of four hundred eighty thousand dollars.

When the media heard the latest "Ken Kirkby story" they once again descended on the studio. Then one day, Salvador dropped by. He had been working on Ken's idea of secretly erecting Inuksuit and dismantling them as mysteriously as they had been deployed. He had half a dozen ready to go, so one night in a chilling, February winter storm, he and Ken and a crew of men took to the streets of the city. In the morning when people woke and commuted to work, Inuksuit towered over them.

A few nights later they went out again and moved them to new locations. They moved them once again and then removed them completely. The media was in another uproar. What was going on, they asked Ken, who denied having anything to do with it. The Inuit had powerful spirits, he said, and it seemed that those spirits must have made their way south to Toronto.

In the spring of 1987, he painted the last brush stroke of Isumataq's sky then flew back to Keith's lodge with Michael and his film crew. They documented this trip that retraced the steps of their last visit.

One day the crew motored up the lake to Joan's old home and Keith followed with Ken an hour later. When they pulled into shore, the cameraman began to film. Ken took a step toward the small rise that hid most of the camp and stopped. Coming over the rise were three grandmothers, flanked by their family. Ken's heart pounded in his chest. His breath left his body and slowly he moved toward them as though in a dream. Joan came toward him and introduced him to her mothers and her large family, who had come to meet him. On the other side of the rise, they had set up tents where the blowing wind drove the bugs away. Near the tents stood an Inukshuk in two parts – a tribute to Joan's father.

Bessie, Joan's mother, invited Ken to her tent. She told him that she remembered him, but when he searched his mind, he could find no memories of his own. He wondered if the trauma of the events he had witnessed had erased some of his memories. She told him stories from her past and the past of her ancestors. She also gave him a paper rolled up and tied with a ribbon. When he opened it, he saw a drawing of himself on the ice with his Inuit friends. The other grandmothers also gave him drawings, exquisitely rendered in the Inuit tradition.

At Bessie's signal people slowly drifted out of the tent. When she was alone with Joan and Ken she questioned him about Nunavut. Was this a good idea? What was going to happen? Would the same bosses who were running things now still be heading the government?

Ken explained that it was not up to him to know how it would turn out or to decide how the government would be run. He was a painter and a messenger. His job was to tell the stories of the North and to make Canadians aware of the people and the conditions that existed there.

When she asked to meet his son, he stepped out of the tent and fetched

Michael. She gazed at him with sparkling eyes and a smile that split her deeply wrinkled face. "Very beautiful," she declared. "Like you."

He laughed, "Thank you, but I've never considered myself beautiful."

"Very beautiful," she said. "Very beautiful."

Stepping outside the tent, she ordered a big feast. Watching her, his memories of his life in the Arctic flooded back – how powerful the grandmothers were! She orchestrated the festivities without a word. A raised eyebrow was a good sign. A crinkled nose sent a signal that something was not right. Watching her quiet power, Ken wondered what would happen when Nunavut was formed. How would these people ever communicate with the people from the south?

By contrast, Egidio and Roberto were arguing stridently with Franco, who had told Ken he would follow him. Once again, as if by magic, he had arrived on the scene some days ago with his camera; and the arguments between him and Roberto had escalated to operatic proportions.

When the feast was well under way, a float plane arrived from Rankin Inlet carrying a couple of the bosses who nodded pleasantly at everyone and wandered around the fringes, watching and listening. Another Twin Otter followed, landed on the island in the bay and disgorged a small, wiry man named Jim Erickson, who was the head of tourism for Bob Engels' company, North West Territorial Airways. When he smiled, his mouth stretched so wide it threatened to slide off his face in both directions.

Thanks to Roxy, he'd heard about the party and had flown in to meet Ken. They took a short walk. What was he doing here? Jim asked. Was he helping Keith attract tourists to his lodge? Was he involved in politics? What was his agenda? Ken explained, for what seemed like the hundredth time, that his only agenda was to tell people about the North. "I'm not here speaking on behalf of anybody," he said. "I'm not some kind of *Lawrence of Arabia* wandering in the desert."

"Well you look the part," Jim said. "And you behave like it."

"I don't want that kind of story out there," Ken said.

Jim laughed. "It's already out." He knew that Ken had had conversations with Keith about attracting tourists, he said. What were his thoughts?

Ken outlined his ideas. First, they had to find a cheaper way to get Canadians to come to the Arctic. Who was going to spend ten or fifteen thousand dollars for two weeks in the frozen North? They would come, but only if there was a compelling reason – and that reason had to do with stories. He told him about his painting for the Yellowknife Airport The giant Inukshuk in the painting was the symbol of the North, he explained, as powerful as Stonehenge, the pyramids, and the mysterious stone faces on Easter Island – people would travel for something iconic. Forget the polar bears, Ken said. There were no polar bears on the tundra and people would only be disappointed when they arrived expecting to see the bears and found none existed except on the ice floes. However, the Inuksuit would not disappoint.

Could Ken fly with him to Yellowknife, right now, to decide where to hang the painting, Jim asked; and minutes later they were on an airplane flying to Rankin Inlet and then on to Yellowknife. At the airport, they surveyed the giant foyer and Ken picked the spot for the painting. Then he met with representatives of the organizations involved and they cemented the deal whereby the painting – donated by them to the Prince of Wales Northern Heritage Centre – would be loaned to the airport indefinitely.

A week later, when he was back in his studio painting Isumataq, Antonio Correia, the Consul General for Portugal, called. He needed help, he said. He was a champion sailor – one of the best in the world – and he was determined to compete for Portugal at the Seoul Olympics. However, Portugal was a small country and raising funds was a problem. Ken was good at this sort of thing – could he help? Ken called Virgil, the most affluent Portuguese businessman he knew, and the three men met for lunch and concocted a plan inviting support from other prosperous Toronto Portuguese community members and inviting them to several fundraising events. The highly successful campaign caught the attention of the Portuguese media, and President Mario Suarez who couriered an invitation for Ken to visit him at his palace in Lisbon. Rocco, Virgil, and Antonio received similar invitations.

Lisbon matched his memory. It was the same and yet completely different. The suite at the Florida Hotel was the one his father had used when he was making important deals. Gazing out the window at the teeming traffic below, Ken felt the past mingle and blend with the present until he was no longer quite sure where or when he was.

Ken, Marsha, Rocco, Virgil and Antonio took a taxi to the gates of the palace where they were greeted warmly and brought to an anteroom. The President's secretary entered and led them to Mario Suarez's office suite. The President was a tall man with a commanding presence. Politically, he stood left of centre and had escaped to Brazil during the civil war. When the war had ended he returned to take over the reins of government.

After Suarez had greeted them he took Ken aside. "I want to talk to you about your dad," he said. "What a magnificent human being. This country owes him a great deal. How wonderful it is to have you back here." He asked him about his wanderings around the Canadian North and his work in the Arctic. "I want to hear all the stories," he said.

Ken told him how it had all started – with an old Portuguese fisherman named Francisco who had lived on the beach not more than twelve kilometres from this very spot.

The following day they travelled to Virgil's hometown where they were grandly feted and on another day, he and Marsha visited the village that had been his home. They walked up the Avenue of Princes and stopped in front of number twelve – his home. In the garden, he saw a couple talking with the gardener. Ken leaned over the garden wall, introduced himself, and asked if he could look inside his old boyhood home. The couple frowned, turned their backs on him, and walked into the house, locking the door behind them.

The gardener said, "You're Ken."

"Yes."

"I'm Francisco's nephew."

"How wonderful to meet you. But why are they so upset?"

"They think you've come back to claim the house."

Ken laughed. "I just wanted to go inside and look. I thought it might be very nice."

"Oh no. People have been wondering when you would return to take back what is yours."

"I've never considered it mine," he said.

They walked on through the village and then down to the beach. Nothing had changed. The wall he and Francisco had built was still there and still trapping the sand to create a beautiful stretch of beach. Even the remains of Francisco's cabin still clung to the cliffs.

They drove to Peniche, the home of their friend, the Count. Even here Ken was recognized, not so much for himself, but for his father; a saint according to the owner of a restaurant, who closed the café in celebration of Ken's visit and served up a feast for his honoured guests.

Back in Toronto, Ken settled into a routine that was continuously interrupted. When he was not working on Isumataq he painted canvases for the gallery and for the financial company's new collection. His biggest challenge was that the media liked him too much. They wanted to know why he was meeting with presidents in Europe; they wanted to know his plans – what was next? Too much good press was boring so they sought out the malcontents – those who had accused him of appropriating a culture that wasn't his. He needled them until they fired back. He had come back from his latest Arctic trip with letters from the grandmothers, written in Inuktitut and translated into English, stating that they not only approved of his art, but had also asked him expressly to do what he was doing. The letters were tucked in a file that Ken suspected might be useful one day.

Bad press was interesting but outrageous press was better. He had about twenty unfinished paintings, stacked in a corner of the studio, that he would likely never complete. He spread them out on the floor and paced between them.

"What are you doing?" Diane asked, poking her head into the studio.

"I'm going to sand them all down," he said.

"Why not just finish the damn things and sell them?"

"No. It's not worth it. I'm going to sand them down and then I'm going to take all my old oil paints and thinners and other material, and get some gold and silver leaf and some red enamel and I'm going to paint eighteen fabulous abstracts – completely different from anything I do – as wild and woolly as possible – and in each one I'm faintly going to paint people from different parts of the world – Africans, Arabs, Mongolians, Indians – and until it comes to you, you won't see the face; but once you see it, it will dominate the painting."

He was inspired: and splashed paint and thinners about with such abandon that he frequently had to throw open the doors of his studio before the vapours sent him reeling.

One day Salvador dropped by with a bottle of red wine and two glasses. "What on earth?" he asked

Ken explained the plan that had been brewing in his mind – possibly aided by the fumes of the various chemicals he was breathing in.

Tengri was the name of the Mongolian God. What if an artist from Mongolia had created these canvases – an artist named Tengri who signed his name in blood red paint. An agoraphobic who never left his rooms? It would mean that Ken had to mount an exhibition for him – a black tie event – by invitation only!

Salvador clapped his hands, downed a couple of glasses of wine, and hurried off to begin arranging the exhibition. He booked a charming and exclusive new Italian restaurant for the evening of the exhibit and helped mail out the invitations. Meanwhile, Rocco, who expressed concern over the consequences of such a hoax, got measured for a tuxedo.

On the evening of the exhibition, the paintings were beautifully displayed on ornate easels throughout the restaurant. The crowd was massive. Ken stood at the podium, telling the sad story of Tengri and explaining that because there was very little of the man's work available, the prices were quite high. Money didn't matter. Everyone wanted a Tengri painting and the show sold out.

Some of the smaller newspapers in the area had sent reporters who wrote that the paintings were the "Work of a genius!"

A few days later, when the focus turned back from Tengri to Ken, one of the press members who liked to snipe at him confronted him again with the accusation that he was appropriating someone else's culture.

"Do you read Inuktitut?" he asked, walking toward his file cabinet and pulling out the grandmothers' letter.

The reporter shook his head.

"Well I have a translation in English," he said, pulling the second letter out of the file. "This letter comes from the grandmothers." And he read their request that he paint Isumataq and let the world know of their plight.

"I have given up my own ambitions in order to carry out a promise that I made," he said.

The Toronto newspapers reported the confrontation, and culture appropriation ceased to be an issue.

Nick Peros was one of his unexpected visitors. He was a young man with dark hair that flopped over on his forehead like a young colt's forelock. A classical composer, who was writing his final thesis and who had been following Ken's story in the newspapers, he wanted to compose a symphony for Isumataq using an augmented orchestra and a choir. Would Ken commission such a piece of music?

Ken offered a painting in trade and Nick became a regular at the studio, watching Ken paint, listening to his stories, and occasionally jotting musical notes on his sheets. When people asked, Ken said, "He's composing a symphony."

"What?"

"A symphony for Isumataq – and not just any symphony. It's for an augmented orchestra and a choir."

"So you're going to have a bigger-than-full symphony orchestra and a choir! You can't have just a symphony?"

"Of course not."

"And where are you going to do this?"

"I have no idea. Tomorrow will reveal itself. Today we're in the business of composing a symphony."

"But what does a symphony have to do with it?"

"I don't know. But what does a symphony not have to do with it?"

"On the other hand," Salvador cried, "Why not an opera?"

While Nick was writing his symphony, Joe Canavan, one of the young professionals brought his brother Patrick to the studio. Patrick was a rock and roll musician and composer who played in several local bands. "Forget the symphony," Joe said. "What Isumataq needs is rock music."

Patrick joined Nick in the studio, asking for stories, turning them into song lyrics and giving them titles like "Rifles, Bibles and Booze".

Ken told the ancient stories: the moon chasing the sun and the girl whose chopped-off fingers became all the animals in the world. While Ken talked, Patrick strummed on his guitar and one day he brought the rest of his band members. When they asked about money, he offered "Ken dollars" and after several months of talking and composing, they took their songs into a recording studio to cut a CD.

Ken fulfilled his promise to create slide shows to lure people to the North. He sorted the photographs he had taken into a twice weekly studio exhibition for about sixty people each evening. Although they loved the photos and stories, they balked at paying three thousand five hundred dollars for ten days in a cold, forsaken land. When Ken pointed out that the price had been whittled down by more than half, they remained unmoved.

The one group that did not attend was the young professionals. They insisted they were too busy working and completing their first annual charity project, raising funds to help street kids – a project Ken had inspired one day when he had rounded on them for being stupidly selfish and short-sighted.

"Here you are. You have your expensive condos, your beautiful shades, your designer clothes, and your shiny Porsches; but what do you do for others? I haven't seen you do anything for anyone. Why don't you get together and look around you? Look out at the street in front of this restaurant. There are kids out there that are sleeping on vents. Are you blind? Couldn't you take some time and energy out of your lives to look after them?"

They had risen to the challenge and were staging a fundraiser. When they asked Ken to donate a painting to auction, he said, "It's a tired idea. It's been done a million times. Be authentic. Be new. Be different. Tell you what, I'll come up with a really neat drawing and we'll do a raffle."

Ken forgot about the drawing. During the dinner, when the raffle was announced, he stood up. "I would rather not do a drawing and present it to you," he said. "I would rather that the winner of the raffle come to the studio and sit beside me, and I will make a drawing for that person. It will be much more personal and far more interesting for both myself and the winner."

Enthusiastic applause greeted his words and when it died down, he added that the price per ticket would double since the prize was now so much more valuable.

The winner and her friend, Karen Wristen, both lawyers, were the first to commit to a trip to the Arctic. Once the first tickets sold, more followed and when a dozen were confirmed Ken called his old friend Gary McLaren. Did he and his cameraman Bailey want to come along as his guests?

"Well, of course," Gary said.

"Good. We're leaving on July 15."

Before the trip he gathered the group together for a briefing. "You're going to a place that words can't describe," he told them. "Still, I'm going to do my best to give you some understanding of what you're going to encounter. We have ten days but if the weather closes in, we have forever. Make no appointments. The weather rules in the North and there is no such thing as a schedule."

"Given that you are going to be in an environment utterly removed from anything you have ever known, at some point you are going to experience some very strange emotions. You'll feel wobbly and this is a very natural thing to happen. Don't worry about it. Imagine being in a place where all the things that are common in your life don't exist. Imagine a place where the only things that do exist are things that are uncommon to you. You will be in a state of sensory deprivation and sensory overload at the same time. There are no trees. There are no cities. There is nothing – but there are vast numbers of insects so pray that the wind blows. There is almost no night. The size of the horizon is so immense that the prairies by comparison are claustrophobic. It will just eat away at you and you'll have to go through the experience of feeling a bit wobbly and perhaps teary and that's fine. I would be worried if you didn't have an emotional moment or two. You would have to be completely insensitive."

In the weeks leading to the departure day, dozens of incidents demanded his attention. First on the list was the long-planned show at the Ontario Legislature buildings, which was a great success. The Premier steered Ken from group to group, demanding that Ken tell the stories that explained the paintings – even relating some himself that he had heard so often he had committed them to memory.

Then Ehor Boyanowsky, his voice almost incoherent with excitement, called him. Ken must fly out to Vancouver right away for an emergency meeting of the Steelhead Society. There were problems with the dam project in Quebec.

He drove into town to deliver a painting to London Life on Avenue Road, on the day of his flight. When he got back into his car, a large cheque in hand, he heard Peter Gzowski, radio's "Mister Canada", interviewing John Fraser, who was now Speaker of the House. The interview had almost ended. "So, Mr. Speaker," Gzowski said. "Your life seems to be completely taken up by your office."

"Well, it is," Fraser, replied.

"I know you're a fanatical fly-fisherman," Gzowski said. "Do you ever get to do that?"

"As a matter of fact, yes," Fraser said. "This afternoon I'm getting on an airplane to go to Vancouver and I'm going to meet my good friend Ken Kirkby, the painter, and I am going to be honoured at the Steelhead Society dinner. I couldn't imagine being in finer company. I'm just delighted. So yes, we are actually going to steal some time – but don't tell anybody – and we're going to have a few meetings to talk about some problems, which I'm sure we'll resolve, and then we're going to go fishing. And the people putting this on have some surprises for us too."

Ken chuckled. So, that was why Boyanowski had insisted he fly to Vancouver. He knew that Ken would never have pulled himself away from Isumataq for a mere fishing trip.

When Ehor greeted him in the baggage area, with an immense bear hug, Ken told him that the jig was up. Ehor shrugged. "I wondered if you might be listening to Gzowski's program. But I do have one or two more surprises for you."

The first was Ted Hughes, the poet Laureate of England who was waiting at Ehor's home in Deep Cove. The next two were Sasha Tolstoy, Leo Tolstoy's grandson and Jack Hemingway, Ernest Hemingway's son, who joined them at the celebratory dinner that night.

The next day was devoted to meetings. The campaigns to stop the Camano dam in northern British Columbia and the Great Whale project in northern Quebec had taken on a global significance with the Inukshuk used as the symbol of survival.

The Steelhead Society had stopped trying to manage the campaign protesting the proposed dam and had turned it over to conservation groups around the world. Chief Billy Diamond, the leader of the Quebec Cree Nation, headed one of the most powerful of them. Through his efforts it had become widely known that the power harnessed by the project was to be sold to the United States for billions of dollars. Matthew Cooncome joined the campaign and set out with giant war canoes down the coast of the United States and up the Hudson River. The United Sates Senators, led by Ted Kennedy, investigated the deal. They had been completely unaware, they said. Along with contracts and several signed agreements, a copy of one of Ken's speeches also circulated in the senate.

"If you, the American people, can get up earlier in the morning, work harder, accomplish more and do better, good on you. But if you, the American people, can get up in the morning and before you go to bed at night participate in a set of activities that will eradicate the last great herd of four-legged animals on the North American continent then I have nothing to say to you. If you, the American people, can get up in the morning and before you go to bed at night do things that you know will eradicate the very people who live on that land and need those animals to survive then I have nothing to say to you."

Vermont was the first state to pull out. New York and Maine and then the others followed suit. Every contract was cancelled.

This was an example that I very much wanted to push forward into the consciousness of people across North America. This is what a handful of people can do. This is power – it is not about money. Canada was going to get more than forty billion dollars and everyone was very caught up in the money. But the money was not power. This was power. Throughout my life, I have tried to get this point across – without success.

The next day Ken, Ehor, John Fraser, Ted Hughes and a small entourage drove to Hilltop Garden, a farm on the banks of the Thompson River, just off the Trans-Canada Highway. The Thompson was once one of the top fly-fishing rivers in the world and had attracted the Hollywood elite like Clark Gable, Spencer Tracy and Katherine Hepburn, who had stayed in the cottage at Hilltop Garden while they camped and fished in blissful peace.

16

The Arctic

Ken wanted to confront one last situation before leaving for the Arctic. He and Marsha had grown apart and scrapped constantly. There was also the matter of Karen Wristen. The first sight of her had attracted him immensely and the attraction grew every time he saw her. But he could never find the right time to talk to Marsha and decided to put it off until his return.

Karen Wristen and her friend had left two weeks previously and met them in the baggage area at the airport in Rankin Inlet. To Ken's surprise he felt his body vibrate as he hugged Karen. This was a new phenomenon for him, and he realized, in that instant, that she was a magnet he could not escape.

They tossed their luggage into the twin otter that was already loaded down with provisions for the lodge. Keith had finished the building since Ken's last visit and the accommodations were new and clean and the rooms furnished. They arrived in bright daylight at 1 a.m. and a temperature of one hundred and one degrees Fahrenheit, without a hint of a breeze. Swarms of mosquitoes attacked them. One unfortunate traveller drew them like honey and his face was swollen within minutes. Bailey, oblivious of the murderous insects, set up his camera the instant he hit the ground, and filmed everything that moved.

Ken wanted them to learn something about the North and to enjoy themselves in the process. He gave them each a four-foot length of string with instructions to walk across the tundra and choose a one-foot square section, which they would outline with the string. "Choose your square carefully," he said. "There are hundreds of millions of acres here but take time to choose your very small section. When you've outlined it, come back."

When they returned he gave them each a small spyglass. "I recommend that you get down on the ground on your knees and look at what's in that square foot – and I mean really look. I'll be back in an hour or so and then we can all go in and have coffee and talk about what you saw. Oh – one last thing – while you're looking at your square foot, keep your mind's eye on the horizon – it's the most giant horizon on earth."

"What are you doing?" Keith whispered.

"How can we start this until everyone gets a real understanding of what it is they are standing on," Ken said. "And then begin to comprehend the immensity of the place? Just about everything that grows on the earth grows in the Arctic. Orchids that in the tropics would grow to three feet are one-thirty-second of an inch in the Arctic. Tea grows here – sassafras, cotton – everything. The Arctic is a peculiar place and few people have any understanding of it."

An hour passed. No one had moved. Shouts erupted now and then. "Hey, that's amazing! Look at that! Do you have one of those?"

Over coffee in the lodge, they interrupted each other in the excitement of describing the things they had seen. Ken explained that one square foot of tundra viewed through a spyglass was like looking down on the Amazon rain forest from an airplane. That square foot was as full of tiny life as the rainforest was full of mammals and reptiles. "So now perhaps you will understand that wherever you put your foot down you are killing something and whenever you breathe in, you are drowning life forms smaller than your eye can see. That said, you have looked at a square foot and you have looked at it in the context of the world's biggest horizon. My suggestion is that you think about this and instead of babbling about it, form coherent thoughts and sentences."

They wandered outdoors where they sat on the high boardwalk that ran in front of their rooms. They pointed out caribou in the distance, and marvelled at the light that never faded. They hadn't slept in almost thirty-six hours but they behaved like children who had forgotten that sleep was necessary.

Ken cracked open a crate he had shipped to the lodge in advance of their arrival, revealing every imaginable kind of liquor that a distillery could brew. He poured drinks for everyone and after a glass or two, they began to yawn, and stretch sleepily, and head to their rooms – and bed.

When they were alone Ken conferred with Michael and Keith. Now that he had these people here, what was he to do with them? He wanted to give them at least one stunning experience each day. For starters, Keith told him, the grandmothers and Joan were going to camp at their deserted homestead again, so that they could re-enact their meeting for the television cameras.

The next morning, Mel, the lodge chef, who was as temperamental as any prima donna and as talented, dished up a magnificent breakfast. Keith had flown in food to impress his guests, including the finest caviar, cream, eggs, ham, and bacon. After breakfast, while everyone piled into canoes to explore the lake, Karen and Joan volunteered to stay behind to fish, and Ken remained with them.

When they had caught enough fish, they delivered their catch to Mel and joined the others at a pebbled beach a couple of miles down the lake.

They were marvelling at the line of diminutive Inuksuit that curved along the water's edge toward a far-off boulder that seemed to reach almost fifty feet into the sky. The Inuksuit told a story, Ken said, and after a lunch of fresh fried fish he led them toward the boulder. As they walked the boulder diminished in size until they stood beside it and found it was about three feet tall, pink, perfectly smooth, and resting on top of an immense gray rock that had been partially heaved out of the tundra.

"This is a fishing Inukshuk," he told them. "It tells you that this is a good place to go fishing. How does it say that? If the fishing is good, the Inuit take a stone out of the water and put it on top of another stone with little Inuksuit leading the way. A passerby who had never been in this land would know immediately that he could catch fish here. Other configurations of stone describe what kind of fish are here. Essentially, this is a language."

He explained that the permafrost lurks just under the surface of the tundra, and below that lay thousands of feet of ice. The ground above the permafrost where the ice melted consisted almost entirely of rich humus built up over eons by the tiny plants that grew and died there. An eight-inch tree takes hundreds of years to grow to that height in the Arctic's short season. The fibres of the humus stretched out along the surface and down to the permafrost, siphoning the water from the ice and sending it into the atmosphere. As the wind travelled across the surface of the land in buffeting gusts, it created rudimentary magnifying lenses of the millions of tiny water bubbles streaming into the air. The farther away you were from an object the more lenses you were looking through and the larger the distant object appeared.

That night after supper he walked down to the dock with a fly-fishing rod. Arctic grayling congregated in the shallows here and after a few causal casts, he landed a fine three-pound fish. As he unhooked it and slipped it back into the water he noticed Karen sitting on an overturned bucket at the far end of the dock.

"I'd like to try that," she said.

He handed her the rod and described the process but even after all these years he still had no idea how to explain that it was a line with no weight and it needed to fly guided by minimal strength and energy, and perfect timing.

She cast a couple of times and smiled. "I like this," she said and while the fly lay on the water, a large grayling took the bait. Ken disengaged it, gave the rod back to her and left her to sort out the tangles and continue casting. He sat on the overturned bucket at the far end of the dock and watched.

At that moment I realized, I was about to fall off a cliff and I wanted to. It had been a very long time since I had had these feelings. This was almost like dealing with a power from another place. And at this time it wasn't even remotely sensual or sexual – there was something utterly different going on here. What is happening to me? I don't know myself. I wondered how wise it was for me to meet this woman. What is going on here is alien to me and I'm losing control of myself.

When she had caught a couple of fish and had managed to untangle the snarls she had made, she was beaming. She pulled another bucket close and sat down. Ken asked questions about her life that she answered in monosyllables, turning the conversation back to him and his stories of the Arctic. Politics was the only subject that animated her. She had hoped to go into politics, she said and confessed to being a great admirer of Pierre Elliot Trudeau.

What kind of lawyer was she? Ken asked.

"I'm a litigator," she said.

Ken imagined her, five foot nothing in her stocking feet, standing in front of a judge and facing down a host of burly male lawyers.

Early the next morning, he met her on the dock to take her fishing, his mind and heart in turmoil. He had found the thing he had always been searching for – and at the same time the one thing he had not allowed himself to look for. He was as excited as a child on Christmas Eve and as afraid as an acrophobic on the edge of the Grand Canyon.

Later that day, Ken led the group to the mouth of the lake where the river poured out on its way to the ocean. He told them to hide behind the surrounding boulders and wait. In less than an hour, caribou surrounded them. They shot roll after roll of film and stared in undisguised astonishment when Ken walked toward the beasts and wandered through the middle of the herd, the animals parting for him as though he were a rock in the river.

The temperature climbed to one hundred and four degrees Fahrenheit. They began to wilt inside the long-sleeved shirts and pants they wore to defend themselves against the voracious mosquitoes. They covered themselves with DEET, slathered on sunscreen, and plopped hats with mosquito netting on their heads, to cover their faces.

The next day, they went in search of muskoxen. They took the boats down the lake and Ken ordered them to stay away from the shore because unlike caribou, muskoxen could be dangerous. The animals came to the shore, drawn by their curiosity. Ken repeated the stunt he had done with Michael, jumping out of the boat into two feet of water and wading ashore where a giant bull pawed the ground and mock charged. When the bull stopped it blew froth over him in a mighty snort.

Wading back to the boat, he submerged himself in the water, shook himself and climbed back in, pouring the water out of his cowboy boots. He told them that muskoxen down, called qiviut, was stronger than steel and softer than the softest eiderdown on earth. Worn next to the skin it was like being touched by the breath of angels. The Inuit women gathered the down at certain times of the year in gullies where willows grew four or five feet high and where the muskoxen liked to browse. As they moved among the trees, they left clumps of down behind on the branches. The women would gather it and weave it into the warmest, lightest garments on earth. Ken led them to one such gully where they each gathered a handful of the down.

In the evening, they once again sat around the dining table long after they had eaten. Keith's children had overcome their shyness and joined them. One of the tourists, Bruce Muir, gave them stacks of paper and crayons that he had packed and they began to draw the most marvellous pictures. Bruce became their Pied Piper for the rest of the time the group stayed at the lodge, and everywhere he went a group of children tagged along behind him.

The next day, Keith and Ken re-enacted the visit to the grandmothers. When Ken arrived and the grandmothers walked over the edge of the hill, Bailey began to film while Gary McLaren hopped from one foot to the other. "This is going to be such an amazing film!" he shouted.

The grandmothers had brought more drawings. Ken had also brought gifts: Swiss army knives for each of them and for Bessie, a Konica camera and many rolls of film. The Inuit were the most photographed people on earth and were invariably represented as short, plump and smiling – but what did the photographers who had taken those pictures know of them? Ken wanted to see the images they would capture of each other. The gift of the camera was so appreciated that before he left, he gave his other four cameras away, along with all his film.

While the grandmothers prepared a feast, float planes arrived carrying several of the "bosses," accompanied by a government minister from Yellowknife. They were the same tired men asking the same stale questions and this time they talked to the others as well. What was Ken doing here? What was their purpose? They were here to enjoy the Arctic, was the uniform response. No one travelled on vacation with an entire film crew, they protested.

"I do," Ken said. "And so do the people who buy my paintings."

The next day, some of the group set off with Keith and his oldest son to explore the tundra while Joan and Michael went off on their own adventure. Karen and Ken launched a boat and went fishing for Arctic grayling. Ken angled over to an esker, a collection of boulders and rock deposited by the glaciers, where they cast their lines into the water. They sat quietly and, after what seemed like a long time, a thin black band appeared on the horizon. It was no wider than a jet stream but stretched to infinity on either side and moved toward them at a furious clip. "I've never seen anything like that before," Ken said pointing it out to Karen. Within minutes the band had widened until it engulfed them with winds that rocked the boat and stirred the water of the shallow lake into heaving whitecaps. Rain poured down as though a tap had been turned on in the heavens.

Ken fought to turn the boat into the wind, powering it up so that it would drift backwards slowly with the eighty-mile-per-hour gales. Karen hunkered in the back of the boat baling water furiously with her bare hands. They had nowhere to go except to drift backward toward the island where the airplanes landed. The entire sky turned black as sharply as though a light had been switched off. Lightening filled the sky and thunder echoed off the tundra. Rainbows flashed briefly through the turmoil and disappeared again, devoured by sheets of lightening.

The temperature plummeted and their waterlogged clothes stuck to their shivering skin. Grayling floated belly up in the bottom of the boat. With more luck than intent, Ken reached the lee of the island where they huddled waiting for the wind to ease, bailing water with their cupped hands. When the wind died down enough to chance it, Ken made a run for the Lodge.

Inside, the others were drinking hot tea, shaking out soaked clothing, and laughing. What an adventure!

After a dinner of filleted grayling, while the sun dipped down to touch the horizon, Karen sat beside him on the boardwalk. One by one, the others went to bed. She uncapped two miniature bottles of scotch, offering one to Ken. As he turned toward her their eyes met.

"Do you know what you're doing?" he asked. "You're married."

"I know," she said. Taking his hand, she led him past the rooms where people were dreaming quietly and into a storage shed, where they made a bed of sleeping bags and chased loneliness away all night long.

Days of magic followed. Everything Ken had ever done or felt had led him to this. They talked little and loved much. He found out that she was not happy in her marriage, that she was trained in environmental and Aboriginal law and that along with politics, those were her passions.

Their time together drew to a close. "I'll call," he said. "This is not a fling. I want you."

"We don't even know each other."

"I know. This is not logical. Something inside tells me this is lunacy but I don't care."

"It's just the hormones talking. You won't call."

"I'll call."

Had they known each other a week or an eternity? It didn't matter. A week was an eternity – an eternity only seven days long.

Ken, reluctantly, waved good-bye as the plane left carrying Karen and most of the rest of the group back to Toronto. For the next week, Ken,

Michael, and John Harris, a journalist, travelled deeper into the tundra to one of Keith's remote summer camps. They took few supplies, expecting to find food and warm bedding at their destination. When Ken assessed the situation after the float plane dropped them off, he realized they were ill-prepared for their stay, and the trek back to the lodge. The supplies at the camp consisted of a boat, a tent with no tent poles, a large can of dried mushroom soup, and a few bedrolls and fishing rods. To make matters worse, the weather turned and the hot summer winds were replaced with the chill of an early fall. The grays and greens of the tundra began to turn scarlet and heavy rain fell, which then turned to sleet and later, to wet snow.

Blindly, they putt-putted around the shore, searching for the river that would lead them back to the lodge. When they found it, it was too shallow to navigate because the waters had drained to their summer depth. Resigned, Ken and John jumped into the water, one pushing and one pulling the boat, while Michael walked along the shore searching for obstacles.

The cold, wet, backbreaking labour continued all day. In the evening, they propped the tent up with paddles, lit two Coleman stoves inside their shelter and fried the fish they had caught, augmenting the meal with vile-tasting mushroom soup.

They pushed on for four days, the time collapsing into itself until all they felt was cold, wet, and bone weary. When they finally made it to Ferguson Lake they were as thrilled as though they had found the elusive pot of gold. A helicopter circled overhead and a large boat motored toward them. They were well overdue and Keith was relieved to find them alive and uninjured.

When Ken got back to Toronto he had one priority. After showering at the studio he called Karen, "How about supper tonight?"

In the week Karen had been back, she had filed for divorce. Ken told Marsha the next day that it was over. When he told Diane about the situation she quit her job.

Karen rented a house on Belsize Avenue off Yonge Street and gave Ken a key. The chaos of broken relationships roared around him and he had never been happier in his life. With Diane gone, Ken turned the entire space into his studio and hired his lawyer's sister-in-law, Elaine Ross, who had a background in publicity. She skillfully kept contact with the media who hovered constantly in the background like hungry jays.

Michael visited frequently and he and Karen became good friends. Watching them together, Ken was often startled by the intensity of his feelings. At times, he could hear the beating of his heart, pounding like a steady and welcome ache in his chest.

Karen applied to write the bar exam for the Northwest Territories on the assumption that, with the creation of Nunavut almost a certainty, the government in the North would need lawyers. Canada's northern territories contained the richest mineral deposits on earth and many corporations were poised to rape the land.

Ken accompanied Karen when she was called to the bar in the summer of 1989 and flew to Yellowknife to take her oath. While they were there, Ken arranged to hang the "Yellowknife Airport" painting, which had been shipped and stored in a nearby warehouse some months previously.

The media and what seemed like half the population of the city came to the airport to witness the installation of the painting. There was one hitch – it was one inch taller than the height of the wall. While officials, builders and architects stood around muttering and scratching their heads, Ken lit a cigarette and considered the dilemma.

While the professionals toyed with the idea of tearing down a section of the wall, Ken hit on a simpler solution. He proposed that they cantilever the top of the painting out just slightly. Not only would it solve the problem, he said, it would actually give the viewer on the ground a better perspective.

Back home again, Ken put a major push on Isumataq. But, where once he would happily have slept in the studio, now he was eager to be home. Nothing, not even Isumataq, was as important as spending time with Karen and Michael.

At night, they talked. Ken had never met a woman who matched him in so many ways – in her intellect, her visions and ideals and even her political leanings. They talked about the future. What would they do when Isumataq was finished – when his great life's work was done? Ken talked about the unveiling, which he imagined might take place in Yellowknife. Karen said no – "the bosses" who still ran the far North didn't like him and he might get a mixed reception.

"What about Rome?" he asked "Much as I want this project to be one hundred percent Canadian – the painting, the symphony, the pop music, the merchandising – wouldn't it be something to take it to the Coliseum in Rome and unveil it while walking two lions on leashes?"

Karen looked at him as though he had suddenly sprouted an alien antenna on his forehead. "No – just picture it!" he protested. In his mind he saw himself on a podium flanked by two lions. He imagined his photo on the front cover of every magazine and newspaper in the world – now that would be media attention!

Why, Karen asked, was he so attracted to the media and why was the media so attracted to him? It was all quite simple, he replied. There was only one story in the entire field of mythology and literature – it was the same story, retold in countless ways: a hero with a cause succeeding against all odds. He was one man against big odds.

Ken played with the hours of his days like a master juggler. He had to paint Isumataq in the scraps of time he had left over – when he wasn't working on the canvases that he sold to his clients – they paid for keeping Isumataq alive. Then the Steelhead Society called on his services again. It was running low on funding and Ken created a series of sketches that were silkscreened and made into limited edition signed prints and sold at fundraisers. He created another series of his Tengri paintings – his Mongolian alter ego – and organized another black tie dinner event where he sold the lot.

He woke up every morning, not with the anxiety of facing an almost insurmountable pile of work, but with deep gratitude for the gift of his life. Karen had washed his pain away. Her love was a benediction. The absence of heartache made him realize how much darkness he had been carrying inside for so long.

In their many talks about the future, Karen told him that when Isumataq was done, she wanted to move to British Columbia where she could practise environmental and Aboriginal law. When Michael heard that he said, "Me too!"

"You too?" Ken asked.

"I might want to go to university there. And I love the gray skies. I love the rain."

And what about the future, he asked Karen. What would happen when Isumataq was done?

"Give me the same support I'm giving you," she said.

As he imagined that future life, a great blanket of peace settled on him. Yes, this was a tomorrow he could embrace.

In the present, plans for the unveiling of Isumataq began to take shape. Ken envisioned a cross-Canada tour to rival the Rolling Stones "Steel Wheels" production. To pay their expenses they would manufacture and sell an immense amount of merchandise. He designed a logo – a circle with a rising sun behind a silhouetted Inukshuk – that would be emblazoned on all the products.

Elaine contacted Beaverbrook Brothers, a promotional products company, and Ken bartered some paintings for the first run of merchandise: sweatshirts, buttons, baseball caps, pins, pens, mugs, and other paraphernalia.

Winter was giving way to spring, in 1990, when Ken and the documentary camera crew travelled to the Arctic once more. Egidio had hired a new cameraman, Chris Porter, a big Maritimer. Roberto came along to shoot stills and Franco flew over from Italy. Keith, who lived in Rankin Inlet during the winter months, had rented a house next door for Ken's crew while Ken bunked in with his family.

After two weeks of filming on the ice, Ken got back to work on Isumataq and for two months rarely took a break; until he received an invitation from Jim Erickson, of North West Territorial Airways (now NWT Air). Jim invited Ken and Karen to join him, the other heads of the airline and a couple of hockey stars, on a fishing trip to Victoria Island, in the high Arctic. The trip took them to Cambridge Bay and then to a remote tent camp far north of the Arctic Circle. They fished for giant Arctic char in the icy waters and watched the sun circle the sky in perpetual, disorienting daylight. The rolling landscape was dotted with rocks and boulders, but when they moved, they were revealed as herds of muskoxen.

After a week of fishing, and shooting hundreds of photos of the muskoxen, they flew back to Cambridge Bay just as the weather closed in. For the next few days the fog would lift for tantalizingly brief periods, only to quickly settle in again.

They made the most of their enforced stay, borrowing a pair of ATVs and riding to the top of Pelly Mountain, a thousand-foot high rolling hill. From the top, when the fog lifted briefly, they could see forever – below them was the Northwest Passage while behind them the tundra stretched away to infinity. In this great silence at the top of the world, sitting among dozens of eccentrically shaped Inuksuit, they talked about many things – their life, their love, and their country. Ken talked about his passion, recalling a song lyric he had heard once: "Canada is somewhere above the timberline" – that was his Canada.

I think Karen finally got what was driving me. How do you explain this place where we were sitting to a world that had never been here? It would be like explaining an orange to a person who had never tasted one. I talked about how near impossible it was to describe these things in words or images. Isumataq was my attempt and it required all the shenanigans of our world to impart, not an intellectual understanding, but an understanding that would grab the audience in the pit of its stomach. I wanted it to create a flood of emotions so huge it would suffocate the intellect – to bring everyone back to the sensory creatures they truly are.

Karen took in the vast expanse. "There have been men who have gone into the desert and had an experience but they've all made the same mistake – they came back and told people about it," she said.

I wondered. Am I just falling into the same trap that all those other people fell into? Is the magic of this place so personal that you can't describe it? All I want to do is take people to the gates. What they do afterwards is their business. I want to at least give them their own emotional experience – not my understanding of it. Each individual who sees the big painting – it will be a personal thing for each one. Canadians have this strange identity crisis. Anybody who sat on that mountain and looked out would see the soul of a nation and there would be no crisis. Whether you spoke English or French or Inuktitut or Swahili – it would make absolutely no difference.

When the fog finally lifted, they flew across the Strait to Coppermine –

a journey through time. It was here that his Arctic adventure had begun. As they walked around the ramshackle town, whose only buildings of note were the grand churches of competing denominations, he described his first sight of the place and how he had come to buy food for the people who were to become his family.

An Inuk man, named Amy Ahangona, asked them to have tea at his home. As they walked toward his house, people smiled and nodded. Amy explained that the people in the Arctic knew about Isumataq and about the spotlight of attention Ken had been focussing on the story of the Inuit. "What can we do to help?" he asked.

Ken made one request. Could Amy take them out on the Coppermine River? They spent a day on Amy's boat, motoring up the river to Copper Mountain where the natives had mined the yellow mineral and beaten it into knives, and had thus become known as the Yellow Knives. They went to Bloody Falls where Ken stood on the same boulder he had straddled when he first crossed from the western into the eastern Arctic. He saw again the boulder where Samuel Hearne had carved his name in the sixteen hundreds and felt the emotional rush of history overwhelm him.

From Coppermine, they flew to Rankin Inlet where they discovered that Keith had asked Michael to spend the summer at his camp, working as a guide. They flew across Hudson's Bay, east to Iqaluit (Frobisher Bay), another ramshackle settlement, except for the new high school in the shape of a giant igloo.

They continued on to Pangirtung, an ancient settlement at the far end of Cumberland Sound on Baffin Island, where the Inuit had made camps for many centuries. But, it was also an old European whaling station and remains of the industry and skeletons of giant blue whales were still scattered on the shore.

They visited the local high school, where Ken gave a talk. When one young student asked him what he would do with Isumataq when it was finished, he said he wanted not one opening as was common with works of art – he wanted many openings, all of them to take place across the Arctic. Yes, the student persisted, but where would he show it first. "Well, first I have to take it to Parliament," he said.

Afterwards, Karen said. "I've never heard you say that before. What's this idea of going to Parliament?"

"It was just a joke," he said. "It just came off the top of my head."

"Some joke! It's perfect."

"Maybe."

"Seriously – it's perfect. That's it!"

"First I want to bring it here."

"Fine, but I tell you I love it – I love it a lot more than your crazy idea of going to Rome and unveiling it in the Colosseum with a pair of lions.

That was nuts!"

"Nuts is what people pay attention to. We're a lunatic society and I'm just talking to lunatics in a lunatic way. That way they'll pay attention."

The idea of presenting Isumataq at Parliament took root. They talked about taking the painting to the Arctic but soon saw the impossibility of the logistics. In the entire Canadian North, only one building could accommodate its size – the community hall in Yellowknife – and it was unheated and that could present serious problems.

But, if he was going to present his painting in Parliament he would need a first-rate manager. Karen laughed. "That's pure lunacy. Now you're really going over the top. Don't you understand? You're unmanageable. When you get up in the morning, you have clarity of some sort, and you launch into it as if you had an army a million strong. There's no stopping you and there's no talking to you. You are a pure, one-hundred-percent autocrat."

Maybe so, he admitted, but he would find a manager regardless.

17

Isumataq Unveiled

Ken turned his attention once again to Isumataq and put Elaine in charge of finding a manager. After a thorough search she gave him a list of candidates. He narrowed it down to two: Bruce Allen, in Vancouver, who was successfully managing the careers of pop bands like Chilliwack, Bachman Turner Overdrive and the Guess Who; and Bruce Davidson, in Toronto, who promoted events like the Messiah production and large congresses across the country. He chose Davidson. When Bruce arrived for their meeting, Ken was on his scaffold. He watched his initial reaction – the stopping, the head swivelling from side to side, the eyes growing larger and finally, the exhalation of breath and the words, "Jesus Christ!"

"I assume you're Bruce Davidson!" Ken called down.

"Yes, I am!"

Ken climbed down.

"What do you want me to do with this?" Bruce asked.

"It's a long story," Ken said. "I can't explain it to you in a blurb. It's not going to mean a damn thing. If you're interested I'll give you the very quick blurb and then I'll tell you the details – but don't say anything until you've heard the whole story."

Ken gave him the bare facts – how he had travelled to the Arctic and lived with the Inuit – how he had come to embrace their cause and how Isumataq was meant to draw attention to their plight. What he needed was someone who would go on the road with the painting – with the whole show – and stage events across the country. Most importantly, he wanted a major unveiling. Ideally, he told him, he'd like to do that in the Arctic but his only choice of venue was Yellowknife. Alternatively, what did he think of the Roman Colosseum with a couple of lions in tow?

Bruce laughed – he liked the idea of Rome, he said, although he could see logistical problems. They also discussed Parliament as a venue for the unveiling although that option simply wasn't available. No one was permitted to stage stunts in Parliament.

They met several times while Bruce wrestled with the idea of Isumataq. One day he said to Ken, "But I can't see how you can make money out of this!"

"But I'm not really after making money," Ken said.

"You don't want to make any money?"

I didn't say that I didn't *want* to make any money. It's just that that's not the main purpose."

"Fine but your ideas are extravagant and they're going to cost a lot of money. How are you going to pay for it?"

"Merchandising – we have a whole merchandising department."

"This isn't a painting," Bruce said. "It's an industry."

Ken nodded. "Yes, it is."

Bruce brought two assistants into the studio. "What do you think?" he asked them. His uncertainty, despite his years of experience as a promoter, convinced Ken that he was the right man. He was willing to question, to listen and to learn. They came to an agreement: Ken was the boss. He would tell Bruce what he wanted and Bruce's job was to "make it so".

Bruce flew to Yellowknife to assess the climate and returned to say that under no circumstances should they attempt an unveiling there. "Talk about people who love you or hate you! There are certain politicos up there who would just as soon see you dead."

"Fine", Ken said. They would find another place to unveil Isumataq.

Ken was wholly absorbed in completing the painting. But he was not destined to concentrate on only one mission. While he painted, he repeatedly heard the echo of his grandmother's words in his head talking to him about magic. When the words resolved into a vision of a sword in a stone he acted on it.

With Elaine and Salvador's help, he found an enormous boulder that weighed at least fifteen tons and had a diameter of about twelve feet. He bought a sword that he took to a Hungarian metalworker who adjusted and modified it so that it became a slim, sleek ribbon of steel. Late in the evening, workers smashed through the walls of his studio, rolled in the giant boulder and rebuilt the wall and door. He had a sliver-thin slit cut into the rock that the sword slid into where it was held in place by a trick release. Ken knew how to draw the sword out of the stone – he and no one else.

He offered a purse of ten thousand dollars to anyone who could pull the sword out of the stone. During the day, the purse was displayed beside the boulder. At night, he locked it in a vault. Hundreds of people came to make the attempt: plumbers and priests, schoolchildren and doctors – no one could accomplish the feat, but several times each day Ken effortlessly slid the sword from its prison of stone.

The media returned to the studio in swarms. Some saw the humour of the stunt – others took the "Who do you think you are?" attitude. Ken informed them that the sword was named after *Excalibur,* King Arthur's legendary "sword in the stone".

Bruce Davidson assessed the spectacle and said, "You're an agent's dream. Usually we have to concoct all this crap and get the artist to go along with it. But here – man, it's hard to keep up with you. It's never going to be boring."

"No," Ken said. "It's never going to be boring."

When the fuss died down he had the boulder removed and put the ten thousand dollars back into his bank account. Summer turned to early fall and Nick's symphony for Isumataq neared completion. The rock CD had been recorded. But they still had no site for the unveiling and the more they discussed it the more they came back to the idea of Parliament as the venue. But how do we get our foot in the door there? Bruce asked. Ken scheduled a breakfast meeting with the Honourable John Fraser, Speaker of the House and they met a few days later. Over bacon and eggs, Ken laid out his ideas for the unveiling of Isumataq.

"I know it's not done," he said. "People don't take over the Houses of Parliament for exhibitions or art openings."

"Well," John said. "Let me think about it. I think it's a wonderful idea. We'll have to get approval from all the parties, because you have to have everyone on board when you do something like this. If you're going to do something that hasn't been done before you don't want to just shove it down somebody's throat. You want to get everybody on side, so the story has to be told very well. I know your story and it's wonderful. You're the one who should come and tell it, but then there are the logistics of getting all those people together. And then, depending on the particular day, they may be angry with each other – it gets so complicated. Let's just work away at it."

The winter of 1990 settled in, and Ken received a call for help from Keith. As president of the Arctic Tourist Association, he was scheduled to make a presentation in a downtown Toronto convention centre to Tom Hawking, the Federal Minister of Arctic Affairs. The snag was that as he was driving his caterpillar over the ice to his island airstrip, the machine had crashed through and he had to get it out before it leaked diesel fuel into the river. Would Ken make the speech in his place, and would he present the Minister with one of his paintings?

The comedian Dave Thomas emceed the event. Ken was the last to speak and he talked about the importance of tourism to the Arctic and how important it was to allow those who lived there to make the decisions about the infrastructure – let them build it in their own way. Let Nunavut be their land and a land of their ideas.

Hawking requested a private talk and they met for a drink the next day. He asked to hear his story – the long version – all the details of his travels through the Arctic and the road that had led to the creation of Isumataq.

Hawking listened intently. When Ken had reached the end of his story Hawking asked him what would happen to the North if Nunavut was created.

"I think that it could be one of the most important things that ever happens in this country," he said. "If we can come to terms with the folks in the Arctic and create a new territory in which all the people have a say – everyone living in the area, not just the Inuit – in which they are able to take responsibility for their own governance, it could be a tremendous change."

He told Hawking that the Inuit were essentially treated like children or wards of the state. "Here are people who have lived for thousands of years and survived – and the most difficult thing they had to survive is us. They survived the cold, the famines, and disagreements with each other – and then we came along – and they even managed to survive us. Nunavut could set a blueprint of self-governance for various native peoples across the country. Then, we can let them show us how good they are at it. My bet is that they're a lot better at it than we are."

"You know, there are those who feel quite differently," Hawking said.

"Yes, I know. Most people would like to continue with the status quo. There are those who are interested in what goes on in this country but, unfortunately, that is probably less than two percent of the population. The ignorance about our Arctic and, in fact, about anyone living a hundred miles from the Trans-Canada Highway, is appalling – they may as well not exist."

If Nunavut was indeed created, wouldn't other aboriginal groups want their own land as well? Ken asked. What about the Inuit of northern Quebec? They were not to be included in Nunavut and why shouldn't they want self-governance? He predicted turbulence among the Inuit and among the northern Cree in Quebec, led by Chiefs Billy Diamond and Matthew Cooncome, and suggested there could be a chain reaction. He also pointed out that Nunavut could not be created without a referendum but it would not be a vote that all of Canada could participate in – only the people who would be directly affected. The outcome of that referendum would have repercussions far into the future. Other aboriginal groups would inevitably want their own referendums – and why not? This should have happened a hundred and fifty years ago – or more. He deplored the ignorance of Canadians who complained when native groups asked for more and more. How could they find fault, when every treaty that had ever been made between Europeans and Natives had been broken or ignored entirely?

"How interesting it is," Hawking said, "That it takes an immigrant to see these things more clearly than we do ourselves. How interesting that the fire grows in you and how interesting the way you visualize this as a great moment not brought about by a single individual but by those who stand on the shoulders of those that went before. How interesting that it might well be a painter, born in another country, who may be the giant banging boulders together to create that last little bit of sand that makes a beach."

Hawking asked him how the government worked in the Northwest Territories. Each year a billion dollars was allocated to the region – a region that was comprised of fewer people than walked through the lobby of First Canadian Place each day. Somehow, the government lost track of the money each year and it wasn't being spent on the social programs it was earmarked for.

Ken told him about "the bosses" – those who used to work for the Hudson's Bay Company and who now ran things. It didn't take a genius to understand where the money was going. If it was meant to build new houses, then those houses were not being built.

Hawking asked Ken to go to Ottawa with him and talk to his staff and other ministers who should know what was going on.

Reluctantly, he agreed. He had been avoiding politics. Instead he had been focussing on disseminating the Arctic story only through his work. He flew to Ottawa and met with the politicians and bureaucrats. When they asked questions he reframed them and tossed them back. But he told them bluntly that the issue of the disappearing money was the biggest boondoggle in the country, though he had no statistics and no proof – just stories.

"If you want to get to the bottom of it, do you own work," he said. "My work is to tell the stories about the Arctic by painting and talking."

"The Prime Minister should hear this," Hawking said.

"It's your job to tell him," Ken said. "Not mine."

No, the ministers said, it would be better coming from you. "He should at least have knowledge of you," Hawking said.

"I'm quite sure he already does," Ken said. "In a short meeting I will have to water all this down and take the thunder out of it. However, one day I am going to march in here and take this place over. You understand that, don't you?"

"I wouldn't doubt it," Hawking said.

Despite Ken's protests, Hawking and his colleagues convinced him to meet with Brian Mulroney the next day. When Mulroney entered the office where Ken was waiting, he reached out a hand and pulled Ken forward, throwing him momentarily off balance. Ken gathered his thoughts and said, "I've been asked to come here and tell you in a few minutes what it took me two and a half days to tell these folks. I am here at their request. I have not sought an audience with you or them. I am not being paid for this and I don't want to be."

"I know who you are," Mulroney said, waving his hand. "Just make a statement."

"We can't build a nation on a foundation of lies," Ken said.

Mulroney's eyes flashed. "Are you calling me a liar?"

"I'm not calling you a liar and I don't give a shit if you are. What bothers me is the behaviour of all those who went before – they make all of us liars."

Mulroney leaned back. "How the fuck did you get in here?"

"I'm here by invitation. I have the distinct impression that your ministers don't have the balls to tell you what needs to be said. I guess I'm the one that's going to say it. Now, don't take this personally, but I don't like you. I can think of a thousand things that I would rather be doing, but, having been dragged up more or less right, when people ask me to do something, I try my damndest to do it."

"About this business of building a nation on a foundation of lies," Mulroney said. "Do you want to expand on that?"

They talked far beyond the allotted ten minutes. Ken told Mulroney his ideas about Nunavut, and near the end of the conversation he played, what he believed was probably his trump card. "Prime Minister, today you are not the most revered person in the country. I would imagine that people from some other country would elect you but not Canadians. Not to say you're the most hated man in the country, but you haven't exactly endeared yourself to the people. But imagine this. It you could do what no man has been able to do for more than three hundred years, how do you think history would see you then? You would be the man who pulled the sword from the stone and I would have to take a back seat."

"You should be in politics," Mulroney said.

"What the hell do you think I'm in? I've been a politician masquerading as a painter all my life."

"So you really think Nunavut would do it, do you?"

"Of course. And by the way, Prime Minister, if it's the last bloody thing you do, you'll sign the act that creates Nunavut. It's going to happen. It is written."

On September 1, 1990, to celebrate his fiftieth birthday, Karen and Ken flew to Yellowknife and boarded a float plane that settled them down on Whitefish Lake where they were greeted by the sight of an enormous Arctic grizzly prowling back and forth.

It was close to the cabin owned by Tom Foess, known as Tundra Tom, one of the northern bush pilots. Tom explained that he had just installed a new outhouse, and the bear seemed displeased with its location. The normally shy animal continued to grumble and pace, then reared to its full height of about ten feet, picked up the outhouse, moved it a few feet and lumbered off.

That night, Ken and Karen stepped outside to watch one of the most glorious displays of Northern Lights they had ever witnessed.

There is no such thing as old hat when it comes to this. It's like it all happens for the first time each time. It grew more and more intense. We lay there on the ground and I don't know how long we lay there. The shafts of light rippled up in an arc all around us, and they came to a centre point directly above us and that point was a black hole. All the rest was light, and the colours were showering down – purple, gold, green, blue, red. The words don't work. It was as if we were laying on the floor of a cathedral the size of the universe. The earth was no longer an issue – we weren't even part of the planet. I can see how religions began. It was stuff like this – it undoes one. All the rational explanations we have for this are nonsense. They just don't work. You have to find a bigger answer. This is too big, too beautiful, and too mysterious.

Something holy descended on their souls. Ken felt as though they had had a direct experience of God and the magic of that night clung to them during those ten days in the Thelon.

The Thelon was like no other place on earth. When the glaciers had retreated they had left behind a vast amount of chirt, a very dense stone that had formed into eskers or low humpbacked hills from forty to a hundred and fifty feet high. The stone was so dense the permafrost could not penetrate it and as a result the vegetation that grew there, born from seeds carried by migrating birds, was that of a more southern landscape. But because of the severe winters and punishing winds, it was a landscape in miniature. Trees that might grow to a hundred feet in the south grew to only a couple of feet here, but they were flawlessly formed. At the base of each esker was a perfectly round small lake, so thick with Arctic grayling you could almost reach your hand into the water and pull one out.

When they got back Ken promised himself that this time he wouldn't leave on another trip until he had finished the painting. He locked himself in his studio and from October 1990 to May 1991. He emerged only long enough to eat and sleep.

The epic project neared completion. Elaine suggested a decorous and dignified gathering to commemorate the event. Ken and the word "decorous" were obviously never meant to meet. He insisted on a "last brushstroke" party that would be more extravagant than his "first brushstroke" event ten years earlier. Decorum in his studio? A studio that had a sign at the entrance identifying it as "The Zoo?" Karen had even presented him with a road sign he had admired in Yellowknife: Ragged Ass Road and Lois Lane.

Ken had actually tried to steal the sign more than once, but each time he had attempted it, someone had gotten to it before him and taken off with it. He guessed that the City of Yellowknife works department likely had a full time employee doing nothing but erecting a new road sign at that intersection each week.

Elaine ordered stacks of memorabilia for the party and sent invitations across the country and press releases to the media outlets.

About five hundred people thronged into the studio on June 21, the longest day of the year and eternal day in the Arctic. At the height of the festivities, Ken climbed up a ladder carrying one of his smallest brushes. Ceremoniously, he made a tiny brush stroke on the centre Inukshuk.

"I want to thank all of those who supported me and who supported this idea," he said. "There were many and you know who you are. I also want to thank all of those who stood in my way throughout my entire life. You know who you are. You turned ordinary iron into steel and that is why this was possible."

In the press release he handed to the media, he quantified the one hundred and fifty-two foot painting. It consisted of 570 linear feet of canvas, 266 bolts to hold the panels together, and 39,360 ounces of oil paint. The actual painting time was 6,840 hours. Looking very carefully at the painting one could see that the centre Inukshuk was placed at the head of Pangirtung Fjord in front of the glacier that had once existed there – and if one looked even more closely at the glacier a stylized Canadian flag was revealed. Behind the Inukshuk was Mount Thor and beside that Mount Asgard – proud Viking names.

Sales of memorabilia were outstanding. The reaction to the painting was everything he could have hoped for. The media was all over it – and yet it rankled. The provincial television, radio and newspapers had covered the event thoroughly. Reports even turned up in newspapers abroad. But within Canada, beyond the borders of Ontario, Ken Kirkby may as well not have existed. What did he have to do to get the attention of the entire country? Elaine estimated that television had given him five hundred and thirty hours of coverage since the beginning of Isumataq. Manitoba had given him about three hours and British Columbia barely one hour. Short of going on a killing rampage, what did he have to do make the entire country pay attention?

Bruce flew to Yellowknife one last time, on the chance that the political atmosphere there might have changed. He came back with the news that Ken had more enemies than before. The river of federal government money that had previously poured so easily into the pockets of "the bosses" had mysteriously dried up and they laid the blame squarely at his door.

Fine, he told Bruce. "If not Yellowknife, I want Parliament."

"You know better than I, that you can't use Parliament for stuff like this."

"Well, let's change that mindset."

"I suppose now you're going to change the whole god-damned system."

"Look, I'm only interested in doing things that haven't been done. If it's been done, I'm not interested."

"Politicians should do politics and painters should paint," Bruce argued.

"Oh no, you've got it completely wrong," Ken said. "Just what the hell do you think I've been up to this entire time? This is politics – this is politics writ large! And I want Parliament. It's the proper place for it."

Karen turned to Bruce. "I told you that he's unmanageable. He'll have his way just because he's bloody-minded enough. Don't forget that his growing-up years were spent in two countries ruled by dictators – and it rubbed off on him. You may as well go along with it. He's not going to shut up until you do something about it."

Ken picked up the phone, dialled John Fraser's number and made an appointment for Bruce.

"But why don't you just come to Ottawa yourself?" John asked.

"Because I have people," Ken said. "And it's time for my people to talk to your people."

John laughed, and Bruce flew to Ottawa. When he came back he was shaking his head. "You've got Parliament!" he said.

The Prime Minister was enormously supportive of the event, John Fraser said. The official unveiling of Isumataq was scheduled for March 30, 1992. In the interim Ken toured with the twenty-five foot model. His first stop was a dinner meeting of the Italian Canadian Business and Professional Association, then the Orillia branch of the Canadian Club, where his audience consisted mostly of older women who greeted his stories of the grandmothers with thunderous applause and the suggestion that he should be the next Prime Minister of Canada.

Many of his presentations were held in towns in the Ottawa area as anticipation began to build for the unveiling in Parliament. Ken and his team had the enormously difficult task of working out the logistics of transporting the painting to Ottawa and later to venues around the country. Since the hall in Parliament could not accommodate all thirty-eight panels of Isumataq, Ken arranged to have the model shipped along with the first four panels, so the audience could view both the scope of Isumataq and the full painting. Isumataq had never been assembled in its entirety and Ken obtained the use of a warehouse for a test run. The panels bolted together seamlessly, just as he had envisioned. Stretched from end to end, the painting was more than impressive. Television cameras covered the event and recorded a remark Ken casually tossed off while he and Karen walked along the length of the panels. "Now I'm satisfied," he said. "When I die, I want you to wrap me in this thing, put me on a Viking ship, pour gasoline over the lot, set it alight, and let me go to Valhalla with the bloody thing."

John Fraser called. "You have to write a speech and you have to present it to me. No one has ever done this before and we're going to make sure it's okay. Don't come in here for God's sake and go off on some wild-ass tangent. This has been enough trouble already!"

"Who me?" he protested.

He wrote a speech, rewrote it and then rewrote it again – and again. In the process, he distilled his thoughts and began to appreciate the power of putting his words on paper.

The countdown to the presentation of Isumataq in Parliament was on. It was running neck and neck with the countdown to the creation of Nunavut as a territory. It was a race that Nunavut won by only days and Ken triumphantly rewrote his speech one more time.

A couple of days before March 30, Ken, Bruce, Karen, Michael, Elaine and a crew of men loaded their cube van and drove in a cavalcade to Ottawa. Along with Isumataq, Ken also took a painting of two Canadian flags; not the painting that had raised such controversy and that he had vowed he would one day present to the country, but a new one. He had assessed the political situation and created a painting to give to Canada – one that went to the heart of it all.

He also took sweatshirts, T-shirts, ball caps and mugs that he distributed freely to the security staff in Parliament who helped with the set-up. When he mentioned the flag painting they hung it without question in the space he had chosen across from the Prime Minister's office. When the morning of March 30 dawned, Ken asked Karen and Michael to precede him. He wanted to walk to Parliament alone.

In my mind, I went right back to the very beginning of the whole thing – back to the beach in Portugal where it all began. There's a well-designed wrought iron fence extending along the front of Parliament Hill and as I walked along it, running my fingers along the intricate scrollwork, I was thinking – what a long story this has been. I thought about my father who was gone; Francisco who was gone; Miloo who was gone; Jessica who was gone – all the people in my life who I had loved and who were gone – I have lived such a wreckage, I thought. I'm not prone to this sort of thinking but I wondered. I thought about this thing that was about to happen – this thing that was unheard-of – and it struck me what an unlikely figure I cut and what an unlikely path I had trod to come to this place. I was an immigrant, wearing black cowboy boots, black pants, and a black sweater that Karen had knit during our journeys in the Arctic. I wondered if the people I had loved could see this. Did they know this? What I would give to have those people here now. Each had played such a large role in the making of me and in me making this. I got so carried away with my thoughts that I forgot to be nervous. You would think that a fellow who had spent a lifetime preparing for this would at least be somewhat nervous, but I was just in this golden place inside me.

When he arrived at the front doors of Parliament he was ushered into the hall where Karen and the crew were putting the finishing touches on the exhibit. He was led to the Speaker's office where Michael was sitting on a desk, his feet dangling, telling stories to the staff of his adventures in the Arctic.

John led Ken into his office and a photographer arrived to immortalize the occasion. He posed Ken and John in front of the Karsh portrait of Winston Churchill and for the next hour shot Ken with various members of Parliament. Jean Chrétien, leader of the opposition, offered his congratulations, as did Joe Clark, who was standing in for Brian Mulroney who was otherwise engaged.

In the hall at the foot of the stairs people stood or sat shoulder to shoulder. Not an inch of space remained.

I had the most amazing feeling. It was a feeling I have never had before or since. It was a feeling that I was standing at a point in the universe where for some minutes and seconds reality was different. This was the magical moment I had been seeking my whole life. Usually, I had foreseen important moments in great detail. But this one – this was different. This one had somehow manufactured itself. It was not the vision I had had in my head.

John Fraser stood on the podium and spoke. "Almost fifty years ago a young boy sat at the feet of his tutor – an old Portuguese fisherman – and heard tales of whaling in the Canadian North. These tales were so wonderful that the boy vowed some day to see Canada for himself and to clarify his mental pictures of the land."

"In his late teens, circumstance found the boy and his family living on Canada's West Coast and several years later he set out on his boyhood dream to see the great Canadian North. For five years, he walked from one end of this great land to the other, travelling with families of Inuit as they pursued their nomadic lifestyle. Often he was alone, walking endlessly – experiencing first-hand Canada's Arctic North, all the while sketching thousands of miniature drawings of what he saw."

"Toward the end of his journey, like a great mirage in the desert, he saw a giant of a man standing on the distant horizon. It was a stone Inukshuk, an Inuit guide to hunting and fishing grounds. Try as he might for the next twenty years, his efforts to portray the splendour of this vast and spectacular landscape resulted in dissatisfaction and personal frustration. Finally, he realized that only a painting which was larger than any ever painted could properly depict the unseen spectacle which he felt compelled to bring to the rest of the world."

"The result of five years of trekking and twenty years of painting was completed on June 21, 1991, the longest day of the year. It is the largest original oil on canvas portrait in the world, measuring one hundred and fifty-two feet long by twelve feet high."

"I would now like to introduce Mr. Ken Kirkby, a truly great Canadian, whose unique vision of this country is an example for us all, especially in this period when the question of Native rights and the very existence of Canada itself is at the forefront of our minds."

Ken took the podium. "Thank you, Mr. Speaker, for this opportunity. Mr. Clark, Ms. McLaughlin, Mr. Chrétien, guests. I am honoured to be invited to unveil Isumataq here today, in Parliament. Unfortunately, we couldn't fit the entire painting into this building. What you will see here is the small twenty-five-foot model I prepared before painting Isumataq and the first four panels of the painting itself, depicting an Inukshuk. Isumataq itself is twelve feet high and one hundred and fifty-two feet long – or half a football field, if you wish."

"I called the painting Isumataq, which is an Inuit word that means "An object in the presence of which wisdom might show itself."

"I intend it to convey a message to all Canadians. Right now, my Canada believes itself to be faced with Solomon's wisdom: 'perhaps the sword will fall, perhaps not.' Consider the infant country we might be about to slice in two. Understand the quiet wisdom of the Inuk grandmother who taught me the meaning of Isumataq. She explained that a nation is composed of its landscape and its people. For a nation to be great it must know, respect, and trust itself."

"In my opinion, ninety percent of Canadians don't know ninety percent of Canada. How can we be a nation if we don't know our own backyard? We are so disappointed with each other when we haven't even met. Understand, compared with ancient cultures, the concept of Canada is only five minutes old."

"We Canadians all have gifts to give each other. Let's not sit in our corners yearning to belong to each other, wondering how to give and receive those gifts. We must offer them freely to each other. If we can't understand the nature of those gifts, let's ask the people in line at Canadian embassies all over the world why they want to come here. Perhaps they understand better than we. As a Canadian who was not born here, but one who came from other places – with a heritage of warring peoples – I feel compelled to tell you that I did not come here to recreate that which I sought to escape."

"Let's be at least as patient with each other as the Aboriginal peoples of this place are with us. As a Canadian, I embrace all the people who live in this country. Isumataq is my tribute to Canadians. It is my homage to the Canadian Arctic and its peoples who inspired me to paint it."

"Isumataq is made of years of personal effort and millions of individual brush strokes. As Canada has been made of the efforts of millions of individuals. Isumataq is an invitation and it is a demand. Let's join each other and be worthy of this place. Let's go forward with a single purpose and a good will."

"I dedicate Isumataq to Canada and all Canadians from sea to sea to sea. Thank you." With that, Ken nodded and Jean Chrétien pushed the button that parted the soft gray-blue curtains to reveal Ken's masterpiece. The model, imposing in its own right, rested on a series of easels that stretched across the room. Elevated behind the model were four of the giant panels of Isumataq.

The hall, which had been so still a feather would have made a sound wafting to the stone floor, erupted in a roar of applause, the noise crashing off the stone walls and soaring ceilings like freight trains colliding in mid-air. A lightening storm of flash bulbs erupted and through the blinding light Ken was pleased to see that among the gathered glitterati were many of the security people who had been of such immense help in the previous days.

My feelings were different from anything I had ever felt in my life. And all of a sudden into my mind, crystal clear, came the face of the old grandmother with a smile on her face as if to say, "I told you so". Along with that I heard the words my grandfather in Spain uttered just moments before he died when he placed his hands on my shoulders, "One day you will understand all of this. Destiny rests here." And here I was, at the moment when the meaning of those words – the words of my grandfather – and the words echoed years later by the grandmother – came to fruition. How do you describe such emotion as I felt at that moment?

Wave after wave of applause surged through the giant hall until finally Ken put up his hand. When it died down, he stepped back to the microphone and thanked the staff – and as he surveyed the throng, he saw something magical – tears in the eyes of the powerful – the rulers and lawmakers of the nation, unabashedly allowing their emotions to spill over, here in this majestic hall.

Then John Fraser stepped up to the podium and took Ken by the arm, "We have to go."

"Where?"

"My office."

"But why now? I have to do all this signing..."

John propelled him forward, parting the crowd with a majestic wave of his hand, "Don't worry – they'll all be here when we come back."

In his office, John opened a bottle of fine white wine and poured glasses for those who had been invited to the private gathering: Jean Chrétien, Joe Clark, and Audrey McLaughlin. The Parliamentary photographer again snapped dozens of photos.

Joe Clark, who was full of congratulations, was also intensely curious about the painting and the events that had led to its inception and completion. When Ken tried to answer Jean Chrétien stepped in before Ken had a chance. Chrétien had been watching Ken's career ever since he had first heard him speak at the Columbus Centre. Ken was surprised to realize how closely the man had been following his progress. His answers to Clark's questions were accurate and precise and there was passion in his words. He cared about Nunavut. He and Pierre Trudeau had been behind the creation of Auyuittug, the first Arctic park ever created – a park that was the centrepiece of Isumataq.

Chrétien talked about the importance of people who had visions – how it was these people, who built nations. Audrey McLaughlin said, "Mr. Kirkby, you must be a very persuasive fellow. You convinced the Speaker of the House to have us, the leaders of the parties, here as props. We didn't get up to make speeches. We were as quiet as church mice. I gather that's what you asked Mr. Speaker to do."

"I did," Ken said. "It was time for one of the people to walk into this place and speak. The needs and wishes and desires of the people have been filtered through the voices of those elected to represent them. That doesn't always mean it's the people's voice. I – a single individual – am actually here as 'the people' and I wanted you to hear the people's voice through me."

Clark grasped Ken's hand and shook it again, and John Fraser ushered them back out into the hall where the crowd had multiplied. The Italian and the Portuguese ambassadors had arrived and smiled at him benignly, like fathers might who were witnessing their son graduate from university.

John stepped to the microphone and announced that Ken was available for interviews and to sign brochures. "I remind you that this is the largest brochure ever made and the most expensive brochure ever made," he said. "It has been made by this artist and he will autograph it for anyone who cares to have it. There is one for every Member of Parliament; there is one for every Senator..." He turned and whispered to Ken. Smiling, he turned back to the microphone. "And there is one for every ambassador of every country in the world."

Ken signed brochures for two hours, Jean Chrétien standing at his side, helping him spell the names. When the last brochure had been signed and the last hand shaken, he sat back. He was trembling, his body soaked in sweat, the adrenaline pumping through his blood, almost making him dizzy. And it wasn't over yet. He had a dinner that night with John Fraser and a meeting with Brian Mulroney in the morning.

Later that night, Ken woke from a dream convinced the day had never occurred – somehow he must have dreamed it. Quietly, he crept out of bed and padded to the window of his hotel room. Drawing back the heavy curtains, he looked out – there were the Parliament buildings, lit like a fairy-tale castle.

I guess it did happen – an immigrant, wearing black cowboy boots, black pants, and a black turtleneck sweater – I had done it. It was as though I was at the centre of a thousand avenues of the past all coming toward me. What a journey! If I ever told this story – well, this story is not possible. You can't tell this story. The convolutions, and the complications, and the bits and the pieces, and the pain and the joy – all of it. It's a story that can't be told. When I realized that, I was relieved. I'm not going to tell this story. I can't tell it. I was there and I don't believe it. The idea that an immigrant can end up at the centre of an event in Parliament. I don't think there's another country on earth where you can achieve so much – no other country except Canada.

Here I was, far, far away from the place I had been born – born in an air raid, which was an omen for how my life had been. I knew how to relentlessly battle. I knew how to be a warrior artist. I didn't know how to do or be anything else. I'm a warrior who has only done one thing, in different forms, and for different durations. All I know is how to be relentless and how to battle. Now, it was done. Now, what am I going to do? Then the face of the grandmother appeared again, as crystal clear as a person sitting in front of me. There we were – looking at each other – nothing said. She was just there. I felt that we would be looking at each other like this forever – and so far we have. This aged woman's face is a connection to a sublime thing. It's as if I have the privilege of looking into the face of God. This face appears at all sorts of different times. It's immensely powerful and it's not just in times of doubt. I can be fishing or painting and all of a sudden – there's that face. For many reasons I consider myself the most fortunate creature that I've ever encountered. It's as if I have a small troupe of very powerful elders who are with me. There are times in my life when I have no idea what I'm doing. Then all of a sudden these elders are guiding me along. It's not an ego thing. Deep inside me I know that I don't know. I have no idea what the hell I'm doing. But there's this quiet place where I know that if I just keep going it will all work out. As long as the intent is right, just keep going relentlessly, and forever, and ever, and ever.

Afterword

The story of Ken goes on – but that is another book. The story of Isumataq also goes on and has not yet come to its end. Ken took Isumataq to New York, to Ontario Place, and to Vancouver. Everywhere it went, it was greeted with wonder, awe, tears, and stunned admiration.

Today it is housed in a little-known hockey arena on Canada's West Coast. But Isumataq was never destined to live in obscurity. Its time will come and it will come soon when once again it will inspire a new generation of people – and perhaps move them to great compassion and to great deeds.

Today, Ken lives in one of the two places he loves most in the world – near the mouth of Nile Creek on the east coast of Vancouver Island where he has dedicated his life to saving the streams that empty into Georgia Strait and restoring the depleted salmon runs. He is president of the Nile Creek Enhancement Society that in 2007 won the Restoration and Rehabilitation Canadian Environmental Award.

Ken attacks the work of restoration as he once approached Isumataq – with single-minded dedication and pigheadedness and while local developers may deplore him, the salmon, if they could talk, would be immensely grateful.

Half the royalties from the sale of this book will go to the Nile Creek Enhancement Society to help carry on its vital work.